"WE ARE ALONE, BECCA. DOES IT FRIGHTEN YOU?"

"Should it?" Waves of heat washed over her and she took a deep breath.

Talon came to her then and took her in his arms. "There can be nothing between us, my Becca," he whispered huskily. "Nothing but a few stolen days in this haunted valley. Will you steal them with me?"

She stood stiffly in his embrace for long seconds, then slowly, her resistance melted. "Talon," she answered. "Talon, I—"

"Do not say it. Do not say that we are enemies, or that you belong to another. Do not say that once we leave this place, we can never think or speak of this time again. There is no need to say what we both know."

"I don't care," she whispered. "Stop talking and kiss me."

THIS FIERCE LOVING

JUDITH E. FRENCH

An Avon Romantic Treasure

AVON BOOKS ◆ NEW YORK

THIS FIERCE LOVING is an original publication of Avon Books. This work has never before appeared in book form. This work is a novel. Any similarity to actual persons or events is purely coincidental.

AVON BOOKS
A division of
The Hearst Corporation
1350 Avenue of the Americas
New York, New York 10019

Copyright © 1994 by Judith E. French
Inside cover author photo by Theis Photography Ltd.
Published by arrangement with the author
Library of Congress Catalog Card Number: 94-94091
ISBN: 0-380-77704-5

First Avon Books Printing: October 1994

AVON TRADEMARK REG. U.S. PAT. OFF. AND IN OTHER COUNTRIES, MARCA REGISTRADA, HECHO EN U.S.A.

Printed in the U.S.A.

RA   10   9   8   7   6   5   4   3   2   1

For my dad, Les Bennett,
who read me Zane Gray as a child
and taught me a little
of what he knows about the woods.
You were my first hero.

"But the bravest are surely those who have the clearest vision of what is before them, glory and danger alike, and yet notwithstanding go out to meet it."

THUCYDIDES

Chapter 1

The Maryland Frontier
Winter 1751

*I*ndians! Rebecca had dreamed of them again last night, and the vivid images of that terrifying nightmare raised goose flesh on her arms. She shivered. She'd not had a peaceful night's sleep since an Ottawa war party had massacred the Johnson family and barbecued Clarence Johnson in his own fireplace.

Rebecca Brandt draped a worn homespun shawl over her shoulders and pushed open the cabin door a crack. *Where in God's name was that boy?* A gust of icy wind whipped through the room, scattering ashes on the hearth and rattling the panes of the single barred window. "Colin!" she shouted. "Colin! Hurry up! I need that water if you want breakfast."

With a sigh of exasperation, she shut the heavy oak door and thrust her stocking feet into high leather moccasins. She was not normally this skittish, but her dream had left her uneasy. If Colin was dawdling along the stream bank instead of bringing up the bucket of water she'd sent him for, she'd take a switch to his backside.

Her little brother was getting out of hand, there were no two ways about it. Simon said she spoiled him rotten, and maybe he was right. Lately, Colin had been bordering on cocky, not just with Simon, but with her. It was time she jerked his leadline up tight.

It hadn't been easy on any of them, her raising Colin off here in the deep forest so far from any white settlement. There were no churches or schools, and no boys of any age for him to play with. The only male company he had was her husband Simon, and that was usually worse than none. Simon had no patience with a ten-year-old child; he was too quick to lash out at Colin with his fist.

She loved the boy so much that it was hard for her to discipline him. Simon didn't love him at all. If she'd had babes of her own, maybe she would have felt differently about an orphan brother. As it was, Colin was her whole world.

And he'd been gone far too long to fetch water . . .

Indians. The possibility of savages lurking in the hills around the cabin made her mouth go dry. It was long past Indian summer—those balmy weeks in late autumn when attacks by hostiles were most likely. Simon had scoffed at her fears when he'd ridden out for Fort Nelson. Common sense told her that Simon knew the wild tribes if anyone did; there'd be no real danger until spring. And maybe not then, she reasoned, if this new peace treaty was signed between the British and the Delaware and Shawnee.

Rebecca finished lacing up her second moccasin, took her hooded cloak off a peg by the door, and stepped outside. It was a bitter gray day—one that seeped into your bones. More snow was in the air, she could smell it. Already, a good four inches lay on the ground, crunching under her feet as she walked.

On the wooded rise behind the barn, a wolf howled and Rebecca cast a nervous glance in that direction. "Colin!" she called again.

She listened hard for an answer, but it was quiet—too quiet. Not even the caw of a crow broke the stillness of the frosty morning.

Rebecca started for the creek on the run.

She was halfway across the clearing of burned stumps when she realized that she hadn't stopped to pick up a weapon. Their only musket hung over the cabin door, primed and ready to fire.

She stopped short and called her brother's name again. Nothing . . . For the hundredth time, she damned Simon for not letting her keep a dog.

A dog would bark and give warning of Indians. A dog might have driven off the wolves that had killed her calf last spring. In her mind's eye, she pictured a huge Irish mastiff prowling the far corners of the farm, protecting them with his keen sense of smell and hearing.

"Colin!" Her heart was racing; her mouth tasted of hammered metal.

He's playing along the stream bank, she told herself. The rascal's forgotten the water and gone to check on his muskrat traps, or he's tracking some animal in the new fallen snow. He'd done it to her before, often enough.

But she'd never before had this overwhelming sensation of impending doom . . .

A sick sensation rose in the pit of her stomach, and Rebecca forced herself to retrace her steps to the house. If Colin was in trouble—if there were Indians out there—she'd need the gun.

The musket was heavy, but she was strong from

years of chopping wood, hoeing corn, and carrying water to her garden. She snagged Simon's old hunting pouch from a pair of deer antlers, secured the knife and powder horn, and slung the strap over her shoulder.

"If you've worried me half to death for nothing, Colin," she murmured under her breath, "I'll make you rue the day . . ." She prayed that he had—that this was just a boyish prank.

She dashed back across the yard, then slowed her pace on the slippery incline that led to the creek at the bottom of the gully. Colin's tracks were plain as day, a single set of small footprints, then a wide, flattened place in the snow where'd he'd slid on his bottom with a separate skid mark for the empty bucket.

Simon had cut two cedar logs and set them into the bank horizontally to make a firm spot to dip up water in all kinds of weather, wet or dry. The snow was scuffed across the surface of the cedar platform. She could see where Colin had dropped to his knees and leaned over the edge. The creek was too swift to freeze over unless the temperature dropped far below normal, but ice crystals formed along the banks. As Rebecca peered over the logs, she caught sight of a half-submerged bucket floating in an eddy.

"Colin." This time his name came out a harsh whisper. Colin might be flighty, but he was never careless. He wouldn't have left the bucket unless . . .

"Rebecca."

She spun around to see an unruly thatch of dark brown hair and two frightened eyes staring over the top of a fallen log. "Colin!"

"Shhh," he warned. He pointed to the far bank of the stream. "I saw something—" he began.

Relief washed over her, making her all shaky, so weak in the knees that she wanted to drop into the snow. "Lord, boy, you scared me."

"Shhh." He stood up cautiously, looking hard and long at the grove of big oaks beyond the creek. "A deer," he began. "A big doe ran down the ravine and crossed there." He pointed to a rocky spot a few hundred feet from where Rebecca stood. "She was running like the devil's hounds were after ..."

"A deer?" Anger was fast replacing her gut-wrenching terror. "You put me through this because you saw a deer?"

Colin scrambled over the log and ran to her side. "Don't be dumb. Something scared that doe plenty." He dropped flat on his stomach and reached down to seize the rope handle of the bucket and pull it up.

"Your imagination is getting away with you," she chided. "Why didn't you answer me when I called you? I—"

"Quiet," he snapped, sounding like a miniature version of their father when he was at the end of his patience. "Voices carry a long way in the woods. Move out slow, up the hill."

"Colin." He was really in for it now. Not only had he caused her a terrible fright, but he was trying to bluff his way out of ...

"There!" he cried. "Look!"

She saw a movement in the shadows of a pine bough fifty yards away. A single ray of sunshine glinted off something bright—something that might have been metal—and the woods echoed with the hunting cry of a gray wolf.

"Run!" Colin ordered.

As she turned to flee up the slippery, snow-covered path, a second wolf howled from the right, and then a third joined in from the hill behind the house.

"That's no wolf pack," Colin yelled. "It's hostiles!"

Together, they plunged up the slope. Weighted down by the flintlock musket, Rebecca was hard pressed to keep up with Colin. She was gasping for breath when she reached the top.

"Come on!" he yelled, offering her his hand. "Faster!"

She glanced back over her shoulder and stifled a scream. Splashing through the creek was a painted savage. Another warrior raced up the ravine, and the chilling sound he uttered was not that of a wolf—it was a Shawnee war whoop.

Rebecca swung the musket around, knelt, and took careful aim at the closest brave, and squeezed the trigger. Smoke and shot burst from the barrel. The stock slammed into her shoulder, but she didn't feel the pain and she didn't stop to see if she'd hit her target. She leaped up and ran toward the cabin.

Colin reached the house first. He threw open the door. "Run, Rebecca!" he screamed. "Run!"

She was inside barring the door before the first Indian charged across the clearing. "The window!" she said urgently.

"Got it!" Colin replied. He slammed the inside shutter closed and rammed the bolt in place.

Her teeth chattered as she shrugged off her cloak and began to reload the musket. One gun—she had a single flintlock musket to hold off a Shawnee war party.

"What if they fire the cabin?"

She ignored her brother, concentrating on tamping down the lead ball. She knew she'd dumped in too much powder in her haste. She only hoped she hadn't put in so much that it blew up the barrel and her to boot.

Colin jumped up on a stool and looked out a small opening carved in the chinking of the log wall. "Jesus!" He gasped. "There must be a hundred of 'em!"

"Hold your blasphemous tongue," Rebecca admonished. She put the musket barrel through the hole, sighted in on a stocky brave with roached hair, and fired. The Indian tumbled backwards and lay still. "That's one," she said with more bravado than she felt. "Only ninety-nine to go."

Colin had armed himself with his bow and arrows. He'd begged Simon to teach him to shoot the musket, but Simon would have none of it. Instead, he'd brought the boy a worn bow and a few sorry arrows. The bowstring was shredding, and the shafts were missing some of their feathers, but that hadn't stopped Colin. He'd practiced day after day with the bow until he was bringing home rabbits, squirrels, and an occasional trout or turkey. Rebecca knew that the boy was a good shot, but against armed warriors his efforts would be useless.

Lead balls were striking the cabin like hail as she withdrew the musket to reload. Powder— patch—lead. She rammed the ball home, glad for once that she had a musket instead of a long rifle. A rifle shot farther and truer, but she could load a musket in half the time. And at this distance, you didn't need to be a marksman to hit your target.

Her fingers trembled as she loaded the frizzen

pan with fine powder. Some of the precious stuff spilled on the hard-packed floor, but she didn't waste time worrying over it. She wasn't as good at this as Simon. He could load and fire ten times in three minutes—and hit the bull's-eye dead center every time at thirty yards.

When the gun was ready, she ran to a loophole on the far side of the door and fired again. This time, she missed her shot, and the savage hurled a tomahawk against the log eighteen inches from her head.

Reload. Fire. Reload. Fire. Rebecca stopped thinking rationally. If she let herself reason, she'd know they didn't have a chance. Already flaming arrows were striking the shingled cedar roof. How long before the cabin went up in flames?

This time when she went back to the nearest opening to shoot, the clearing was empty of all save the two dead men on the ground and the one crawling away through the muddy snow. She hesitated, waiting for someone to move.

"What is it?" Colin demanded. "Why aren't you firing?"

"They're not out there," she said in disbelief.

"We ran 'em off? Yaay!" He jumped up and down at her elbow. "They turned tail and—"

"Quiet!" she ordered. "Here, you hold the musket while I look." There were too many unanswered questions. Why had the attack been so half-hearted? Why hadn't someone slipped up to the cabin and fired inside through one of the gun ports?

She checked the other sides of the cabin. No signs of hostiles anywhere. The war cries had stopped, but the silence was somehow worse than the screaming. She could feel her own blood pounding in her temple, and her heart was beating so fast it was a wonder it hadn't burst from her chest.

Simon's bloody tales of Indian atrocities committed against white women and children coiled in the recesses of her imagination like diamondback rattlers. "Never allow yourself to be captured," Simon had warned. "Never. Five minutes with a Shawnee warrior and you'd pray for the mercy of hellfire."

She scooped up a double handful of water from the bucket on the table, drank a little, and splashed the rest over her face. Returning to Colin's side, she lifted the musket's weight again and curled her finger around the trigger.

"We can't hold them off with one musket," Colin said. His brown eyes were wide with fear.

"The walls are thick, they'll hold."

He shook his head. "Not if the Injuns set fire to the roof."

"If they burn the cabin, we'll go out through the root cellar and follow Simon's tunnel to the hill behind the house," she said patiently. "He dug it for an escape route in case of trouble."

"This is trouble. I think we better go out now, while we can."

"No, not yet." She took a deep breath and tried to sound sure of herself. "We're safer in here for now."

"I ain't seen hide nor hair of 'em," he said. "Maybe—"

"Hide nor hair of them," she said, correcting him automatically. Keeping Colin from sounding like an ignorant backwoodsman was a never-ending task. Simon claimed she was "too high in the stomach" for a bastard Irish slut, but it was a habit she couldn't change. Illegitimate or not, she and Colin were James Gordon's children, and they would speak the King's English as properly as he had.

Colin threw her an incredulous look. "Hide nor hair of *them*. Maybe the *In-di-ans* hiked up their pants and ran."

"Shhh." She gazed intently at the tree line. "You go to the back wall and watch," she said. "In case they sneak up on us."

He obeyed without a whimper, and a lump rose in her throat. Colin was only ten, but he was tough. Whatever happened, he would face the worst head on, eyes open, back straight. Papa would have been proud of you, she thought. You're a Gordon, through and through.

Christ's sacred wounds! Ten was too young to die. Too young to end up scalped or burned alive. If only Simon would come back—or some of his friends. She hadn't seen a hundred Indians out there, only a dozen or so. A few riflemen could drive them off before—

Suddenly, something white caught her attention. A brave stepped out of the woods waving a cream-colored deer hide. "Wife of Simon Brandt!" he called in perfect English. "Wife of Simon Brandt! This man, Fire Talon, would parley with you!"

"What do you want?" she shouted back.

"Surrender or we burn your house!"

Rebecca's mouth went dry, and she dug her nails into the musket stock. The brave was tall and muscular, not as tall as Simon, perhaps, but sleek as a mountain cat. He wore his hair long. Blue-black as the devil's own locks, it fell to his waist in shimmering waves.

He was too far away for her to see the color of his eyes, but she knew they would be black and cold as obsidian. His brows were slashes across a hawklike face; his high prominent cheekbones were marked with yellow and black war paint. He was half-naked in the cold; his chest was bare, adorned with heathen bear claws. A wide band of copper encircled one sinewy bicep, and a single eagle feather dangled from the back of his head to trail insolently against his naked shoulder.

His waist was as narrow as a girl's, his loins barely covered with a fringed loincloth. Leggings reached from mid-thigh to the tops of his moccasins. He carried no weapons, but she recognized him just the same. He was the first Indian she had seen splashing through the creek—the one she'd fired at from the top of the slope.

"Surrender, wife of Simon Brandt!" he thundered. "Surrender and you will not die this day!"

"Go to hell!" she replied, drawing a bead on the amulet in the center of his bear-claw necklace. Then she pulled the trigger, solidifying her position with a .75-caliber musket ball aimed two inches to the right, directly at his black heart.

Chapter 2

Sh'Kotaa Osh-Kah-Shah, Fire Talon—war chief of the Mecate Shawnee—recoiled in shock as Rebecca's musket ball tore a furrow along his left upper arm. "Treacherous white witch!" He gasped as pain replaced the initial numbness and bright red blood spilled over his beaten copper armband to drip on the trampled snow.

Releasing the white deerskin robe which served as a parley flag of truce, Fire Talon shook a clenched fist at the cabin. *What manner of humans were these English?* he raged silently. *Honor means nothing to them.*

"Get out of the line of fire!" shouted his friend Fox from the safety of the trees. "Will you stand there like an untried boy until she reloads?"

"Use common sense!" argued another, a dark-skinned warrior from beyond the Ohio, a man Talon knew only as The Stranger.

Talon's nostrils flared as he breathed deeply of the crisp morning air, laced with the scents of pine, burning leaves, and the acrid scent of gunpowder. He drew himself up to his full height and pointed deliberately toward the cabin, waiting until the barrel of the musket appeared once more in the small round loophole. "You have broken the peace, woman!" he called in precise English. "What happens is on your head!" He motioned to

Counts His Scalps and switched to his native Algonquian tongue. "Burn them out!"

Seconds later, three flaming arrows flew through the air toward the house. One struck the stone chimney and fell to earth, but the other two stuck upright in the cedar shakes. Counts His Scalps had wrapped the arrow shafts with dried grass; in seconds, an orange tongue of fire licked against the wooden roof and began to smolder. Counts let out a long triumphant whoop and raised his outspread arms over his head.

We'll hear about that deed around the campfires, Talon thought wryly. Counts His Scalps was a boastful man, one who would not let his successes go unnoticed, but he was brave and trustworthy. Talon was glad Counts had come along. In spite of his prickly disposition, he was an asset to the raiding party.

On the hillside beyond the house, Counts' companion, Osage Killer, saw the smoke and responded with a perfect imitation of a hunting wolf's howl. Counts His Scalps grinned from ear to ear.

Talon slapped him on the shoulder and nodded. "Good aim. Shoot a few more, just to be certain."

"The roof will burn," Counts grumbled. "I hate to waste fine arrows."

Talon scooped up a handful of snow and held it against the place where the white woman's musket ball had grazed his arm. The bleeding had slowed, but the gash stung like the poison of a hundred wasps. "Just the same, shoot another volley," Talon ordered. "We want to frighten them as badly as possible."

"Maybe they are too stupid to be afraid."

Talon frowned as he slung his embroidered war

bag over his shoulder and slid his knife back into his fringed leather sheath. "Don't underestimate Simon Brandt's woman. Skins Two Elk and Shadow of Rain are dead because of her." He motioned toward the clearing where the still bodies of his followers lay. "Joins the River is badly injured."

"I am sorry for their families, but Shadow of Rain was a fool. You should not have brought him with us."

Talon nodded again. "His luck was bad. You are right, I should not have allowed him to join us. But after men die, it is easy to say they should not have come. Would that I had your vision."

"I would not have chosen either one of them. Skins Two Elk has mocked me many times at the council fire. A lesser man would take pleasure in his death, but I do not." Counts His Scalps's handsome face grew sullen. "I accept people as they are. But still, I would not have brought him."

"Perhaps I should ask your opinion the next time I assemble a war band," Talon mused.

"Yes. It would be wise."

Talon averted his eyes so that the brave could not read the amusement there. "I'll keep that in mind," Talon said gravely. The loss of the dead men cut him deep, but now was not the time to reveal his emotions. Counts His Scalps would follow so long as he believed that Talon was a strong leader. Any sign of weakness, and Counts would desert him; and if Counts His Scalps went, Osage Killer would leave as well. The companions had their faults, but they had proved their valor against the Iroquois. He would be a fool to alienate them unnecessarily.

Talon thought briefly of the dead warriors. Nei-

ther were married, and that was good. There
would be no widows to mourn their passing.
Skins Two Elk had grown sons with families of
their own, but Shadow of Rain left only an aging
mother. She lived near The Forks in *Shannopis*, the
big Lenape town. He would remember to see that
there were men to hunt meat for the old woman,
and he would send her enough skins and trade
goods to make her wealthy. He could not replace
her only son, but he could make her last days
comfortable.

A war chief carries a heavy burden, he thought.
He leads men to victory—if he is good at what he
does—but he also marks a path to the grave for
others. And this time his responsibility was greater
than it had ever been; his own father's life hung in
the balance.

Talon picked up his long rifle from where it
leaned against a pin oak, raised it, and checked the
priming.

"I tell you it is a waste of good arrows," Counts
complained as he shot two more fiery missiles into
the cabin roof.

Talon barely heard him; the familiar features of
his father's lined face formed in his mind's eye
and a blast of cold wind chilled the war chief's
heart. "Only for my *no'tha*, my father, would I
break my own rule," he murmured under his
breath.

"What did you say?"

"This business does not sit well on my stomach," Talon replied.

Choosing an arrow from his beaded quiver,
Counts squatted beside the small fire and began to
wrap shredded bark along the shaft. "I have not
noticed that the *Englishmanake* shy away from

burning our villages or murdering our women and children."

"The whites behave like crazed animals. Must we, who know better, lower ourselves to imitate them?"

Counts shrugged. "Sometimes, when it is necessary."

Talon shrugged. "Stay here, but keep a sharp eye and listen for my signal." Leaving Counts His Scalps by the fire, he moved back into the woods and circled around the cabin.

It was no small thing for Talon to lead his warriors against Simon Brandt's woman. For more years than he wanted to remember, he'd followed the war trail. He had killed many men in honorable battle, burned many cabins, and taken more scalps than he wanted to number. But he had never made war against his enemy's women and children. To do so meant breaking an oath he'd made on his mother's grave. "Forgive me, *Anati*," he whispered through tightly drawn lips. *I do this in hope of saving my father.*

When the English soldiers at Fort Nelson had sent the belt of white wampum to many of the Delaware and Shawnee villages, including the Mecate, asking for a peace conference, Talon and his father had argued. Medicine Smoke was a shaman, a holy man, and it was natural that he should seek peace—and just as natural that he should see good in the whites where Talon saw none.

"I fear my son has begun to take pleasure in the scalps he takes," Medicine Smoke had said sadly. "Taking life is always a bad thing. A spiritual man—a man whole in mind and body—does what he must to protect his people, but he finds no joy in the stench of death."

"The English cannot be trusted, Father," Talon had replied. "The soldiers of King George do not love the Delaware or the Shawnee. They love only our land and the soft beaver pelts they steal from us."

"Their messenger says that they weary of this war as we do. They say they will make a treaty between us, one that will not strip our people of honor."

"Who says? Simon Brandt?"

"Even the mightiest enemy can become a friend," his father had murmured hoarsely. Medicine Smoke had survived a Huron's knife wound to the throat in his youth, and his voice sounded like the rasp of dried corn husks.

"Have you forgotten my mother? My sister? I will make peace with Simon Brandt when his soul walks the star path and not before," Talon had insisted hotly.

"You will listen to the wisdom of your elders."

In the end, the council had listened to the words of Medicine Smoke and other old men instead of Talon's warnings. They had sent a delegation to Fort Nelson to talk with the white colonel and the long rifles, led by Simon Brandt. And the price of that mission was death for many and imprisonment for his beloved father.

Talon had not gone—would not willingly place himself behind enemy walls. From a distance, he'd heard the shots and the screams of men both red and white when talking ceased and killing began.

The toll of the Mecate Shawnee had been terrible. Four members of the high council fire had died: Plunging Raven, Cloud Man, Quiet Bear, and

Shadow of the Sun. Raven's wife, Sees Red, had been shot down like a fleeing doe, and the council woman, Remembers Yesterday, was clubbed in the head so terribly that she would surely die. Raven's oldest son, Pipe, had carried her away from the fort, but it had cost him an eye and the knowledge that he had left his dying father's side.

Other tribes had suffered equally. Not one member of the delegation from the Tax-cox Lenape village had survived. In all, the death count of Indians was fifteen, with three men and one woman taken prisoner. Four escaped uninjured. English had died as well, but Talon didn't know how many.

Not enough.

The whites were as numerous as leaves in a forest, and the great sea was not wide enough to keep them in their own land. They were like spoiled children, taking what they wanted and destroying what they could not use. And if the white men could not be driven back across the salt water, it would mean the extermination of his people.

The bitter thoughts hardened Talon's heart. Simon Brandt was responsible for Medicine Smoke's capture. Now the wife of Simon Brandt would pay the price.

Thick, acrid smoke from the burning cabin seeped along the narrow, dirt tunnel and made it hard for Rebecca and Colin to breathe. She went first—crouched low on hands and knees—pushing aside cobwebs and dragging the loaded musket behind her. "Stay close," she whispered to her brother. Her eyes stung, but she was afraid to wipe them because her hands were so dirty. The walls of the passageway were narrow and crumbly, and the floor was covered with loose soil and gravel.

She was so scared that she was trembling all over. She'd never liked the dark, and being hemmed in by the earth terrified her. She hadn't realized that it was so far to Simon's secret hillside entrance.

Rebecca had no idea what they would do when they came to the mouth of the tunnel. Would it be hours or days before they'd dare to venture out? Would they freeze to death without a fire when night came?

It had been impossible to bring much with them in the frantic attempt to escape the fire. A flint and tinder box, the hunting bag with its knife and powder horn, a single wool blanket, and a canteen of water. Colin had slung the canteen around his neck by the leather strap, rolled Simon's small camp ax in the blanket with some pemmican and cold biscuits, and tied the blanket together with a short length of rope. At the last moment before climbing down the hole he had dashed back across the smoke-filled cabin for his tin box of fish hooks, folding knife, and bows and arrows.

"Don't stop," Colin warned.

"I can't see."

"Don't be a baby, Becca. I been through here lots of times, and I never even seen a snake."

"Uggh, did you have to mention snakes?"

"Look," he whispered excitedly. "I see light. We're almost there."

Rebecca squinted. Yes, there was a pinhole of daylight ahead. She raised up, hit her head on the roof of the tunnel, and caught her breath as dirt rained around her.

"Keep going," Colin said. "The smoke's getting worse."

The last few yards were all uphill. As she crawled closer, the air became fresher. "Stay here," she whispered. "I'll see if it's safe."

Cautiously, she pushed aside a woven screen of wild grape vine. A fallen tree and a pile of brush shielded the entrance from sight. "I think it's all right," she said, wiggling through. Smoke was drifting out of the mouth of the tunnel, and she hoped that the breeze would dissipate it before the savages noticed. She brushed the dirt off the musket and checked the priming.

"What do you see?" he asked. "Let me—"

"Stay there until I tell you to come," she repeated. She looked back in the direction of the cabin. A black column of smoke spewed into the sky.

"Take the blanket," Colin said. He scrambled to his feet. "Now what, Becca?" His face split into a grin. "You should see your face. You look like a blackamoor."

She took a scarf from her pocket and rubbed her aching eyes. "You don't look so great yourself." Her heartbeat slowed to normal as she took deep breaths of the fresh air.

We did it, she thought. *We got away. And with luck, the Indians will think we died in the fire.* She didn't want to think about the miles of wilderness between them and the nearest white settlement. They were alive, and for now, that was all that mattered.

"We best hide until dark," Colin whispered. "You never know if—"

"I told you to stay in the tunnel," she admonished. She had no intention of venturing out until she was sure the hostiles were gone, but neither did she relish the thought of spending hours inside the damp passageway.

Reluctantly, she crawled back into the opening, keeping the musket ready to fire if she saw any sign of movement. Colin pressed close to her and she draped the blanket around them. Her fingers and toes were numb with cold; she wiggled them to start the blood flowing.

"I'm scared, Becca," her brother murmured.

"Shhh, we'll be all right. Simon's probably on his way home now," she soothed. "Like as not, he's seen the smoke and will come in here with all guns blazing." She hugged Colin's sturdy shoulders, suddenly realizing how much he'd grown in the last year. He wouldn't be a child for long.

The thought that he would be leaving her in a few years was more chilling than the cold. Colin was all she had. If Simon sent the boy east to be indentured to a blacksmith as he'd threatened, she'd have no one left to love.

No one to love her . . .

I should have had babies by now. Colin is my flesh and blood—all that's left of my life before I crossed the ocean from Ireland. But, still, it's only natural that he'll sprout to a man and want his own family.

If he lives that long . . .

She swallowed against the tightness of her throat and took comfort in the warmth of Colin's body against hers. His legs were long and gangly; his hands and wrists thrust out of his shirt sleeves like a scarecrow's.

His thin fingers tightened around hers. "Simon said I was to kill you myself before I let Injuns get you," he whispered. "But I don't think I can do it." She felt a shudder run through him. "I love you, Becca." His last words were barely audible, and all the more poignant to her for being so.

She laid her cheek against his head. His thick, dark hair was clean as always; soft as an otter pelt, it smelled of wood smoke and pine. "I love you too," she murmured close to his ear. "And I couldn't kill you—no matter what Simon said."

"He said it was my duty—but I couldn't ... I know I couldn't."

"It will be all right," she repeated, "I promise."

"Cross your heart and hope to die?"

"Yes, Colin, cross my heart and hope to die." She hugged him fiercely.

And they waited.

Hours passed. It seemed to Rebecca as if the sun crawled across the sky; she couldn't see it for the clouds, but she could guess at the time. Sometime in the afternoon they allowed themselves a swallow of water from the canteen. Colin slept fitfully, but she couldn't. She simply waited, staring out and listening, praying that the Indians had given up the hunt and left.

Just before dusk, a cardinal swooped down into the thicket and scratched aimlessly at the fallen leaves. Then two grosbeaks landed on a branch and frightened the cardinal away. Colin stirred beside her and the grosbeaks took flight.

"Becca?"

"What?"

"I'm cold."

"Me too."

"No." His voice was thinner than usual. "I mean I'm really cold." He burrowed closer. "I'm cold to death, Becca."

"No, you're not."

"We've got to start walkin'. If we stay here after dark, without a fire, we'll freeze."

Snow was falling again, big lazy flakes that drifted around them as silently as late autumn moths.

"I haven't heard anything but squirrels and birds for hours," she confided. "We'll go as soon as it gets good and dark."

"Where?"

"East to the settlements," she said with more confidence than she felt. "I'm sure I can find the way to Fort Nelson."

"It wasn't finding the trail that I was worried about," Colin said. "It's the weather. There's no safe place to build a fire—"

"Then we'll do without one. We've got to get away from here."

"I never thought I'd miss Simon."

Rebecca tried not to smile. At times even a stern husband was a welcome presence. "Mind your tongue," she said. "You forget who's given you a roof over your head and food in your belly these last eight years."

"And his fist."

"Simon's hard, I admit, but he's fair. You're wild as a Mohawk, Colin. If you'd be more obedient, he wouldn't have to—"

"He hits you."

"Not often, and like as not, I deserve it. I've a harsh tongue for a woman. I sometimes fail to show Simon the respect a husband—"

"Simon's a swivin' bully. I'll beat the tar out of him when I'm a man grown."

She gasped in astonishment. "Colin Gordon. Bite your tongue. Where did you learn such foul talk? I've taught you better."

"It's true. He's mean as a wounded opossum. I owe him nothin' and neither do you."

"Stop it," she hissed. "No more." A vein throbbed in her temple. There was no mistaking the venom in her brother's voice. She'd known he harbored ill feelings against Simon, but she'd not guessed the boy's contempt ran so deep.

She'd tried to keep peace between them, shielding Colin from the worst of her husband's temper and urging the child to show proper respect. Most men beat their wives, and she'd never known a father who didn't use physical punishment to curb a child's mischief. *Spare the rod and spoil the child*, the Bible said.

Except for their father ... James Gordon, dead in his grave these past ten years, was the sweetest, gentlest man she'd ever seen. God, how she missed him and mourned the fact that he'd died too soon for Colin to remember him or his loving arms around them. Oh, Dadda, how I wish you were here now, she thought. Just for a minute ... just so that I could hug you one last time.

"It's time," she said to Colin. "Follow me. Keep close, and don't make a sound."

Her muscles were almost too stiff with cold to stand. Her legs were as awkward as a newborn colt's. Her nose felt as though it was a chunk of ice.

Cautiously, she parted the bushes and stared into the twilight. Nothing moved. Holding the musket ready, she took one step and then another. "It's all right," she whispered. "They're gone." She glanced over her shoulder at Colin and then a huge dark form hurled itself out of the branches overhead and knocked her flat on the ground.

Chapter 3

Rebecca's musket went off, firing harmlessly into the air as it spun out of her hand. She screamed and tried to squirm free of the heavy weight pinning her down in the snow. Gasping for breath, she flailed wildly with her fists, and the second her attacker got to his knees, she began to crawl away.

"*Chitkwesi!*," he ordered. "Be still."

Strong fingers closed around her bare ankle and she kicked out with all her might. "No!" she cried. "Run, Colin! Run!" From the corner of her eye, she saw her brother fighting with a swarthy brave wearing a chestplate of battered armor.

"I said, *be still*, woman!" her captor repeated in carefully enunciated English.

She kicked again, this time striking flesh. She heard him grunt in pain, but she had no time to see what damage she'd done. Shrieking with anger, she threw herself against the Indian who was assaulting Colin. Climbing his back, she pounded him on the head with both hands and tried to scratch his eyes.

Colin lowered his head and butted the Indian in the pit of his stomach. The brave doubled over, sending Rebecca pitching into the snow.

"Enough!" the first man commanded.

25

Rebecca whipped the hunting knife from her sheath and whirled to face him. "Run, Colin!"

To her dismay, he didn't obey. Nocking an arrow, he drew his child's flimsy bow and took a protective stance at her back. She could hear him breathing hard, but he didn't say a word. He just stood there, braced against her, showing as much grit as any man full grown.

"Colin . . ." she began. But it was too late for retreat. The bushes parted, and she caught sight of a third hostile, and then a fourth, as the war party surrounded them. Time seemed to slow as she stared hopelessly from one cruel, painted face to another.

A man's deep chuckle seeped through her terror. "*Qua neeshk won ai,*" Talon said in Algonquian. "Not a soft white woman, but a she-panther and her cub. See their sharp teeth."

One of the other warriors called out in a mocking voice, but the Indian words were meaningless to her ears. She turned to the creature who had laughed, realizing with shock that he was the same brave she'd shot outside the cabin when he demanded her surrender—and also the one who'd knocked her to the ground and wrestled with her. Her foot had evidently struck his nose because it was trickling blood.

"Put down your knife, wife of Simon Brandt," he said in perfect English. The amusement vanished from his face, and Rebecca felt the intensity of his ire. She stiffened involuntarily.

His eyes were as black as pitch; they seemed as lifeless as glass in his sharp-featured, bronze face as he stared at her with a fierceness that made her blood run cold. She could not keep from trembling.

"You have no chance," he said in a low, rumbling voice. "Surrender your weapon and the boy will not be harmed."

"No!" Colin said. "Don't trust him."

She looked back over her shoulder to her brother holding his bow drawn tight, his arrow aimed at the dark-skinned warrior in armor.

"The boy is brave," Rebecca's assailant said. She could see the others glancing toward him as if waiting for a signal to strike, and she surmised that he was their leader. "Such a panther cub should not die for his courage."

Simon's warnings flashed through her mind, and it came to her that she could turn and drive her knife into Colin's back before any of them could stop her. *"Better to end it quick, than slow over a Shawnee torture fire,"* Simon had said. But the thought of harming Colin sickened her. Instead, she lunged at the devil-eyed savage, thrusting her steel blade toward his heart. She knew she had no hope of escape, but she intended to die fighting.

The Indian stood his ground, waiting until the point of her knife was barely inches from his skin, then he caught her wrist in an iron grip. Before she could react, he knocked her feet out from under her and she fell. Her head hit the snow-covered earth with enough force to take her breath away. When she opened her eyes, he was on top of her, pinning both arms.

"Let go of the knife," he said.

Knife? What knife? Her head spun, and blackness threatened to overcome her. Did she still have the knife?

"Drop it, or I will break your arm."

She became aware of the pain in her wrist as he tightened his grasp. His face was so close that she could feel his hot breath on her cheek. His lips were drawn back in a snarl, and she caught a glimpse of white, even teeth.

"No!" Colin yelled.

Rebecca gasped as the Indian flattened his nearly naked body against her, and Colin's arrow flew over the man's back, just missing him. Someone let out a shout, and Colin was silent.

"Colin!" she screamed. "Don't hurt him! Please!"

Then the Indian was on his feet, yanking her up. He bent and retrieved her knife—she hadn't been aware that she'd dropped it, but her right hand was numb. She struggled to see around him. He was taller than she was, but not so tall as Simon. Half naked, the brave seemed all muscle. His red-brown skin was only a little darker than Colin's, but it glistened as though it were oiled. She twisted, trying to break free, and he held her out at arm's length, too far away to hit or kick him.

"Colin!" she sobbed.

"Silence," he ordered her. He said something in his heathen language, and the armored warrior dragged Colin into view.

"Becca." His child's voice revealed his fear, but he wasn't crying—and as far as she could see, he wasn't hurt. They had tied his wrists behind him, and his clothing was wet from rolling in the snow, but his face was unmarked.

Her captor peered curiously into her face. "Your son?"

"She's my sister," Colin cried stoutly. "She's my sister, and you leave her be."

A faint smile played over the lips of the savage that held her fast. "He does not have the look of Simon Brandt, this small panther cub." Then he grew stern again. "I am *Sh'Kotaa Osh-Kah-Shah*—Fire Talon. War chief of the Mecate Shawnee. You are my prisoner."

"You son of a bitch, you're hurting my arm!" she protested.

He released her and she jumped back. It was easier to breathe—easier to think—when he wasn't clutching her with that blood-stained hand. She inhaled sharply as she remembered that the blood was his, and that she had been the one who'd given him the wound . . . and killed several of his war party.

Her face must have given away her fright because he scowled at her. "You cannot escape, wife of Simon Brandt. I—"

"You'll rue the day you burned our cabin, you heathen bastard. When Simon catches up with you, he'll—" He scowled so harshly that her words died in her throat. Her knees suddenly went weak as a newborn pup's. God in heaven! Hadn't Simon always told her that her mouth would be the death of her? "Please," she said in a shaking voice. "Please let my brother go. He's only a child. Do whatever you want to do to me, Colin has no part of it."

"I'm not a child!" Colin said. "Let her go. I killed those Indians. I shot them. It's me you want—not her."

"That's not true," Rebecca protested. "I shot them. You must believe me. It wasn't Colin. He didn't even have a gun."

Talon glanced from one to the other. He had not expected such valor from the family of Simon Brandt. The woman had a warrior's heart for all her treachery, and the boy . . . Well, the boy was not his worry. The Stranger had captured the

white boy. He was his to do with as he pleased.
The Stranger was not a cruel man; Talon didn't believe he had it in him to harm a child, especially
one with such promise. His own worry was the
woman, and making a bargain with the English
for the safe release of his father.

"Bind the woman," he ordered Counts in Algonquian.

"Beware of her claws," his follower quipped, as
he drew her hands behind her back and secured
them with a leather thong.

"Becca," the boy called. He would have run to
her but The Stranger blocked his path.

The woman trembled like a willow tree in the
wind as Counts tightened the cords on her wrists,
but no hint of tears showed on her pale face. Her
striking eyes were large and intelligent, framed by
thick lashes. The exact color of a spring sky, Talon
mused. Strange eyes for a woman, hardly human
in appearance, but memorable just the same.

Talon wished she'd stop looking at him as
though she expected him to strike her head from
her body. Guilt washed over him. Many men took
perverse delight in making war on women; the
whites and a few depraved renegades even sought
sexual pleasure from their helpless prey. He would
never understand such logic. This was dirty business, and it weakened his manhood to be part of
it.

A branch snapped and he turned to see Osage
Killer appear from the forest. He raised a hand in
salute.

"We are not alone," Counts' partner said without commenting on the prisoners. He gestured toward the hill. "Two Frenchmen, two hands of

Huron. They have seen the smoke, I think, and come to reap our harvest of booty."

Talon nodded. Huron. Sworn enemies of his people. He did not fear them, but neither would he risk an encounter with so few men. Enough had died already. "We have done what we came for," he said in his own tongue. "Let us leave this place." He glanced at the prisoners and switched to English. "There are Huron close by. If you cry out, it will mean your death. Do you understand?"

The woman nodded. The boy looked at her for an instant, then back to him, and gave his reluctant consent.

"Gag them," Counts said. "I'll not lose my scalp for a foolish squaw's wailing."

Realizing that his follower was right, Talon gave the command. He could not risk his life and those of his men on a frightened woman's fancy. She uttered only a low moan as Counts bound a leather strap over her mouth.

Talon motioned downhill toward the stream. Quickly, Osage Killer, Counts, and the others melted into the trees. The Stranger led the unprotesting boy away, leaving him alone with Simon Brandt's wife. She stared at him with accusing eyes.

I do only what must be done, he thought, as he seized her and slung her over his shoulder. It was not as if she hadn't tried to kill him repeatedly today. Ignoring her struggles, he picked up his long rifle and set out after his men at a steady lope.

The water was cold as he crossed the stream, taking care not to wet his powder. The woman was a heavy load, but he adjusted his stride, taking care where he put his feet down. It would not do to trip and fall with her, thereby making him look a fool in front of his men.

She was as tense as a crouching wolf. It would have been far easier to carry her unconscious, but at least she had ceased to fight him. It pleased him; it was what he would have done in her position, and it showed her keen mind. He did not fool himself that she was subdued. No, this *equiwa* would bear close watching. Given half a chance, she would run a knife into his gut without shedding a tear.

He climbed the ridge beyond the creek, walked along a fallen log, and dropped onto an outcropping of bare rock. He walked the rock for the distance of an arrow's flight, taking care not to put a foot where it might leave sign for the Huron to track them. Each man in his party would be doing the same; it was the reason he carried the woman instead of making her walk.

From time to time, he caught sight of Walking Bear, Fox, or Osage Killer and Counts. The pair were taking turns carrying the injured man, Joins the River. Others bore the two dead bodies; he would not leave them unburied, without proper ceremony to see them to the spirit world. Talon hadn't seen The Stranger since they'd waded the stream, but he was a competent warrior. He had no doubt that The Stranger was ahead of him, moving fast with the boy, putting distance between them and the Huron. For the Huron would find their trail, no matter how cautious they were. So many men could not pass through a forest without leaving sign; it was impossible.

When he reached the last of the rock, he lowered his prisoner to the ground. "Now you will run," he told her. "If you give trouble or do not keep up, I will leave you for the Huron." It was a lie. She was his captive now, and he would not give her up—not without shedding his last drop of blood. But it would not do to tell her so. Fear would lend wings to her feet.

Her blue eyes sought his, full of pent-up hate. He had thought to remove her gag, but decided to leave it on a while longer. A woman's scream carried a long way in these woods, and he had no wish to end up roasted over a Huron cook fire.

Without speaking to her, he untied her wrists and fastened them together in front of her with a foot of slack cord between her hands. Then he looked down at her long skirts and exhaled in disgust. White women—they made even less sense than their men. Running or climbing in such garments was ridiculous.

Her eyes widened in fear as he drew his scalping knife and cut away the layers of cloth below her knees, then slit the sides to her hip. With satisfaction, he noted that she wore sturdy skin moccasins that laced tight around her trim ankles. Bundling the precious wool and linen scraps, he tied them with a strip of leather and slung them over her shoulder. Fox had picked up her hunting bag at the mouth of the tunnel; he made a mental note to retrieve it. Such a shrewd woman would have brought items of value with her, perhaps even powder and shot.

"Come, we go," he said. They began to run downhill. They were behind the others now; stopping had cost them time, but now that he didn't have to carry her, they would make it up.

They ran for as long as it took a man to skin and butcher an elk, and then he paused to let her catch her breath. Her blue eyes showed weariness, but they had lost none of their defiance. Sweat streaked her face and darkened her red hair. Her free hand was scratched and bleeding where she had scraped it against a thorn tree.

He caught that small hand in his and held it up to examine the wound. The tip of a broken thorn was embedded in her palm. He raised her hand to his lips and felt the splinter with the tip of his tongue. She gasped and pulled her hand back.

"Be still," he admonished. "Do you want me to cut it out with my knife?" A thorn could fester and turn flesh black with poison. Dead, she was of no use to him.

She shook her head. Her hand trembled as she held it out to him. Her sky eyes were wary, the expression like that of a doe he had once seen crossing a frozen lake in winter. The ice had been rotten, and it creaked ominously with each step the deer took. Still she had continued on until she reached the far bank and safety. He wondered if firm earth waited for this female with the strange blue eyes. Eventual safety or . . .

A shudder of revulsion rippled through him. War should be between men, he thought. And no matter how much contempt he felt for Simon Brandt and those he led to Indian country, he could not find it in his heart to despise this courageous woman, even if she was without honor.

Gently, he bent and brushed his lips against her hand, then, when he found the thorn with his tongue, he closed his teeth on it and pulled it free. Blood welled up from her palm as he spat out the bit of wood. He scooped up a handful of snow and pressed it against the injury.

She blinked. Moisture glistened in her round eyes and for a second he thought she might begin to cry. Then her eyes narrowed and the expression gleaming there hardened. Again, Talon reminded himself that she was his enemy's wife, and that she wished him dead.

"If I take away the cloth from your mouth, will you promise not to cry out?" he asked her. She will run farther if she isn't gagged, he told himself. "Try any of your English tricks, and you will regret them, I promise you."

Her chin quivered.

"Yes or no?" he demanded, deliberately making his voice as cold as morning frost.

She nodded.

"Disobey me and you die," he warned, cutting the thong.

The corners of her mouth were rubbed by the cloth; she touched the raw spots gingerly, but uttered no sound.

"Good. Can you run some more?" he asked.

She nodded again.

"Not far. When we reach the river, we will travel by canoe."

"My ... my brother?" Her tone was low and husky, as melodious as water trickling over rocks.

"We value bravery. He will live."

"He won't be ..." She swallowed and moistened her lips with her tongue. "Tortured?"

"We are not English. We do not torture children—or burn them alive in Jesu houses of worship. Nor do we crush their infant skulls against trees or cut them from their mother's bellies." For a terrible moment, he remembered again the faces of the women and babies he had carried from a burned church long ago. By sheer will, he pushed the awful images away and tried to picture his mother's face when he had last seen her alive and laughing.

The woman moved back and his eyes snapped open.

The blood had drained from her face until the freckles stood out like a spattering of brown paint on her ashen skin. She knew of the atrocities committed against his people—of the evils done by her own husband's hand, and she knew that he knew.

"Snow will stop the bleeding," he said gruffly, breaking the silence. "I do not wish to leave a trail for the Huron scouts."

She stooped and scraped up a handful of snow. "What are you going to do to me?" she demanded.

"Your husband holds my father prisoner. I will trade your life for that of my father. So long as he is safe, you are safe."

"Simon? But you must be mistaken," she said. "He went to witness a peace treaty at Fort Nelson."

"So did my father. But he was betrayed by Simon Brandt and made a prisoner." He took her arm to pull her up and spied a flicker of red through the trees where no red should be. Instinctively he shoved her to the ground and knelt beside her. "Huron," he whispered urgently, bringing up his long rifle, checking the priming, and drawing back the hammer.

His heartbeat quickened; the hair on his neck rose like the hackles of a dog. Huron. He was certain of it. He could almost smell them.

Then a red-coated figure darted out from behind a tree and Talon's breath caught in his throat. His finger tightened on the trigger as he followed the sprinting target with his rifle sight. Another tree blocked his line of vision. And when his quarry moved into the light again, he fired.

Chapter 4

⌒∽◯◯∽⌒

The explosion nearly deafened Rebecca. She turned her head in time to see the Huron in the red coat sprawl face down in the snow. Immediately, shots rang out from the forest. Puffs of white smoke drifted up and the air buzzed with the ring of hot lead.

A chilling "*Ki-yi-yi-yi*" burst from the throat of a nearly bald warrior wielding a massive war club. He leaped a fallen log and charged down upon them. Fire Talon—her Shawnee captor—sprang to meet him, dodging the deadly swing and slamming his opponent in the chest with the butt of his rifle. As the Huron fell, Talon finished him off with a second blow to the head. Blood flew and Rebecca closed her eyes in sick horror.

Two more braves sprinted across the clearing. Talon heaved his tomahawk into the first man's throat and met the second with a drawn knife.

The remaining Huron was shorter than Talon and older. His roached hair was streaked with gray above a black-painted face, and a circlet of mummified human fingers dangled around his neck. His arms were long and thewy, crisscrossed with healed scars, and his earlobes were distended with beaten copper disks. Shrieking a challenge, he rushed at Talon, then feinted left, bristling like a fighting cock. Clutched in his right hand he

brandished a French trade hatchet, in his left a
butcher knife.

Rebecca slipped the cord off one wrist. She
crawled across the ground to the place where Talon's rifle lay, picked it up, and looked around for
lead and powder. He saw her from the corner of
his eye, shrugged off his hunting bag, and tossed
it to her.

"Load it," he said.

She had already dumped the contents into the
snow and was frantically scrambling for a rifle ball
and wadding. What was the proper measure of
powder for a rifle? Was it the same as a musket?
She couldn't remember, but there was no time to
think. She pulled the wooden plug on the powder
horn with her teeth and dumped in what she
hoped was right.

Her fingers were stiff with cold as she fitted a
patch over the end of the barrel and seated a
round rifle ball. The two Indians slashed at each
other, leaped and circled. Talon had drawn first
blood, but the wound on the Huron's arm was mi-
nor. Rebecca concentrated on pouring a tiny
amount of fine powder into the frizzen pan. She
was just lifting the rifle to her shoulder when the
Huron threw his tomahawk at Talon.

The Shawnee war chief ducked, passed his knife
from his right hand to his left, and hurled the
weapon. The steel blade flashed through the air
and plunged into the Huron's heart. As the
roached warrior fell back clutching his chest, Rebecca swung the rifle barrel and took a bead on
Talon.

For an instant, their eyes met. She felt sweat
trickle between her breasts. Her mouth was dry.
She willed herself to squeeze the trigger.

"Behind you!" he yelled.

She twisted around to glance back over her shoulder, half expecting to see only empty forest. Instead, another Huron in knee-high red leggings raced toward her, taking aim with a flintlock pistol.

"Shoot!" Talon shouted.

The two shots sounded as one. The Huron ran another ten yards before pitching face down. He gave two awful groans and lay still.

Talon snatched the rifle from her hands. "Come," he said, snatching up the powderhorn and bag.

"But . . . but they're dead," she whispered. Now that the immediate danger had passed, she felt faint. "I don't—"

He tucked the Huron's tomahawk into his waistband. "No!" he said. "We go, before their comrades come." He hesitated just long enough to pick up the pistol. "Do you come, or do I leave you?" he demanded.

With a tiny whimper, she set her teeth together and followed him at a hard run.

She thought they would never stop. Uphill and down they sprinted, through ancient trees that shut out the sun overhead, down the marshy lowlands and into a frozen meadow. After the first two miles, she developed a stitch in her side. She ignored it, trying with all her will to keep up with the tireless Shawnee. She knew she couldn't escape him now, but she could best him by refusing to cry quit.

In time, her breathing steadied and the pain receded to be replaced by a tight, aching chest and a sore spot on one heel. She fixed her eyes on the green, quill-worked turtle design on Talon's hunting pouch strap. The turtle rested and bounced in the exact center of the war chief's bare back, and it gave her focus for her ordeal. Her anger lent her strength, and she vowed silently to follow that green turtle to hell and back before she'd stop running.

When Talon did stop at the edge of a bluff, she nearly slammed into him. He turned and caught her with both hands, and her legs turned to porridge. She dropped to her knees, breathing hard, her head light and giddy. He left her for ... seconds? Minutes? She couldn't be sure. But when he put an arm around her shoulders again, he cupped a brimming shell of water.

She seized the cup and downed the water in one long gulp. "More," she gasped. "More."

"Wait," he said. "Too much will founder you like a sick horse." He helped her down the brush-covered bank to the river's edge and refilled the shell for her. She reached for it and he dashed it in her face.

"Damn you," she sputtered. "You fiend of Satan!" She shoved him aside and knelt beside the ice-encrusted flow. The water was so cold it made her teeth ache, but nothing had ever tasted so good in her life.

When he beckoned, she rose and followed him. Each step now was an agony. Her heels burned; her knees were as stiff as those of an old woman. Her head pounded and her eyes refused to work together.

They walked only a few hundred feet before coming to a birchbark canoe drawn up on the bank. Beside it were two of the Shawnee braves she had seen at her capture. The three men exchanged a few words, and Talon motioned for her to climb into the boat.

Realizing suddenly that Colin was nowhere to be seen shocked her out of her stupor. "Where's my brother?" she demanded. "Where is he?"

Talon frowned and spoke to his friends. One pointed up river and said something she couldn't understand. "They say he was ahead of us," Talon answered.

"I don't believe you," she cried. "We can't leave him here. The Huron will—"

"The Huron will have all our scalps stretched on hoops if we don't go quickly." He tapped the knife at his waist. "Do as I say, woman."

She scrambled into the light canoe, kneeling on the frail cedar ribs in the center and clutching both sides to hold her balance. Talon gathered a wolf pelt from the bow of the canoe and tossed it to her. She wrapped it around her, hair side in for warmth.

The war chief took a position in front of her, a second man sat directly behind her, and the third man crouched in the stern. That brave made no attempt to lift a paddle; instead he checked the priming on his musket and scanned the shoreline with narrowed eyes.

Talon slid his rifle sling over his shoulder and grasped a paddle in his sinewy hands. Pushing away from the bank, he drove the canoe out into the current and turned the bow upriver. Sleek back muscles rippled under his copper-brown skin as he dipped deep into the icy water and propelled the vessel along with powerful strokes.

In spite of her intense hatred for him, it was impossible not to admire his animal strength and coordination. The rhythm of his repeated motion was almost hypnotic. The drops of water spraying from the blade of his paddle sparkled like diamonds in the fading afternoon light.

Her eyelids were heavy; she was long past exhaustion. Her agony over Colin's safety tore at her belly and brought tears to her eyes, but she blinked them away. She'd not let these heathen see her weep. She'd die before she showed them any scrap of fear.

The canoe glided along as though by magic, the only sound the faint swish of water and an occasional cry of a startled bird. In spite of her determination not to, she drifted into sleep.

When she woke, it was dark and she was alone in the boat with Talon. There were no stars; only a faint crescent moon lit the black surface of the river.

"Where are they?" she asked.

He did not answer, and at first she thought he had not heard her. He continued dipping the paddle, first on one side of the canoe, then the other, without missing a beat.

She gathered her courage and spoke again. "Where did they go? And where's my brother?"

"Shhh," he cautioned. "A woman's voice carries far over water."

"I'll scream my head off if you don't tell me where Colin is," she threatened.

"Scream and I'll throw you into the river."

"Bully." His soft chuckle burned hotter than a curse. "Please," she tried again. "Where is Colin? He's only a child. He'll be frightened by—"

"That one would face a she-bear with an eating knife."

She tried reason. He had given her the fur wrap when she was cold. Perhaps he wasn't a complete monster. "You don't understand," she began. "I'm all he has. If what you say about your father is true, I'm sorry—but both of us would make a better bargain for a trade than just me. Simon doesn't—"

"No more talk."

"Heartless devil," she flung back.

He turned and raised the paddle. She shrank back, certain that he was going to strike her, but instead, he dipped the blade and steered the canoe to the far shore. He leaped out and pulled the vessel onto a narrow sandy beach. "Get out," he ordered.

Her limbs were so stiff that she could barely obey, but somehow she managed to get herself and the wolf robe onto the shore without getting wet. Talon took the paddles, his rifle and pack, and pushed the canoe back out into the river. The boat drifted slowly into midstream. He turned away from the water and walked into the forest. Uncertain what else to do, she hurried after him.

After only a short hike through the trees, he waded into a creek. She hesitated, knowing how quickly the water would soak her moccasins.

"Come," he said.

She sighed and obeyed. The cold was worse than she had imagined. In minutes, she was stumbling along, unable to feel sensation in her feet or ankles. When she staggered and nearly fell, he gave a sound of irritation, picked her up, and threw her across his shoulder. She dangled there, miserable and chilled, feeling for all the world like a side of venison.

At last, that torture came to an end. He climbed out of the stream, scrambled up some rocks, moved in what seemed like endless circles, and bent to squeeze under some hemlock boughs. He dumped her onto hard ground, rolled away a rock, and pointed into a pitch dark hole. "Crawl in there," he said tersely.

"Not to save my soul from eternal torment."

"Woman, you try my patience." He didn't sound angry, just tired, and she took heart from his tone.

"I hate the dark."

"It's a cave. Crawl in, so that I can close up the entrance."

"What if there are snakes? I'd rather freeze to death out here."

"You won't live to freeze to death. I'll throttle you with my bare hands if you don't do as I say."

She crawled into the stygian blackness, her heart in her throat. Spider webs clung to her face, and she shuddered, certain that she would put her hand in a nest of rattlesnakes at any second. She heard him move the rock into place, then he followed close behind.

The passageway was narrow. She could feel the wall along her left, and once, when she raised her head, she struck the rock ceiling above.

Then she touched something warm and hairy and shrieked loud enough to raise the dead.

Talon gave a grunt as she kicked him in the face. Panic-stricken, she doubled back and tried to crawl under him, still screaming at the top of her lungs. He stood up, caught her ankle, and yanked her back. She fell flat on her face and covered her head with her hands while he struck flint and steel to make a light.

When her heart slowed enough for her to open her eyes, he was staring at her in disgust. "You are a curse for some sin I have committed in another life," he said softly.

She chewed her bottom lip and looked around the small cave. The tunnel had opened into a room half the size of her cabin. The ceiling, low and uneven, was still high enough for Talon to stand upright with ease. The floor was solid rock, covered with a few scattered bones and a layer of dust. There was no sign of the bear she had touched.

"Where is it?" she asked.

"Where is what?"

"The grizzly."

He pointed to raccoon tracks and scat near her head. "Not even a mountain lion," he said. "Just a raccoon, seeking shelter from the cold as we are."

She sat up, feeling foolish. "If you mean to ravish me, do it and get it over with," she said. "I'm too tired to fight you any more. I just want to sleep." Had it been only this morning that he had led the attack on Simon's cabin? Time seemed to have lost all meaning. Even dying would be better than this endless running and walking through the snow. "My feet are frozen," she said. "I probably won't live until morning."

He made a sound of derision and proceeded to gather dry twigs to start a fire. Then he snapped the paddles into sections and fed the seasoned wood into the new flames. "Take off your moccasins and put your feet close to the fire," he instructed.

She watched him with dull eyes. What did it matter? Colin was lost. She was about to be raped and murdered, and she couldn't feel the cold in her feet anymore anyway. She closed her eyes, then snapped them open as she felt him tugging at her shoes. "Don't," she protested weakly. Was he undressing her so that he could have his way with her? She only hoped that he'd show her the mercy of cutting her throat when he was done.

Instead, he stripped off her wool stockings and briskly rubbed her blue, cold feet between his hands. "Stay awake," he ordered. "Later, when you have eaten and driven out the chill, then you can sleep." He bent down and blew warm breath on her bare skin. "You have been a warrior this day," he said. "Don't ruin it by acting like a Dutchman."

"Leave me be," she said, curling into a ball.

He took her other foot and repeated the process. It only made her colder. Her teeth began to chatter.

"Come to the fire," he said.

"Damn you to an icy hell," she muttered. She wanted to stay away, but she couldn't. The flickering orange tongues of living heat drew her with almost primeval power.

He shoved a measure of parched corn into her hand. Automatically, she put it into her mouth. Chewing seemed the hardest thing in the world, but the corn was sweetened with dried berries and maple sugar. She swallowed and then took more when he offered it.

The food strengthened her. He passed a skin of water and she drank. Now her lips felt numb. She'd never been so weary in her life, and she knew she was ill-prepared to defend herself against whatever assault he might make.

All her life she'd thought of what she'd do if a man attempted to defile her. Now it didn't seem as important as lying down by the fire. Tomorrow, she would kill him, if she could. Tonight, she would only take what came and try to survive.

He touched her shoulder and she started,

throwing up an arm to protect herself. "Do not," he said, drawing back. "Do not fear my touch, wife of Simon Brandt."

She swallowed her terror. "My name is Rebecca."

He frowned. "That which a man and woman share is not a thing to be taken like a scalp. It would shame me to lie with you."

"Shame *you?*" she cried in indignation. "I'd sooner sleep with a pig than an Indian."

He smiled thinly. "If you share Simon Brandt's bed, you do."

"Simon is my husband."

"For that, I pity you."

"He is a good man—a respected man."

"And brave when he faces unarmed women and children."

"You dare to say that—after what you've done to me this day?"

He scoffed. "You are hardly helpless. You nearly killed me outside your cabin door, and again, when I fought the Huron with my knife. You would have shot me, if—"

"I should have shot you! I'd been better to take my chances with the Huron."

He spread his hands, palms down, in a quick, dismissing gesture. "Woman, I have had enough of your evil tongue. If I was an Iroquois, I would have split it by now, or cut it out."

"And if I was a man, I would have sent you to your maker."

"Then it is lucky for us both that you are not."

"Go to hell."

"I don't believe in your white man's hell. The Creator who made the world and all in it would never have conceived of such—"

"Tell me none of your pagan beliefs. I am a Christian, and a Christian I shall be until I die."

"Which may be sooner than you expect if you don't be still." He glared at her one last time, then put the fire between them. Settling down with legs folded under him, he laid his rifle across his lap. "Move from that spot and I will make moccasins from your skin," he threatened.

She turned her back to him and lay there, pulse pounding, wrapped tightly in her wolfskin blanket. She closed her eyes, willing sleep, but now it would not come. Scenes from the day played over and over in her mind, but the most vivid and heart-wrenching was Colin's face when they'd dragged him away.

"I'll survive this," she whispered. "I'll survive it, and I'll find you, Colin. I swear I will."

But deep down inside, she fought back the fear that he was already dead—the victim of a Huron tomahawk or the dark-skinned warrior who'd captured him.

Chapter 5

Rebecca tossed and turned, crying out in her sleep and waking Talon from his light doze. He laid down his rifle and went to her side, but despite her obvious distress, she was not awake. He slipped a hand inside her wolfskin blanket to see if her clothing was damp, then, when he was satisfied that she wasn't wrapped in wet garments, he pushed a gnarled maple limb into the glowing coals in the crude, stone-lined hearth.

Within minutes, the hot hardwood fire began to raise the temperature in the small cave. Talon fingered his captive's moccasins and turned them inside out so that they'd receive the greatest amount of heat without harming the tanned leather. Then he hung her wool stockings over sticks so that they too would dry through and through. Her bare feet were streaked with dirt, but they had lost their pallor. He stroked first one slender, high-arched foot and then the other to make certain that she'd suffered no permanent injury from the icy water.

She groaned and he saw that tears left a wet path down her cheeks. Uttering a small sound of sympathy, he returned to his place on the far side of the fire, picked up his weapon once more, and settled down to wait out the long hours until morning.

* * *

Rebecca sighed. "No," she whimpered. "No, don't take him away. He's my brother. I'll tend him... I'll tend him." Her eyelids fluttered, and then the nightmare pulled her back eight years into her own clouded past.

Waves crashed against the side of the ship; ribs creaked, and water trickled down the stinking inner hull of the Dublin Princess. *Rebecca, her face flushed with fever and stomach wracked with cramps, waved away the dour faces that surrounded her.*

"Colin is my brother, I tell you," she repeated. "I'd be grateful for a little tea and sugar, but I'll care for him." She dipped the rag in the bucket of cold sea water, wrung it out, and patted the toddler's hot red face.

"Some folks think they're too good for their own kind," a pock-faced woman muttered. "When that boy is wound in his death shroud, you'll be sorry."

Seven children had died since the Dublin Princess *had set sail from Ireland bound for the Maryland Colony in America ... three in the last week. Sickness and bad weather had hounded the merchant vessel from the first hours of the voyage.*

"Shhh, shhh," Rebecca had said, soothing and rocking the fitful child against her chest. For five weeks, she had kept Colin well and happy when most babies were in misery. She'd done it by taking him on deck for most of every day—regardless of the weather—and by forcing him to eat a little sauerkraut every day. She'd not eaten meat herself, or allowed Colin to have any, and she'd only given him goat milk when she'd milked the goat herself, fresh from a herd that a German couple was taking with them to America. They'd lived on dry biscuit, moldy cheese, milk, and sauerkraut. She'd earned the last two items by caring for the German matron's seven-year-old twins.

But now, in spite of all her precautions, Colin was ill, and she was frantic with worry. She was just shy of fourteen to his two years, and the stress of being her brother's sole protector was almost too great to bear. Country girls might marry and have their own babes by thirteen, but she'd led a sheltered life until she'd been tragically orphaned and left penniless. "Let her be a child a while longer," her dear father had repeatedly told her mother. Now, she and Colin were reaping the fruit of that harvest.

Had it been just six short months since she was playing with dolls and having her hair washed and combed by servants? She pushed back a stiff, sticky braid and concentrated on trying to lower her brother's fever. Here, there was no French soap and no white linen towels, only cold salt water and an aching dampness that kept anything from drying properly.

The dream darkened, becoming more bizarre . . . losing all semblance of reality, no longer playing out what *had* happened, but what *might have happened.*

The swaying ship's whale oil lanterns glowed with a hellish light, and the faces of her fellow travelers took on fiendish proportions.

Colin's wailing became incessant. He screamed louder and louder, until his cries blocked out the relentless slap of waves and groaning of wood. She was weeping—weeping tears of salt, and she was so cold that her bones ached, but not so cold or pale as Colin. His dark eyes glowed with fever and his tiny heart fluttered like a caged bird.

"Make him a winding-sheet of ship's sail," the old woman intoned. "Close his eyes with copper pennies and wrap him tight against the sea."

"No," Rebecca protested. "No! You can't. He's not dead. He's not dead!" But they wouldn't listen; gnarled

hands pulled Colin from her arms—other hands kept her from reaching him. "He's alive!" *she shouted.* "Can't you see he's alive?"

Panic-stricken, the baby stretched out small fingers to her—one thumb pink and swollen from constant sucking—and called her name. "Bec'ca!"

She fought them tooth and nail, but there were too many and they were too strong. In horror, she watched as they wrapped the death cloth round Colin's squirming body, pinning his sturdy arms and legs with the death shroud, muffling his baby cries until they faded to silence.

Rebecca stood on the deck of the ship watching as they carried the gray bundle to the rail. "You can't!" *she screamed again.* "He's not dead! He's not dead!"

Then she was staring in horror as Colin's body sank into the black water, swirling down and down, until—

Talon rocked her against his chest, cradling her as one would a feverish child. "Shhh, shhh," he soothed in Algonquian. "He is not dead."

She opened her eyes, and he knew from her glazed expression that she wasn't seeing his face, but the haunting shadows of the spirit world.

"*Nuwi,*" he coaxed. "Come back to me." He dared not handle her roughly. Did not the shamans speak of dreaming souls that broke free from sleepers to drift away into the spirit world and never return? "*Nuwi,* Becca."

She whimpered and slipped her arms around his neck. He felt the shudders rack her body as she clung to him. "He's not dead," she whispered hoarsely.

"No," he repeated in English. "He is not dead."

She took a deep breath and her eyes closed. Her trembling lessened and color flowed into her cheeks. This time when her lashes parted, she saw him.

She stiffened and gave a fearful cry, striking at him with her hands and trying to break free.

"*Ku,*" he said. "No—do not be afraid. I will not harm you." He released her and she tore loose from his arms and scrambled away until she reached the walls of the cave. "Do not be afraid," he said impatiently.

"You . . . you . . ." She gasped, clutching her arms against her body.

"You cried out," he explained, feeling foolish. "You had a dream."

"Yes." Her voice was dry and rasping, her eyes wide with alarm.

"You were very loud," he chided. "I thought your screeching would bring the Huron."

"You . . . you touched me," she said accusingly.

"I touched you—as I would a terrified child or a startled horse."

"A horse?"

He noticed spots of high color in her fair-skinned, oval face, a startling contrast to her vivid blue eyes and dark arching brows. Her fear was quickly turning to indignation. He gazed intensely at her delicate English features. Her nose was thin, sprinkled with freckles and slightly tilted at the tip.

Without realizing that he was doing so, he smiled. Such a foolish nose for a woman—he didn't think he had ever seen one quite like it. Her mouth was full, her lips plump and red as the first wild strawberries in May.

"How dare you compare me to a horse?" she demanded hotly.

"A horse?" He chuckled, remembering his

words. "A horse was not the best comparison," he conceded.

"I may be your prisoner, but I have rights."

His mood shifted. "No," he said sharply, remembering too how she had fitted neatly into his arms. "No. A prisoner has no rights—none but those her captor gives her. You are the wife of my enemy. Expect nothing from me, and be grateful for what I give."

"Barbarian!"

"An Englishwoman has little reason to call—"

"I am not English," she flared. "I'm Irish. Irish born and bred."

He shrugged. "To me, English and Irish are the same. I—"

"They are not the same, and you are a fool if you think so!"

Hot blood infused his cheeks and his belly grew tight. Did this woman believe his English was so poor that he didn't know the insult she offered him? He had seen a man touched by the spirits in the town the whites called Philadelphia. A twisted creature with misshapen limbs and drooling mouth, he had been chained to a post at a fair and taunted by cruel children who threw rotten eggs and spoiled vegetables at him while their mothers laughed. Even the most primitive tribes of Indians knew that those with injured minds were not to be harmed; they were in the care of *Inu-msi-ila-fe-wanu*—the Great Spirit who is a grandmother—and any who dared her wrath did so at their own peril.

Among the Shawnee and Delaware, such a person was called blessed. Men and women vied for the honor of showing kindness to the afflicted, and children were taught the proper respect for the weak and helpless. An act of mercy performed for a blessed one was the same as if the service had been done for *Inu-msi-ila-fe-wanu* and counted heavily in the donor's favor when his soul was judged at the time of death.

The whites did not understand these simple truths. Instead, they mocked the deformed and the mindless. It was further proof of the European lack of values in their daily lives.

Talon stared at Rebecca in shock, unable to believe she would use the English word *fool* in such a thoughtless manner. He had believed that she might be different from her husband ... that she might have more wisdom and heart. It was clear she didn't.

He had shown poor judgment in treating her differently from any other captive. Shame flooded over him as he remembered how he had held her in his arms. She was his enemy, and he would do well not to forget it just because she was pleasing to look upon.

"You are ignorant," he said. "Ignorant and dirty. When is the last time you bathed?"

"What?" She looked at him as though he had suddenly sprouted wings and begun to fly.

"Swim. Bathe. Wash your hair and body? Surely, you know what I'm talking about."

The insult stung and he was glad. She trembled with anger and balled her fists into tight knots. "How dare you say I'm dirty, you filthy Indian?"

He smiled. "You do not answer my question, woman. When did you bathe last?"

"Saturday night. Not a week ago," she flared. "And you—your hands are covered with blood."

Talon looked down and nodded. "You are right.

When the danger is past, we shall both wash away the stink of our bodies."

"I don't stink," she protested. Her voice wavered, and he thought she might burst into tears at any second.

"I could find you in the darkest night in the forest by your scent alone," he insisted. "All Englishmen stink—and Irish," he added. "Your husband's stench would sicken a badger."

"That's not so. Simon bathes, maybe not as often as I do, but he washes. And our clothes—"

"White men wear their sheep's wool garments until they rot off their backs."

"Leave me alone," she said. "I'm not talking to you any more. Kill me if you want to, but I won't listen to your lies about my husband. He's a decent Christian man and—"

Talon leaped to his feet and she shrank back. "Simon Brandt is a heartless murderer of women and children. He will go to his Christian God soon enough, I promise you that. For I, Fire Talon, will send him there."

Her lower lip trembled. "You mean to kill him . . . kill my Simon."

"His scalp will hang at my belt."

"You're nothing more than a cold-blooded murderer."

"And you, Becca Brandt? What are you? Did you not shoot down two of my warriors? Did you not try to shoot me under a flag of truce?"

"That was different," she argued. "I was under attack. I wouldn't deliberately hunt someone down to kill them."

"No? Then it is too bad your husband doesn't share your feelings. He has spent a lifetime murdering my people."

"He has reason. You killed his first wife, scalped his brother and sister-in-law, carried off their children."

"Not my people, but the Susquehanna did this thing."

"They were Indians," she cried. "Indians are Indians."

"As French and Irish and Dutch are English?"

"Damn you." She turned her face away.

He clenched his teeth and tried to control his anger. This woman was nothing but trouble. He should have let her go on dreaming her bad visions. He flexed his arm and was rewarded with a fresh trickle of blood seeping from the gunshot wound in his upper arm. The injury had been throbbing most of the night, but he had ignored it. Now, the woman's accusation that he was dirty made him think of possible infection.

The cave was without water, so he bade her remain where she was, took his rifle, and crawled back outside to scoop up some snow. It was still dark; he judged dawn to be a good two hours off. He listened hard, but could hear nothing but the howl of wind through the empty branches and the far off hoot of a hunting owl.

When he returned, the woman was huddled at the far side of the fire, head down. Her eyes were nearly shut, but he could feel her watching him and he sensed her fear. "Sleep," he said. "I will keep watch." She didn't give any indication that she'd heard him. "You will need your rest," he added. "We have far to go."

Leaning his rifle against the wall, he squatted by the fire and proceeded to pack his wound with snow. The musket ball hadn't lodged in his flesh, but it had torn a jagged furrow through skin and muscle. Certain kinds of moss were good to pack in a cut, but he didn't care to go out stumbling around in the dark searching for a fresh supply.

His friend, Fox, carried medicine in his war bag, but Fox wasn't here. There was nothing to do but purify the gunshot with flame, Talon decided reluctantly.

He hated the thought. A good hunting knife would take only so much fire. With a sigh, he slipped his weapon from his sheath and heard a faint gasp escape from the woman's lips. Without speaking, he laid his knife blade in the hottest part of the coals and waited until the steel glowed redorange. Then he held his breath, picked up the bone handle, and placed the hot steel against his wound.

Blood and skin sizzled; the flesh burned and darkened, and tears gathered in the corners of his eyes. The woman scrambled up and covered her mouth with her hands. Talon waited, mentally counting, as sweat beaded on his forehead. By sheer force of will, he kept his features immobile. Finally, after what seemed an eternity, he removed the knife.

She was looking at him.

He averted his eyes and pushed the weapon back into his sheath. He felt sick to his stomach and his head was full of swirling mist. He swallowed, wishing he could wash his face with cold snow.

"Was the fire hot?" she asked.

"What?" He blinked, still not free of the blinding waves of pain.

"Perhaps it will give you a taste of what's to come in hell," she said, "or of what you meant to do to us when you set our cabin afire."

"I do not burn women and children."

"You tried hard enough."

"I ordered the fire arrows to drive you out. We knew of the tunnel."

"Liar. You couldn't have," she accused.

He smiled thinly. "I have been in your cabin, Becca Brandt. Over the fireplace was a clock with a moon painted on it."

She shook her head. "I don't believe you."

"And at the foot of your bed a carved chest."

"You sneaking—"

"Save your insults, Becca Brandt. But know this. As much as I hate your husband, as much as I desire his death, I will not harm your smallest finger—so long as my father lives."

"And if he dies?"

"If he dies, you must die as well."

"Out of revenge."

"For honor's sake."

"How would an Indian know anything of honor?"

"If I do not, then your husband must blacken his face with the ashes of mourning. For if I, Fire Talon of the Mecate Shawnee, have no honor, then you have no hope of life no matter what happens to my father."

Chapter 6

"I won't take off my clothes for you! You'll have to kill me first," Rebecca shouted at Talon. It was early morning the following day; they'd left the shelter of the cave and were standing beside an ice-sheened forest pool about a quarter of a mile away.

"Lower your voice, Becca Brandt," Talon warned. "I mean for you to wash, not lie with me. Again you prove your ignorance. A Shawnee brave who shares pleasures with a captive woman on the war trail gives away his power and his luck. Your charms do not tempt me enough to risk failure of my mission."

"To hell with your luck. I may be a country girl, but I'm not stupid. If you want my dress, you'll have to cut it off my dead body."

His rough-hewn features darkened like a thunder cloud. "Now you do tempt me," he threatened.

He'd used a bone comb to dress his long hair and fastened it back away from his face with a simple rawhide thong; it fell over his shoulders and caught the rays of light like skeins of raw black silk. The war paint that had seemed so garish to her yesterday was smudged and faded, making him seem more human.

"I'll wash my feet, nothing more," she said.

Slowly, step by step, she edged away from him until a fallen log lay between them. She didn't know what he would do, but she meant to fight or run before she'd give in and remove her dress.

The rest of last night had passed in fitful starts with her nodding off to sleep and then jerking awake. Her head hurt, and her belly growled with hunger, but she had made it this long alive. She was still afraid of Talon, but not so fearful as she had been, and she was in no mood this morning to be bullied.

Dawn had broken cold and clear. The storm had passed, leaving the crusty snow and frost-decked branches a fairyland of sparkling splendor. Their breaths made little puffs of white in the crisp, clean air. It was her favorite kind of winter day. Often, she and Colin had tramped through the woods for hours in weather like this. The thought made her throat tighten.

Where was her brother today? Was he following the river? Or did he lie stiff and cold somewhere in this endless forest, unburied and unmourned? Never unmourned . . . He was all she had, and so long as she drew breath, she would never cease searching for him and hoping he was alive.

"You smell bad, white woman," Talon said rudely, interrupting her thoughts. "I do not wish to make hunting us too easy for our enemies. You will go into this water and clean your whole body. You will scrub your skin with sand, and you will wash your hair."

"I am a decent Catholic woman," she replied. "I take off my clothes for no man but my God-given husband." She glanced around breathlessly for a stick, anything to defend herself with. Was he mad that he thought she would disrobe because he told her to? He must be, she decided. Only a crazy person would expect her to go willingly into that frigid creek.

If that was truly what he intended . . .

She looked into his eyes, trying to read what was behind the flashing obsidian irises. She'd been chastised by Simon too many times not to be wary. If her own husband would lose his temper and hit her, what might this savage do?

Ravishment by the Indians was the black terror in every white woman's soul. There were tales . . . whispers. Once, a Dutch family had stopped at the farm where she and Colin had worked when she'd first come to America. The oldest daughter—unmarried—had been large with child. "An abomination," the farmer's wife had informed her after the guests had left. The pregnancy was the result of unholy union between the Dutch girl and a Lenape Indian, and the resulting bastard would make mother and babe outcasts. "Better if they both die when it is born," the goodwife had insisted stridently. "Any Christian girl would have killed herself before letting a red heathen touch her." And hadn't Simon said the same thing to her—not once but many times?

Rebecca's stomach knotted into a tight ball. Frissons of fear rippled down her spine, and her mouth went dry. She didn't want to die this morning. She didn't want to die at all.

"Please," she bargained with Talon. "I won't make trouble for you. I won't try to escape. Just don't force me to—"

He leaped the fallen log without mussing a hair on his head and strode within inches of her. His black devil eyes bored into hers; his half-naked chest was close enough for her to feel his body heat. She could smell the black powder on his hands, hear the soft hiss of his breathing.

And then she remembered something else that had happened last night, and her heart skipped a beat.

Sometime between the time he had branded himself with his knife and the time they had awakened at dawn, she had dreamed again, of him.

Shame flooded her; tears sprang to her eyes. She was no decent Catholic woman—not even a good Christian to have such hidden desires. For an instant, the dream flashed across her mind.

She was home in her cabin. It was night— winter, as it was now. A fire crackled on the hearth, and she could smell a haunch of deer smoking in the chimney. The room was shadowy, and she was lying in her bed with her rose quilt pulled round her shoulders. She was warm and happy, joyous almost.

Then Simon stepped between the bed and the hearth; his nude form was backlit by the glowing fire. She called to him, rose on one elbow, and raised the quilt to beckon him into her bed. He moved closer and she held out her arms in anticipation. But when he bent to kiss her, a mass of black hair fell over his shoulders to brush her face with silken promise.

And when she looked into his eyes, they were not Simon's eyes. Not Simon's lips pressing hers, or Simon's hard hands on her breasts. The lover she had welcomed so eagerly into her bed was Talon.

Reality replaced the unthinkable dream. Rebecca's eyes widened; she let out a short scream, and turned to flee.

He caught her before she had gone three paces.

"No! No!" she cried hysterically. She thrashed from side to side, tossing her head and kicking at him.

"When I say you will bathe, Becca Brandt, you will bathe," he hissed.

She shrieked as he swept her up into his arms. Suddenly, she was flying through the air. Before she could scream again, she hit the water. The shock of the numbing cold stream drove everything but self-preservation from her mind. She struggled to get her head above the surface, came up sputtering and gasping for breath, lost her balance, and fell under again.

Strong hands closed around her shoulders and lifted her to her feet. As the panic receded, she realized that the water was only waist deep and she was in no danger of drowning.

"By the great deeds of *Glooskap!* Are you possessed of a demon, woman, that you try me so? Can you not bathe without drowning yourself?"

She stared at him through dripping strands of hair and cursed him with the foulest expletive she could muster.

"Good," he said. "If you can call me names, you've enough breath to survive." He let go of her and waded out of the creek. "I will go downstream," he said, "and wash my own body. See that you clean your hair properly, or I will throw you in again and do it myself."

"You . . . you're crazy!" she said with chattering teeth. "I'm . . . freezing!"

"Then wash quickly and return to the fire. I'll try and find us something to break our fast."

"Fiend!" she shouted at his broad back.

He must be an animal not to feel the cold, she

thought, as she splashed half-heartedly in the shallows. Her feet and legs were solid ice. Her body shook with chills. "Damn him," she muttered. "Damn him to a frozen hell."

It was impossible to wash in her dress, but she wasn't even certain she could get it off. With stiffened fingers, she fumbled with the ties of her gown, unlaced it halfway down the front, and pulled it off over her head. She stood shivering in her long-sleeved shift and stays and was about to throw her gown up onto the bank when she heard a gunshot. Instantly, she clutched the soaking wet garment against her bosom.

It sounded to her as if the rifle had been fired on the far side of the stream and down to the left. Yet she was positive that Talon had gone right. She waited, unsure of what to think, when suddenly she caught sight of a gray shape streaking down the hill toward the water.

A dog? The gait was not a deer's gait. As the animal came closer, she gave a little gasp. It wasn't a dog—it was a gray wolf, a big one.

It came at a dead run, and when it reached the edge of the creek, it didn't hesitate. It leaped in and began to swim across. One front paw, Rebecca noticed, was missing toes and bloody.

Rebecca didn't move a muscle. Terrified, she stood where she was and didn't utter another sound. The she-wolf came close enough for her to see the white hairs around her muzzle and glimpse sharp yellow teeth.

Paying no more heed to her than if she'd been a tree stump, the wolf scrambled up the rocky overhang at the water's edge and vanished into a thicket in two bounds.

"A wolf," Rebecca murmured. "He tried to shoot a wolf for our breakfast?"

Seconds later an Indian appeared near the spot where she'd first seen the wolf. He came loping down the incline, rifle in one hand and tomahawk in the other. He saw her at the exact instant she realized that he wasn't Talon. She dropped her dress and dove under, swimming toward a pile of brush and fallen trees in midstream, but not before she'd heard the high-pitched Huron war cry.

She reached the logjam and climbed over the twisted timber as the Huron splashed into the creek after her. Brandishing his hatchet, he charged. Branches tore at her shift and dug into her skin, but she didn't stop. She clawed her way into the tangle, walked an icy branch, and burrowed deeper into the intertwined morass.

He was right behind her. She crawled through a small opening, half-climbed and half-fell down a partially submerged log, scrambled up the icy bank, and reached for an oak sapling to steady her balance. With a sickening thud, the Huron's tomahawk splintered the tree inches from her head. The blade passed so close to her head that a lock of her red hair was pinned between the axe and the sapling. Crying out in fear and anger, she jerked free, snatching the weapon loose, and whirled to face her pursuer.

The Huron stopped short and a wide grin spread across his face. He said something to her; the guttural sounds were like nothing she'd ever heard, but she didn't need to translate. His eyes told her what he meant to do.

His knife hissed as he pulled it from the sheath at his waist. Strips of braided yellow hair dangled from the antler handle; the nine-inch iron blade bore stains of rust or blood. He laughed and raised the knife.

She hurled the tomahawk with all her strength—straight into his right kneecap. He howled like a panther, and staggered forward, grasping his wound and trying to pull out the hatchet. The knee spewed blood; it couldn't bear his weight. When he crumbled, she seized a fist-sized rock and threw it at his head. The rock struck his temple and he fell forward groaning. She picked up a second rock, larger than the first, and advanced on him.

Suddenly, his hand shot out and grabbed her ankle. She screamed and hit at him with the rock. She twisted, trying to get away, but he pulled her down and dragged her inch by inch toward him. He pinned her to the ground; his bloody face loomed over her and his hands reached for her throat.

His fingers dug into her neck and the earth began to sway under her. Then, without warning, another face appeared behind the Huron's. The weight was jerked off her chest, and she realized the second man was Talon. She drew in deep gulps of air and tried to crawl away. When she stopped and looked back, the Huron lay face down, no longer moving. Talon knelt on the prone man's back, took hold of a section of his scalp lock, and sliced free a dollar-sized piece of hair and skin.

Rebecca moaned and tried not to gag.

"I told you to bathe, not hunt Huron," Talon said, calmly wiping his knife in the snow and replacing the weapon in his sheath.

She began to shake.

"Come," he said, touching her arm. "You must

warm yourself at the fire." She didn't notice when he bent to pick up the section of her hair that had been hacked away by the tomahawk and never saw him ball it up and tuck it into his waistband.

She rose and followed him, too cold, too exhausted and hungry to do anything else. "The Huron," she stammered. "Will you leave him here for the wolves?"

"No. There is a deep ravine near here. I will come back and throw his body down there. It doesn't matter. I have taken his scalp. The Iroquois say a man cannot cross the great river to the sky without it."

"You mean he cannot enter heaven?" She forced herself to think of the warmth in the cave, to take one step after another. She remembered her dress. Where was it? Had it sunk in the creek? She wanted to beg Talon to look for it, but she wouldn't ask him for any more favors, not even if it meant her death.

Talon scoffed. "I doubt he was any more of a Christian than I am, although my mother allowed the French priest to spill water on my head when I was a child. What need has a Huron of a Christian heaven?"

She crossed her arms and hugged them to her breasts. Her hair hung in her eyes, but it was too much effort to push it away. All she could think of was the fire. Her limbs were stiff with cold; she wanted to lie down and rest, but she knew she couldn't. "Surely you know you committed a mortal sin when you took that man's scalp," she said. Arguing with him would keep her moving, keep her from giving up and freezing where she stood.

He shrugged. "I am a warrior. I kill because I must. I kill to protect those who cannot protect themselves—and you did not thank me for saving your life, but you are welcome, just the same."

"Killing is one thing. I would have killed him if—"

"You nearly did. I must remember to keep my tomahawk far away from you."

"Killing in self-defense is not the same as mutilating—" She broke off abruptly. "He might not have been dead."

"I cut his throat from ear to ear. He is surely dead."

"Still, to take a trophy from a human being, it is barbaric, beyond the bounds of—"

"The Shawnee and Delaware are few. The Iroquois—the Huron, the Seneca, the Mohawk, and the other tribes of the league—are many. If an Iroquois is a little afraid for his soul when he faces me, so much the better. It may give me an advantage."

"And if he kills you and takes your scalp, what then?"

"I said the Iroquois believe it. I did not say I believe it. I am not a superstitious man."

"You are not superstitious? You who prattle on about luck and power."

"Be silent, wife of Simon Brandt. I tire of your incessant tongue." He paused near the entrance to the cave and turned to glare at her. "You are the captive. You should fear torture, not me. You flay me with your barbed tongue."

"I ..." She started to answer back, to tell him just what she thought of him. But the fierce gleam in his eyes made her remember the wolf. Talon was as dangerous as that ravenous beast. He had saved her from the Huron, but for what? Not for herself, but for his own purpose. And when he no

longer needed her, he might kill her as easily as he
had slain the enemy warrior. She needed to keep
that in mind at all times, and not be lulled by his
glib English.

She kept telling herself that as he built up the
fire. She huddled close, trying to warm her entire
body at once. He didn't speak to her, which was
just as well. She didn't think she had the energy to
reply. Worst of all, she couldn't stop shivering,
deep, bone-rattling shakes that made her feel
wretched.

He was still damp, but he didn't seem to notice.
When the fire was hot enough to suit him, he
stood up. "I will tend to the Huron now," he said.
"Take off your garment and wrap yourself in the
wolfskin. I will leave you alone long enough to
dry, and I will call out before I enter the cave."

"Thank you," she managed. Somehow, the
thought of being naked didn't matter as much as
the cold. He said he wouldn't come in on her—but
after all, if he intended to rape her, he could do it
any time, couldn't he? "My feet are so cold I can't
feel them."

"Cover them with warm ashes from the hearth.
Stay here. I'll try to find us food."

"Where do you expect me to go? With wet moccasins, I wouldn't last an hour outside."

"That's what I thought."

She waited until she was sure he was gone, then
removed her stays and shift. She wrapped the
wolf pelt around her, hair side in, and crouched by
the fire.

If anyone saw me, she thought, they'd take me
for a savage. Naked, barefoot, with my hair hanging every which way. When she was warmer,

she'd try to tame her tangled locks. Now, all she wanted was to stop shivering.

She did not mean to sleep, but somehow she did. She was awakened by the smell of something delicious roasting over the fire. "What's that?" she cried, opening her eyes.

Talon was seated across from her. Between them, a large bird sizzled and dripped fat into the glowing coals.

"Oh," she said. "I—" Realizing that she was clad only in the fur, she pulled it tight around her, trying to cover her legs, her shoulders, and her breasts all at the same time. "You monster!" she said. "You promised me you'd call out before you came back. You tricked me." She grabbed her shift and retreated to the shadows in the back of the cave.

"I did call you," he said. "You were sleeping like a bear in winter. I killed the turkey, plucked it, and cooked it. Still you slept. I think Simon Brandt has a lazy woman for a wife."

Rebecca sputtered, too angry for words, as she struggled to get into her shift without dropping the wolfskin. She did notice that not only was she dry, but her garment was dry as well. She had been asleep, and not just for a few moments.

"You seem to have lost your dress," he said, "so I brought you the Huron's French coat instead. I think it will fit you if you tie his belt around your waist." He reached over and held up a blue men's military jacket.

"You expect me to wear a dead man's coat?"

"You will wear it, woman, or I will take your last garment and leave you only the wolf pelt to wear."

"Go to hell!" she shouted.

"If the English are right about their god, I will. But what if the Shawnee are right, and you are wrong. Have you thought of that?"

"No."

"Think of it while you eat my turkey and sit at my fire. Perhaps it will help you to be properly grateful to a man who has gone to great lengths to keep you from harm."

"I'll never be grateful to you."

He smiled. "But you will eat my turkey."

She nodded. "Only to have enough strength to live long enough to see you hanged for the savage you are."

Chapter 7

⌒───∞───⌒

Fort Nelson
The Virginia Frontier
December 1, 1751

Inside the barred gates of Fort Nelson, hooves, paws, and human feet had churned the hard-packed dirt and choking dust of summer to ankle-deep mud. and sink holes overflowing with manure and scummed standing water. Around three inner sides of the stout log enclosure ran a low lean-to, divided into quarters for common soldiers, officers, and horses. A small pound to the left of the fort entrance held cattle, and a cedar-shingled building on the right was used as a combination church and infirmary. In the center, sunken into the ground, stood the powder store, a crude, octagonal structure of square-hewn timber.

Ten paces to the east of the powder magazine, carpenters had erected a free-standing wooden cage, four feet wide, four feet high, and five feet long. The trap door was nailed shut with iron spikes, and there was no solid roof to protect the prisoner from the elements.

The feeble December sunlight offered little warmth to the captive or the other inhabitants of the English stronghold. Men slapped their hands together against the cold as they wandered toward

the cattle pound. There, they arranged their clothing and emptied their bladders against the split
rail fence. Soon the pungent scent of human urine
filled the air, mingling with the strong odors of
livestock, black powder, dogs, wood smoke, and
unwashed bodies.

Women and children left their tents and wagons,
retreating to the corner between infirmary and
stockade wall to obey the calls of nature. Most ci-
vilians passing the cage stopped to stare at the
stoic Indian shaman inside. A few gawkers looked
and did nothing more; some shouted insults, a
gray-haired woman with a huge goiter on her
neck threw the contents of her chamber pot at the
old Shawnee.

Medicine Smoke ignored them, ignored the mud
and feces that littered his cell, and ignored the
cold that had turned his toes and one finger black
with poison. His eyes were closed; he barely drew
breath, and he sat cross-legged, arms folded over
his chest, waiting with almost animal patience.

The ring of the blacksmith's hammer stirred the
fort to action; a platoon of red-coated soldiers
marched half-heartedly to and fro in front of the
commandant's door. A cow, her udder distended
with milk, lowed repeatedly. Settlers tidied their
makeshift camps and prepared for another boring
day locked inside the strong, upright log fortress.

The smell of boiling corn mush and frying ba-
con drifted past Medicine Smoke's cage. A cat
streaked over the top of the wooden pen, pausing
just long enough to hiss a challenge to the three
hounds in hot pursuit before leaping over the
heaped snow and scrambling up on the roof of the
powder magazine. The dogs howled; a baby cried,

and Reverend Allan rang a small bell to summon worshipers for his Sunday sermon.

A tall, buckskin-clad English scout walked over to the Indian's cage and slammed the butt of his rifle repeatedly against the bars. "Wake up, ye old son of a bitch!" he called.

Medicine Smoke opened his eyes. "Simon Brandt." His words were stilted, his voice cracked and rasping.

"No, ye stupid bastard. It's King George."

The aging Shawnee smiled thinly. His white hair was matted with dried blood and mud; his lined face was streaked with dirt. His mouth was swollen; one ear had been nearly ripped from his head.

"Are ye ready to listen to reason and sign the peace treaty?" the scout asked.

"The land is not mine to give."

The white man reversed his rifle and drove the steel barrel through the narrow bars into the shaman's ribs. The resulting dull snap and Medicine Smoke's hiss of pain made Simon's pale gray eyes widen with obvious pleasure. He waited for some further reaction from the Indian, but when there was none, he said, "You're a stubborn fool. I'll hang you. By God, ye know I will."

The older man spread his hands, palms up. One finger was broken so badly that the bone pushed through the torn skin. "It matters not what you do to me. I am finished. I have given my people bad council. Now the Shawnee will strike the war post and blood will feed the forest floor. Your women and ours will mourn their fallen sons and husbands."

"It ain't too late to stop the hostilities. You kin rein in your son, Fire Talon. Force him to—"

Medicine Smoke's rheumy eyes glowed with

amusement. "You of all men should not suggest such a thing. Have you not tried to kill him for twenty years?" He shook his battered head. "*Mahtah*. No man, red or white, controls Fire Talon. His heart is hot—his fist is strong. You lit the torch, Simon Brandt. You killed his mother, my wife, when my son was little more than a child. You taught him hate. You made of him a war chief such as the old ones tell about in legends. And you will reap the whirlwind of his fury."

"Not before I see your neck stretched on the gallows and your mangy carcass thrown to the dogs."

The prisoner shrugged, almost imperceptibly, and closed his eyes.

"I'm late for church services, or I'd have them drag ye out of there and give you a taste of the whip," Simon threatened. "I don't have—"

Zeke Taylor, a balding man in homespun, came toward the two at a trot. His oversized shirt was untucked and his beard half shaven. "Simon! Simon!" he shouted. "Bad news. Amos Dodd just come into the fort. He heard from a half-breed Nanticoke that yer cabin is burnt to the ground."

"What?" Simon spun to face Taylor. "What's that you say? My place burned?"

"I swear to God. Dodd just told me. He said the Nanticoke, Red Jim, has a message fer ye, but he's scared to come into the fort, 'fraid of what you'll do to him."

"Red Jim? That drunken whoreson? Why would I believe anything he said? He ain't got half a brain. The other half's rotted away from drinking trade whiskey."

"Dodd says Red Jim's got proof. Your woman's dress and a piece of her hair. You'd best come quick, Simon. The Nanticoke says Shawnee have got her," Taylor continued excitedly. "This one's son, Fire Talon. Red Jim says another Shawnee told him that Fire Talon took your wife and her little brother and they're holdin' them 'til you let old Medicine Smoke here go free."

Simon scowled and gripped his rifle tighter. "The hell, you say."

Taylor nodded. "A dress could be any white woman's. But this sure looks like your missus' hair. Ain't many got that fox color. Red Jim claims that Fire Talon's messenger says he'll swap you. His pa, alive and unharmed, for your wife. If anything bad happens to Medicine Smoke, Fire Talon claims he'll kill your missus and send you the rest of her scalp."

"Did Dodd see the burned farm for hisself?" Simon asked.

"No, he didn't, and that's a fact. Dodd would soil his breeches if he ever come up on a real Injun in these woods. You know he keeps close to the fort. But Red Jim sells him a lot of beaver pelts. Dodd says that Red Jim's tellin' the truth about your place."

With a smothered oath, Simon set off across the parade ground in search of Amos Dodd. Medicine Smoke pulled his ragged deerskin around his shoulders and smiled.

After dark that same day, Talon left Rebecca sleeping in the cave and went out to meet Fox near the stream where the Huron had died. The war chief exchanged formal greetings with the Shawnee brave and then asked about the safety of the rest of his companions.

"Joins the River will recover. Counts and Osage Killer have told the story a dozen times to our camp. Now they can't wait to dance the story at the Shannopins Big House council fire for our Delaware brothers at the feast of child naming. Counts has already made himself a new wolfskin headdress to match Osage Killer's."

"But not good enough to match your eagle-wing dance costume," Talon teased.

Fox grinned. "I paid dearly for that garment."

"I'm sure you did. Just how old was that widow you spent the winter with?"

"Old enough to teach me a few tricks even you don't know," Fox retorted good-naturedly.

"You never seem to have any trouble getting women to sew for you," Talon said, looking with envy at his friend's thick beaver-skin cloak that hung to the tops of his fur leggings.

"It's because I take the time to make myself attractive to them, and I have something more to say than boasting of my battle feats." Fox struck a pose and both laughed. The younger man wore his hair cut at chin length on either side of his face and long in the back. Tufts from an eagle's plumage hung from his silver earrings.

"It's time you settled down and found a wife."

"Right after you do," Fox answered.

Talon laughed.

Fox removed a few strips of dried meat from a pouch at his waist, and they shared the meal in fraternal silence.

When he had finished, Talon drank from the cold stream and glanced at his friend. "Has my message reached Fort Nelson?"

Fox shrugged. "Who can tell? The Nanticoke has had enough days to get there. I paid him with an English musket to carry the word to Simon

Brandt, and I put the white woman's dress into his hands."

"And her hair?"

The slim man nodded. "I gave him the lock of her hair."

Talon's features took on a grim visage. "Then we wait for Simon Brandt's answer."

"We wait," Fox agreed. "Will you bring her to the village now?"

"No. And make certain that the white trader, Clancy, and the French priest come to camp. They will both ask questions. The Frenchman is a spy for the English. When both sources report that Brandt's wife is not with the Mecate Shawnee, Brandt and the soldiers will search for her elsewhere, and leave my people in peace."

"It is not safe, you being alone with her. There are many dangers for a warrior without friends."

Talon shook his head. "No. What I do is for my father. I will not bring ruin on the village for this. I have the blood feud with Simon Brandt. I will not risk another Shawnee life unnecessarily."

"Counts, Osage Killer, Badger Scent, and I, we could come with you." Fox smiled and clasped Talon's arm. "We killed our first buck together. You pulled me from the river when I hit my head and nearly drowned. It grieves my heart to let you face the English wrath alone."

"So long as I am your war chief, I will say who walks the forest and who guards the people. As soon as the priest and the trader leave, move the camp south to the banks of the Salt Lick River. And if there is trouble, say to the council that I want them to take the people west of the Ohio."

Fox's high forehead creased with concern. "At

least, let me accompany you. If Simon Brandt comes—"

"When Simon Brandt comes after me, I will travel faster alone."

"You have the woman to slow you down."

"On the day an enemy woman slows me down enough for Simon Brandt to catch me, you can take my place as war chief."

"Don't underestimate him, Talon. He's evaded you for many years."

"His days are written on the drifting smoke from my mother's pyre. I cannot change them; he cannot change them. I only know that I must hunt him down and destroy him."

"And the woman? Counts says you do not have the belly to kill her if her man will not release your father."

Talon scoffed. "Counts talks too much."

"Will you? You have never stained your knife with the blood of a woman."

"You carried my word. Have you ever known me to break that word?"

Fox exhaled softly. "No."

"A war chief who does not speak the truth is not fit to lead."

"Then, for all of us, I hope Simon Brandt and the English soldiers see the sense in this bargain."

"He will—in time," Talon said. "But first, he will not be able to resist the urge to try and rescue her."

"Maybe."

Talon made a quick gesture with his right hand. "No. Not maybe. He will come. I know him all too well. Sometimes, I think I know him better than I know my own father."

"Medicine Smoke is a wise man, a good man.

Don't blame him for this one mistake. He believed that a treaty would be good for the Mecate."

"He is too soft, my father. He has never learned that they will not rest until our forests fall to English axes and the spring grass grows green on our graves."

Fox pointed to a bundle that lay on the ground a few yards away. "I have brought leggings and fur robes for you both—and some good corn cakes that Sweet Rain made. Take care, Talon."

"And you, brother." He rose to go.

"What of the boy? Does The Stranger still have him? Is he well?"

"I don't know. No one has seen them since the day of the raid. Does it matter?"

"The woman asks after him. She will give me no peace."

"I will send a runner to his village if you wish."

"No . . . yes, find out what you can. If The Stranger wishes to sell him, say that I will pay his ransom. If not, tell The Stranger that I would consider it an act of friendship to give him back to the English."

"You do care about him."

"He showed courage. We should not make of such a boy an enemy."

"It may be that you are right." Fox touched his chest lightly with a closed fist and loped off into the trees. Talon picked up the bundle and turned back toward the cave and his prisoner.

Rebecca moved closer to the fire and held her hands over the glowing warmth. She had awakened when Talon went out, and she'd lain sleepless since then, wondering what he was doing and where he'd gone. She'd even entertained the thought that perhaps he was leaving her—that he wouldn't come back. She wasn't sure whether being alone in this wilderness was worse than being a captive.

The Shawnee terrified her, made her furious with him, and intrigued her, all at the same time. He was everything she'd expected a hostile savage to be . . . and nothing. In the nine days that she'd been at his mercy, he'd never once touched her in a way that made her fear for her virtue. He'd bullied her and dragged her through forest and stream against her will, but he'd never actually hurt her.

Common sense told her that for all his paint and bravado, he was not a wicked man at heart. And she'd had enough experience with men to know that Talon was a rarity. Hadn't her own husband blacked her eye for far less than she'd said or done to this Shawnee? What in God's name would Simon's reaction be if she tried to kill him—not once, but repeatedly?

Simon was like most men, neither all good nor all bad. He had a quick temper, and he lived by a harsh code. He wasn't the man she'd have picked to marry if she'd had half a chance. But he was her husband, and she owed him loyalty and respect. At least she'd been taught that she did.

Sometimes, they were hard to give . . .

"If Dadda hadn't died." Her whisper echoed in the cave. "Hadn't died . . . hadn't died . . . hadn't . . ."

She shivered. Truth was, James Gordon would turn over in his grave to see his only daughter married to a rough frontiersman like Simon. Be she illegitimate or not, her father's money would have provided enough dowry to see her wed into

the Irish gentry or even to the second son of an
English nobleman. Dadda had loved her well, and
he'd weep to see how low she'd come.

Her father had loved books and works of art; he
would have thought Simon an ignorant, impover-
ished man without social graces. Her husband
could write little more than his own name, and he
could barely read at all. Simon was poor by her
parent's standards. He didn't own much that he
couldn't wear on his back or carry as he ventured
ever deeper into uncharted Indian country. Even
the land he claimed had no deed, only squatters'
rights.

Not that Simon was a man to be scorned. He
was honest and brave—well respected by colonial
and military commanders. He had taken her in
honorable wedlock, giving her a ring and the
blessing of the Church, when most indentured
girls were at the mercy of their owners. Simon was
not old, or deformed, or a drunkard. And if he
was a hard man, it was a hard country. She should
be grateful to have such a husband.

She *was* grateful, she corrected mentally. If only
he could have showed her more tenderness,
shared laughter, been more of a companion . . .

If only he didn't hit her.

Her father would have cut off his right hand before he'd ever have struck her mother, and she
wasn't even his legal wife—only his Irish housekeeper. Many's the time Rebecca had heard them
speak harsh words, usually about religion or poli-
tics. Her mother's disposition had been as fiery as
her bright red hair. But heated words were all that
had ever passed between them when they were
angry.

Rebecca had inherited her mother's sharp

tongue—but not her luck in love. When she'd accepted Simon Brandt's proposal at the Maryland
dock, she'd agreed because he promised she could
keep Colin with her. A Catholic priest and the
sheriff had vouched for his character. No one had
told her that Simon would discipline her with his
hand or his belt. And no one had told her that she
would be a wife in name only.

Rebecca sighed and pushed another stick into
the coals. She had known the facts of life when
she'd wed Simon, but she'd still been an innocent
in sexual matters. It hadn't occurred to her that a
husband might be unnatural when it came to the
marriage bed.

Or that she might someday find herself lusting
after a half-naked Indian . . .

Chapter 8

Talon crawled into the cave and rose to his feet, stamping off fresh snow and filling the cave with the sharp scent of evergreen and the deeper musk of damp furs. His eyes met hers across the fire and widened in mild surprise. "You are awake, woman."

Rebecca saw that he had brought a bundle of what seemed to be pelts with him. He dropped to one knee, untied the thongs, and unrolled an assortment of Indian garments across the dirt floor. His waist-length hair fell carelessly forward over his left shoulder as he concentrated on the task, and Rebecca's heart gave an odd leap as dancing stars of firelight reflected off his crow-black tresses.

Would his hair feel as soft as it looked, she wondered ... or would it be coarse, like a horse's mane? Instantly, the unspoken questions shamed her, and she covered her mortification with forced anger. "I have a name," she snapped at him. "Rebecca! How many times must I tell you? Stop calling me *woman!*"

She glared at him, while confusion blurred her reason. What was happening to her? She was a decent Christian matron—eight years wed. Was she losing her mind from the strain of her ordeal? Or had she finally succumbed to the total lack of morals that Simon insisted her mother had revealed when she gave birth to two bastards.

Why she was having these intimate fantasies about Fire Talon didn't matter, Rebecca told herself sternly. She must gain control of her wayward emotions and fight this unnatural physical attraction she felt toward him.

"You are my prisoner," he replied, matter-of-factly. "You have no rights but those I give you."

"I would expect as much from you," she flung back. His expression was solemn, but he was making fun of her. She knew it, and it made her angrier still. "You savages treat your squaws like beasts of burden," she accused.

He looked at her with those fathomless, sloe eyes and her skin prickled. The air seemed charged between them, and she found it hard to draw breath.

"Doubtless, you have known many Shawnee women."

"No . . ." She swallowed. Where did he get this keen sense of wit? With his quick tongue, he should have been born an Irishman; he was using her language to make her look foolish. "It . . . it's common knowledge," she stammered awkwardly.

"Wrong knowledge." His pronunciation was proper, each syllable enunciated . . . but still, the words rang with a hint of music.

She shook her head. "Simon is an expert on Indians. He told me—"

"*Tah hah shee!* You are wrong. Your man is wrong. Shawnee and Delaware women have more rights than any white woman."

"I don't believe you."

"*E-e!* Yes, I speak the truth," he retorted. "I have no wife, but if I did, I would own my weapons, my moccasins, my pipe. Our wigwam would be hers. Our food, our blankets, clothing, my canoe—even our hunting ground would be hers. My sons and daughters would inherit her family clan. To you, as a European, that means my wife's surname. And if she wished to be rid of me, she need only put my moccasins outside of the house and declare that she had divorced me."

"I don't believe a word of it."

He shrugged. "Do I care what the wife of Simon Brandt believes? You are ignorant."

"Rebecca. Say it."

"Becca."

She winced. Only Colin called her by that childish nickname. On Talon's lips, it sounded—no, she argued, trying to ignore the shivers playing up and down her spine. She would not allow herself to be cajoled by her captor. These days in the forest must have affected her mind. What matter if he said her name in a husky tone that brought moisture to her eyes? He was the enemy—a cold-blooded murderer.

Still, her awakening curiosity would not be denied. "How do you speak my language so well?" she demanded. "You did not find your English mannerisms and vocabulary in a greenbrier thicket."

He nodded. "Correct. My mother accepted your Christian religion. She even had me baptized as a young child. She believed that her children must learn European ways if we were to survive."

"A wise woman."

"Not so wise. Her love of Christianity killed her. She was in a church when Simon Brandt and his friends burned her alive."

Rebecca turned her head away. "I don't believe

you," she protested, but something deep inside told her that he wasn't lying. She'd heard Simon boast of Indian villages he'd burned—of scalps he'd taken. Burning a church to kill savages inside wasn't beyond his capability. "Simon is my husband. I won't listen to lies you tell about him," she said. But her stomach constricted and a lump rose in her throat. If it was true—if Simon had done this awful thing—Talon would have little mercy for her once his father was released.

"My mother's devotion to her new religion ran deep, so deep that she sent her oldest son to the English at Williamsburg. They have a school at the College of William and Mary where small naked natives are dressed in proper coats and breeches and taught their catechism. She knew that a young child learns best, so I went at four and stayed two years. Since I was too little to manage the doors in the Wren Building, I lived with a physician and his family. They were kind enough to let me sleep on the kitchen floor with their dogs."

"Two years you lived there?" His eyes reflected flickering light from the fire, and for an instant she forgot who he was and looked into the soul of a lonely, frightened little boy.

"They whipped me when I spoke Delaware, so I learned quickly. They say leather stimulates the brain if applied often enough to the back. When I passed the moon of my sixth birthday, I stole my benefactor's best horse and rode away. I was halfway to the Ohio River when a Shawnee hunter found me."

"It must have been a difficult experience for you," she said stiffly. "But I can't believe that you mastered our language at so young an age."

"So my mother thought. She sent me to

Williamsburg again when I was eleven. This time, I was housed at The Brafferton on the college grounds with boys from a half-dozen tribes. We studied religion, grammar, mathematics, Latin, and other subjects. Religion was the favorite class of our instructors, but I preferred the history of your Greek and Roman generals. Do you know that the library at William and Mary contains detailed accounts of the battle tactics of Alexander the Great?"

"You are an educated man?"

He shrugged. "My teachers thought I had a gift for learning languages. Naturally, they kept us locked in Brafferton House. Who would sanction savages roaming the streets of town—coming in contact with decent folk? At night, a friend and I would climb down the brick walls from the upper floor and run for hours. It was a way to keep myself fit and to remember who I was."

She swallowed, and her voice came out softer than she intended. "Why didn't you escape again?"

His lips tightened into a thin slash across his inscrutable face. For a long moment, she thought he wouldn't answer, and then he said simply, "My mother made me promise that I would stay until I knew enough about your people to be an asset to mine."

She almost laughed. "Your mother? You stayed because your mother wanted you to?"

"You do not honor your mother? You would break your word to her?"

"She's dead."

"Then you realize her value, if you did not while she lived."

She shut her eyes as the pain knifed through

her. Once again, the awful scene that was seared on her brain came to mind . . .

She was thirteen again—coming down the stone stairs from the new wing of her father's house with an armful of linens, a gift for the itinerant tinker families that camped every summer on her father's land, when she'd first seen her mother lying at the foot of the steps. She lay moaning, sprawled in a spreading pool of blood and birth fluids from a babe brought to birth too soon. Standing over her body was father's cousin, his pious face twisted in a smug grin. "Murderer!" *Rebecca had whispered, as she knelt in her mother's blood and looked into her ashen face.* "Murderer!"

"Becca."

Talon's voice dragged her from the past. "I always knew my mother's value," she murmured. "I loved her . . . more than anyone else." She looked up into his chiseled male face and remembered who he was and who she was. "My mother has nothing to do with this. If you are a Christian—"

"I am not a Christian. The Shawnee and their grandfathers, the Delaware, have their own religion. We have practiced our faith for time out of time, long before the Irish ceased worshiping standing stones."

"All Christians are not perfect. You cannot blame our God for—"

"Your God and mine are the same, Becca. It is your eyes that are clouded by ignorance. Does it matter whether we call him *Wishemenetoo* or *Keshaalemookungk* or Jehovah? There can be only one *Creator*, a Supreme Being of love and benevolence."

"If you've been given the advantages of our culture—if you know us so well—then how can you hate us?" She was beyond anger now. He disturbed her in a way that went far beyond his burning their farm and holding her hostage.

In a heartbeat, he crossed the distance between them and seized her hand. She tried to struggle free, but he was stronger than she remembered. "Don't—" she began.

He held her hand firmly, not twisting it or hurting her, but so that she knew that she had no chance of pulling away. Fear possessed her and she clamped her other hand over her mouth to hold back her screams.

"Be still," he ordered. Almost gently, he turned her palm so that it was lit by firelight.

"Please," she whimpered. "I don't—"

He raised his eyes and gazed into hers. "I do not hate you, Becca," he said. "I mean you no harm. So long as my father lives, you are safe with me." He clasped her hand with his lean, brown fingers. "There is something I do not understand," he continued softly. "Your flesh is no different from mine."

She shuddered with terror as he pulled his knife from his sheath and sliced the skin on the back of his hand. A thin trickle of blood ran down over her palm.

"Do you see?" he asked. "Do you see that my blood is the color of yours? I am a man. I thirst and hunger; my heart is glad when the first flowers bloom through March snow, and I know sorrow when those I love come to grief. Am I so different from an Englishman—an Irishman—a Frenchman? Am I?"

She shook her head.

"Then why do the Europeans come to our land

and treat us no differently from the game they slaughter for sport?"

"I am Irish. I told you that. The English stole my country as well. You can't blame me for—"

"We have a treaty signed in the name of King George. It says that no whites will settle on Indian land. Simon Brandt built his cabin on Delaware hunting grounds."

Rebecca dropped her gaze, unable to answer. It was true. Simon had no right to be there. "I didn't choose where to clear the forest," she protested. "I go where my husband tells me and—"

He would not let go of her hand. "And you dare to say that Shawnee women are without rights?"

Her chest felt tight and she was dizzy. She desperately wanted him to release her . . . and yet she took perverse pleasure in his touch. His half-naked chest was very close, and she had the strangest urge to reach out with her other hand and stroke his bronze skin.

Mary and Joseph! What was she thinking? She turned her head away as tears welled up in her eyes and spilled down her cheeks.

Instantly, his mood shifted. He opened his hand and let her slip away. "I did not want to frighten you," he said. "I only wanted you to see that I am as much a human as—"

"No." Her voice cracked with emotion and her lower lip quivered. "No, you are not human. You are a cruel, heartless barbarian, and you'll never convince me otherwise until you return me unharmed to my husband."

He retreated to the far wall of the cave, moving on silent feet with the lithe grace of a hunting animal. "There is nothing I would rather do, wife of my greatest enemy ... as soon as my father is free."

Inside the commandant's quarters of Fort Nelson, Simon Brandt, Amos Dodd, and two members of the Virginia Free Militia met with Colonel Pickering, the ranking British officer. Pickering was seated at a table with his second, Major Brooke; a young, red-haired orderly stood just behind the two.

Simon leaned across the table and slammed his fist down with so much force that an ink stand fell to the plank floor and shattered. "Damn ye, Pickering! This is yer fault," he accused. "If you'd taken action immediately, my cabin wouldn't be in ashes and my wife wouldn't be in the hands of that red devil."

Brooke motioned toward the broken glass and the orderly hastened to clean up the mess. "I'll thank you to keep a decent tongue in your head, Brandt," the major admonished. "Colonel Pickering is new come to the wilderness. He must have time to adjust to our rather *unusual* circumstances here."

"My orders were to placate the savages, not stir them into frenzy," Pickering said. He was a meek man, the fourth son of an English baron, and had had the good fortune to serve in London for most of his career.

The extremes in weather that Colonel Pickering had experienced since coming to Virginia had strained his frail body. This morning he was suffering from a sore throat and a hacking cough; his throat was wrapped in red flannel to protect him from the chill, and he gave off a strong odor of garlic.

Simon sneered. "Ye treat Injuns like ye do all vermin. Hot lead and cold steel is all they understand."

Pickering covered his mouth with a monogrammed handkerchief and coughed into it. "My superior in London . . ." he began. His voice lost volume and he repeated himself in a louder tone. "My superior in London is deeply concerned by the rising French influence among the natives. He fears treachery from that quarter. If I anger the Indians by—"

"I ain't askin' ye to do anything, Colonel. My militia can handle this job. All we want from you is powder and protection for the men's families while we move west and cut us a swath through the hostiles."

"And recover your lost wife, I presume," Major Brooke put in. "My condolences, Brandt. I understand that this is not the first time Indians have—"

Simon's face darkened with rage. "Aye. They killed my first wife," he lied glibly. "Scalped and murdered my brother Peter, his wife, and their youngins. I buried 'em with these two hands— what was left of 'em. And I struck down the beasts that caused their deaths."

"This Indian captain . . ." the colonel said. "What is his name? Fire something . . . Are you certain he's the one who . . ."

"He's the one," Amos Dodd said. He shifted his cud of tobacco from one cheek to the other and leaned forward on his long rifle. "He sent word by Red Jim the Nanticoke that he had Missus Brandt. Claimed he'd trade her for the old man we got locked up here."

"Fire is Medicine Smoke's son," Major Brooke explained. "He's a big war chief—a real hothead.

He leads the Mecate Shawnee, but he draws braves from a lot of other tribes."

"Aye," Dodd agreed. "You snuff him, and you'll stop a lot of the killin' on the frontier."

"Fire Talon," Simon corrected brusquely. He paused, glanced around, and aimed a stream of tobacco at the brass spittoon beside the fireplace. He missed by six inches. "His name is Fire Talon," he said. "Half Shawnee, half Delaware, and half devil. Him and me go way back." He fixed Major Pickering with a malevolent stare. "If he's got my missus, she's dead. You kin count on it. Or if she ain't dead, she's prayin' to be. The Shawnee love to get their bloody hands on white women. And my woman's got red hair. Hell, they'd boil up their own grandma for a chance at a red scalp."

Pickering paled and wiped the corners of his mouth. "I am so sorry for you. My deepest condolences."

"Best be sorry for her," Simon replied, *because if she ain't dead yet, she soon will be.* His gut twisted until he tasted bile rising in his throat. He'd not expected this. All the nights he'd left Rebecca alone in that cabin, he'd never thought the hostiles would dare to touch her. Now Fire Talon had taken her, and they both had to die.

He couldn't believe it was happening again. It had been so many years since Injuns had killed his brother and family and run off with his first wife, Jane. She should have died with the others. It was God's will that she die with them, but she hadn't. She'd let some filthy brave crawl into her and fill her belly with his seed. She'd shamed him over and over—clung to her pitiful life when any decent woman would have killed herself. Until he found her . . . and did what had to be done.

He'd had his revenge . . . near twenty years of it. He'd suffered but he'd made sure that the red bastards suffered more. Foot by foot, he and good men like him had pushed the savages back to the Ohio. They'd did what God's chosen showed in the Old Testament, slaying the heathen, young and old, burning their towns, and plowing over their graves. Now it was time to finish them off, and to settle with his old enemy, Fire Talon, once and for all.

"Mister Brandt had requested that we send to Philadelphia for certain items," Major Brooke said. "Blankets to give out to the hostiles as gifts. Good wool blankets from the smallpox hospital on Water Street."

"Smallpox hospital?" Pickering said. "I wasn't aware that . . ."

"The Quakers run a charitable institution for the dying," Brooke answered. "The blankets can be purchased reasonably. There is military precedent. It's been done before in the lower Pennsylvania Counties."

"But why send to Philadelphia?" the colonel asked. "If you want blankets, we have some here that you can—Oh." His face turned from white to tallow. "You specifically want . . ."

"Exactly," Brooke agreed. "Smallpox kills more hostiles in a month than we can in a year."

"But smallpox cannot distinguish between combatants and women and children," Pickering said. "Surely, you don't want to . . ."

"The cost of war," the major said. "If the Indians would see reason and move back across the Ohio, this wouldn't be necessary."

"I can't be responsible for . . ." Pickering began hesitantly.

"You will be responsible for nothin'," Simon said. "I tole ye. Me and my militia, we'll tend to the dirty work. Ye sit here in the fort and wait. By spring, yore problems will be over, and all this land will be open for white settlement."

"But the treaty?" Pickering argued. "What about . . ."

"We don't need a treaty if there aren't any hostiles to make it with," Dodd said.

In the next room, a half-breed laundress paused in the act of stripping the sheets from Colonel Pickering's bed and crept close to the door on moccasined feet. She brushed aside a long hank of greasy black hair and pressed her face to the door.

Her eyes were bloodshot from last night's bout of drinking, and her mouth tasted like a chicken run. She was no longer young, and her once firm breasts swung when she walked. Ready Mary they called her at the fort. She had once had another name and another life, but she rarely thought of that. In fact, she rarely thought of anything but her next meal and where she would find another mug of whiskey, but the word *treaty* had broken through her stupor. Ignoring the obvious danger, she listened to the ongoing conversation.

"I don't know," the commandant said. "There's our prisoner to think of. You insisted that we hold him until he signed the agreement, ceding the land in question to the crown, and now . . ."

"Yes, Brandt," the major said, rising to his feet. "What do you propose we do with old Medicine Smoke? From the looks of him, he's close to death already."

"Hang him," Simon said.

The colonel's eyes widened in surprise. "Hang him?"

"Yes, hang the bastard," Simon snapped. "He's of no use to us if he won't sign and useless if he's dead."

"Then why kill him?" Pickering asked.

"Would ye see white women kidnapped up and down the frontier?" Simon answered sharply. "He's a party to the deed—as much to blame as his son. Hang him, I say, and hang the Nanticoke as well."

"But if this Fire Talon offered to trade Mrs. Brandt for his father," the colonel said, "shouldn't you arrange her release before . . ."

"The only bargain I'll give Fire Talon is a quick trip to hell," Simon said. "These Injuns see any weakness in us, they'll set the frontier aflame. We'll trade with Fire Talon if it comes to that—we just won't tell him his old man's a little ripe."

"Yep," Dodd agreed. "An' if ye don't kill the Nanticoke, he'll soon get word to the Shawnee that Medicine Smoke is dead."

"I don't know . . ." Pickering said. "It seems dishonorable . . . not something his majesty's forces should . . ."

"If it will insure peace for the settlers and safety for our soldiers, then Brandt's plan is a solid one," Major Brooke said. "Your mission here is to subdue the area, Colonel. The decision is yours, of course. You are the commandant. But if you ask for my opinion, I say let the Free Virginia Militia handle this matter." He pursed his full lips and brought both palms together, then brushed his chin with his joined fingertips. "And if anything goes wrong . . . ," he smiled wryly, "no one can attach any blame to you or to high command in London."

"This isn't easy to decide," Pickering said. "Mrs.

Brandt's life may be lost if we make the wrong decision." He glanced toward the door. "There's a terrible draft in this room. Does anyone else notice it? This is going to be another foul day, I'm certain of it."

The major motioned to the orderly, who draped a heavy dressing robe over the colonel's shoulders.

"Thank you, Wales," Pickering said. "I believe the fire needs additional fuel, as well. This accursed place is as drafty as a barn."

"Not so drafty as where my wife stands this morning," Simon put in. "And if she dies, ye kin be sure a lot of complaints will be made to London."

"It's best to finish this quickly, sir," Brooke suggested, pouring Pickering another glass of port. "You should be in bed. I don't like the sound of your cough. Mister Brandt and his militia have had a lot of experience with these natives. A good military leader knows when to delegate . . ."

"Exactly my feelings," the colonel said. "Do what you think best, Mister Brandt. Do it quickly, and without involving my troops. Godspeed."

"Aye," Simon replied thickly. The hate in his gut was so fierce it drove steel needles into his vitals. "Godspeed." Godspeed Fire Talon's death and Rebecca's. And Godspeed the last Injun from this country straight to the bowels of hell.

Chapter 9

Rebecca hadn't thought of her mother's death in days. Now, since the memory had returned so vividly this morning in the cave, her mother's dying face haunted her. Automatically, she put one foot in front of her, following Talon's moccasin prints in the crusty snow. But while her body continued moving in a steady rhythm, her mind was fixed on the past.

They had gathered their belongings and left the campsite before the sun was fully up. For hours they had walked west—at least she thought it was west—over rugged terrain and among trees so massive that she felt dwarfed by their size.

The day was bitter, but the forest blocked the wind. She felt only occasional gusts of cold wind and heard it whistling through the bare winter branches far overhead. Now and then, evergreens bent and swayed, lending the rustle of their snowy boughs to nature's symphony.

Rebecca had to admit she was warm enough. Talon had given her a second pair of knee-high moccasins to slip over her own; these were hard-soled, in a fashion she hadn't seen Indians use before. Under the Huron's military coat she wore a short, fringed squaw's dress of thick green kersey and otterskin leggings with the fur inside. On her hands were fur mittens, and a wolfskin robe cov-

ered her shoulders and laced close around her
face.

He was dressed much more simply: high moccasins, leggings and loincloth, a vest, and a fur wrap.
One arm was bare in the frigid air, and he wore
nothing on his head. A rifle was strapped to his
back; he carried a second in his right hand. Talon
was further weighed down by his tomahawk,
knife, hunting bag, powderhorn, and the hunting
bag of possessions she'd carried from the cabin.
Still, she was hard pressed to keep up with his
long strides.

They had not spoken for more than an hour. She
didn't know or care what his thoughts were—hers
were back in Ireland with her lost childhood.

Her father's accident had brought an end to her
former existence as surely and swiftly as Fire Talon's attack on Simon's cabin. In one brief day, she
had gone from adored child to an Irish housekeeper's bastard girl. It was weeks before she was to
realize the extent of the disaster, but only hours
until she noticed that the servants looked at her in
a different way and villagers whispered behind
her back.

Her mother had been devastated, too overcome
by grief to offer much help with funeral arrangements or even legal matters. It fell to Rebecca at
thirteen to send for a physician and a Protestant
minister, and after the funeral, to write to Father's
solicitor in Dublin.

James Gordon had been wise enough to leave a
will, and loving enough to provide handsomely
for his wife, his son and daughter, and the unborn
child that Mary Caitlin carried. He had supposed
that his family in England would not be pleased to
see the bulk of his substantial estate go to his mis-

tress and children. But he hadn't realized just how far his cousin would go to rob the bereaved family of everything.

Cousin Abner had descended on them in record time, bringing with him an entire household of relatives and servants. They had taken over her father's house like a horde of hungry fleas, creeping into every corner and setting everyone's nerves on edge. Her mother, always so strong and articulate—the woman who had ridden horseback up until the day of Colin's birth—made little objection. Instead, five months gone with child, she took to her bed.

In a week, Cousin Abner had dismissed her mother's physician and appointed his own. Cousin Resolve, Abner's wife, settled her own children into Colin's nursery and pushed him out. Rebecca had taken him into her bed, grateful for the company. From then on, her baby brother had been her responsibility.

The new physician drew the shutters in her mother's bedchamber, declared that she was suffering from a *melancholy of the spirit*, and prescribed laudanum three times a day. Her mother's cheeks had gone from rosy to gray, her unwashed hair became tangled, and her sparkling eyes dulled. Soon, she wept day and night. She was unable to bear the sound of Colin's laughter or look into the little face that was so much like his father's.

Cousin Resolve had hinted that the bedroom with the rose-tinted windows, the one Rebecca had slept in since she was tiny, was too grand for a housekeeper's daughter. And when Rebecca had reminded Abner's wife that they were merely guests in her mother's household, Abner had caned her severely.

She had not been ignorant. She had known of the Penal Laws enacted by the English crown against the Irish Catholics. To name but a few of the restraints placed upon those who followed the old religion, there were the following:

A Catholic was forbidden to hold public office, engage in trade, enter a profession, or vote.

A Catholic could not buy land, lease land, or inherit land from a Protestant.

Practice of the Catholic religion was forbidden. Catholics were not permitted to attend mass. They must attend and support the Protestant church. Priests were to be hunted down like criminals.

Catholics were forbidden to educate their children at home, enroll them in school, or send them abroad for an education. Catholic teachers were also outlawed.

A Catholic could not stand as a child's guardian, and Catholic orphans must be raised as Protestants.

Her father had warned her how dangerous it was to be a Catholic in Ireland. To protect his children, he'd had both Colin and her christened in the Anglican faith—hours after her mother had had them christened by a priest. By law, if not in their hearts, she and her brother were Protestant. Dadda had counted on that to keep them safe and preserve their inheritance. He had named his solicitor and friend, John Ledger, Esq., good Protestant, as their legal guardian.

But an English judge had set aside the guardianship of honorable John Ledger and replaced him with Cousin Abner. Shortly after that, Abner produced a second, *later* will giving him everything, and she, Colin, and their mother were stripped of all they owned. Rebecca—and even John Ledger—had suspected that the new document was forged, but no one paid them any mind.

The following day, her mother—who had not stirred from her bed for weeks—had somehow walked the length of the house in her night rail and tumbled down the steep old steps that led to the kitchen.

Her mother's grave was not yet green when Abner signed indentures for her and her brother and sent them off across the ocean to the American Colonies . . . where she had met Simon and become a wife too soon.

What would her mother think? Would she blame her for losing Colin? Did she know from heaven's gate that Colin was missing? And had her eyes regained their bright—

"Stop!"

Talon's order brought Rebecca up short. Startled, she looked around her. She had been so intent on her memories that she'd forgotten where she was. "What . . ." she began.

"*Chitkwesi!* Be quiet. Listen." He pointed to a nearby tree. The bark had been sliced and torn just above her head level.

She stared at the oak, then dropped her gaze to the trampled, muddy snow below. Bear tracks. Big ones. She glanced around uneasily. The animal that had made these marks in the snow would go to four hundred pounds.

"Do you smell him?" Talon whispered.

Rebecca sniffed the air. To her surprise, she did catch the faint stench of rotten meat lingering in the cold stillness.

He eased back the hammer on his rifle. "Can you not sense *maxkw's* pain?" he asked her.

She shook her head. Other than the tracks and the marks on the tree, everything seemed peaceful.

Talon closed his eyes for a few seconds and

went perfectly still. Then his eyes snapped open. "Back," he said urgently. "Move back the way we came. The wind carries our scent to him. We'll try and circle around."

She looked at Talon with questioning eyes. "Simon always said a bear would run from a man, given half a chance."

"Most bears. Maybe not this one." He knelt and examined the tracks. "See here. *Maxkw* walked on four legs; here he rose on hind ones. It is a male in his prime, fat and ready to go into his long sleep. Why then does he behave unnaturally?"

"I don't see that he has," she answered. "Bears claw tree bark to get at the insects underneath."

"But he should be slow, sleepy. See there." Talon pointed to a yellow stain in the snow. "He makes water."

"So?"

"And again there." He pointed to a spot about twenty feet away. "He is confused, this bear. His paws are not injured. He walks without a limp, yet is angry. He rips the tree in fury, not in hunger."

Her eyes narrowed in disbelief. "You can tell all that from these tracks?"

He made a quick motion with his hand for her to be still and they retreated in silence back down the gentle incline. They followed their own trail for nearly a mile, and Talon kept his thumb on the hammer of his gun all the way. They walked quickly, and his eyes scanned the forest for any movement. It was evident to Rebecca that the signs of the bear had disturbed him greatly, and she couldn't help being puzzled. Talon hadn't seemed so vigilant when they were fleeing the enemy war party.

Finally, he seemed satisfied that they'd come far enough. He turned off the faint game path and led the way across country, around a burned out section, through an open meadow, and over a narrow stream, before starting up the mountain once more.

Rebecca's legs ached. Her feet hurt, and she was hungry. She didn't see the need for retracing their steps and making this long jaunt over rough country just to avoid a bear that probably would have lit out running as soon as he smelled humans. She wondered if it was possible that the great war chief, Fire Talon, was afraid of bears. If he was any kind of shot at all, he should have been able to bring a bear down with the rifle he was carrying.

"I thought the Shawnee were great hunters," she murmured, half under her breath.

"What?" He spun around and stared at her. "What did you say?"

She stood her ground. "You're afraid of that bear, aren't you?"

"The man who does not respect *maxkw* does not live to see his hair turn gray."

"Simon killed two or three every winter for their hides, meat, and fat."

Talon stiffened. "Do not speak to me of Simon Brandt."

"I am his wife."

"And will be his widow—if you can't hold your tongue."

"You're wrong! Simon will see you dead."

"And that will please you?"

"Yes . . . no. I don't know," she admitted honestly. "Maybe it would."

"Your hate runs deep."

"You've burned my house, kidnapped me—done something with my brother . . . I don't know what. Why shouldn't I hate you?"

Some of the hardness seeped out of his features. "I asked Fox—the man who brought the warm clothing for you—about the boy. He said no one has seen your brother or the warrior who captured him."

"If you knew Colin was dead, would you tell me?"

Talon nodded. "I would tell you. It would not give me pleasure, but I would tell you the truth."

She swallowed. "I wish I could believe that."

"Believe what you will." He shrugged, and his face became a granite mask once more. "Come, enough talk. We have far to go before the sun sets."

"Where are you taking me?"

He didn't bother to answer. He simply started off. She followed, knowing full well that to be alone and without shelter in these mountains at night would mean her certain death.

The uphill climb grew steeper. Low brush and scrub trees clung to the rocky soil, interspersed with larger pine trees and cedar. Rebecca found herself scrambling to keep up. She removed her fur mittens, tucking them into her coat for safe keeping. The slope was so rugged that she had to take hold of branches and protruding rocks to pull herself up.

Once, Talon offered his hand to help her over a particularly rough spot. For an instant, she nearly refused his assistance, but he waited, dark eyes expressionless, hand extended. Against her better judgement, she clasped his fingers. His touch was warm and strong and—she had to admit to herself—oddly comforting.

Ignoring the curious fluttering sensation in the pit of her stomach, she let him lift her up. When her feet rested on level ground, she pulled free. He let her go instantly.

"You are welcome," he said.

She felt her cheeks grow hot. "Thank you."

"I did not . . ." He broke off as a huge gray owl rose flapping from a hidden branch and flew off over their heads.

Startled by the sudden appearance of the bird, Rebecca gasped and threw her hands up over her head. Talon uttered something in his own language and his face grew grim.

"A bad omen," he said. "*Kok hose* does not hunt by day."

"It was just an owl," she said, as her heartbeat slowed. "Don't tell me you're afraid of owls too."

"Pah," he answered with disgust. "You are ignorant, woman. You know nothing."

"At least I'm not scared of a horned owl."

He set off up the hill. They'd not gone more than a hundred yards when she heard a snort, almost the same sound a pig makes. "What . . ."

"Halt," he said, moving away from her. "Stay right where you are and be quiet."

"But . . . Oh!"

The bear rose out of the underbrush on two hind legs and kept rising. He went up and up, until she thought he must be the size of a team of oxen. Her cry died in her throat as the massive brown creature waved huge front paws with long, hooked claws as creamy-white as old ivory. The animal threw back his head and roared, a deep, rumbling growl that turned her bones to jelly. His small eyes were yellow and piglike—his head as big as a wagon wheel. His red mouth flashed curving teeth that were the stuff of children's nightmares.

She wanted to run. Every instinct for survival bade her run, but she couldn't. The bear swung his great head in her direction, wrinkled his nose, and sniffed the air. His bloodshot eyes rolled from side to side, and Rebecca knew that he was searching for her exact location.

He growled again, bellowing out a challenge. The sound made her tremble with fear. Then from the corner of her eye, she caught a flicker of movement, and Talon's tomahawk quivered in the trunk of a pine tree. The bear turned and snorted, then dropped to all fours and charged across the clearing, faster than Rebecca could ever believe he could run.

When he reached the tree, he rocked back on his hind feet and struck the tomahawk a mighty blow with his right paw. The shaft shattered and flew through the air like straw in a blast of wind, and with the ruined weapon went a piece of the tree trunk as thick as her thigh.

For what seemed an eternity, the beast worried the pine tree, slashing at it and biting chunks of wood with his teeth. Then he sniffed again, lifted his head, and waited motionless, clearly listening.

A Shawnee war cry rang out from almost the same spot where Rebecca had first sighted the bear. Enraged, the bear snorted, emitted a deep cough, and stood upright again.

"*Maxkw!*" Talon shouted. "Come, you lazy pig! Come!"

The bear charged again, racing toward Talon with a roar like thunder. But halfway to his tormentor, the animal stopped short and swung his head around.

"Maxkw!"

Rebecca's terrified gaze met that of the bear. Then he squealed and swung toward her. Talon's rifle spat lead and smoke and a great puff of fur rose from the bear's spine.

Panic spilled through her veins. She fled into the woods. Behind her, she could hear the bear's guttural snarl. She could feel the earth shudder under the weight of his feet.

"Climb a tree!" Talon yelled.

A second shot vibrated through the forest.

She looked frantically for a tree with branches low enough to grasp, dodged around a pine that seemed too small, and slammed into a cedar.

Branches were snapping behind her. Rebecca could almost feel the bear's hot breath on her neck. She grabbed a limb and pulled herself up as a great force smashed into the trunk.

"Arrrannngg!" The bear's roar deafened her.

Bark and twigs scratched her face and hands, but Rebecca didn't stop. She climbed higher. The tree swayed and groaned, but she didn't look down. She fixed her eyes on a patch of white cloud outlined in azure blue sky and kept going. The tree shook so hard that debris rained around her. She lost her grip with one hand, but held fast with the other.

When she had gone as high as she could, she glanced down into the face of the bear. He was trying to climb the tree after her.

She screamed and the bear uttered a horrendous growl. His mouth opened and the sickening rotten meat odor floated up to hit her face. He raised a paw to strike at her.

"Talon!" she cried. "Talon!" Then the branch she was clinging to snapped with a dull crack and she began sliding down toward the bear.

Chapter 10

Time slowed as Rebecca tried desperately to hold on to the slippery, snow-covered tree trunk. The blue sky and the green pine needles overhead flashed before her eyes. The bear's growls deafened her. She tried to scream, but sheer terror paralyzed her vocal cords and she could not utter a sound.

I'm going to die, she thought. *Mother of God, I'm going to be eaten alive by this damn bear and leave Colin lost in this wilderness . . .*

And then she was falling. She hit the ground hard; her head slammed against the tree. Everything went black. Was it night? Had minutes passed or only seconds? Pinwheels of light spun through the murky fog. She fought to regain consciousness. The bear? Where was the bear?

She could hear him roaring. His snarls shook the forest. She could smell him. But where . . . Wiping snow and bark from her face, she tried to stand. Her head hurt but—

Sweet Mary and Joseph! The bear was only a few yards away. He reared high on his back legs and raked the air with terrible claws. His maw gaped open as he thrashed from side to side and tried to throw off the man on his back.

Talon! His war whoop rose above the snarls of the bear. His blood-soaked arm rose and fell, driving a knife into the massive animal's neck over and over.

It was impossible. No mortal could cling to such a raging beast. And yet he did. Naked but for his loincloth and leggings, hair streaming down his back, soaked in a river of blood, the Shawnee warrior rode the bear like a burr on a bull's neck.

The bear was crazed. He knocked down trees and clawed the earth. Each time the knife blade struck his flesh, he moaned in pain. Blood poured from his mouth in a river; his eyes were blinded with it.

The tendons on Talon's arms and naked back stood out like ropes; his contorted face showed the strain of the unequal contest between man and animal that could only end one way.

Unless . . . Cold reason flooded Rebecca's mind. Talon would die, and then she would die—horribly—unless she intervened.

To reach one of the fallen rifles she had to cross the open space, the place where the bear raged. If he saw her, she would have no chance. But if she remained where she was and did nothing . . .

She willed herself to take a single step. Her body seemed not to belong to her but to another. She was a wooden puppet. Her muscles refused to obey.

And then the bear gave a mighty shrug and Talon went flying through the air. He landed on the trampled snow and the bear threw back his head and howled in triumph. Then the bruin's blood-streaked eyes focused on his tormentor, and he lumbered toward him.

Rebecca dashed toward the rifle, raised it to her shoulder, and pulled the trigger. There was no sound but the dull click of the hammer.

Empty. Of course—Talon would have fired off the shot before charging the bear with only his knife. She looked around frantically for the powder horn and hunting bag.

The bear struck Talon a horrendous blow. Talon's body was lifted off the ground and thrown. He fell like a sack of wheat and lay still. Down the length of his back four ribbons of scarlet unfurled. The bear cocked his head as if listening and sniffed the air.

Rebecca dumped the contents of the hunting sack on the ground. She would not look at the bear. She would not think of Talon. She would load and fire the rifle.

She could do it. She had done it before. Bite the lid off the powder flask, hold the rifle away. Measure powder into the barrel; place the patch over the end, seat the ball and tamp. Her stiff fingers seemed made of wood as she loaded the frizzen pan with fine powder, lifted the rifle to her shoulder, and sighted in on the raging bear.

He had struck Talon a second time; now he prepared to finish him off with his teeth. The great head hovered over the man's crumbled body.

"Bear!" Rebecca shouted. "You bear! Have this with your tea!"

The shaggy body swayed; the reddish-brown head turned and red pig eyes sought her out. The smell of blood was heavy and cloying in the air; Rebecca could almost taste it.

A low, rumbling roar spilled from the bear's throat. He rose up and took one step toward her.

One shot, she thought. If I miss this one . . . The bear lowered his head and she squeezed the trigger.

The sound of her weapon firing was lost in the

bear's growl. He kept coming—coming at her like a crazed mountain. She gripped her rifle and closed her eyes.

"Holy Mary, Mother of God, pray for me now," she whispered. She waited for the death blow.

She opened one eye and watched him fall at her feet. Rebecca sprang back as the bear pawed weakly at the ground, then gave an almost human moan and went limp. He shuddered and the single eye that remained glazed over. Her shot had taken out the other neatly.

She poked at the animal with the rifle barrel, but there was no more movement. "Bear?" she cried, half in triumph, half in hysteria. "Are you dead?"

Tears spilled down her cheeks and she dashed them away. Cautiously, she circled the outstretched bear and walked to the man.

Was he dead as well? He lay sprawled on his side, one arm flung over his head, his ruined back open to the sky. He still held his knife in his clenched fist.

"Talon?" She dropped to her knees beside him and took his limp hand in hers. "Talon?" He felt so cold. Could any man be so cold and live? Could any man lose so much blood and survive?

She put her hand over his mouth, but she couldn't feel any movement of breath. She glanced at his back and her stomach turned over. The bear's claws had cut him to the bone. Snow was caked over the wounds, but the blood seeping through it was bright red.

Did you still bleed if you were dead? she wondered. She scooped up fresh handfuls of snow and packed it against the torn flesh. He gave no sign that he felt either pain or the cold.

"Talon? Damn you, you son of a bitch! Don't

think you can die on me and leave me out here alone. I won't let you. Do you hear me?" she shouted. "I won't let you."

She rocked back on her heels and looked around. It would be dark soon. She was cold. She needed a fire and shelter if she was to survive. But if she took the time to try and make a fire, Talon might die of loss of blood.

"Might die? Might die? You fool," she admonished herself. "He's already dead. You can see that. He's already dead. You've killed the futtering bear, but he's going to have the last laugh after all. By morning, you'll be as dead as the two of them."

The sound of her voice in the now silent clearing seemed louder than the bear's growling. Anyone who heard her talking to herself would think she was as mad as May butter. Her head still ached, but the giddiness was leaving her.

Reluctantly, she left Talon's side and gathered up both rifles, the packs, and the fur cloak he'd thrown off. She carried them to where he lay. Then she draped his robe gently over him.

"Are you alive?" she murmured. His face was dirty and blood streaked, but untouched. His eyes were closed. She cupped his cheek in her hand and leaned close to see if she could feel any warmth. "Talon," she whispered.

Nothing.

An uneasiness threatened to push her over the brink to true madness. If he was dead, she was lost. If he was dead . . .

She shook her head. She wouldn't let him be dead. Fool that he was, savage, barbarian—he was her only hope of reaching the settlements again.

"Oh, Talon." She sighed. It was more than her

own safety that plagued her. She didn't want him dead . . . not just for her sake, but for his.

She cared if he lived.

The thought hung in the air defiantly.

"I don't care," she said.

But she did. No amount of lying to herself could change it. He was her sworn enemy—the man who'd burned her farm and vowed to kill her husband. But he was also the man who had leaped on the back of a bear to save her life when he could have run away. No, she didn't want Talon to die. What she did want, she would face later. For now . . . She exhaled softly and began to pack his wounds once more with snow.

His back was the worst, but a single claw had ripped open his flesh on his right arm from shoulder to elbow. A glancing blow had gouged his chest, cutting deep to expose his collar bone. She tried not to think of the poison those claws had carried. She would stop the bleeding now, if she could, and worry later about infection.

She took hold of his right hand and tried to pry free the knife that he still gripped as tightly as if it were an extension of his arm. The wicked steel blade was sticky with blood and hair. "Let go of the knife, Talon," she said. "It's all right. The bear is dead. You can let go of the knife now." His fingers were as cool and hard as ivory. "Let go," she repeated.

She thought she heard a groan.

"Talon?" She shook him. "Talon?" She slid her numbed hand inside her coat, then when it had warmed a little, pressed it against his chest to try and feel a heartbeat. Still nothing.

"Damn you," she muttered. "You're doing this on purpose." The bleeding was slowing. She wondered if the snow was doing the trick or if he really was dead.

Reason was returning. Her vision had cleared. Suddenly, everything that had been hazy with soft edges and softer colors slipped into place. "Talon is alive," she said to herself. "A dead man can't bleed."

She looked around her. The sun was much lower than it had been. She needed a fire, but not here where the wind would keep a spark from catching. There! She saw an enormous fallen cedar a few yards away. The trunk reached nearly to her chest and a huge branch curved around to make a natural shelter. There, a small fire might ignite and flourish, and the boughs would provide some relief from the frozen ground.

Again, she left him. Quickly, she began to gather wood for her fire. She found the head of the tomahawk and used it to scrape away rotten bark to reach the dryer inner lining. At home, this had been Colin's job for years. Boy that he was, he'd taught her how to find the driest wood when it rained. I wish I had you with me now, she thought fervently. I need you, Colin.

But she had only herself. And if she made a mistake, there would be no second chances.

When she had all her tinder and fuel, she crouched down beside the cedar log, took flint and steel from Talon's pack, and set to work to build a fire.

Her first attempt failed, as did her second and her third. On the fourth try, the tiny spark brought curls of smoke from the cedar bark, but no flame. But on the sixth, her spark flared, ate through the tinder, and began to burn. Patiently, she added twigs and then sticks the thickness of her finger.

When she was satisfied that the fire was a good one, she braced it with larger branches and went to drag Talon to the shelter.

His waist was so slender that she wouldn't have believed that he could be so heavy. Futilely, she pulled and tugged at his dead weight before seizing on the idea to roll him onto the cloak and slide that across the snow. As she pushed him over onto his stomach, he groaned.

"You are alive, you son of a bitch," she said. But her heart leaped, and she felt the same sudden joy that she'd felt when her feet had touched solid ground after so many weeks on the Atlantic.

She began to drag the cloak, an inch at a time, toward the fire. She was halfway there and it was pitch dark when she slipped on the frozen ground and fell flat on her face. And when she lifted her head, she found herself staring into the slanting yellow eyes of a mountain lion.

Simon Brandt stepped away from his friends at the fire and moved into the darkness of the surrounding forest. A fierce need had come over him after the incident with the Delaware this afternoon, and he could not sleep until he'd satisfied the racing in his blood.

They'd stayed at the fort just long enough to see Medicine Smoke kicking from the end of a rope, then nineteen militia men and one Ottawa scout had set out to find Fire Talon's Shawnee and take back Rebecca. The commandant had retreated to his bed, pleading illness and refusing to dignify the execution with his presence, but Major Brooke had brought out enough soldiers to make a good show.

The Nanticoke had died quickly. His neck

snapped when they'd dragged the Dutch cart out from under him, but the old man—Talon's father—hadn't been so lucky. His hanging had been slow and painful, and Simon had enjoyed every moment of it.

The weather had held, and he and the boys had made good time, reaching Coverdale's trading post by high noon. They'd been careful not to make mention of Medicine Smoke's hanging when they stopped for a bit of ale and pork pie. One of Coverdale's boys had married a Miami squaw, and another had a Delaware woman for a wife. Simon didn't want either Injun woman learning of the shaman's death. If they knew, word could travel to the Shawnee faster than the militia could march. So long as Fire Talon believed that Medicine Smoke was alive, the old man could still be valuable to them.

At Coverdale's they picked up three more good men. Two were farmers, looking to settle farther west as soon as the country was clear of hostiles. Jeb Steiner was the third man, a German preacher—as much a dyed-in-the-wool Injun hater as Simon had ever seen. Jeb carried a long rifle he'd named Gabriel; it had twenty-three notches carved in the stock, one for every Injun scalp the preacher had taken.

In midafternoon, the militia had come across a Delaware hunting camp, three braves, two kids, and a young squaw. One of the bucks had come out grinning with his hand in the air in a peace sign. Amos Dodd had put a musket ball right through his hand just before Davy Clarke had shot the Injun in the gut. The fight didn't last a quarter of an hour. When it was over, all the men and the young ones were dead. The boys had taken sport with the woman. Her screams were near loud enough to raise the dead.

He'd taken no part in the rape. He didn't mind what other men did; he had his own reasons for not joining in—reasons that went back as long as his feud with Fire Talon.

Nigh on to ten years the two of them had tried to kill each other, and he had to admit he'd never come up against another hostile as wily as Fire Talon. They'd both been little more than lads when they'd first come face to face. He'd wished many a time that Fire Talon had been in that church with his kin when they'd burned it.

The campfire was just a red glow over his left shoulder when Simon stopped and leaned his rifle against the tree. Thinking about that Shawnee nearly drove the urge out of his head . . . nearly, but not quite.

Simon had caught sight of the woman's bare breasts when they'd stripped her, small, pointed little tits, the kind that always excited him. Rebecca had had breasts like that when he'd first married her. He always liked to watch her bathe when she didn't know he was looking. She'd changed in time, filled out. To his way of thinking, she wasn't as fetching now as she had been at fifteen.

She'd been different in a lot of ways back then. He'd knocked some of the fancy ways out of her since then, but she didn't show him the respect she used to. Her or the boy. If the Injuns had scalped Colin, so much the better. He would never have amounted to much, not to Simon's way of thinking. Bastard stock never did.

Rebecca had seemed promising when she'd stepped off that boat from the old Ireland country.

She'd been scared and easily led by her husband. Young women made the best wives for a man like him. Once Rebecca was dead for certain, he'd show the proper mournin' for a full year, then he'd find himself another young bride, maybe a Mennonite girl this time.

Jeb Steiner said Lancaster was full of Mennonite families, and most of them had an eligible daughter or two. Mennonite girls were taught to obey their men and they were good cooks. He'd need a strong girl to help him rebuild his cabin and to work in the field. This time, he'd choose careful, and not take one that was too high in the stomach, thinkin' herself a lady when she weren't nothin' but a woods colt.

He tried to picture a Mennonite girl bent over his hearth, but thoughts of the Injun woman kept interfering. He swallowed hard as he remembered the sight of that squirmin' dusky red thigh Davy had been holdin' on to. She'd put up quite a fight, but Davy wouldn't be bested by a wench. He'd taken his turn with the squaw, Simon was sure of that. But if any of them wondered why he didn't, they daresn't have the gall to ask.

Fire Talon had nearly killed him more than ten years ago, back on the Susquehanna that Christmas Day they'd fought each other to their knees. He'd sliced the Shawnee's side open with a butcher knife and put a lead ball through his thigh, but Fire Talon had nearly turned him into a woman with his own knife. Simon left one ballock and a quart of his life's blood on that river bank, along with something a man couldn't taste or smell. Fire Talon had robbed him of a man's pleasures in life. His jock worked good enough when he was alone, but he couldn't keep it stiff with a woman. That was something Simon would never forgive or forget.

He meant to see the Shawnee pay. He meant to skin him alive, cut off his male parts, and stuff them ... Simon chuckled. Maybe ... maybe, he'd think of something better.

Thinking about Fire Talon and Rebecca made his blood boil. The Shawnee had made free with his wife. He knew it wasn't customary, but the war chief wouldn't miss a chance to shame his greatest enemy. He'd lain with Rebecca all right, and the worthless slut had probably enjoyed it—enjoyed those naked red legs wrapped around her. Damn if it didn't make a man want to vomit to think of a Christian white woman with such vermin. But it wasn't heatin' he needed just now, it was coolin'.

There'd be time enough to deal with those two. Time enough to consider what to do with Rebecca if she was still alive when he caught up with her. It wouldn't do to let anyone know. Just like Jane, he'd take care of the problem by hisself. He'd clear his honor and his wife's, whether she had sense enough to know what was right or not.

He summoned up the image of that Delaware squaw again. How old had she been? Thirteen? Fourteen? It was always hard to tell with Injuns; they weren't made like normal women. Pretty little thing she'd been. Round little arse. Delicate hands and feet, and a slender neck. If he'd found her alone, maybe he could have ...

A waste to think of that now. She hadn't been as strong as she'd looked. One man had had to use her after she was already dead. A damn shame, he thought. Loud as she'd yelled, a man would have thought she'd have stayin' power.

Simon undid the buttons on the front of his

breeches. His need was making itself felt now ...
a strong need, stiff and throbbing.

His breathing became ragged as he thought of
the little squaw. "Fetching critter," he whispered
hoarsely, as his hand closed around his thick upright member. Then he stopped talking and concentrated on satisfying his intense desire.

Chapter 11

Rebecca was too astonished to breathe. Her heart thudded wildly as she stared in utter terror at the big cat. The mountain lion's eyes caught the reflected light from the fire and glowed an unholy green in the tawny face. For what seemed an eternity, the cat didn't move a muscle, then the long, ropelike tail began to flip nervously from side to side.

First a bear, now this, Rebecca thought, and she steeled herself for the lion to spring on her.

"Meshepeshe!"

A human voice broke through Rebecca's fright. She couldn't tell if the speaker was male or female; the tone was raspy, as though it hadn't been used in a long time.

"Meshepeshe." A ghostly figure swathed in white furs moved from the trees. "No move."

Rebecca swallowed the imaginary lump in her throat. Don't move? She couldn't have moved— not for anything in the world.

The mountain lion made a rumbling sound deep in her belly. The tip of a red tongue appeared. Rebecca closed her eyes and felt a wet rasping sensation down one side of her face. The thing was licking her as though it was an overgrown tabby cat.

The ghost spoke again, a quick order that Re-

becca couldn't comprehend. When she opened her
eyes again, the cat crouched beside the newcomer
rubbing its huge head against his leg.

"Please, I need help," Rebecca said as she rose
to her knees. "We were attacked by a bear.
My—my companion is badly hurt."

The mountain lion hissed a warning, and Rebecca shrank back in alarm.

"I won't hurt you," Rebecca said. "He's bleeding. He'll die if we don't do something." She
looked into the ghost's face and realized that he
was wearing a fringed white doeskin mask that
covered his face from brow to chin. The only human aspect she saw were two dark brown eyes
and a glimpse of bare skin at the throat. "Please."
She tried again in desperation. "Do you speak English? Can you understand anything I'm saying?"

A white fur mitten stroked the animal's head,
and the beast dropped to the snow and began to
groom a front paw. "Losowahkun hear."

"Low-so ..." Rebecca's tongue stumbled over
the alien sounds. "Losowahkun? Is that your
name?"

"Talk, no fast. *Englishmanake.* Losowahkun
have white-hair talk. Some." He glanced down at
the mountain lion. The animal was chewing con-
tentedly on his high fur moccasin. "Meshepeshe
have ..." He struggled for the English. "Have curious. No hurt. Is bairn ... baby." He made a
chuckling sound. "Best you not move. Curious
Meshepeshe dangerous."

"My companion," Rebecca insisted, bordering
on hysteria. "He is close to death." Was she to
stand here fencing with this odd pair while Talon
bled to death?

The stranger moved to examine Talon's wounds,

and Rebecca noticed for the first time that the white-garbed Indian carried no weapons. But then, who would need any with such a creature by his side? Then Rebecca heard a sharp intake of breath.

"*Ku!* Sh'Kotaa Osh-Kah-Shah."

"You know him?" Rebecca cried.

"Losowahkun know. Is my brother."

Together, they dragged Talon to the fire. When he was lying on a bed of cedar boughs and covered with the fur robe, Losowahkun left them alone with the big cat for the space of an hour. When he returned, he was leading a shaggy brown pony with thick, stocky legs and an oversized head.

With great effort, the two managed to get Talon over the pony's back. Losowahkun tied him on, and they gathered the rifles and belongings. Rebecca didn't know where Talon's brother wanted to take him, but it was beginning to snow again and the temperature was dropping. Any place was bound to be better than this windswept mountain. She held onto the pony's tail and followed as Losowahkun led them over the mountain and through forest so thick and black she couldn't see her hand in front of her face.

Eventually, when she was so weary and cold she didn't think she could take another step, she caught a whiff of hot, baking bread. It seemed a form of delusion, and she tried to ignore it, but within minutes, they stopped short. Rebecca walked smack into the pony's rump.

She heard wood grating on wood, then Losowahkun pulled open a high door of branches and hide, revealing the interior of a long hut with a fire built at one end. He clicked to the pony, and the animal stepped over the sill and walked inside, followed by the mountain lion. Rebecca didn't wait for an invitation. She stumbled past them and ran to the fire, pulling off her mittens and holding out her stiff hands to the crackling flame.

Losowahkun shed his outer robe and mittens and led the pony to a wide platform that ran along two sides of the longhouse. The structure was about waist high and used in various spots as bed, table, and storage area. Losowahkun halted the pony beside a heaped pile of furs and motioned for Rebecca to help him get Talon off the animal's back.

Once Talon was on the platform, Losowahkun clicked to the pony, and the gentle animal walked to the far end of the longhouse, away from the fire, and began to nibble at a heap of dry corn stalks. The cat circled around behind Rebecca and watched her every movement with narrowed eyes.

Losowahkun seemed to have forgotten that she was there. He went to the fire pit and brought back a copper tea kettle of warm water, then got a small clay pot from the storage area. The domed ceiling was braced with saplings stripped of their bark; numerous skin bags, woven baskets, and leather pouches hung from the poles. Losowahkun chose two pouches, sprinkled powder from each into the bowl, poured water from the kettle on top, and stirred with a peeled stick.

"Is he still alive?" Rebecca asked. Talon hadn't even groaned when they'd lowered him, face down, onto the sleeping platform. "He lost a lot of blood."

"Sh'Kotaa Osh-Kah-Shah lives. His spirit walks

the star path. Losowahkun call back or he die before morning sun."

Firelight gleamed off a terrible knotted purple scar that ran down Talon's brother's exposed arm. His chest and his other arm were covered by a white fox fur vest and sleeve. He had not removed the deerskin mask, but he had taken off the fox hood. His hair was thick and black, chopped off short at shoulder length. In the front, a fringe of dark bangs fell to cover the top of the eerie white mask.

Rebecca peered at him from the corner of her eyes, no longer certain if he was indeed a man or a woman. He was not so tall as Talon, and more lightly built, but his arm was lean and muscular. His voice was husky, his movements decisive like a man's, with none of a woman's deference.

His clothing was male, an undecorated white buckskin apron—front and back—worn over the fur leggings and moccasins. He wore no jewelry that she could see. He must be a man, she decided. But there was something . . . something she couldn't quite put a name to that made her unsure of his sex.

"Who are you?" she asked. "And why do you live here alone in the mountains?" There was no village nearby, she was certain of that. If there were other Indians, she would have smelled their campfires and heard the dogs.

As if on cue, Rebecca heard a whining and scratching at the side of the hut. Losowahkun turned and pulled aside an elkhide, and a wolf slunk into the longhouse. "Wonderful," Rebecca murmured.

The wolf laid back his lips and snarled. Losowahkun silenced the animal with a word and turned back to Talon. "Eat," he said. "There." He motioned to a flat rock on the edge of the fire pit.

Rebecca looked toward the hearth and noticed the small round cakes, realizing that they were what she'd smelled when they'd approached the longhouse. Losowahkun had evidently left the bread cooking, far enough from the fire to keep them from burning. Rebecca reached for one, and found the rock hot to the touch. She as unfamiliar with the texture of the patty, but hungry enough to try anything.

She bit into one gingerly, and was surprised at how good it tasted. "What is it?" she asked. "It's delicious." She recognized a maple-sugar flavor and the sweet bite of blueberries, but the flour was something she hadn't seen before.

"Acorn," Losowahkun answered. "Acorn and squash, mix with *xaskwim*—corn." He came back to the fire and took a flaming branch, using the light to inspect Talon's back more closely. "Aiyee," he murmured. He tossed the wood back into the fire pit and began rummaging through a basket of small birchbark containers.

Rebecca finished a second cake and dusted the crumbs off her fingers. Absently, Losowahkun handed her a gourd. She unstoppered the end and took a small sip. The liquid was much like herbal tea. "Thank you," she said and took a deeper drink.

Talon's brother found a box that satisfied him and returned to the patient. "Bring gourd," he said.

"This?" He nodded, and she joined him. When she looked down at Talon's back, she shuddered. Now that the blood had been cleaned away, she could see the full extent of the damage the bear's claws had done. Muscle and tissue had been ripped away; pieces of flesh were missing entirely. "He can't live, can he?" she asked. Her heart sank. She had known that the injuries were critical, but the fact that he'd survived so long had given her hope.

Losowahkun had cleaned the wounds and rubbed a grayish paste into the gashes. Now, he gestured for Rebecca to take one of Talon's arms. Together, they raised him to a sitting position, and Losowahkun began to drip the herbal tea into Talon's mouth. Most ran over his lips and down his chin, but his brother was persistent. He continued to give Talon the liquid until every drop was gone. "Good," he said. "Make sleep."

"Make sleep?" Rebecca said. "But you gave it to me, too."

"*E-e.*" He motioned for her to help lay Talon back on the furs, then took a sharp steel needle and a length of silk thread. "Sew?" he asked Rebecca.

"Sew him?"

"*E-e.* Sew." He handed her the needle and pointed to the deepest of the claw marks. "Sew!"

She shook her head. "You do it." Her stomach was beginning to feel queasy, and her head felt as if it was full of uncarded wool.

"*Ku.* Sew!"

Rebecca took a deep breath, glanced at the watching mountain lion, and gritted her teeth. "All right," she agreed. "You show me where, and I'll stitch. My stitches are probably better than yours anyway."

Talon's brother sprinkled black powder onto the open wounds and pointed to the place where he wanted her to make the first suture. Fresh blood sprang from the needle entrance, and Losowahkun wiped it away with a compress of shredded cedar bark. "Sew," he repeated.

Rebecca drew the silk tight and worked the needle through a second time. I wanted you to suffer, she thought, as sweat beaded on her head. I hated you ... but I don't now. I don't know why I changed, but I did. Best be careful what you pray for, she decided. You may not want what you prayed for when it comes.

Losowahkun brought a clay pot of lit tobacco and moved the container back and forth over Talon's back as Rebecca worked. The smoke made Rebecca's eyes water.

She blinked; it was hard to focus on her patient. She seemed almost detached from the task. Stitch—knot—stitch. Then she realized with a start that she had finished.

Talon's brother dusted the lines of raw flesh with more of the black powder, then indicated that Rebecca should help to move the patient onto his side so that they could administer to the wound on his right arm. This tear was particularly nasty. She watched in disbelief while Losowahkun sucked blood and dirt from the injury and spat it into the fire. Then he rinsed his mouth out with water and treated Talon's arm in the same way he'd repaired the lacerations on his back.

Rebecca could barely keep her eyes open to sew up the deep slash. She swayed on her feet as she finished tying the last knot. Vaguely, she was aware of Losowahkun guiding her to a place on the platform piled with furs. She crawled between them, unable to summon the energy to remove her moccasins. When she next stirred, sunlight was pouring through the smoke hole over the hearth.

She sat up and looked around. Immediately, her senses were assaulted by a myriad of strange smells and sights. Curing hides, tobacco, mint, pine, she recognized; but the majority of the odors were totally alien to her. A somewhat unpleasant smell could only come from the mountain lion staring back at her from the far side of the fire.

"Well, if you didn't eat me while I slept, I guess I'm safe for the moment," she murmured. Nothing else moved in the longhouse. She reached out and touched the wall next to her sleeping shelf.

Tightly curling hair covered the immense hide that must belong to a woods bison. Other skins were stretched over the inner bark panels that formed the structure of the hut. The floor was made of hard-packed earth. Fur rugs were spread beside the platform and next to the fire pit. Overhead hung a pair of snowshoes, a beaded quiver full of arrows, fish spears, strings of dried squash and pumpkin, dried fish, and an assortment of deerskin clothing in various stages of construction.

Along the platform were baskets of corn, acorns, and unfamiliar roots. There were sealed containers woven of grass, and of reeds, and stacks of dry firewood. A fishing net was folded on top of a small sled. Beside that stood a copper kettle large enough to boil a goose. One wall held wooden masks, several rifles, and a hunting bag and powder horn. The hut was so well supplied that it was evident to her that this was Losowahkun's permanent home, not just a hunting camp.

Rebecca took a deep breath and stretched. How was it possible for her to sleep so soundly here in this Indian stronghold, she wondered. Then she remembered the herb tea Losowahkun had given her to drink.

Talon.

Mother of God! She clapped her hand over her mouth. She had lost her mind if she'd forgotten Talon. She began to get off the sleeping platform when the cat growled. Instantly, Rebecca froze. The tawny lion's tail was twitching back and forth, and she could see a hint of curving ivory fangs.

"I'm not going to hurt anyone," she said soothingly as she lifted the furs slowly. "I just want to—"

The cat snarled.

"All right. All right." She settled back into her warm nest. Her host was absent, along with the pony and the wolf. It seemed that the mountain lion had been left as guard. She wondered if she could creep down the platform to where Talon lay without disturbing the cat, but as soon as she moved, the animal snarled again. "No one would believe this," she murmured, half to herself.

Then the larger door opened and Losowahkun entered, leading the pony. The little pack animal was weighed down with the bear skin and huge chunks of meat.

"Talon," Rebecca called. "Is he still alive? I tried to—"

"My brother sleeps."

"He isn't dead?"

"He has not crossed the river."

"River?"

Losowahkun shook his head and pushed back his fox hood. "You look." He pointed to where Talon lay.

Rebecca took that for permission to leave her bed. She slipped down onto the floor and crossed to Talon. He was stretched on his side as she had last seen him. He was very pale, but there was no mistaking the steady rise and fall of his breathing. She laid a hand on his forehead. "He has no fever," she said, glancing back at Losowahkun. "Why isn't he feverish? Bear claws are poison—everyone knows that."

He nodded solemnly. "Fever will come. I give blood of bear and liver. Make medicine. Burn *kinnikinnick*—tobacco."

"Will it be enough?" she asked.

He shrugged. "Sh'Kotaa Osh-Kah-Shah strong." From a pouch at his waist, he took a sticky ball of cedar gum and handed it to her. "Make ..." He sighed in exasperation, then went to the storage area and took a small English copper pot. He put the gum in it and added water from a tall clay container. Adding a pinch of dried leaves, and a bit of this and that, he went to the hearth and propped the pot over the coals. "Watch," he instructed. "No burn. You watch."

Rebecca went to crouch by the fire pit. Losowahkun added another log to the flames. Almost at once, the hut was filled with the pungent aroma of cedar. Then, in another clay pot, he began to heat a mixture of wild cherry bark, water, and maple sugar. "We give drink," Losowahkun explained. "Medicine woman teach me. Good."

"Will you make me drink it too?" Rebecca dared.

The dark eyes behind the mask flashed amusement. "You sleep good," he said.

"Yes," Rebecca nodded. "I did sleep good."

Later, when the potions were ready, she helped Losowahkun spoon the cherry liquid between Talon's lips and applied the cedar gum to his wounds.

At midmorning, she and Talon's brother shared

a breakfast of grilled bear meat, corn porridge, and dried fish. Losowahkun managed to eat small bites without removing his mask or looking the least bit awkward. Still, Rebecca wondered if the scars she supposed lay under the buckskin mask could be as frightening as the mask itself. It gave Losowahkun an unearthly look. Her first impression had been that he was a ghost; it still might be true, she thought. He didn't seem quite of this world, even for an Indian.

By afternoon, when Losowahkun left the hut, followed by the mountain lion, Talon had begun to run a fever. Rebecca sponged off his forehead with cool water and pushed his thick hair back away from his face. It worried her that he hadn't yet regained consciousness. The notion of being left here with Losowahkun was nearly as scary as being alone.

When did I begin to think of Talon as keeping me safe, she mused. Once, she shrank from his touch; now she was bathing him as gently as she'd bathed Colin.

She sighed. Where in God's name was her little brother? Was he safe or—no, she wouldn't let herself think otherwise. Colin was sound as a Dutch dollar. She just had to rescue him.

"This is all your fault," she said to Talon. "You're responsible." But the sting had gone out of her words. He was still her enemy, but she no longer hated him.

"I don't want you to die," she whispered. "I don't."

Without warning he seized her wrist with his left hand. She gasped as he opened his eyes and stared into hers. "I am glad you no longer want me dead," he murmured hoarsely. "If you did, I would be easy to kill."

She tried to pull free. "Let me go," she insisted.

"Will you wipe my head again, if I do? I'm hot."

"You're feverish." He was looking at her in such a strange way—for an instant, she had the oddest notion that he might kiss her.

"And you care for me?"

"If you die there will be no one to take me back to the white settlements," she said. Her words were harsh, but her tone revealed the joy that bubbled up inside her and made her giddy.

He smiled and glanced around the longhouse. "Siipu found us?" He caressed her hand with his thumb, making slow, gentle circular motions against her skin.

Sweet sensations rippled up her arm and made her pulse quicken. "Siipu? No," she protested. "It was your brother, Losowahkun, who saved us. He—"

"No." He frowned. "Do not use that name. Siipu. Not my brother, Becca."

"Losowahkun," she repeated in bewilderment. "He said he was your brother—he wears a deerskin mask." She was no longer trying to free her hand. She wanted to leave it in his grasp. She fought an impossible urge to throw her arms around his neck and hug him against her. "There can't be two such—"

"Another like her," he finished. "You are right. But I have no brother. Her name is not Losowahkun—the Burned One. She is Siipu, Creek Water, and she is my beloved sister."

Chapter 12

"Your sister? I couldn't tell if she was a man or woman because of that mask. I couldn't imagine a woman living alone here with these wild animals," Rebecca said to Talon as she offered him a water gourd. "Are you thirsty?" He nodded. "Drink all you can," she said. "It will help hold down the fever."

His lips were dry and cracked; he released her hand and reached for the liquid eagerly, but she could see how much the effort cost him. It seemed the most natural thing in the world to cradle his head against her breast and hold the cup to his mouth for him to drink. A section of his hair slid over her wrist.

His hair feels as silky as it looks, she thought, as quiet excitement rippled through her. She swallowed, trying to ease the constriction in her throat. His nearness was like tasting a forbidden sweet—one bite and she wanted more.

Her instincts screamed that she was treading on dangerous ground, but she pushed the warnings away and held him a few seconds longer than necessary.

"More?" she asked him. Talon's cheek was as beardless as a boy's, but there was nothing of youth about him. He was a man in his prime. Despite his loss of blood, she could feel the pent up power in his body.

"Thank you." He stared at her until she felt her face grown warm. Then he smiled, closed his eyes, and lay back.

Rebecca busied herself with the cup and compress, trying to ignore the odd sensation that she'd just run a long way uphill. She was so clumsy that the gourd cup slipped from her fingers and rolled across the floor.

What's wrong with me? she thought. I'm a respectable married woman. I'm too old for foolish fancies. There can be nothing between me and Talon—nothing.

But as she made the silent declaration, she knew that it was already too late. She'd run too far across thin ice. This Indian warrior had already settled firmly into a place in her heart.

The realization shocked her almost speechless. Desperate to turn her thoughts from the unthinkable, she stammered out, "Siipu, your sister, is she terribly scarred beneath that mask?" When Rebecca was small, she had played with the tinkers' children for a few weeks every year. One boy, Gilvarry, had fallen into an open campfire as a toddler. Half of his face was burned and his mouth twisted. But Gilvarry had the merriest laugh and knew the most games and stories of the lot. It had never occurred to her to feel sorry for Gilvarry. Instead, she'd envied him his carefree life of traveling and adventure. "Talon? I asked if your sister hides a deformity."

For a moment, he didn't answer, and she thought he'd fallen asleep. "Yes," he answered softly. "Siipu is scarred." His eyelids flickered and then he fixed her once more with that riveting dark gaze. "She was with my mother in the fire. My mother broke a window and pushed her out."

For an instant, the black stare wavered. Behind the wall of obsidian she glimpsed a pain so deep and wide that tears welled up in her own eyes.

When he spoke again, his words were dry and emotionless. "My sister tried to run, but the white men caught her. She was a child, but they used her like a woman. When my father came, she would not speak. She used to sing all the time, but after the fire, it was two years before I heard her voice again."

Rebecca looked away and a sob rose in her throat. Simon and his followers again, she thought. This time, she did not call Talon a liar. She had heard whispers of atrocities, but she'd not suspected that they'd stooped to raping little girls. She covered her face with her hands. "I'm so sorry." She wanted him to be quiet—she didn't want to hear anymore, but he went on.

"My people say she is touched by the spirits. Some are afraid of her and call her witch. I know only that she is happy here with her friends. It may be that the world of men is too hard for her."

Rebecca tried to imagine the loneliness of rainy nights and cold mornings when fog lay thick over the endless mountains.

His voice softened. "I come when I can, but she is not at ease with me, either. She blames herself because she did not die with our mother in the flames."

"But it wasn't her fault," Rebecca protested.

"No. It was not. Each man and woman has a path to follow."

"And ours took us into the way of that bear?"

"Yes."

"Then you don't believe it was an accident—
Siipu finding us on the mountain."

"I was bringing you to her wigwam. I meant to
leave you in my sister's care while I went to face
Simon Brandt."

"And the bear? I still don't understand why it
attacked us. Most bears run from the scent of man.
They—"

"They fear us. That is true. But this bear was
different. He had already lost a fight with a porcupine." Talon motioned for her to give him more
water. "*Gatusemwi*—I am thirsty," he said.

"*Gatusemwee?*" she echoed. The Indian words reminded her of the native Celtic she'd often heard
as a child in Ireland. It wasn't the same, but both
languages shared a lilting, almost musical sound.

He smiled. "*Gatusemwi*. I am thirsty. You have a
good ear for Delaware." He drank deeply, then
continued explaining about the bear. "Quills were
embedded in his muzzle and mouth, and they had
become infected. He couldn't eat and the poison
maddened him. He thought we had caused his
pain, and he struck out at us."

"You risked your own life to save me," she said.
"I won't forget that."

His face grew expressionless again. "I told you,
Becca. You belong to me. I will not let you go until
my father is released."

You belong to me. You belong to me. The words
echoed in her mind. "I belong to no one but myself," she said throatily. But deep inside, she
wished . . .

"You are my captive."

"I could have left you to bleed to death," she reminded him.

"*Ahikta*. It is true. But my father is old. If I do

not save him, he will die. It shames me to use a
woman for a weapon, but sometimes a man must
do what he must."

"I think I understand that now," she said. *As I
must return to a husband that I can never love, as I
might have loved this man were we not born mortal enemies.*

Talon did not speak again, and in a little while
he drifted off to sleep. She sat beside him, hands
in her lap, gazing at his sleeping face.

How alien he is, she thought, and how beautiful. His skin tone was a warm red–bronze, his
cheekbones high and prominent. His lips were
thin but sensual, his eyes slightly slanted beneath
raven–black brows. His forehead was high and
broad, his chin and nose ruggedly defined. It was
all she could do to keep from touching his face
again. She wanted to stroke the smooth lines of his
beardless jaw, to trace those fierce arching brows
and commit them all to memory.

I have a husband, she thought. But eight years
in his bed have never caused these feelings in my
breast. She wondered if Talon would believe her if
she told him that she had never known a man's
physical love—that she was so many years a wife,
and still a virgin.

She allowed herself to pull the fur robe close
around his shoulders. Despite his pallor, spots of
fever colored each cheek. He was not yet out of
danger. Often, fever and infection came days after
an injury. Some wounds caused spasms of the jaw
that ended in slow, painful death; others turned
gangrenous.

Once, she'd watched Simon saw a man's leg off
to keep the rot from killing him. Despite their efforts, he'd died from loss of blood. Talon would ei-

ther survive the bear claw poison or it would kill him.

She rose and went to the entranceway of the longhouse, then pushed aside the door skin. The sun was shining, but the air was very cold. She was surprised at how comfortable it was inside the wigwam compared to the raw winter temperature. Throwing a fur wrap around her shoulders, she stepped outside.

Tall trees grew very close to the hut. A few feet from the door was another fire pit, now frozen, half-covered with snow. A few racks for drying meat stood empty; a large pile of firewood leaned against the side of the longhouse. Beyond that was a small log pound for the pony. The small clearing seemed deserted. This house is well hidden, she thought. A few steps from the wigwam and I wouldn't know it was here.

The wind was cold on her face, but she turned into it, welcoming the bite of the raw blast. She needed something to blow the cobwebs from her mind. Inside the warm hut—near Talon—she couldn't think clearly.

My marriage to Simon is a failure, she reasoned. *No matter what happens to me, I can never live with him as I did before, knowing what awful things he's done.* Yet, how could she not? She was a Catholic—bound to him so long as they both lived. She could not divorce him, and if she ran away, who would shelter her from her rightful husband?

But Talon had sworn to kill Simon.

That was even worse. If Simon was dead, how could she find happiness knowing that she'd wished him ill? Only a depraved and evil woman could think rationally about the murder of a husband who had cared for her for eight long years.

"But he's never been a husband . . ." she argued softly. She would never put Simon's babe to her breast or know the joy of seeing a toddler take a first step. She doubted that Simon could father a child . . .

Since they'd first wed, Simon had never undressed in front of her—he always slept in his breeches when he shared her bed. She'd never even seen him bathing. But once, several years ago, she'd come upon him accidentally near the creek. It was a windy day, and she'd been gathering firewood. The wind blowing through the trees had kept Simon from hearing her until she was almost on him.

She'd been shocked by the sight of Simon's breeches down around his ankles and his man parts exposed. One of Simon's testicles was missing, the other horribly scarred. But what had horrified her most was not his being maimed; it was the fact that she'd caught him in the act of seeking out his own pleasure.

Simon had been as startled as she was. He'd ranted and raved, cursing and threatening her life if she told anyone. He'd come after her, but she'd outrun him. Long after dark, when she'd finally come back to the cabin, he'd slapped her—not once, but twice—cutting her lip. Colin had tried to come to her aid, and Simon had slammed him up against the wall so hard he'd given the boy a bloody nose. Later, he'd said that he was sorry and told her that his injuries were the result of a knife attack by an Indian.

Neither Simon's violence nor his apologies had made any difference to her. She had been so glad to finally understand why he had never claimed the rights of a husband, and why he'd mocked her when she tried to invite him to her bed. The victory was hers, and nothing Simon could do to her would ever change things. From that day, she had grown stronger and more sure of herself, and Simon had grown less powerful in her mind.

She had wondered at the time if Simon's lack of ability made her eligible for an annulment in the Church. It was an idle whimsey, of course. Annulments were for the wealthy and influential. No backwoods wife could ever hope to procure one. Had she asked, she had no doubt that it would be the last thing she ever asked of her husband. Simon would not be shamed publicly.

She lay her face against a sapling, not feeling the roughness of the bark on her cold cheek. She clutched the tree so tightly that a fingernail snapped.

What did she feel for Simon? Not love or even compassion. It was a debt of honor that she fulfill the bargain she'd made when they met. The Church was clear on the duties of marriage. Once made, a union was for life. Anything less would risk her immortal soul.

Simon dead would free her. But she felt no hate for him in her heart. She had often wished, childishly, that he would just go away and not come back. She and Colin could have lived happily in the cabin without him. But now?

"I still don't hate him," she murmured into the wind. "I am ashamed of him, but I can't seek to take his life—not by word or deed."

She sighed, feeling suddenly wise. Fire Talon is a better man than Simon Brandt, she decided. Barbarian or not, I could have been happy with him if I were an Indian maiden. If?

She chuckled. Was she losing her mind to have

such fancies? There could be no future for her with Talon. His customs, his people were totally different from hers. He wasn't even a Christian. And any white woman who took up with an Indian would be ostracized, cut off from decent society forever. Men would spit at her, and women would turn their heads when she walked by. Not to mention the everlasting shame that would fall on the heads of any children she might bring into the world!

Bastard half-breeds. Bloods. Abominations. She had heard the whispers and the taunts directed to the offspring of Indian squaws who hung around the forts and trading posts. She had seen the dirty, ragged children with tangled, dark hair.

She had thought them beautiful ... with skin like wild honey and black currant eyes. She remembered one laughing little boy, naked and barefoot, peering around his mother's skirts. A fairy child. What kind of God would not love such a babe as well as any born with yellow hair and sky blue eyes? What kind of mother would not?

Perhaps it wasn't the half-breed children who were to be blamed, but the hypocrites who despised them for the color of their skin. Perhaps ...

But she had another child to think of—Colin. So long as he was too young to care for himself, she had to look after him. If she left Simon, how could she see Colin fed and decently garbed? Could she be assured of putting a roof over his head or seeing to his education? A woman alone might go south to the Carolinas and pass herself off as a free widow or a servant seeking employment. But how long could she hide from runaway notices that might advertise for a red-haired wench and a ten-year-old black-haired boy?

Simon would never let her go. He'd bought and paid for her—as he'd told her many times. She belonged to him.

But Talon said she was his.

Damn them both to an eternal hell. She belonged to no one but herself. And once she found her brother, she'd find a way to look after herself. She'd ask nothing of any man—red or white.

Talon's sister, Siipu, returned to the longhouse before dusk with the big cat padding silently by her side. The pony carried additional cuts of bear meat. There was no sign of the wolf.

Siipu went first to Talon's side. He was sleeping, a deep unnatural slumber. She felt his cheeks and lifted his eyelids. He didn't wake, and she made a sound of concern.

"He was awake earlier," Rebecca said. "He drank water, and he seemed clear in his head."

The cat curled into a ball and watched Rebecca through glowing slits. She wrinkled her nose. Sharing a bed chamber with a mountain lion left much to be desired. Did Siipu even notice the feral odor the beast gave off? "Where is the wolf?"

Talon's sister glanced at her, and again Rebecca was struck by the eerie air of mystery that the mask gave her. The brown eyes were heavy with sorrow. "*Tumma* feeds on . . . on remains of bear. She runs with pack."

"She's wild then—she's a wild wolf?" Rebecca said.

"*Tumma* is free like Losowahkun."

"Your brother told me to call you Siipu. He doesn't like that other name."

Siipu shrugged. "A name is name. Call this one what you want. In heart, I be Losowahkun."

Rebecca took a deep breath. "Talon also told me that Simon Brandt was responsible for your mother's death. Do you know that I am Simon's wife?"

The Indian woman nodded. "This one know. Talon tell me he go for you. For father's life. To trade."

"I want you to know that I'm sorry. It happened long ago—before I came from Ireland—from across the salt sea. I think what Simon does is wrong, but there is nothing I can do to stop him."

"*Bischi*. It is so." Siipu's voice dropped to a whisper. "The bones are rolled. The runners of the Lenape carry the black wampum. The raven and the wolf scent the feast to come. *N'wishasi*—I am afraid. Red and white blood will soak the forest floor. The streams will run red. This is a green land. Men will turn it black with their hate and women will weep."

"Siipu, my brother was taken in the raid on our cabin. He's just a child, only ten years old. All we have is each other. Do you know anything about where he is?"

She shook her head.

"His name is Colin. He has black hair—our father's hair. I must find him."

"What does Sh'Kotaa Osh-Kah-Shah say?"

Rebecca sighed. "He says he doesn't know either. How could he just disappear? He was with a man Talon called The Stranger."

"Ah. The Stranger."

"Please . . . if you could help me in any way. I have to find Colin."

Siipu began to untie the packs. "Some meat we freeze. Some we dry over hearth. Tonight—when moon rises—I look into fire for face of small brother."

"Into the fire? I don't understand," Rebecca said. "How could—"

"First I treat Sh'Kotaa Osh-Kah-Shah's wounds. You must hold him. Much pain."

"Me? Hold him? He's too strong for me. How could I hold him?"

"Man have much pride, even man who . . . who bad hurt. Young woman hold, he lay still, no cry out. Have pride. We use pride." She dropped a chunk of bear meat into a large woven basket. "We make grease. Bear grease good for wound. No heal stiff. My brother use arm again."

"You think he'll live then?" Suddenly, it was the most important thing in the world to her that Talon would survive.

"We do what we can. Sh'Kotaa Osh-Kah-Shah fight. We see."

Together, they unloaded the pack animal and put the meat aside. Then Siipu set several Indian pots on the rocks over the coals. In one, she prepared a stewed squash, in a second, a rich stew of bear meat and vegetables. In a third, she brought a potion of roots and herbs to a simmer.

"What is in it?" Rebecca asked. "Is it for Talon to drink—like the herb tea?"

"I make . . ." She searched her mind for the English. "Poultice. Bloodroot and painted trillium. Smartweed. I mix with honey and apply to wounds. From willow bark, I make tea for fever. Willow bark very powerful."

"I know," Rebecca replied. "A woman at the fort told me about it. I made a drink for Colin when he had the measles. He was only four and his fever was high. He was sick nearly a week, but he got better once the spots came out."

Siipu nodded. "Measles bad. This one sees nine

children die one day from red spots. My people want to lay sick children in water to stop fever. But they die anyway."

"You must keep a patient warm and away from light when they're taken with the measles. Light's bad for their eyes."

"*Ahikta.* Light is bad when they burn with fever. Some children who not die lose sight of eyes. Lose mind. My people no know this *measles.* White man bring from across ocean. Indian catch—most all die."

"I've heard that the smallpox is very bad for Indians as well. Many people die in my country from it. But I caught the cowpox when I was young. I'll never take the sickness."

"Once, Mohicans friend to Delaware. Many village, many warriors. Pox come. Mohican drop like falling leaves. Now, not so many. Soon none. Pox is demon sickness. Ghosts make."

Talon groaned, and they both went instantly to his side. Rebecca saw that his face was red. She touched his cheek and his skin felt hot. "Talon," she said. "Can you hear me?"

He mumbled something in Indian, but didn't open his eyes. He thrashed from side to side, and tried to push away her hand.

"We must treat him again," his sister said. She pulled the fur robe down to his waist and looked at the angry streaks of color around the stitches Rebecca had taken. "Here and here . . ." She pointed to a swollen spot. "We will cut the thread and drain poison."

Rebecca was troubled by Talon's sudden change for the worse. "Why now?" she asked. "He seemed so much better this afternoon."

"He will not die tonight," Siipu pronounced.

"Now help me. We fight until battle is won . . . or lost."

For nearly an hour, they washed his injuries, dripped willow tea into his mouth, and laid poultices against his back and arm. His sister brought handfuls of snow to cool his forehead. Rebecca held it there until it melted, then wiped his face dry.

His arm was greatly inflamed. When Siipu had done everything she could with her potions, she still wasn't satisfied. "We need more," she said.

To Rebecca's horror, his sister laid an iron blade in the red hot coals. When the metal glowed orange, she bade Rebecca hold Talon's head. Siipu put a roll of soft leather between his teeth and whispered in his ear.

He sat bolt upright when the smoking brand pressed into his flesh. Rebecca felt a shudder go through him. His fist tightened until his knuckles stood out white through his tanned skin. But he did not cry out.

The smell of charred flesh turned Rebecca's stomach. The pony stamped his feet and rolled his eyes in fear, and the lion hissed.

"There," Siipu said, when the awful deed was done. "Two men could not hold him. You, he did not fight."

They laid him back against the furs. His face was ashen, his breathing harsh. He looked to Rebecca as though he had aged ten years in the last few hours.

"Now what?" Rebecca asked. She was trembling with emotion. She wanted to run outside and cry.

Siipu shrugged. "When the sun rises, we will see." She turned back toward the fire. "I will look now—for your brother."

She went to a weasel-skin pouch, tanned with head and feet intact. From it, she removed a small skin bag. Then she crouched by the fire pit and began to chant in a low, monotonous voice.

Gooseflesh rose on Rebecca's arms. Witchcraft. She knew she should have no part of it, but she could not stay away. She knelt beside the Indian woman.

Siipu threw tobacco into the flames. The odor curled upward, filling the longhouse and drifting out the smoke hole in the ceiling above. She continued to sing in Algonquian. Then she scattered a white powder over the glowing hearth.

The smell was acrid. Smoke stung Rebecca's eyes. She shut them, and when she looked again, the fire flickered with strange shades of blue and green. Suddenly, she felt the air grow cool. The fringes on Siipu's mask fluttered as a strong breeze whipped through the longhouse.

The big cat snarled.

Siipu gave a low moan and turned away from the fire. She staggered back and put her hands over her face.

"What is it?" Rebecca demanded. "What happened?" The wind was gone as quickly as it had come, and she felt the heat of the fire again. Her mouth was as dry as if she'd been eating sawdust—her heart was pounding like hail on a cedar roof. "What did you see?"

Talon's sister leaned against the platform and drew in a long, slow breath. "I saw the face of a boy," she said. "A white boy. Here, and here . . ." She made imaginary slashes across her cheekbones. "I see paint. He warms himself by a fire as we do. He is alive. Safe. He calls for you."

"I don't believe you," Rebecca said. She wasn't

certain what had happened here, but it had frightened her. "What does he call me?" she asked. "What name does he use?"

"Becca. He says, Becca."

Hair rose on the back of Rebecca's neck. Colin had always called her Becca. When he was little, he'd been unable to say Rebecca, and the nickname had stuck.

Siipu shook her head and struck her chest with her clenched fist. "Aiyee," she whispered. "Aiyee."

Rebecca tensed. "You said he was all right."

"Your brother is safe. He is cared for."

"Then why are you so distressed? What's wrong? That's not what you saw, was it? You must tell me the truth."

Siipu raised her head slowly. "Your brother is alive," she repeated. Rebecca heard a noise that could only be a sob as Talon's sister returned to the fire pit and dropped to her knees. Taking a handful of ashes, she rubbed them on her arms. "I mourn," she murmured. "I mourn."

"But why?" Rebecca asked. "Why?"

"I have seen the face of our father," she said, rocking back and forth. "I have heard his voice on the spirit wind. He calls to me from across the river. He is dead."

Chapter 13

*F*ire Talon struggled through the waist-deep mud of the cold swamp. Mist lay thick over the black, twisted trees and pools of stagnant water. He was weary . . . so weary, but he'd found no dry spot to rest.

Thirst plagued him, but he could not forced himself to drink the foul liquid that oozed around his chest. His head echoed to the beat of a hundred drums, and interspersed with the incessant pounding were the whispers. Women's voices . . . too low to understand . . . They haunted him, but no matter how hard he strained to catch the words, all he could hear were bits and pieces too faint to comprehend.

"Father's face . . . face . . . face . . ." came the tantalizing whispers.

He took hold of a dead sapling to steady his balance, but the wood snapped to dust in his hand. The fog drifted closer, enveloping him, so thick that he couldn't see his own outstretched fingertips.

Talon's back and arm seemed on fire. Pain gnawed at his bones and slowed his step. If he closed his eyes, he could see the bear towering over him, mouth open and slavering, yellow teeth gleaming. He could smell the putrid stink of that gaping red mouth—feel the rending of his flesh.

Then another image hovered between him and the bear. Becca—the white woman—her blue eyes soft with compassion, her hands gentle on his body.

Becca, his enemy's wife . . . Becca, whose walk was as graceful as a doe, whose laughter reminded him of spring water bubbling from the earth.

She was forbidden to him, this pale-skinned woman. But she touched his soul in a way that no human had done for a long time.

He wished she was here with him now. He needed her.

"Becca! Becca!" he called. The only answer was the rattle of bare tree limbs and the sucking sound of the mud under his feet. "Becca!"

Suddenly, he began to sink. He thrashed and tried to swim as the muck rose up to his chest. Frantically, he grabbed for a handful of marsh grass. It broke off in his hand, and the cold goo rose to his throat. "Becca!" he called. Another instant and the mud would fill his mouth. He wasn't afraid of death, but he didn't want to meet it here—like this—dragged down into a black, wet grave.

"Talon."

Her voice reached him just as he began the first note of his death song and his heart leaped.

"Talon. Can you hear me?"

He tried to open his eyes, but they were weighed down with mud. He smelled her. She was very close. He wanted to reach out to her, but he was so tired.

"Talon."

Something warm and alive brushed his lips. Her caress was sweet and powerful. Feather-light, it jolted him with the intensity of a lightning bolt. If he didn't hold on to her, the cold mud would seep into his nose and throat and choke the life from him.

"Talon . . . don't die," she whispered.

He opened his eyes just as she kissed him a second time with infinite tenderness. She gasped as he threw his good arm around her and crushed her against him. She was warm and alive. Vision or flesh and blood woman, she'd not leave him.

Talon pressed his mouth against hers with searing heat. "Talon," she cried, as she struggled free of his embrace and stood trembling, apparently unsure whether to run or fling herself back into his arms. "You're . . . you're awake," she managed.

A slow smile spread over his face.

She covered her mouth with her hand. Her lips were tingling. "I was afraid . . ." she began. "I mean . . . I thought that you . . ." She put distance between them. "Your fever was very high," she said quickly. "We . . . I was afraid that you—"

"I am not dead, Becca," he said hoarsely.

"I . . . can see that." Unconsciously, she rubbed her mouth. "You . . . you kissed me," she whispered.

"You kissed me first."

She felt giddy. "I did, didn't I?"

He closed his eyes again. "We must talk of this later," he murmured. "Now, I can't seem to keep my eyes open."

She reached for the brimming cup of medicine his sister had left when she went out. "You . . . you must have something to drink," she said. "Are you in pain?"

He made a sound that might have been either a low groan or a chuckle. "A man who was not a warrior of the Mecate Shawnee might say that."

"You fought with a bear," she reminded him. "What shame is there to admit that you hurt? You're human, aren't you?"

His black eyes snapped open with the intensity

of a steel trap. "A Shawnee? Human?" he challenged. "Do you hear what you say?"

"By Christ's wounds, Talon! You're as human as I am."

He sighed and his eyelids drifted closed. "Remember that, Becca . . . remember. I am just a man. A man . . . who cannot . . . cannot hate his . . . prisoner."

Siipu didn't tell Talon about the vision she'd seen in the fire. When Rebecca saw her again, she had washed away the signs of mourning. The two didn't speak of the incident again, and Rebecca tried to forget it. Talon's father couldn't be dead. If he was . . . if he was, the consequences were too awful to think about.

Talon began to recover. In two days, he could stand on his own feet. He was wobbly as a new colt, but he was up. By the third day, his appetite had returned, and the two women were kept busy cooking to feed him.

At the end of a week, Talon was outside in the crisp mountain air, naked from the waist up, shooting a bow and arrow at a target tacked against a tree. His back had healed faster than Rebecca would have believed, but many muscles had been badly damaged. Each movement was an effort. Each twist and strain cost Talon dearly; his agony showed in the sweat that beaded on his face. Still, he never complained, and he wouldn't rest until Siipu begged him.

"Even a medicine woman has her limits," she protested, when she'd called Talon three times to stop practicing and come and eat. "Healing takes time."

"Ah, but you are a witch, sister," he replied in English. "A witch can do magic."

"If I could, I'd keep you on your sleeping mat for a few more days," she chided in Algonquian.

"My sister wants me to lie idle," he translated for Rebecca's sake.

She turned away from the good-natured teasing that passed between them. It was obvious to her that Siipu loved Talon dearly and that he felt the same about her. A part of her wanted to join in their banter, but she couldn't. Her own emotions were too confused for her to feel at ease with them.

She wondered if Talon remembered the kiss they had shared. He had said nothing since he'd risen from his sickbed. He no longer treated her as though she was his prisoner, but neither did he behave in an overly familiar manner. It was almost as though they were polite strangers, brought together by circumstances—strangers who would never meet again once they left this place.

She had wanted him to recover; she'd prayed for it. She'd admitted to herself and to him that she cared for him. But now ... Now, she did not know where her brazen revelation would lead. Or if she really wanted it to ...

Had she lost all sense of perspective? It was difficult to remember that this laughing man was the same painted savage who'd burned her farm and nearly killed her and her brother. He'd seemed so violent, so lacking in compassion. Now, she wasn't sure who Talon was or who she was. The only thing she knew for certain was that she had cut all ties to Simon Brandt. She could never be a wife to him again, no matter the cost to her safety or to her immortal soul.

"Becca."

Talon's voice and his hand on her shoulder startled her from her reverie. Surprised, she spun around—right into the circle of his arms.

"Siipu has made fresh corn cakes," he said. "She invited you to come and eat." His eyes locked with hers, and she knew that Siipu's meal was the farthest thing from his mind.

She was standing very close to him, so close that it was hard to breathe. "Her corn cakes are ... are ..." She trembled inwardly. Any second and he would kiss her again, she knew it.

And then the instant passed and he stepped back. She might have believed she'd imagined his intention, but a hint of yearning flickered across those inscrutable dark eyes, and the taut, bronze skin over his cheekbones took on a darker hue of tan.

"Tomorrow I go to find Simon Brandt," he said brusquely. "I leave you here with my sister. You will be safe here."

"Simon ...." she stammered. "But where— how? How do you know that he—"

"Siipu has seen him in the coals of her cooking fire," he replied. "He comes hunting his woman, and he does not hunt alone."

"Seen him in the coals of her fire?" Rebecca scoffed, hiding the fear that curled in her chest. "That's ridiculous. You're an educated man, you know that's ridiculous."

He shrugged.

"It's witchcraft."

A ghost of a smile played across his thin lips— lips that she had tasted and wanted desperately to taste again.

"Talon," she pleaded. "You can't believe it."

"Eighteen centuries have passed since a woman who had never known a man gave birth to your king in a stable. A man who you believe died under torture and came to life again. Eighteen centuries, Becca. You believe, do you not?"

"The death and resurrection of Jesus? Of course. It is the foundation of my faith."

"Eighteen centuries, my Becca, only eighteen. Hardly time for a river to change its course. My people have hunted these forests for two hundred centuries, twenty thousand years. We have danced our dances and sung our songs of power. We have watched the eternal dance of the sun and her sister the moon. We are as much a part of this land as the trees and the grass."

Confused, she shook her head. "What does that have to do with witchcraft?"

"What you call witchcraft, we call wisdom." He smiled at her. "I do not think such things are evil," he said gently. "And I do not know why those that the Great Spirit has blessed see what others do not see. I only know that Siipu sees true, and that Simon Brandt comes with bloody hands to the land of the Shawnee and the Delaware. And I know that this one will stand between him and the Ohio so long as blood runs in my veins."

"And you expect me to stay here as your sister's prisoner?"

"As her honored guest." His eyes filled with warmth.

"While you go and try and kill my husband?"

"Becca." His tone hardened. "I do not know what is between you and Simon Brandt, but I know you. You are not a woman to deceive your husband by smiling at him and looking with doe eyes at another. He is not worthy of you. If I kill him, you will be the better for it."

She shook her head. "I don't understand you. What are you trying to say?"

"There is no love between you and him."

"No, there isn't," she admitted. "But that doesn't mean I want him dead."

"Him dead, or me. Will you choose?"

She winced. "That's unfair."

His fingertips brushed her chin in a motion that might have been a caress. "If my father's life did not hang in the balance, it might be different."

She thrilled to his touch even as his meaning came clear. "You mean to give me back to Simon?"

"If I must."

"If you can't kill him."

"*Ahikta*—it is so."

"And if he kills you—what happens to me?"

"I have spoken to my sister. You will still be traded for our father's life. No harm will come to you. Another will see you back to the English settlement."

"And if . . ." The words stuck in the back of her throat. *If I didn't want to go back,* she wanted to scream at him. *What if I wanted to stay with you?*

"There is no *if,*" he said firmly. "You are my enemy's wife. We will both do what is demanded of us."

"Yes," she answered. "I suppose we must." But she turned away from him so that he couldn't see the tears welling up in her eyes.

Talon shielded his eyes with his hand and squinted into the rising sun. It was just breaking dawn, ten days from the afternoon he'd fought with the great brown bear. He was still stiff, and he'd not regained all his strength, but there was no more time to waste warming himself by Siipu's fire.

Simon Brandt was very near—he felt it in his bones. He'd seen deer, elk, and wolves since he'd left his sister's longhouse, but no sign of humans, red or white. The forest stretched around him, tall and deep, throbbing with its own life force. The weather had favored him; it was cold, but clear. No more snow had fallen. It was easier to track a man or an animal in snow, but it was also easier to be tracked.

Siipu had said she saw many long rifles with Simon Brandt. Militia. They were tougher opponents than the stupid English soldiers who marched abreast in straight lines and wore bright red coats. He wondered how long it would take the British generals to realize that their armies, with their big guns that had to be dragged by oxen, were useless in the wilderness. They could destroy a French fort or blow up Indian villages, but even children could run away and hide from an unwieldy procession of wagons, carts, horses, and soldiers, which moved at a cow's pace.

When the English cut roads through the woods, those wide trails became graves. When the British slowed to drive horse-drawn vehicles across creeks and rivers, they were easy targets for any half-grown Indian boy to pick off from the safety of the trees. Muskets roared like thunder, but an arrow sped with the silence of a plunging hawk.

The long rifles had learned this lesson. Many were trackers and marksmen to match the Indians they hunted. The militia traveled light; they could strike hard and move fast. Simon Brandt's followers were among the best of the white scouts, and

Simon Brandt led them because he was as woods-wise and brave as any Huron.

Talon's hate for Becca's husband glowed white-hot in his breast, but he did not underestimate him. "He is a worthy opponent," he murmured. "And if the spirits are against me, my scalp will hang at his belt."

He grinned, deciding that he'd have to give the spirits a little assistance. Because if Simon Brandt died, then his woman would be free to choose an-other man.

Ruthlessly, he pushed such foolish thoughts out of his mind. A war chief who put his own wants ahead of his people was unfit. The best captains were those who had no family. A man who cared only for his tribe would not hesitate to put himself into danger. No, he needed no woman to tug at his heart and make him soft.

And the last thing he needed was a white woman with sky blue eyes who made his blood run hot when he thought of her . . .

Forget her, he told himself. Think only of your father's life, and of Simon Brandt, who comes with his hunting pack to invade Shawnee land. Keep your mind empty of all things that will interfere with your mission. Kill Simon Brandt, and bring your father home.

If the militia was destroyed, it would buy pre-cious time for his people, and it might hold back the steady press of settlers for a few more years. In those years, the French king might prevail. A French presence in Indian country would be bitter, but not so disastrous as the English. The French came to trade for furs. The English wanted to cut down the forest and chop the earth into small squares. A reasonable man could deal with the

French, but no one could make sense of the English.

Cautiously, Talon worked his way up a ridge that overlooked a rock-strewn, fast-running creek. The water was deep and crusted with ice, too dangerous to travel by boat. Any adult crossing would be wet to the chest—unless he chose the spot that lay directly below Talon's vantage point. Here, scattered rocks jutted out of the creek to form a natural bridge that an agile man might traverse.

Talon reached the highest point and crawled forward on his hands and knees, taking care not to get dirt in the barrel of his rifle. When he was certain he could see without being seen, he dropped flat on his belly to wait.

The sun moved overhead. A rock dug into Talon's knee, and he shifted slightly to avoid it. A pair of ducks flew overhead. The sheltered hiding place was out of the wind; the sun's rays beat into his fur cloak. The urge to doze off teased, but he refused to give in to it. He began to count the rocks in the creek, beginning with the bend to the south and working upstream.

He had counted the rocks three times when a mouse with an acorn in his mouth scurried by. Bright round eyes stared at him in curiosity as the little rodent came within inches of his hand. Minutes later, the mouse was back, pausing to scratch an itchy spot with a back paw, preen long whiskers, and groom his fur before scampering off again.

The cawing of crows snapped Talon into instant readiness. He waited, straining his ears for some sound other than the tumbling rush of water. Then the bushes parted on the far side of the creek and a painted face appeared. Talon recognized the man as Miami by the quill-work on his vest.

The Indian stopped, looked both ways, and took several steps out to the edge of the stream. Then he cupped his mouth and gave an imitation of the crow call Talon had heard earlier.

Talon chuckled silently. Miami crows must speak differently from Shawnee crows, he thought. That caw wouldn't fool an old woman.

A few minutes later, a tall, rangy white man in a wide-brimmed leather hat and a fringed buckskin hunting shirt moved out of the trees. A powder horn and bag hung over one shoulder; he carried a long rifle in his hand. When he turned to beckon to his comrades, Talon got a good look at his face.

Simon Brandt.

Talon nodded. Siipu had been right as usual. Now to see how many more wolves hunted in Brandt's pack.

One after another, the militia men melted into the clearing at the stream bank. Eight, nine—two more, no three. Thirteen, counting the Miami. There would be rear guard as well. If Talon knew Brandt, there would be scouts on either side of the main party, as well as one or two far ahead. He'd seen no sign, but still—

Talon's ears caught the ominous sound of a hammer being cocked, and his blood went cold. He rolled over onto his back and threw up his rifle to protect his head—and stared into the gaping muzzle of a Brown Bess musket.

Chapter 14

Talon looked up at the man holding the musket and gave a low exclamation of relief.

His friend, Fox, grinned. "You're dead," he said.

"Fox!" Talon wiggled backward until overhanging evergreens concealed his movements from anyone watching on the creek bank below and got to his feet. To his shame, Counts His Scalps was standing a few yards away with a smirk on his handsome face.

"It isn't like you to be so foolish," Counts admonished. "What happened to you? You look like you lost a wrestling match with a bear."

"I won one." Talon dusted the sand off his rifle barrel. "Didn't I tell you to stay with the village?"

Fox chuckled. "And if we had? Your hair would have been dangling from Simon Brandt's trophy belt."

"We came up on you as easily as if you were a blind buffalo," Counts said.

"Perhaps," Fox said softly, "perhaps not. If we were white, he would have smelled us."

The cedar boughs parted and Osage Killer appeared. His face was streaked with black and yellow slashes of paint, and his heavy-lidded eyes were hard. He nodded in greeting to Talon, then offered Counts a hint of a smile. "Do not be so

167

hard on our war chief," he said. "A man's guardian spirits do not warn him against his friends—only his enemies."

"How many others are here?" Talon asked. His pride had taken a blow and he wished no more talk about his carelessness. In truth, he should have sensed Fox sneaking up on him, but he hadn't. Maybe he was getting old, or maybe the white woman had stolen some of his power. He looked from one man to the other. "Just you three?"

"Just us," Fox replied. "But there are only fifteen of them."

"Less than four apiece," Counts said.

Talon frowned. "I'm glad to have you with me, but—"

Counts shook his head. "This man dreamed a dream."

"Your sister is a powerful witch," Osage Killer said. "She warned Counts His Scalps of the militia. She showed Counts the face of Simon Brandt."

"This man had the dream," Counts interrupted. "This man will tell what he wishes. Others—" He glared at his companion. "Others should hold their tongues until they have a medicine dream."

"Counts has decided that he is called to become a shaman," Osage Killer continued.

"Who else heard the witch's message?" Counts demanded. "Who else saw Simon Brandt? This man knows the seriousness of such a calling. If the spirits wish my life, can I refuse?"

"I've told him he's too old to begin training," Fox teased. "He would have to grow his hair long like a boy and—"

Talon motioned Fox to silence. "Such a decision

comes from a man's heart," he said. "If Counts His
Scalps is called, it's not for us to taunt him."

"So." Counts lifted his chin and stared off into
space. "Even a man's friends are sometimes jealous of his powers."

"So Counts had a dream and you came," Talon
said smoothly. "But what of the village? Did you
do as I bid you?"

"It's as you said," Fox answered with laughing
eyes. "We followed your instructions precisely, oh
noble war leader. As usual, you were right. The
white trader came running. Both he and the
French priest brought gifts when none were expected. They talked too loud and laughed when
there was nothing to laugh at."

"And both asked many questions about a flame-
haired captive," Counts added.

"You moved the village?" Talon asked.

Osage Killer nodded. "Across the Ohio. So
quickly that not even the crows could follow. We
carried the old people and the children. Some
went by river, but all went. If the white men come
to our village site, they will find only cold ashes
and empty houses."

"The old shaman put a curse on the village
place," Fox said. "Any man who sets foot there
will know the wrath of the winter ghosts. So powerful was his spell that he says we will not be able
to return to that camp for three years."

"I helped him to erect the feather barrier,"
Counts said proudly. "He asked for my help."

"Only because you were treading close on his
heels and staring over his shoulder," Osage Killer
said.

"You do not believe in my power? Even after
you have seen the proof?" Counts asked. "My

dream was strong. The witch knew of my calling, and the old shaman knows."

"Oh, I believe in your calling," Osage Killer said with a smile. "I believe. But I also know that you take great satisfaction in your gift. You were never a modest man."

"Peace," Talon said. "It is true that Counts has always been first to cry his deeds in battle, but it is also true that his accomplishments are many and great." He clasped Counts' hand. "If you are called to be a shaman, I don't doubt you'll be a strong one. And I will not hesitate to seek your advice."

Counts smiled and a genuine warmth spread across his face. "Perhaps I have misjudged you, Talon. You and I think more alike than I knew. Perhaps . . ."

Osage Killer's features hardened.

Talon shook his head. "I value you as I value few men, Counts His Scalps, but my path is not yours. Friends and blood brothers we may be, nothing more. My tastes run elsewhere."

Counts scoffed. "Women."

Talon shrugged. "I have always liked them."

Counts grinned. "It is your loss." He glanced sideways at Osage Killer. "You know I only speak in jest, *ki-te-hi*. Our leader has his qualities, but you and I are pledged until death."

"Will we stand here breaking wind and jawing like old men while the enemy surrounds us?" Fox demanded. "There is a time for jests and a time for war."

"You are right," Talon agreed. His eyes met Counts' and the brave nodded. Talon crouched down, brushed away the leaves, and began to draw on the earth with a twig. Fox, you circle here. Counts, you and Osage Killer . . ." Carefully, he began to instruct them on a plan of attack. His man gathered close around him in silence, their differences forgotten, as Simon Brandt and his militia began to cross the rocky creek far below.

Rebecca stuffed food into a skin bag, threw a fur robe over the French military jacket, and left the wigwam. Talon's sister had been gone for more than an hour. If she followed her usual pattern, she wouldn't be home until dusk. Rebecca didn't know what Siipu did in the woods all day alone and she didn't care. She had chosen this morning to make her escape.

Talon had told her he'd gone to meet Simon. If she was ever to get away, it had to be now. She could not risk staying longer with Talon. He'd said they each had to do what they had to do. He said it, but in her heart she didn't believe he meant it.

She wanted him—wanted him to make love to her. She wanted to stay here with him in the wilderness, forsaking her husband and her own kind. It was wrong—terribly wrong—but she knew she couldn't fight her desires forever.

He wanted her as much as she wanted him.

Regardless of what he said, regardless of how much he protested that she was his enemy, she could feel the tension rising between them. And if she took that step—if she went into his arms—she'd never have the strength to break away again.

There was no chance of their finding happiness together. Simon would follow her to the ends of the earth if necessary. Nothing could come of the fierce passion that threatened to leap between her and Talon—nothing but sorrow and bloodshed. They would be outcasts, hated by Indians and by whites. And if their love produced a child . . . Merciful Father, how could she think of bringing a half-breed child into a world of war and destruction?

The only sensible thing was to put time and distance between them. If she was gone, he would forget her as she would forget him.

Somehow, she would convince Simon that their marriage was over, that her capture by the Indians had ruined her as a wife. They would separate, and she would go her own way. She would find work on a farm or in some small village near the sea, far away from Shawnee country. And if her prayers were answered, Colin would be released and she could make a new life for him.

Delaware. That was a fair spot, she'd heard. The lower three colonies of Pennsylvania had been a Dutch settlement—or was it Swedish? Anyway, she'd heard that Catholics were not persecuted there, and that living was easy. Yes, she'd go to Delaware, near the ocean, and wait for Colin.

And forget she'd ever followed a tawny man through the trackless forest . . . Forget she'd dared to dream of long winter nights, wrapped in his strong arms . . . Forget those eyes as black as the pits of hell and the mouth that tempted her to certain damnation . . .

Her decision to run away hadn't come easily. She was afraid of the woods, fearful of hostile Indians and wild beasts. But she was even more afraid of staying here.

She wasn't being rash or stupid; she'd thought her plan out carefully since Talon had left. She'd walk until she came to a river, then follow it south. When she was far enough away from here, she'd turn east toward the rising sun. She was taking a musket, ammunition, and all the things she'd brought from her cabin. When the food ran out, she'd shoot a deer. She'd keep walking until she found a trading post. If she had to surrender to a Frenchman, she would.

Another white woman, Mildred Emmett, had done it. She'd escaped from her Indian captors and walked twenty-two days to freedom. Of course, Mildred had walked out of the woods in summer. But she'd been with child. If an English-woman could do it, surely an able-bodied Irish woman could.

The trick was to get away from Siipu and her animals. Rebecca knew she'd have to travel fast to-day. She felt guilty stealing Siipu's food after the Indian woman had been so kind to her, but she couldn't go into the forest without supplies. She'd make it up to Talon's sister by going to the fort and making certain that her father was being treated kindly. Rebecca didn't believe for one min-ute that the old man was dead. That was supersti-tious nonsense. She'd been foolish even to consider it.

No educated person could believe in witchcraft. Banshees, leprechauns, and pookas were all of a lot—tall tales to frighten children. Siipu's *seeing* in the fire was the pitiful fantasy of a poor girl whose wits had been damaged by bad treatment and liv-ing alone too long. No, Talon's father was cer-tainly alive and well. What sense would it make for the English military to take a hostage and then kill him when they were trying to make peace with the hostiles?

At first, she didn't feel the cold. She walked fast, following a game trail that led downhill. The sky was overcast, but it didn't smell like snow. She slung the musket over one shoulder, her blanket and hunting bag over the other. The snow was nearly gone, and the ground was frozen solid. Her feet were warm in the double moccasins, her hands swathed in thick mittens. As she hurried along, she looked around her as she had seen Talon do and she listened for sounds of danger.

The air smelled so fresh and clean that she actually enjoyed the rare experience of venturing into the forest alone. Once, she stopped short as a doe and two yearlings crossed just ahead of her. They were so beautiful that she was glad she didn't need to shoot one. The doe stared at her with huge liquid eyes for a long moment, then loped gracefully away. The others followed, and Rebecca continued on, trying not to think how heavy the musket was becoming.

After what she judged to be two hours' time, she paused beneath a chestnut tree to catch her breath. So far, her escape had been easy. She was carrying more weight than was comfortable, but that couldn't be helped. She'd need the weapon later.

The cold didn't bother her. If anything, she was almost too warm in her heavy clothing. She was thirsty, but she didn't want to drink yet even though she'd brought water in a skin bag; she'd wait until she came to a stream. Instead, she dug out a corn cake laced with dried berries and nibbled on that while a gray squirrel scampered down from a tree and scolded her with sharp, chattering barks.

Someday, I'll tell Colin about this adventure, she decided. And we'll laugh about it together. He'd have his own stories to relate, exaggerated, she was sure. Colin always did have a vivid imagination.

Maybe her little brother was already back in the settlement. The Indian who'd taken him away might have found out the boy was too much trouble, or he might have sold him back to the British. Holding Colin prisoner would be like trying to hold onto a summer thunderstorm. No doubt, he was already free, with his feet propped up in front of a crackling fireplace, worrying about her safety.

"Wait until I tell you about the bear," she murmured aloud. "He had a hump on his back and a head the size of a wagon wheel." She could almost picture Colin's wide-eyed look of astonishment.

But thinking about Colin brought a catch to her throat. She got to her feet and shouldered her pack. "I'd best get going if I'm going," she said. The twisting trail led downhill over an outcropping of loose rock and through an area that had burned years ago in a fire.

By dusk, she had entered virgin forest again. She was cold and hungry, and she knew she'd need to find shelter and build a fire. She'd been looking for someplace to camp since late afternoon, but so far, she hadn't found water or the right spot to stop. She was tired, and her left foot had a sore spot on the heel. The shoulder that the musket banged against felt as though it was broken.

She paused and glanced around, hoping she'd overlooked some overhanging ledge or fallen tree. Then she heard what sounded like a woman's terrified scream.

Rebecca's mouth went dry. Badly frightened, she spun around, trying to decide where the cry had come from. Then the scream came again, and she knew it wasn't a woman. It was a mountain lion.

She backed against a tree, lowered the musket, and began to check the priming. A branch snapped, and her heart nearly leaped out of her chest.

I can't run, she thought frantically. I can't run. But every instinct urged her to flee. Hands trembling, she raised the musket, waiting for the lion to spring at her.

"There be no need," Siipu said, stepping out from behind a giant beech. "It be Meshepeshe."

"Siipu!" She lowered the gun.

Talon's sister stared at her as the mountain lion materialized out of the gathering twilight and rubbed against his mistress's leg.

"I'm not going back," Rebecca said defiantly. "I won't. You can't make me."

"This one not want you go back," the Indian woman answered.

Her husky voice sounded hollow; it echoed through the trees, and a shiver ran down Rebecca's spine. In the longhouse, Talon's sister had seemed almost friendly, despite the ever present mask. But here . . .

I thought she was a ghost the first time I saw her, Rebecca remembered. Maybe I was right.

"It's better for Talon if I go back to my own people," she argued. "Once I return, I'm certain I can convince the English to release your father."

Siipu shook her head. The dark eyes behind the doeskin mask were expressionless. "Do not speak of him," she said. "He has crossed river of souls. The Lenape not speak name of dead."

"Stop saying that! There's no way you can know if he's dead or alive."

"This one know."

"Then why didn't you tell Talon if you're so sure?" Rebecca demanded.

"Talon vow kill you. Father dead, white prisoner dead."

"I don't believe you! Talon won't hurt me. He won't. He's no murderer."

"He Shawnee. War chief. Word is honor. He know father die, he must put you to death. No want. Must."

"Then I can't go back. Surely, you can see that."

"Losowahkun see. See Sh'Kotaa Osh-Kah-Shah watch prisoner with wanting eyes."

"You're wrong," Rebecca protested. "He's been good to me, that's all. There's nothing between us. There couldn't be. He's Shawnee, and I'm—"

"A woman."

"It's not the same. I am a Catholic. I could never—"

"A woman's heart sometime lead where head know better not to go. You have want for Sh'Kotaa Osh-Kah-Shah. Best you return your own people."

Rebecca stared at her in shock. "You agree with me?"

"Losowahkun agree. Come not to bring you back. Come guide you to white settlement."

Chapter 15

Simon took aim at the running figure and fired. He was rewarded by the sound of branches snapping as a man's body tumbled down the far side of the ridge. Without wasting a motion, he began to dump powder and shot into the barrel of his silver-inlaid Pennsylvania long rifle.

Despite the cold, sweat gleamed on Simon's forehead. This mission was not going as he'd intended. They'd already lost two men and the Miami scout, murdered by Indians they hadn't even seen.

Amos Dodd had been the first to die, cut down as they crossed the rocky creek. Dodd hadn't wanted to leave the safety of the fort, and he'd whined and grumbled every step of the journey. "Guess you were right," Simon murmured. "Guess you shoulda stayed safe behind the fort walls." He couldn't waste time mourning the likes of Dodd. "Yellow belly." This country was too hard for weak men; if Dodd hadn't caught a rifle ball in the gut yesterday, ole man death would have found him soon enough.

Simon had set the Miami Injun scout and Richard Beaumont to guard the night camp for the last watch while the rest slept. When he woke at first light, he'd found them both with throats cut, minus their scalps. The Injun was no great loss; Simon knew this country about as well as he did. But Beaumont was a man to be reckoned with. The militia could scarce afford to lose his kind. Simon had fought side by side with Beaumont for twenty years, and he'd miss his steady aim and ready laughter.

It was too friggin' bad the ground was frozen hard as a whore's heart, Simon mused. The dead men would end up in some varmint's belly, that was certain. "Hellfire and damnation, Richard. It grates on me to leave ye for wolf bait."

Davy caught his eye and waved. He was crouched about ten yards away beneath the overhanging branches of a pin oak. Simon nodded and moved cautiously to his friend's side.

"Ye hit one?" Davy asked. Tobacco juice trickled from the corner of his mouth and clotted in his six-day beard. He wiped at it absently with the sleeve of his red hunting coat.

"Hit him square, I reckon," Simon answered, as he peered into the surrounding forest for any sign of movement. Someone had been taking potshots at them for over an hour, and he didn't mean to be the next victim.

Davy cleared his throat. Small green eyes peered out from beneath a soft, leather, three-cornered hat that had once been gray but was now stained with a score of colors of dirt and grease and dried blood. "How many of 'em ye 'spose there be?"

"Not as many as us. They'd of come at us afore this if they had us outgunned."

"Maybe." Dave bit off a fresh twist of tobacco. "Maybe not. Injuns is all cowards at heart."

"Some is," Simon agreed. "But they's some got more nerve than brains. Ye take this Shawnee whoreson we're ahuntin', Fire Talon. Me and him, we had a few set-to's afore this. And he ain't no yellow belly, I'll give the devil his due."

"The men don't care much for this, Simon. They shoot one, we shoot one. This ain't gettin' yer woman back or cleaning out the brier patch fer white folk. Wilson and Barrel-head Hooper, they're fer turnin' back afore we all end up like Richard."

"Just like that, huh? We take a few knocks, and then we let 'em chase us home like curs with our tails 'tween our legs. We come to teach 'em a lesson, Davy. That's a good lesson, but I ain't sure it's the one we wanted to deliver."

"Don't go all stiff necked on me," Davy said. "I didn't say I was ready to call it quits. I said the boys was nervous. They got good right to be. Most got women folk and kids at home. I know yer worried about your wife, but—"

A bullet tore a chunk of bark out of the tree inches above Davy's head. "Son of a howlin' bitch!" he swore.

Two militiamen fired off their rifles, and a Shawnee war cry echoed through the trees. Black smoke drifted up through the bare branches. Davy and Simon edged around to the far side of the oak.

"Let's you and me play a little Injun ourselves," Simon suggested. "You go that way." He motioned left. "And I'll try and come around from the other direction."

Davy nodded. "All right by me. Just don't show your ass. Barrel-head's scared enough to shoot anything that moves."

"I'll mind my rear, you mind yer own," Simon replied with a grin. "I've a notion to decorate this hunting bag of mine with some Shawnee hair."

"I hear ye."

Head low, Simon slipped off into the brush. Davy waited for a count of twenty-five, then crept to the next tree.

In the gully, several hundred yards away, Osage Killer pressed his fist against the rifle wound in Counts' shoulder and tried to stanch the blood flow. Counts leaned against a boulder, head down, and eyes shut.

"How bad is he hurt?" Talon asked as he approached the two.

Counts opened his eyes. His face was white with shock and pain. "I'll live," he said.

"Not if I can't slow this," Osage Killer said.

Talon bent to inspect the injury. "Is the ball still in there?"

Counts shook his head. "No."

"Hold the pressure on it," Talon advised. "He always bleeds like this. Remember the time you took that Huron arrow up on the big lake?"

"You'll never let me forget it," Counts whispered.

Osage Killer frowned. "He needs more help than I can give him here."

"Take him to my sister's," Talon said.

"The witch?" Osage Killer's lips thinned.

"Who better?" Talon retorted. "Siipu is good with medicine. "He needs a warm bed and hot food."

"No," Counts His Scalps protested. "We'll not leave you and Fox alone to fight the long knives. I can make it on my own."

Talon clasped Counts' forearm. "Little use you'd be to us dead, old friend. Osage Killer can take you there and return. Meanwhile, we'll try to lead Simon Brandt's men in another direction."

"This man does not like the smell of witches," Osage Killer said. "Better I take Counts to the village."

"Too far," Talon said. "And wounded or not, Counts' powers are stronger than those of any witch woman. What say you, dreamer of dreams?" He glanced back at the injured brave. "Are you afraid of Siipu?"

Counts made a sound of derision.

"Then it's settled," Talon said. "Go quickly, before Simon Brandt comes to see if you're dead. I'll relieve Fox. Watch for smoke when the sun is at its highest. We'll send a signal if we can. If not, we'll meet at the salt licks two days from now. Agreed?"

Osage Killer nodded. "Walk with care, Sh'Kotaa Osh-Kah-Shah. Simon Brandt is a worthy enemy."

Talon shrugged. "His luck has held for many years. And even a worthy enemy makes a mistake in time."

"Unless the spirits are with him and against you," Osage Killer said.

"If that is so, then nothing this man can do will add one breath to his own life," Talon answered softly. "For my father's sake, I hope not."

"If you die, we will free Medicine Smoke," Counts said. "The honor of the Mecate Shawnee will not allow him to remain a prisoner of the English."

"I will hold you to your word," Talon said. "If we do not meet again on this side of the river of souls, remember what you have promised."

Osage Killer nodded solemnly. "I swear as well," he said. "If you do not live, we will become Medicine Smoke's sons in your place. All that you would do for your father, so we shall do. On Counts' life, I vow it."

"Swear on your own life," Counts said as he struggled to his feet. He gasped with pain as the bullet wound began to bleed again. Fighting to keep his balance, he swayed. He gritted his teeth, but remained upright.

Osage Killer put an arm around Counts' shoulders to steady him. "You should lie still until I bandage this."

"Bleeding will clean the flesh. If I cannot stand, how can I walk?" Counts grumbled.

"I left the wife of Simon Brandt with my sister," Talon said as he prepared to leave them. "Treat her gently. She is not to blame for her husband's crimes."

"You think too much about this fox-haired woman," Counts said. "She will bring you only trouble."

She already has, Talon thought, as he checked the priming on his rifle and zig-zagged up the woody incline. She already has.

Rebecca followed Siipu up another ridge and through another stand of pine. They had spent the night together, shared a morning meal, and been walking since early dawn, but Rebecca still wasn't certain she could trust Talon's sister to return her to the white settlements.

The Indian woman had barely spoken since they'd stamped out their small campfire and left the tiny cave where they'd spent the night. She strode along with effortless grace, the big yellow-brown cat padding soundlessly at her side. Rebecca had slept within arm's reach of the mountain lion, and her clothing still smelled of cat. She was grateful for the shelter Siipu had found, but nothing would make her easy around the puma and his curving white fangs.

It was a miserable day for traveling. The temperature rose, and it was drizzling cold rain. The snow had turned to mush, and the undergrowth soaked their clothes every time they brushed against it. The air was heavy with the scents of wet leaves and musty earth. Rebecca's outer moccasins were wet, the inner pair damp; she had pulled her fur hood over her head to protect her from the rain, but icy drops still dripped off the folds and trickled down her neck, making her shiver.

Most cats hated water, but if this one was bothered by the nasty weather, he didn't show it. Siipu had told her that the lion was still young, that it would continue to grow for another year. Rebecca couldn't imagine how large it would be when it reached maturity; the thing was enormous now. His yellow eyes watched every movement through lazy slits as the ropelike tail waved slowly to and fro.

Then, suddenly, the animal tensed and bounded off through the trees. It happened so fast that Rebecca blinked her eyes and stared. One minute the lion was beside Siipu, and the next, it had vanished.

Talon's sister stopped short in her tracks. She put a finger to her mask for silence, and unslung the bow from her left shoulder.

Seconds later, Rebecca heard a rifle shot. The sound echoed through the trees, followed by what could have been a man's shout. Siipu tapped her shoulder and led the way quickly up a steep incline toward several large boulders half buried in the hillside. Another shot rang out, closer than the first. Siipu ducked down behind a rock and motioned for Rebecca to do the same. They crouched there, side by side.

Something large and black swooped down from the branches overhead with a shrill *kik-kik-kikkik* cry, and Rebecca's heart jumped. Then she let out her breath with a hiss of relief as she recognized the red crest and the white underwing of a pileated woodpecker. We probably frightened him out of his hollow tree when we scrambled up the slope, she thought, as she watched the big, awkward bird flap his long angular wings and drift away into the forest.

She was staring in the direction the woodpecker had flown when she saw a white man dash from the trees and run toward the boulders. Right behind him sprinted an Indian. The first man whirled and fired at his pursuer; the Indian dodged aside, hit the ground and rolled, and came up swinging a tomahawk. The feathered weapon spun through the air. Rebecca shut her eyes just before the hatchet struck the victim, but she couldn't shut out the sound of the white man's scream.

When she looked again, the Indian stood over him, stripping his motionless body of his weapons and valuables. He threw back his head and let out a triumphant whoop.

Siipu grabbed her arm. "Run!" she cried.

Rebecca twisted around to see two more white men coming over the top of the rise directly behind them. One militiaman dropped to his knee and raised his musket, sighting in on her.

"Run!" Siipu screamed again.

"No!" Rebecca shouted as she threw up her

arms. "Wait! I'm a white—" The musket roared and the lead ball slammed into the rock over her head. Pieces of granite flew around her like angry bees. Something stung her face. In shock, she touched her cheek. When she looked down at her fingers, they were stained red.

"Becca!" Siipu urged. "Run!"

Rebecca leaped up and began to run. But only a few yards from the boulder, she slipped on the loose scree and fell to her knees just as the second man fired at her. Siipu doubled back and seized her hand, jerking her to her feet.

Together, they dashed down the hill through the pouring rain back toward the place where the puma had left them. Crumbling rock and slick mud made the slope dangerous, but they didn't hesitate. From the corner of her eye, Rebecca saw the Indian off to her right in hand to hand combat with another white man in buckskins. When she glanced back over her shoulder, she went numb all over. One of the men who'd tried to kill her was close behind and gaining with every stride. Terror lent a new burst of speed to her flight, but the strain of running over such rough ground, even downhill, was telling on her. She could feel her strength draining away with each ragged gasp of breath.

Siipu yelled something at her in Algonquian, then, when she realized that Rebecca didn't understand, she switched to English. "Drop musket!"

Rebecca pushed the heavy weapon off her shoulder without a minute's hesitation. Siipu let go of her hand, leaped up onto a rotting log and notched an arrow on her bowstring. Rebecca heard a groan behind her as she followed Siipu over the fallen tree and down a steep outcrop of crumbling shale.

Bullets whistled over their heads. Rebecca had lost one mitten somewhere, and she'd dropped her hunting bag. Siipu stopped behind a tree to let fly another arrow. Rebecca's breath was coming in painful gulps as the two of them plunged into a tangle of fallen pine and briers, wiggled through the morass, and slid down into a narrow stream.

Water soaked Rebecca to her knees. Her exposed hand was bleeding, but she didn't feel anything. She glanced at Siipu and realized that the woman's fringed mask was twisted to one side so that Rebecca had a clear view of her face. To her astonishment, there was no ugly scarring. Siipu's face was as smooth and flawless as a baby's. "Your mask," she blurted out. "I thought—"

The Indian woman snatched the leather covering into place. For an instant, their eyes met and Rebecca thought that Talon's sister was going to answer her unasked question.

Instead, she reached over and pushed back Rebecca's hood so that her hair tumbled loose around her shoulders. "Listen," the Indian woman said. She pointed upstream. "More come."

Above the sound of her own pounding pulse, Rebecca heard men cursing—in English.

"Too many," Siipu said. "Too many long knife." She touched her own chest. "Losowahkun no be capture. Never." Her eyes were dilated with fright behind the mud-streaked doeskin mask. "No more."

"It's all right," Rebecca assured her. "I'll be all right. If they see my red hair, they'll know I'm white. They won't hurt me. I'll protect you. I won't let them—"

"Shhh," Siipu warned.

Underbrush crashed behind them. There was a thunderous growl and a human shriek. Siipu flattened herself against the muddy creek bank.

Rebecca saw a bearded white man come into view along the far side of the creek. He was wearing a red hunting shirt and a shapeless leather hat, and he was definitely not one of the men who'd fired on them earlier. She glanced at Siipu, then sprang forward and splashed through the water. "Help me!" she screamed as loudly as she could. "Help me!" She ran toward the men, away from Siipu's hiding place.

"What the hell!" Red Shirt raised his rifle and took aim.

"No!" Rebecca shouted. "I'm Rebecca Brandt! I'm white!" She stopped short and held up her arms. "Help me! The Indians—"

The bearded man leaped down into the water and seized her by the chin. He twisted her face up and peered into it. "Reckon ye are Simon's woman, after all," he said.

His breath was foul and her stomach turned over as she caught a whiff of stale tobacco from his beard. His green eyes narrowed as his dirty fingers dug into her flesh. "Stop it. You're hurting me," she protested.

"Had ye a good time with 'em savages?" he asked slyly. He let go of her chin and fumbled for her breast. She stepped sideways and threw her weight into him with as much force as she could muster. He bellowed with anger, lunged for her, and lost his footing on the slippery rocks. He went down into waist-deep water.

Rebecca scrambled up the muddy bank, then groaned as his hand closed around her ankle.

"Not so fast!" he shouted. He shoved her face down as he climbed up behind her. She crawled forward on hands and knees, but when she rose to her feet, he backhanded her with a meaty fist.

She hit the ground hard and lay still, stunned.

"Crazy, are ye?" Davy demanded. "Crazy enough to fight yer own kind?"

She tried to get up and he kicked her in the ribs. She doubled up in pain and swore at him as blood ran from the corner of her mouth. "I'm Simon Brandt's wife, you stupid ass," she screamed. "You can't . . ."

"Shut your mouth," he ordered. "Lay right there until I tell ye to move, or I'll knock them pretty white teeth down yer throat." He scanned the quiet woods and began to empty his rifle's frizzen pan of wet powder.

"Simon will kill you for this," Rebecca said. The wet ground was cold under her and rain beat in her face. Her hair hung in matted ropes, and she was covered in mud. "Can't I make you understand who I am?"

"I tole ye to hold yer tongue," he muttered. "Treacherous little red-swivin' slut." He was soaking wet; he'd lost his hat, and even his hair was dripping. "No better than an Injun yerself." He measured dry powder from a horn and wiped the water off the stock of his rifle. The falling rain streaked it as fast as he rubbed, but he didn't seem to notice.

She watched him warily as he took a few steps closer, then looked around again. Nothing stirred. Not even a squirrel moved in the treetops. There was no sign or sound of human life.

"Don't I know you?" she asked. "Are you Davy

Clarke? You're in Simon's militia. Why are you doing this to me? He will—"

"I tole you to shut up!" he warned. "Ye won't tell ole Simon nothin' if the Injuns kill ye, will ye? What Simon don't know won't hurt him. It ain't as if he's pinin' away over ye, ye howlin' red-haired bitch." He glanced around quickly. "Now spread them legs and hike up that dress, girl. Davy ain't got all day. My root's as cold and stiff as a grave marker. I got a notion to warm it in yer jelly pot."

Rebecca curled into a ball. "I won't," she whispered. "You can't expect me to—"

"I expect ye to give me what ye been givin' them red bastards. Ye got nothin' left to lose, woman. Fact is, ye might even like it."

"I won't!"

"You damn sight will, and you'll hold your tongue afterwards. You say a word to that man o' yourn, and I'll make ye the laughin' stock of the territory. I'll tell it that ye begged me fer it, and turned nasty when I wouldn't give it to ye."

Rebecca took a deep breath and let out the loudest scream she'd ever given in her life.

Davy threw himself on top of her. Still screaming, she twisted under him and dug at his face with her nails. He grabbed one wrist and forced her hand back over her head, pinned her with his knees, and tried to yank her dress up with his free hand. She slammed him in the nose with her fist, and he let go of her arm long enough to slap her twice, so hard that she saw stars.

Her head rocked back and she nearly lost consciousness. He's going to kill me, she thought, from some distant corner of her mind. If I just close my eyes and lie still ... if I let him have his way, then maybe—

But the image of his swollen red member tearing into her filled her with a terrible rage. "No!" she cried. "No!" In desperation, she renewed her struggle with the strength of a madwoman.

"I'll ha' ye, ye screamin' bitch," he grunted. "I'll ha' ye, if I ha' to strangle the life out o' ye first."

His threat rang in her ears as his bare hands closed around her throat and cut off her breath.

Chapter 16

Cold, deadly rage possessed Talon as he sprinted toward the bearded militiaman who had knocked Becca to the ground and flung himself on her like a raging beast. He could see that the woodsman was choking her, but Talon couldn't risk a rifle shot that might kill her as well as her assailant.

Instinct told him he was endangering his own life and that of Fox. But he was past the point of reason. The long knife was trying to murder Becca, and for that crime, he would pay the ultimate penalty, no matter the cost to Talon.

He uttered no war cry as he bore down on his enemy. With the silence of his totem, the plunging hawk, he fell upon his quarry with swift, merciless wrath. At the last possible instant, the white man looked up and saw him coming.

Green eyes dilated in terror. His mouth gaped open to scream. Then Talon struck. His weight hammered the white scout to the ground. Before he could do more than struggle, Talon drove the polished steel point of his scalping knife deep into the coward's heart.

The white man gasped, his eyes rolled back in their sockets, and his head fell unnaturally to one side. Talon twisted the weapon free, wiped it clean of blood on the red hunting shirt, and shoved it back into his sheath. Shoving the body away in disgust, Talon turned his attention to the woman.

She lay like an abandoned cornhusk doll, hair tangled, face expressionless. Her eyes were closed, and she wasn't making a sound. It wasn't until he knelt beside her that he saw the ugly purple bruises on her throat.

"Becca," he murmured. "Becca?" Had he been too late to save her? He gathered her in his arms and brushed her pale eyelids with his lips.

She hung limp and lifeless.

Tears clouded Talon's vision as a great wave of sadness washed over him. He crushed her against his chest. "No! I will not lose you!" he cried in his own tongue. "Live, my Becca, I command you to live."

He looked down into her ashen face. Her lips parted slightly and he caught a glimpse of white, even teeth. So perfect, he thought. So beautiful. Without thinking, he bent his head and kissed her mouth, breathing into her his own life spirit ... trying desperately to hold on to what had been her essence.

She moaned.

"Becca!" He shook her roughly. "Becca!"

She drew in a long, gasping breath, then began to choke.

He leaned her upright against his chest and supported her head. "Breathe, Becca," he urged in English. "Breathe."

Her eyelids flickered and she fought to suck air through her swollen throat.

He murmured her name with infinite tenderness.

Slowly, she opened her eyes and looked up into his face. "You came," she tried to say. Her voice was so distorted by her ordeal that the words were little more than rasping tones, barely audible.

But Talon had no need to understand her harsh whispers. Her eyes glowed with meaning, and when she smiled up at him, his soul leaped.

"Are you mad?" Fox called in Algonquian.

Talon looked up to see the Shawnee brave dashing toward them.

"Simon Brandt is still out there with six of his men," the warrior admonished. Then he glanced down at the white man's outstretched body and corrected himself. "Well, five, if you count the wounded. Would you offer them your scalp already stretched for drying?"

Talon was on his feet, helping Becca up. "Can you walk?" he asked her. Still breathing with difficulty, she leaned against him and nodded.

Fox glanced from one to the other. "I found Siipu by the creek bank," he said, continuing in the Shawnee dialect. "She's hiding in the bushes on the far side."

"Siipu? But why is she here?" He glared down at Becca. "Why are you both here? Is Siipu all right?"

"Uninjured," Fox replied.

"I told you to stay at the wigwam," he said to Becca in English. "Why did you disobey—"

"Later," Fox admonished. "This is not the best place to satisfy your curiosity. They're here. Now what are we going to do with them?"

"You're right," Talon agreed. "You take my sister back to her longhouse. Counts and Osage Killer should be there. Counts will need her skill to heal his wound."

"And you?"

"It's not wise for us to travel together with the

women. We'd leave a trail. I will take the white woman with me. We'll all meet at the village in two weeks' time."

"You'll leave Simon Brandt and his militia alive?" Fox demanded. "You said—"

"I said I would kill him and I will. But not today." He clasped his friend's arm. "We have taught the long knives a lesson they'll not soon forget. I think they've had enough of this hunting trip. If we leave them, they'll turn back to the white settlements."

"But you intend to keep the woman?"

"Until I trade her for my father. Yes, Fox, I keep her."

"Hmmp." The slim warrior looked unconvinced. "I hope you have not misjudged Simon Brandt."

"How so?"

"What if he does not want her as much as you seem to?"

"She is his wife. If she were yours, would you want her?" Talon demanded, trying to control his temper. What was Fox insinuating? Did his friend believe that he would put a beautiful white woman ahead of the best interests of the people— ahead of his father's safety? Whatever feelings he had for Becca were private. They would not keep him from his duty.

"So long as you remember that Medicine Smoke's life hangs in the balance," Fox said.

"On the day I forget, on that day you can become war chief in my place."

Fox tapped his breast with a clenched fist. "In two weeks, then. Guard your back, brother."

"And yours." He smiled at Fox. "You may find that Siipu is the woman of your dreams."

Fox shrugged. "Perhaps, but I think not. I'm not a man who likes to sleep with the stench of a puma in his robes."

"Take care of her."

"As if she were my own sister."

Fox turned back toward the stream. Talon covered him with his rifle until he reached cover on the other side, then looked down at Becca. "Come," he said gently to her. "We go."

"Go where?" she croaked. "What ..." She rubbed her throat and tried again. "Why ..."

"Hush," he soothed. "Don't try to talk. Your voice will come back in a day or two."

"But why—" she whispered hoarsely.

"We go," he said. "Unless you wish to see me kill your husband before your eyes."

She shook her head.

"Then you must trust me, Becca." He paused long enough to gather up the dead man's gun, knife, hatchet, and powder horn before leading the way south, up a wooded slope, away from the creek. He didn't look back to see if she was following, but the soft sound of her footfalls told him what he needed to know.

Rebecca didn't know how many miles they walked that day or how many half-frozen streams they crossed. She didn't have the slightest idea where Talon was taking her, and she'd lost all sense of direction. He could have been leading her to Canada or straight to hell for all she knew. All that mattered was that she was tired, wet, and cold. Her throat ached and her face was swollen and bruised from the scout's beating. She wanted something to eat, and she wanted a soft bed near a fire. At this point, hell didn't look all that bad. At least it would be warm, she thought wryly.

She'd made a few attempts to ask Talon what he intended to do with her, but he'd warned her that voices carried a long way in the woods. He had made it plain that he didn't want to talk, and his mood was less than cheerful. Finally, she gave up and concentrated on staying close behind him.

By dark, the misty rain had changed to snow. Her feet felt like wooden stumps, and she was so weary that she didn't think she could take another step. When she stumbled and nearly fell, he picked her up and carried her the last mile. Too cold to protest, she closed her eyes against the falling snow and huddled against his chest, trying desperately to borrow some of his body warmth.

"Here," he said, stopping short. He dropped her onto her feet, keeping one arm around her to keep her from falling. "We will have a fire soon."

She stared at a one-room log cabin that seemed to have materialized out of the forest. She could just make out a small cleared area of raw tree stumps and a smaller log shed a few yards from the cabin. "Who lives here?" she asked him.

"No one. This is a trading post. The Frenchman Adrian Pascal built it. Usually, he spends winters here with his Ottawa wife, but this year, he did not come. Word is that Pascal lost a leg up on the Hockhocking River last summer." Talon raised the heavy wooden bar and pushed up the door. "Come." He motioned for her to follow. "We will be safe here."

"Why?" she wondered aloud.

"Pascal used to be a Jesuit priest. He knew a lot about the failings of men. He chose this site carefully. This valley is haunted by the ghosts of great creatures with leg bones the size of trees. On stormy nights, they say you can hear them trumpeting."

"Haunted by animal ghosts?" She followed him inside, out of the wind, and sank down on the floor, grateful that it was hewn log and not more cold, wet earth.

Talon closed the door behind them and moved across the room. "Pascal always kept flint and steel on the fireplace mantel. Yes, here it is." In seconds, he had struck a spark and then another. In five minutes time, Talon had a small fire burning on the hearth.

Rebecca was relieved to see a large pile of dry firewood stacked along one wall. Gratefully, she edged closer to the flickering flames and held out her stiff hands. Talon removed his fur wrap and draped it around her shoulders, and she murmured her thanks.

He continued to add more sticks until the rosy glow of the fire illuminated the small cabin. It was crudely furnished with a table and benches, a low bed, and a counter that ran along the wall opposite the firewood. An iron kettle was propped upside down on the stone hearth.

Talon took the kettle outside and returned with it half full of snow. "There's a spring behind the cabin, but I'm not going to search for it tonight. We can melt snow for water." He hung the kettle on an iron crane and added a mixture of cornmeal, dried meat, and dried berries from bags in his hunting pack. Almost at once, a delicious smell began to drift from the simmering broth.

Good wool blankets were pegged to the wall. Talon took them down, shook out the dust and mice nests, and spread them on the sapling bed frame. "When it stops snowing, I'll make you a mattress of pine boughs," he said. "For now, it will be hard sleeping."

"I don't care," she said. "I just want to be warm and dry. If it wasn't wet, I could sleep on a brick wall." Her voice still came out as a grating whisper.

He chuckled and some of the lines on his face smoothed. "This man too is grateful for a warm bed," he admitted.

He's not made of stone after all, Rebecca thought. He feels cold and fatigue. He was worried about finding shelter for us tonight; I can see the relief in his eyes.

She pushed back the wrap and went to the plank cupboard and brought back two tin bowls and wooden spoons. The dishes had been turned upside down to keep mice out. Still, she couldn't resist wiping them out with the hem of her coat. A tin dipper dangled from the mantel ledge; she used that to ladle out the stew.

Talon settled onto the floor, legs folded, and accepted the brimming bowl with a nod of thanks. She had already taken the first hot spoonful of her own meal when she realized that Talon was whispering a prayer over his. She remembered that in his sister's house, an Indian grace had been offered before any food was eaten.

"You are an amazing man," she said.

"No, Becca, I am just a man as any other."

"I don't know what to think anymore."

"Nor I." He took a sip of the broth.

"I ran away," she said.

"And nearly got yourself killed."

She looked at the steaming bowl in her hands.

"I thought it would be best for both of us if I wasn't there when you got back."

He shook his head. "Don't talk anymore, Becca. Eat and sleep. Tomorrow, your throat will be better. Tomorrow you will be rested."

"But I want to—"

"No, not tonight. You have been through much. Sleep first. Recover, and then this man will listen to all you have to say."

Nodding, she finished her supper, dashed outside to tend to her personal needs, and returned to warm up by the fire, before climbing into bed. She made no protest when he slid in beside her.

Like husband and wife, she thought. First, we share the evening meal, then . . . She swallowed and her heartbeat quickened.

"There is only one bed," he said.

She didn't answer, but a shiver of anticipation ran through her and her mouth went dry.

"You are safe here, Becca," he assured her, turning his back without touching her. "Sleep now. Tomorrow, we will talk."

She was lying beside a hostile Shawnee warrior, she thought. She should be terrified, both for her honor and her life. And yet . . . yet, she felt more secure than she'd ever felt in Simon's bed. She lay there motionless except for the faint rise and fall of her chest, listening to him breathe, letting his clean, male scent wash over her.

She wanted to touch him. In spite of her bruises, her swollen throat, her aches and pains, she wanted him to hold her in his muscular arms. She wanted him to cover her mouth with his—to claim her with his strong hands and fill her with his sex.

Could it be that Talon found her as undesirable as Simon seemed to? Would no decent man wish to make love to her? They were here, wrapped in the same blankets, sharing a bed. How could he ignore her? How could she sleep when her body cried out for fulfillment?

The lump in her throat grew until it hurt. Tears seeped through her clenched eyelids.

I want you, she wanted to scream. I want you to make me a woman! Here, tonight, before I lose my nerve.

But the words would not come, and somehow, surprisingly, she did drift off to a dreamless sleep, unmarred by night terrors.

She smelled roasting chicken. Sighing, she turned over and opened her eyes, then sat up in bed with a start. "Talon?" she cried.

Had he left her? The cabin was empty. She felt the space where he had slept. No warmth remained from his body.

"Talon?" She threw back the covers, stood up, and looked around the small room as though she expected him to be hiding somewhere. She called his name again, then smiled with relief as she saw the large bird roasting on the spit over the fire.

He wouldn't go to all the trouble of shooting a turkey, picking and cleaning it, then putting it on to cook, if he didn't intend to share in the feast, she decided.

Unconsciously, her hand went to her hair. I must look a mess, she thought. Her voice sounded unnatural to her ears, but much of the swelling had gone down. Her fingertips slid down to brush the bruises on her throat.

Suddenly, a gust of cold air hit her. She turned to see Talon coming through the open door. It was snowing outside and clouds of frozen crystals swirled around him. "Oh," she murmured.

He smiled at her and shook the snow off his unbound hair. The streaks of war paint were gone from his face, and he looked much younger. "There is no need for you to be out of bed," he said. "Today you rest. I will serve you." A contagious mischief lurked behind his dark eyes, an unexpected playfulness that she could not resist.

"Is that an order to a helpless prisoner?"

He made a sharp sign of dismissal with his right hand. "*Ku.* There will be no more talk of prisoners between us, at least not here in this valley of the ghost bones. Here we are only Becca and Talon."

"And . . ."

"And it is my wish that you go back to bed and let me care for you this day."

"Oh." She pursed her lips. "There are some things a gentleman cannot do for a lady."

His eyes expressed puzzlement.

A flush warmed her cheeks. "I must go outside," she explained.

"But the storm. We cannot—" Then a knowing look spread over his bronze features. "*Yuho.* You must go out." He laughed. "Behind the shed. I'm sorry the cabin does not offer other arrangements. But the snow isn't too deep there. You can—"

"You tend the bird and let me tend my needs," she said, a little too sharply. She prided herself on being a practical woman, but some subjects were too personal to be discussed with a man.

She was all too glad to return to the cabin a few minutes later. Stamping snow off her moccasins and shivering, she went again to the fire. Considering the intensity of the wind outside, she was surprised how warm the cabin was. But the single room was small and low and constructed of heavy timber chinked with clay. There was not even a single window. The only light, even in daytime, came from the glowing hearth.

"I was about to come searching for you," he said.

She nodded. "It's bad out there, but I kept close to the house."

"If you lost your way, you could freeze to death out there. The storm may blow for several days."

"I'm glad there's plenty of wood."

"The Frenchman is wise in the way of the forest."

Talon had warmed the remainder of last night's meal while she was outside. He handed her a bowl. She started as his hand brushed hers and nearly dropped the stew on the floor. Their eyes met and then both looked away, too quickly.

"Careful," he cautioned, trying to act as though nothing had passed between them. "The turkey will take a while."

She covered her own confusion by talking about the meal he'd found for them. "It smells wonderful," she said. "How did you find a turkey in the snow?"

"Skill," he replied. "Haven't you heard? This man is a great hunter." He grinned boyishly. "And luck. The stupid birds were roosting in a tree at the edge of the clearing. I caught two with my bare hands."

"Then you deserve to boast. Turkeys are the wariest game in the forest."

"But not in snow. They tucked their heads under their wings and waited for this hunter to pluck them from their perch." His eyes were on her again, and she knew that he wasn't thinking about turkeys.

She concentrated on her breakfast and tried to ignore his admiring gaze. "Will the storm last long, do you think?" she asked.

"Does it matter?" He moved closer to her. "None can reach us while the snow blankets the forest and the wind howls like a wolf."

"No one?" She was warm enough to be uncomfortable. Setting down her bowl, she removed her coat and placed it over the bench. When she turned her back to him, her skin prickled, not unpleasantly, but with curious anticipation.

"We are alone, Becca," he said as she turned to face him. "You and this man. Does it frighten you?"

She moistened her lips with the tip of her tongue, and her stomach did flip-flops. "Should it?" Waves of heat washed over her and she took a deep breath.

He came to her then and took her in his arms. "There can be nothing between us, my Becca," he whispered huskily. "Nothing but a few stolen days in this haunted valley. Will you steal them with me?"

She stood stiffly in his embrace for long seconds, then slowly, her resistance melted. She laid her head against his chest and listened to the strong, regular beat of his heart. She let his scent envelop her. Then, almost as if she was dreaming, she slowly smiled and looked up into his dark, almond shaped eyes. "Talon," she answered. "Talon, I—"

"Do not say it." He closed her lips gently with

two calloused fingers. "Do not say that we are enemies, or that you belong to another. Do not say that once we leave this place, we can never think or speak of this time again."

"But I—" she began.

"No. Do not tell me that what we do breaks the laws of your people and mine." His big hand cupped her cheek and one fingertip stroked a stray lock of her hair. "There is no need to say what we both know."

"Talon." She needed to say his name . . . needed to hear him say hers, not in anger, but in yearning.

"Becca."

How sweet the sounds were in her ears. No one, not even Colin, said her name in just that way. Trembling, not from cold but excitement, she drew in a ragged breath and laid her hand over his. "I don't care," she whispered.

"I care," he said with wrenching emotion. "I care more for you than right or wrong. I care enough to trade my honor for a chance to—"

"Talon." Happiness bubbled up inside her as her barriers crumbled. "Stop talking and kiss me."

He did not have to be told twice. He bent down and brushed her lips with his. And once again, for Rebecca, the earth shifted under her feet. She threw her arms around his neck and pulled him closer, as the kiss that began with hesitant tenderness slowly deepened into something more.

How perfectly we fit, she thought, arms and chins and lips, without effort or conscious thought . . . fit as though we were two halves of a whole that were separated and now have come together. And with that thought came such a wave of pent-up longing that Rebecca closed her eyes and gave herself over to the unfamiliar sensations of delight.

She clung to him, wanting the kiss to go on and on. His tongue slid between her teeth, and she gave a little cry of surprise and then intense pleasure. Two could play this wonderful game. She savored the taste and texture of his mouth, the sweetness of his breath, and the feel of his strong, hard fingers twining in her hair. Simon had always smelled of tobacco and sometimes of rum. Talon's mouth was clean and minty, as fresh as new snow.

His body molded against hers, all sinew and bone, so different from her own, and yet so familiar. She had sensed he would feel like this, and she could not get enough of him.

His fingers moved down to trace the raised bruises on her throat, and she felt him stiffen. When she opened her eyes and looked into his, she saw such a fierce flame raging there that she shivered. His eyes are as wild and untamed as the puma's, she thought. But then he stroked her hair and kissed the bruises with a touch as light as a butterfly's wing, and she knew that the fire in Talon burned to protect her, never to do her harm.

Tears welled up in her eyes, and their lips met again. He trailed a series of soft caresses to her ear and down to her neck. One bronze hand supported the back of her head while his other slid down to support the curve of her spine. And all the while, he murmured endearments to her in the Indian tongue—words she needed no translation to understand.

A strange excitement possessed her. It didn't matter that it was broad daylight, or that she was a married woman. She wanted him to go on kissing her. She wanted to feel his hands on her, his warm skin pressed against hers.

As if reading her mind, he kissed her again and again. And he kept on kissing her until the giddiness in her head spilled over and made her laugh with the joy of it. Her lips parted, and their tongues touched and delved and explored with eagerness.

Never had she imagined that anything could feel as right and good. But the kiss was not enough. She wanted more. She wanted ... wanted ... An elusive desire teased the corners of her mind as sweet languidness spread through her body.

Her head sank back; she lay in the circle of his arms with heaving breasts and trembling hands. He cupped her chin in one broad hand and tilted her face. With feather-light kisses he caressed her brows and cheekbones and the curve of her bottom lip.

She sighed with pleasure. Boldly, she touched his exposed chest, running her fingers over the lean, hard sinew, feeling the silken smooth surface of bronzed skin over muscle and bone. His chest was hairless, the curves of his shoulder a marvel of coiled and graceful brawn.

He groaned.

"Shall I stop?" she asked shyly.

"*Ku.* No—don't stop. Touch this man where you will."

Shivers of delight ran through her. How could a man's body feel so hard and yet so soft at the same time? What brazen woman could find such joy in fondling him?

"Kiss me," he commanded.

This time, she knew to part her lips. This time, she met his passion with a blend of innocence and tantalizing sensuality. And when he filled her mouth with his hard tongue, she welcomed him, and reveled in the spirals of ecstasy that drove all modesty, all restraint from her mind.

His hands were on her, sliding down her back and over her buttocks, molding her against him. And breathless, shaken by the force of the electricity that leaped between them, she made no resistance when he picked her up and carried her to the bed.

"Is this wrong?" she asked him, as he leaned over her.

"Does it feel wrong?"

"No, no," she protested. "It feels more right than anything I've ever known."

His fingers found the hem of her Indian gown and raised it to her thigh. She gasped as his strong hand touched her bare leg.

"Shall I stop, Becca?" he asked. His dark eyes were heavy lidded with desire. "Do you want me to stop?"

"No," she said. "No." The heat of the fire had leaped to her loins as his lips brushed the place his fingers had touched.

"Oh," she cried. His tongue traced tiny circles on her inner thigh.

"Do you like that, Becca?" he asked.

"Yes, yes." It was hard to breathe. She tossed her head from side to side, not understanding the need that drove her beyond reason. "Make love to me," she whispered. "Please, make me a woman."

"But you are a woman," he replied. "The most vital woman this man has ever known." His hand moved higher to brush her nether curls and she gasped with surprise as warm dampness seeped from her cleft.

"Trust me," he said. And he took her hand in his and pressed it against the hard length of muscle beneath his loincloth. "Trust me."

Chapter 17

All shame and modesty was lost as Rebecca gave herself over to the pleasure of Talon's touch, of his whispered endearments, and her emotional fulfillment of finally being desired by a man. She closed her eyes and made no protest when he slipped her dress over her head. Her stays and stockings followed, until she lay beneath him clad only in her unbound hair.

"Why are you afraid?" he asked her.

Trembling, she opened her eyes and looked full into his face. "I'm not," she lied.

"You are so beautiful." He traced the outline of her lips with one fingertip with a touch so light she might have imagined it. "So pale and so beautiful."

"And you," she echoed. It was true. His blue-black hair, his bronzed skin, his eyes as deep and dark as the night sea made Simon's fairness seem a fault. Surely, God's first man, Adam, must have strode the Garden of Eden with glowing, honeyed limbs and flashing midnight eyes. Talon was as hairless as a youth, but there was nothing of the boy about him. His lean, muscled neck, his powerful chest, his hips and legs as hard and smooth as any dancer's revealed his manhood with every movement.

"My sky-eyed Becca," he murmured. "I have always wondered how a human sees out of blue eyes." His hands were moving over her, making delightful sensations run through her body.

"I see well enough," she teased, "to know a seducer when—"

"Is that what this man is?" His fingers drew an imaginary line along her collarbone. "Am I a seducer?"

She sighed with pleasure. "That or a sorcerer. You have bewitched me."

"Perhaps it is this haunted valley."

"Perhaps," she murmured.

They kissed again, their twentieth or hundredth caress. She dind't know or care. His fingers now were cupping her breast, stroking and teasing first one and then the other, until her nipples tingled and grew hard, and she could not lie still under his touch.

And then, when she thought he could not surprise her again, he did. He lowered his head and took one aching bud between his lips, drawing such sweet sensations from her that she cried out and arched her back, pulling him ever closer.

"Oh," she cried.

"Do you like that?" he asked huskily.

"Oh, yes," she replied. "I never knew a man . . ." She left the rest unspoken. He was suckling at her breast again—like a baby, but not like any baby. She hadn't known that men did that with women . . . hadn't known or guessed how wonderful it would feel.

"You have such beautiful breasts," he said. "I want to touch them . . . lick them . . . drink the nectar from your buds."

"Yes . . . yes."

Long, lean fingers teased the folds of flesh at the

apex of her thighs, teased and gently probed within to worry the tiny knot until she was wet and slippery with desire.

"Talon," she whispered. "Talon." Caught up in the heat of his sensual lovemaking, she moaned and dug her fingers into his back. "Please," she begged. "Please."

Gently, he spread her knees apart and knelt between them. Then she felt him nudge her with the tip of his swollen sex. She thrust her hips upward, wanting him as she had never wanted anything before.

And he filled her with his love.

There was a deep tearing sensation and searing pain. Rebecca gasped as she tried to adjust to the raw hurt. He stopped and kissed her again, soothing her with soft sounds and warm fingers. He kissed her breasts and her mouth, and then slowly withdrew and slid into her again.

She caught her breath, waiting for the pain to begin again. But this time all she felt was an uncomfortable soreness.

"Becca, Becca," he murmured. "I cannot . . ." He moved again, plunged deep and shuddered as a spasm rocked him. "Oh, Becca," he cried.

Afterwards, he held her in his arms and kissed her face and hair. She turned her face to his chest and lay there ashamed and confused. And something more . . . something she could not explain, even to herself. She felt . . . unfinished . . . disappointed. All the wonderful excitement, all the wild longing had led to nothing more than pain and . . .

She could not look him in the eye. She had failed him, she knew it. She had failed as a woman.

"Becca, Becca," he said, turning her face until he

could look into it. "Why didn't you tell me that your husband never—"

"Never took his rights?" She began to weeep softly.

"If I had known ..." He trailed off. "Oh, my fox-haired Becca, it isn't your fault. You have never known a man. Many women have pain the first time. But it will never happen again, I promise you."

She turned face down to the blankets. She felt foolish—stupid. Yes, she'd heard that a girl had discomfort, even bled a little when her maidenhood was pierced. But she hadn't thought that she ... Again, she dissolved in tears.

He stretched out beside her and rubbed her back, then kissed the hollow between her shoulder blades. She sniffed and dried her eyes. Talon continued massaging her shoulders and neck, lifting the mass of her hair to brush his lips along her hairline.

In a little while, she sighed and nestled against him. His body was warm, and he made her feel safe. The soothing motion of his fingers drained the tension from her muscles, and his soft words made her lips turn up in a smile. Drowsy, she closed her eyes and listened to the wind outside. It was easier not to think, just to soak up the warmth of the fire and the man ... to let him go on stroking her ...

Until he kissed her lips and she found to her surprise that the excitement had not died, but was only banked like the glowing coals of a hearth, waiting for a gust of wind to ignite the fire.

This time when he kissed her breasts and teased them until they grew hard and tingling, she was brave enough to touch him in his most vulnerable places. With wonder, she discovered the power she had over him, as her fingers explored the length of his satin tumescence and the soft pouch beneath.

Talon groaned with pleasure, and she grew more brazen. Soon they were locked in an embrace so heated that the blankets fell away and neither noticed.

This time, when he entered her, her passion was greater than the discomfort. She strained against him as his engorged shaft plunged deep within her with slow, deliberate strokes. And when he withdrew, she found that she didn't want him to leave her. She cried out and arched against him, clutching his shoulders and murmuring sweet nothings. What seemed so strange at first became natural as she found the rhythm, moving with him ... taking and giving joy with each thrust. Tension rose within her and she felt as though she was caught in a current that swept her faster and faster, until—

Suddenly, an invisible dam burst inside. Pinwheels of light and giddy sensations rocked her, and she cried out with unexpected bliss. She felt Talon stiffen and shudder with his own consummation, and the hot gush of his seed flowed into her womb. And then they were both floating on a lazy tide of shared contentment that lasted for what seemed forever.

"What manner of man is Simon Brandt that he would leave you untouched?" he demanded suddenly.

She shook her head. "I don't know. I always thought it was me ... that I wasn't ... you know ..."

"Never think that, never. You are the stuff of a

warrior's dreams, my Becca. The fault is Simon Brandt's, not yours."

"Not completely. Simon has injuries. His—"

"I know his injuries," Talon answered harshly. "I gave them to him."

"You?"

"We fought hand to hand, each trying to kill the other. He wounded me gravely—I did the same for him. It has always been my greatest regret that I didn't finish him there on the riverbank."

"If he had told me in the beginning, maybe I wouldn't have ..." She couldn't finish, couldn't defend him. In truth, Simon was the last thing she wanted to think of now.

"I am glad," Talon said.

"Glad?"

"It warms my heart that he could not claim you as a husband—that this man should be the first to share pleasures of the mat with you." He kissed her tenderly. "The first time is a gift from a woman to a man," he whispered. "I thank you."

"It was magic," she said, "I didn't know—"

He smiled at her tenderly. "I will teach you, my precious one. This man will show you more than you ever dreamed." Then he rose from the bed and brought warm water to clean the smears of blood from her thighs. He rocked her against him and brushed her hair with an antler comb and then sang to her a Delaware love song until her heart was at peace.

All day they lay in bed, whispering tales of their childhood, some happy and some sad. She told him of her family in Ireland and the tragedy that followed her father's death because of her illegitimacy. He kissed away her tears and expressed shock that such a thing could happen, and then re-lated another funny story about his stay in Williamsburg that made her laugh. Neither mentioned Simon Brandt again, nor the trouble between white men and red, and neither mentioned what would happen when they left this place. Today, there was only Talon and Rebecca and the comfort of freely given embraces and teasing kisses.

As he promised, Talon served her, bringing roast turkey—only a little charred on the outside—to her bed with a flourish. He flavored melted snow with berries and a little maple sugar to make her a steaming bowl of tea, and shared it with her sip for sip. The sipping turned easily enough to kissing, and before either knew it, the bowl of berry tea spilled out on the plank floor and they were in each other's arms.

And neither knew or cared that the storm raged all through the night and into the following morning.

By that evening, after two days of passionate lovemaking, the two discovered that the storm had blown itself out. The clouds cleared away and the velvet blue sky was strewn with stars. Rebecca and Talon dressed in their warmest clothes and walked out into the cold, still night together. The pristine snow lay in heaped drifts, as high as Rebecca's head. Everything was still; no birdcall or animal cry disturbed the forest solitude.

The frozen woods seemed vast and a little frightening to Rebecca. "Is this valley really haunted, do you suppose?"

He shrugged. "Perhaps. But I do not think the ghosts will hurt us. We have not come to disturb their rest."

She stepped closer to him and his hand clasped

hers. For a long time, they stood there, not speaking, then he turned and led her back inside.

Hanging on one wall of the cabin was a pair of snowshoes. Talon took them down, tested the thongs, and made ready to go hunting. "I don't know about you," he said, "but this man is tired of turkey. The deer will be herded up in the deep snow. I'll find us some tender venison. You stay near the fire and keep warm."

She knew that what he said made sense, but it was hard to let him go. Alone, she might begin to think, and she wanted to avoid that at all costs. "Will you be gone long?" she asked. It was a foolish question. A hunt took as long as it took. No hunter could say for certain how far he would have to search for game or if his shot would fly true. "Be careful."

He smiled at her. "Men lie low in such weather, and the bears are all sleeping. So long as I don't break a leg or lose my way, I'll come back to you."

His teasing was little comfort. She sat by the hearth and waited for an hour or two or three, jumping at every rustle of a mouse or creak of the ice melting on the chimney. She paced the floor nervously, and made up the bed, then stripped away the covers and went outside to break pine boughs to make a mattress. Red cheeked and shivering, she carried them in, beat them against the floor to shake off the snow, heaped them on the sleeping platform.

When the covers were in place once more, she hit upon the idea of making a checkerboard and playing pieces. Using a burned stick from the fireplace, she drew squares on the table, then patiently cut sections from pine branches to use as checkers. Half she left natural, half she colored with charcoal to make them black. She was just lining them up in their places when she heard Talon's shout of greeting.

He'd brought home venison as he'd promised. A yearling buck lay across his shoulders. He carried the field-dressed animal inside and hung it by the front legs to a wooden peg wedged in a rafter near the door. "I'd leave it outside," he said, "but I'm afraid it would draw wolves. Two followed me back."

She brought him water to wash and listened to his story of how he'd found the deer and picked his quarry. He'd killed it instantly with a single shot, he explained. He would have gotten back sooner, but the weight of the animal made it difficult to walk in the snowshoes.

While he held his hands to the fire, Rebecca sliced the liver and propped pieces on green sticks over the coals. They talked and laughed as the rich smell of roasting venison permeated the small cabin.

Then Rebecca remembered something that had troubled her. "Your sister," she said. "When we were running away from the militia, we fell down an embankment. Siipu's mask twisted aside. Talon." She looked at him meaningfully. "Talon, Siipu's face is as smooth as mine. She isn't scarred by the fire. So why does she wear the mask?"

He shook his head and sighed. "Losing our mother and what happened to Siipu after—what the white men did to her—scarred her worse than any flames could do. She is scarred, Becca, but her scars are within. Sometimes, they are the worse, the scars another cannot see."

"But I still don't undertsand."

He squeezed her hand. "My sister believes they

are there," he said. "When she looks into a pool of water, or passes a mirror, she sees the scarring on her face. For her, the burn scars are there, and no one can convince her that they're not."

"So she covers a scar that doesn't exist?"

"It exists. It is real. We just cannot see it. It is why she has taken the name Losowahkun—the burned one."

"But can't someone convince her—"

"No, my Becca. This man has tried, her people have tried."

"So she lives all alone with her animals."

"She is happy, or as happy as Siipu can be."

"Are you sure, Talon?"

He shruggd. "Who can say about the happiness of another? Each must follow his own path. Siipu has many who love her."

For a few minutes, silence lay between them. Then she remembered the game she'd assembled. "I made a checker game," she told him. "Do you play?" He shook his head. "I know enough to teach you," she said modestly. Her father had taught her when she was small, and they had often waged a war across the checkerboard that lasted for hours. Her father had been what was politely regarded as an aggressive player, and she had learned tactics from him.

"Show me your game," he said, "and later, I will teach you how to roll bones. But I warn you, bones is a gambling game, and you must be prepared to wager something of value."

"I'm sure," she answered. They nibbled at the hot meat as she showed him the basic rules of checkers. He was a quick study. She won the first two games and he tied the third fairly.

"Tomorrow I will beat you," he promised, licking his fingers clean of juices.

"Never," she countered.

"We'll see about that."

He glanced at the bed. "It looks higher than before."

"I made a mattress of pine," she told him shyly.

"Is it soft?"

"I don't know."

"Then we'll have to try it, won't we?"

He kissed her mouth and neck, and lifted her hair to whisper in her ear. She laughed and tried to turn away. He caught her and kissed her again.

Somehow, they found their way to the bed. It was softer, but they would have been just as happy on the plank floor. He made slow, tender love to her all that night, and the next morning, she watched with sleepy eyes as he carved a flute from turkey bone.

"What will you do with it when it's finished?" she teased.

"I will do what all Shawnee men do for the women they desire. I will play such songs of longing that they will melt your heart and you will welcome me into your blanket."

"I think I already have."

He laughed. "But you will do so again. I am a great musician."

"I think you are a great braggart."

"Wait until you hear me play."

"On a bone?" She giggled. "First you tell me you gamble with them and now play tunes. Why do I think I'm not going to like this music?"

But when he did begin to draw music from the primitive instrument, it touched a chord deep inside her, and she could not keep her eyes from sparkling with tears. So fey was the high, sweet sound that she closed her eyes and listened, letting the ancient melody run through her until the lonely cry of a wolf shattered the mood. Shivering, she went to him and begged him to hold her.

"My playing must be bad if the wolf protests," he said as he lay down the flute.

"You are a man of many accomplishments," she said. "Next you will be reading poetry to me."

"I am a poet," he agreed. "But I have written none of my poems on paper. Sometime, I will recite some of them for you."

She sighed and snuggled closer to him. "Are you certain you're not Irish?" she asked. "For who but an Irishman could be so full of himself?"

"No, Becca. This man is not Irish, or English. This man is born of a Delaware mother and a Shawnee father. You must not forget that. For we are different. This man does not think as a white man does."

A shiver ran through her as she looked into his eyes. Firelight reflected in the black depths. Firelight and something more—a wildness that she could not hope to understand. What have I done? she wondered. What have I done to go willingly to the bed of someone so alien? Will I spend the rest of my life regretting these few days? Or ... She drew in a deep breath. Will I spend the rest of my life wishing that I was here again in this haunted valley with Talon in my arms?

Chapter 18

For seven days Rebecca and Talon shut out the world. They thought of nothing but each other and the giving and taking of sensual pleasure and of laughter. They played at checkers and the Indian gambling game and told each other stories of giants and ghosts and magic springs. The weather turned warm and the snow melted, washed away by a deluge of rain. But they were snug inside the cabin, heated by the fireplace and their love and nourished by venison and sweet words.

On the morning of the eighth day, Talon shook Rebecca awake. "You must divorce Simon Brandt," he declared. "I have decided. This man wants you as his wife. You must break your ties with your husband."

She looked at him with sleepy doe eyes. How long they'd lain awake the night before making love, he wasn't sure. When the cabin door was closed and he couldn't see the sky, it was hard to tell one day from the next. "What?" she murmured, yawning. "What did you say?"

"This man tells you you must divorce your husband," he repeated. He had thought about it for days now. What was between them was more than the pleasure a man took from between a woman's thighs. He wanted Rebecca beside him; he wanted her to be the mother of his children, he wanted her to walk hand in hand with him when his hair had turned gray with age. He loved her as he had never loved another woman, and he had decided that she was the bride he'd waited for most of his life. He knew that they were very different, that it wouldn't be easy, but a good marriage such as his parents had shared was worth fighting for. "Marry me, Becca. Marry me and become a good Shawnee wife."

Startled, she sat up and the covers fell away, revealing her full curving breasts. The cool air made her nipples harden, and he had to struggle with himself to keep from touching them. His throat constricted as his loins tightened with desire. He wanted to possess her again and again. Each time was as exciting for him as the first. Like clear water from a sparkling brook, each drink made him want more.

Her blue eyes dilated with sorrow. "I can't marry you," she whispered.

Rejection stung like the snap of a broken bow string, and indignation turned his voice cold. "Can't or won't? Is it me you will not have to husband, or the color of my skin?"

"How can you say that?" She reached for his hand, but he snatched it away.

His stomach burned and he felt as empty inside as if he had gone days without eating. "Why, Becca? Why can't you marry me?"

Her face paled as though he had slapped her. "I'm married, Talon, you know that. I'm Catholic. My marriage vows are for life. I can't divorce."

"You cannot divorce a man you do not love? A man who does not deserve you?"

She shook her head. "You don't understand. I

married in the Church." She raised her hand to show him the ring on her finger.

"Shawnee mothers frighten their unruly children with tales of Simon Brandt. He has no respect for the aged or suckling babes; he murders them indiscriminately. Your church would ask a woman to stay with such a monster?"

She hung her head. "Yes."

He caught her hand, slipped the hateful ring from her finger, and flung it with such force into the fire that sparks flew. "If you stay with me, you leave white laws behind. I will protect you, Becca. You will have as many rights as any Indian woman. Our women rid themselves of unwanted husbands whenever they wish. It is a simple thing for the Shawnee or Delaware to divorce. A marriage without love is a travesty."

She looked up at him then, and one crystal tear glistened on her ashen cheek. "Not for me, Talon. For me, what you ask is impossible."

"You can lie with this man on a bed of pine boughs, but you cannot wed him?"

"No." She pulled the blanket to her chin.

"Do you love Simon Brandt."

"You know I don't."

He would not ask her if she loved him, Fire Talon. The pain would be too great if she said she did not. "And if you were free," he said. "If Simon Brandt was in his grave, then would you marry this man?"

"I . . . I honestly don't know," she answered huskily. "I . . . can't tell you that." Her lower lip quivered. "Do you hear what you're asking me? Do you expect me to sanction my husband's death? I don't want you to kill him."

"What do you want, *ki-te-hi?*" *My heart.* His voice thickened with sarcasm.

"I want Colin!" she cried. "You took him from me. I want him back."

"I tried to find him, Becca. I—"

"Well, you're not trying hard enough—are you?"

He reached for his loin cloth and belt and wound them over his naked loins. "What a hostage wants does not matter very much. But this man does not speak with the tongue of his enemies the *Englishmanakes.* If your brother lives, I will find him; if I live, I will slay Simon Brandt."

"And if I hate you afterwards? What then, Talon? What if I can't bear for you to touch me with my husband's blood on your hands?"

Anger made him cruel. He stiffened and turned away. "Make yourself ready," he ordered. "We start the journey to my village today."

"And what will you do with me there?"

For that question, he had no answer.

The half-breed Indian woman called Ready Mary by the English, but *Shash-kee-thee* by her mother's people, lay hidden in her nest of soft blankets as the two-wheeled cart rocked and jolted over the narrow trail. For days, she had thought of what she'd seen and heard at the white fort. And then, when she finally made up her mind where her duty lay, the cart appeared as if by magic. No need for Mary to walk through frozen woods and cross ice-covered rivers; the soldiers' wagon would carry her where she wanted to go.

At the fort, she carried water, washed clothes, and dumped pee buckets, when she was not occupied with satisfying the drunken desires of white men. Here in the cart, there was nothing for her to do but sleep and soak up the warmth of the heavy, Quaker wool blankets. Once she had owned a red and blue blanket almost as nice as these; a soldier had given it to her when she was still young with firm breasts and all her teeth. Now, no one gave her expensive gifts. Sometimes, men gave her whiskey or food, but only if she did what they asked.

Mary was glad she'd decided to carry word of Medicine Smoke's death to his tribe. It was the right thing to do. It made her heart feel glad, and as reward, she was leaving behind the white fort and the men who treated her so badly. She hoped that Medicine Smoke's son had whiskey and that he would share it with her. At night, her teeth hurt and she had bad dreams. The whiskey made her sleep. If she went too long without it, her head ached.

When the soldiers camped, she crept from the cart in the darkness and helped herself to food and drink. Once she stole a flask of rum from an officer's tent. At daybreak, when he discovered his loss, there was much shouting. But Mary didn't care. Let the blue-eyed soldiers be blamed. She clutched the flask close to her sagging breasts and sipped at it until the mules brayed and the cart began to sway again.

At last the British troops reached a small Delaware town and Mary slid from the back of the wagon and hid behind a wigwam. She realized at once that these people were certainly not Shawnee, but the soldiers didn't seem to know the difference. The big-nosed sergeant began handing out blankets from the first cart to anyone who came forward. They had no sense of order, these white men. They did not offer the wonderful gifts of the wool blankets with proper ceremony, and they didn't wait to receive presents in return. In less than an hour, they had turned back toward the white fort while the Delaware stared at them in utter dismay.

Mary came out of hiding in time to snatch two blankets for herself, a green and black one and a gray one with a blue stripe. Mary was not a Delaware, but she understood the language well enough. She quickly introduced herself and told the gape-mouthed women to help themselves to the blankets.

"The white soldiers are ignorant," she explained. "They know no better. Their mothers beat all common sense out of them with sticks when they are still on the tit. Take the blankets before they realize this wasn't the Shawnee village they were looking for and come back for them."

It was a very cold day, and swirls of snow and sleet were falling. This village site was new; these people had been driven from their cornfields farther east on the Juniata. Their old village had been burned, and they had lost most of their belongings. When Mary urged them to take the blankets, the women surged forward. But even in their need, they did not push or take more than their share.

Mary almost felt greedy, having two blankets, when some women got none. But she told herself that she had come from the white fort with the precious blankets. That made her almost one of the gift-givers. She was entitled to a double share. After all, other than the silver flask which was now as dry as last year's bone, she had no other possessions.

They made her welcome, these Delaware. They did not mind that her dress was torn and dirty, or that her hair was matted. No one laughed at her toothless grin or called attention to her worn moccasins. Instead, she was offered a sweat bath and new clothing. And she found herself the guest of honor at a feast that night.

Yes, Mary thought, as she stuffed another bite of fat, roasted raccoon into her mouth, she was truly receiving the blessings of the spirits for her courage. Even respected warriors leaned close in rapt attention to listen to her tale of perfidy. And when she told of Medicine Smoke's hanging, there were groans and cries of outrage.

"I must carry the word to his son, the great war chief, Fire Talon," she concluded. "It is only fitting that he know of his father's death and Simon Brandt's plot to trade a dead body for a live captive."

"*Yohu! Yohu!*" her audience called. Yes! Yes! It was only right that she do this. And a handsome young man with a shaved head and red-dyed scalplock leaped to his feet.

"Chimhe will guide you to the village of the Mecate Shawnee," he shouted. "My cousin lives there. They have moved across the Ohio, but this hunter knows where they pitch their wigwams."

Mary nodded with dignity. The brave had broad shoulders and hard thighs. Doubtless, when they were away from his village, he would come to her arms for comfort. In the darkness, her missing teeth did not show, and a man might take her for years younger than she was. "I accept your offer," she said graciously. "The war chief, Fire Talon, will be pleased that you help to carry the message. He may even reward you with a place in his band."

"Ahikta," called a stocky matron whom Mary took for his mother. "Chimhe should go. The Shawnee are our brothers and Fire Talon would do the same for us."

"Tomorrow, then," Chimhe said.

"Yes, tomorrow," Mary agreed, reaching for another corn cake. For tonight she would be content to fill her belly and sleep beside a crackling fire. She was sorry that the Shawnee Village had moved so far away. Walking would not be nearly as pleasant as traveling in the soldiers' cart, but then . . . She smiled. She would have the company of young Chimhe on the journey . . . and she would have the warmth of her good Quaker blankets.

Rebecca followed Talon with shoulders squared and head high. Her legs had adjusted to the long days of walking, and the weight of her pack no longer troubled her. What did bother her was Colin's fate.

When they'd left the cabin, Talon hadn't gone directly to his own village. Instead, they'd traveled four days to the camp where The Stranger had lived to look for her brother. Her high hopes had been dashed when they'd found no trace of Colin or his captor. The Stranger's Delaware wife had died recently, according to her relatives. The Stranger had mourned her passing, had given away all her possessions, then left the village with the boy. He'd not told anyone where they were going. The only thing that had made Rebecca feel better was that several people spoke of the white captive's good health and the kind treatment he'd received.

"The Stranger seemed fond of the English child," an old woman had assured Rebecca. Talon had translated the Algonquian for her, but the smiles and repeated hand patting didn't need explanation.

"I don't understand how they can just vanish," Rebecca had said to Talon later. "Where would they have gone?"

Talon had shrugged. "I cannot say, Becca. The Stranger was a brave warrior, but I didn't really know him. He said he came from the west, far over the plains toward the setting sun. He may have gone trapping for the winter, or . . ." He spread his hands, palms up. "I do not know. Perhaps he returned to his own tribe, or perhaps he took your brother to the French at the Big Lakes."

"This is awful," she'd replied. "He's missing, and it's all your fault for separating us."

"So you've told me."

Their relationship, which had not been the same since he'd asked her to marry him at the cabin, seemed to suffer even more. He'd slept beside her every night, wrapped in a blanket, but he'd not made love to her since they'd left the haunted valley.

And she desperately wanted him to.

Talon had distanced himself from her emotionally. They still spent every hour together, ate together, dressed and bathed within an arm's length of each other, but he was once more the Shawnee war chief. And she was again the wife of his greatest enemy.

He had told her this morning that they were only a short distance from his village. The day before, they'd crossed the Ohio River in a canoe Talon had found buried in some bushes. The boat was old and it leaked, but it was sufficiently strong to carry them across the swift body of water. She'd asked him how he'd known where to look, and he'd explained that it was courtesy to leave a canoe on either side in a certain place for passage.

Today, they had risen and started walking without even cooking breakfast. "We will eat at the village," he'd assured her. She hoped so; she was starving. The cold duck they'd shared the night before had hardly been enough to feed one, let alone two.

"How much farther do we have to go?" she called to him. He looked back over his shoulder and raised a finger to his lips. "But you said—" she began.

"Quiet. Village guards will—"

Suddenly, an Indian dropped from a tree directly in their path. Talon rushed forward and clapped the man on the shoulder. The lookout spoke to him in Algonquian and Talon replied in English for Rebecca's benefit.

"It's good to see you, Water Snake. This man does not need to ask about your leg. If you can climb trees, then you are healed."

The thin young brave grinned. A scar marred his top lip and chin. He was dressed for the cold in long leggings, fur-lined moccasins, and a beaver skin cloak. In one hand, he carried a French long rifle with silver engraving on the stock. He motioned in the direction they were heading, then said something more in his own tongue.

"Water Snake tells me that Counts and the others are already here. He says a stranger has come to bring me a message."

"A stranger?" Becca asked excitedly. "Does he say anything about a white boy? Is it the man who took Colin prisoner?"

Talon shook his head. "A stranger, not The Stranger," he corrected. "This is not the one you seek. This is a woman, a mixed blood. Water Snake says she brings word from the white settlements—word for my ears only."

Water Snake said something more in quick, low tones.

"He also says the woman is unwell. She suffers a fever and muscle aches."

"Is the village far?"

Talon asked, then shook his head. "About a mile. Water Snake is one of several roving scouts. There should be no whites on this side of the Ohio, but Fox is cautious. Come, you can rest before a fire and fill your hunger in the wigwam of my father's sister."

Dogs began to bark as they neared the village. More men came out to greet Talon, and then a few women, and finally children. Mongrel dogs crept close to sniff and growl at her. A small flock of turkeys scattered, and a large Canada goose flattened his long neck and hissed at her. A little girl in braids, no more than seven years old, clapped her hands and chased the goose away.

There were more houses than Rebecca expected. This was obviously a large village, not only big, but new. The remaining small trees showed signs of fresh trimming. There seemed to be no order, no streets as an English town might have. Wigwams, some round, some oval, and some that reminded her of Siipu's longhouse, were scattered around a natural meadow. Most of the houses were constructed of saplings and bark, but some were roofed in animal hide, or even woven reeds. Near the center of the encampment stood a long, unfinished building of logs without any chimneys.

"What's that?" Rebecca asked Talon. "Is that your chief's house?"

He chuckled. "No. That's the Big House, a religious gathering place, almost like your church. It will be used for political meetings as well."

Rebecca counted more than a hundred onlookers before she gave up. Women with babies, old people, everyone seemed to be happy to see Talon; it was obvious he was popular. Then she saw a familiar face, the man Talon called Fox.

"My friend," Talon shouted.

Fox threw his arms around him. "Counts is here and Osage Killer. We convinced your sister to come back with us, but the hard part was to get her to leave that cat. She says she will only stay until Counts recovers."

"The wound does not turn bad, does it?" Talon asked.

Fox shook his head. "Your sister is a powerful witch." He grinned. "Besides, Counts is too mean to die." He glanced at Rebecca. "Do you draw breath?" he asked her.

She looked at him in confusion. "What?"

"It is a traditional greeting," Talon said.

"I'm glad to see you too, Fox," she said.

He nodded. "There is someone to see you, Talon. A woman from the white fort. She arrived several days ago with a Delaware named Chimhe. He says he hunted buffalo with you. Do you know him?"

"Yes. He is trustworthy," Talon answered. "I will see this woman. Take her"—he motioned to Rebecca—"to Squash Blossom's wigwam. Ask the sister of my father to treat her kindly. This man has not provided food today, and she is hungry."

"No," Rebecca said. She didn't want to be

stowed away at Talon's aunt's house. She wanted to hear the news from the settlements first hand. "I want to come with you," she insisted.

Talon frowned. "It would be better to do as this man suggests."

"I want to come," she repeated stubbornly. There might be some news of Colin or even of Simon. There might be word of Talon's father. She didn't want to think about that ... about what would happen if Siipu had been right—if the old man was dead. A shiver ran down Rebecca's spine. "Please, Talon," she said.

He turned and strode away. No one tried to stop her when she followed, but her skin tingled from the stares of dozens of eyes. Children ran after her, reaching out to touch her skin or the edge of her clothing. The dogs continued to bark and run in circles.

The village smelled of wood smoke and leather. The curious people watching her with such relish had red-brown skin, but other than that, they could have been Irish peasants from the little hamlet near her father's house. Some were short, some were tall; a few were fat, but most were handsomely built with clear, bright eyes and intelligent faces. The children were relatively clean and obviously healthy. They were all warmly dressed against the cold. She could detect no hostility toward her, in spite of the difficult relations between whites and the tribes.

I could learn to like these friendly, laughing people, she thought. If I spoke their language, I could gossip with them and share their jokes. And for just a brief instant, she wondered what her life would be like if she could do as Talon had asked her ... if she could set aside Simon and take Talon as husband.

She was so engrossed in her own musings that she nearly ran into Talon. He had stopped in front of a wigwam that looked much like all the others. He followed Fox through the low doorway and held aside the deerskin flap for her.

Inside, Rebecca paused to let her eyes become accustomed to the dim light. The hut was similar to Siipu's home, but here the smell of wet fur and simmering stew was tempered with an unpleasant scent—the odor of sickness.

Talon circled the fire pit and went to the far side of the wigwam where a gray-haired woman was spooning broth into another woman's mouth. The patient coughed and turned her face away. Rebecca gazed at her intently. In the shadows, it was hard to tell, but she looked like ... Yes, she knew the sick woman from the fort. She was a laundry woman named Ready Mary. "Isn't that Mary?" she asked Talon.

"This is Shash-kee-thee," Talon said. "In our tongue, her name means Virgin. She says she did work for the white soldiers at Fort Nelson."

The woman's face was drawn and pasty. Two unnatural spots of color tinted her cheeks. Seized by a spasm of coughing, she covered her mouth with her hands. Her nurse looked at Talon and shook her head gravely, then retreated to the far side of the hut.

"You are the war chief Fire Talon?" Shash-kee-thee demanded hoarsely, when she could speak.

He nodded. "What message do you bring me? Has Medicine Smoke sent you?"

"I have come—" She broke off with another fit of coughing. "Come at great personal risk, to tell

you of your father's death," she said in Algonquian.

"Medicine Smoke no longer lives?" Talon asked
in the same language.

"Simon Brandt hanged him."

"When?"

Shash-kee-thee shook her head. "I don't remember how many days ago. Before the long-knife militia rode out to hunt your warriors. Many suns."

"You saw this with your own eyes?" he demanded of her.

The sick woman nodded solemnly. "I saw," she
said. "The shaman died bravely."

"What is she saying?" Rebecca asked.

Talon turned back to her, and his face seemed
carved of sun-dried cedar. "My father is dead," he
said in an emotionless voice. "Hanged at the English fort."

"It's not true," she protested. "It can't be." She
looked back at the coughing woman. "Why are
you saying that, Mary?" she cried. "They wouldn't
hang Medicine Smoke. If they did—"

Talon knelt and gathered a handful of cold ashes
from the edge of the fire pit and scattered them
over the flames. "Then your life would be worth
no more than this," he said. "If the Shaman has
been murdered, then of what use to the Shawnee
is a hostage?"

Chapter 19

Sick numbness spread through Rebecca as she watched Talon kneel by the fire pit and rub ashes on his face. He began to chant, a low eerie song that could only be a mourning hymn for his dead father.

"Talon, I'm so sorry," she whispered. Her first instinct was to put her arms around him and comfort him, but she was afraid. This wasn't the man she'd made love to so passionately; this Shawnee warrior with the features of carved cedar was someone she didn't know.

"Talon," she tried again. But he didn't respond; he didn't even seem to hear her. It was as if a wall of solid ice divided them.

What Siipu had seen in her witch's vision was real. Rebecca's worst nightmare was coming true. It didn't seem possible to her that the commander at Fort Nelson would do such a thing, knowing that the old man's execution would put her life in such terrible danger. Deep inside, her suspicion grew that it was not the commandant, but Simon and his blind hate for the Indians who was responsible.

Gathering her courage, she reached out to touch Talon's arm.

"Ku!" The gray-haired woman who had tended

237

Mary pulled her away from him and shook her head. *"Ku!"*

"I didn't mean any harm," Rebecca said. "I only . . ." She trailed off as she saw the old squaw's forbidding expression.

Ignoring her, Talon rocked back and forth. Rebecca saw the gleam of firelight on his knife blade as he slid the ten-inch weapon from the fringed sheath at his waist.

Her heart skipped a beat. She clapped a hand over her mouth and backed away as full realization hit her. Talon had repeatedly promised that he would kill her if his father died at the hands of the English. Until this instant, she had never believed he would. Now . . . It took all her will power to keep from fleeing the wigwam.

He's going to murder me, she thought. I'm going to die here and now.

But pride wouldn't let her grovel. She was Irish born and bred, and if he wanted to kill her, he could do so with her staring him full in the face.

But he made no threatening move toward her. Instead, he slashed his own arms until blood ran down to sizzle in the flames of the fire.

Sickened, she turned away. I will never understand him, she thought. Never. Cold air brushed her cheek, and when she looked again, he was gone.

The squaw's seamed face contorted in grief as she crouched down and began a high-pitched keening. Rebecca glanced back toward Mary, but the laundress's eyes were shut and her head was slumped to one side. Rebecca wondered if she was dead, but when she drew closer, she saw that Mary's chest still rose and fell, and she heard her harsh breathing.

Rebecca wasn't sure what to do. Staying here with these two was unthinkable, but if she followed Talon outside, would he remember his threat and carry it out? Cautiously, she pushed aside the deerskin and peered out. Men and women were gathering beside the unfinished Big House. The steady throb of a drum rose from the left. No one looked at her, and she stepped into the cold air.

"Becca!"

A familiar voice called her name. She turned to see Siipu coming around the wigwam.

"You come," Talon's sister said in her dry, rustling voice. "Not good people see white woman."

Rebecca didn't need to be told twice.

Siipu led her a short way to a round dwelling near the edge of the trees and motioned her to enter. This must be the aunt's home, Rebecca thought, and was surprised to see Counts and Osage Killer inside instead.

Counts His Scalps sat on a sleeping platform with a fur robe drawn up to his waist. His chest was bare; wrapped around his shoulder was a thick bandage of cedar bark. He glanced at her and gave a grunt of recognition as she stood up.

The other man, Osage Killer, sat cross-legged by the fire sharpening a knife on a whetstone. He said something to her in Algonquian and made a hand sign of welcome.

This wigwam was smaller than either Siipu's home or the hut where Ready Mary was being cared for, but Rebecca was struck by the neatness of this dwelling. Weapons, animal skins, and baskets hung from the ceiling and walls, but each piece seemed in its proper place. The fire pit was lined with round fist-sized rocks, and wood was stacked carefully beside it. The house smelled of tobacco and fresh pine.

Siipu waved Rebecca to sit. Awkwardly, she knelt and then crossed her legs. Osage Killer watched her with dark, hooded eyes.

"My brother knows," Siipu said.

Counts frowned. "You should have told him." His English was heavily accented, but Rebecca understood his words. "Wrong for witch to keep word of shaman's death from him."

"What will happen now?" Rebecca asked Siipu.

"He go for father's body," Counts replied tersely.

"To give burial," the masked woman added.

"And me?" Rebecca gazed into her eyes. "What of me?"

"That is for Fire Talon to say," Counts answered. coldly. "He has no time for you now. He must send the shaman across the river with prayer and reverence." He nodded toward Osage Killer. "This warrior will go with him."

"Until my brother come back, you stay this wigwam," Siipu said. "Best you not anger people."

"Unless her moon-time comes," Counts said. "Do you bleed, woman?" he demanded.

Heat scalded Rebecca's cheeks. "No," she stammered. She had had her woman's bleeding while she stayed with Siipu, and Talon's sister had provided her with a soft skin belt and cedar bark padding to keep herself clean.

"This man will have no moon-time woman in his wigwam," Counts declared adamantly in Algonquian. "White or red."

"If her cycle comes, I will take her to the woman's hut," Siipu assured him. "I know the customs of my people. I would never endanger you so."

"A woman's moon blood is taboo for a warrior," he continued. "Female power does not mix with a hunter's weapons. You will cause my rifle to misfire, my arrows to fly crookedly, if you let this white captive defile my house."

"I give you my oath," Siipu replied. "It is not her time. It is safe for her and for you to sleep here."

"Just so we are clear on that," Osage Killer said with a wink. "Counts fears nothing like a bleeding woman."

"I fear nothing, least of all a moon-time female," Counts retorted. "But a man must guard his luck, and a man who has been called to be a shaman must follow the laws of custom more carefully than an ordinary man."

Rebecca looked from one to the other in confusion. What were they arguing about? And why had Counts His Scalps asked such a personal question of her? Even Ready Mary and the old woman seemed more hospitable than the cold and scowling Counts. She could feel the hostility in the air. Counts blamed her in some way for Talon's father's death, and he would not hesitate to kill her without remorse. "Please," she said to Siipu. "If he does not want me here—"

"This best place for you," Talon's sister answered.

"I need to talk to Talon before he goes," Rebecca said. "Will you ask him if he will see me?"

Siipu shook her head. "He mourns our father, he whose name we do not say. No see wife of Simon Brandt."

"But I must," she argued. Talon cared for her—she knew he did. And she loved him, in spite of all that had happened. Memories of her own father's death assaulted her, and she felt Talon's pain. If she could make him understand how sorry she was, then perhaps . . .

But Siipu would not be swayed. "No," she said. "When he return with the body of our father, when we have sent him to the spirits with ceremony, then will be time to do what must be done with prisoner."

The next two days passed slowly. Rebecca did not leave the wigwam except to attend to her personal needs, accompanied by Talon's sister. Fortunately, the injured man, Counts, was seldom there. The village was in mourning for their dead shaman, and Counts His Scalps joined other men in the unfinished Big House for the greater part of every day and evening.

Drums beat continually, and the sound of many people chanting filled the nights. A fire burned in the center of the village. Women gathered there, and Rebecca smelled the odor of roasting meat coming from that direction. But Siipu didn't join the others; instead, she remained in the wigwam and busied herself by stitching a pair of beaded moccasins for Counts.

"He has no wife to sew for him?" Rebecca commented, when the silence between the two women had gone on for hours.

Siipu's soft laughter filled the wigwam. "No. Counts have no wife." She punched another series of holes in the soft buckskin, matched the top and bottom and laced the sole tightly with sinew. "Counts His Scalps not like women."

"But this is his wigwam."

Siipu nodded. "His and Osage Killer's."

"So why are we here, if he doesn't like women?"

"This one heal Counts' wound. You, my brother leave with Counts. Counts honored warrior in tribe. You no run, stay safe until he come back."

"I think I'd rather sleep in a rattlesnake den," Rebecca replied tartly.

The Indian woman held a needle to the firelight and threaded it. "Maybe best you do sleep rattlesnake. Best you, best my brother. Trouble you make for each other."

"You could let me go again. This time, I'd run so fast and so far—"

"No." Siipu shook her head. "No run. Wait."

On the third morning, Rebecca was awakened before dawn by Counts nudging her arm with the toe of his moccasin. "Siipu say you come," he said.

She sat up and rubbed her eyes. She had slept fully dressed, so it was no trouble to rise, throw her coat around her shoulders, and follow him out into the bitter gray dawn. The wind was howling around the wigwams like a wild beast, and she lowered her head against the stinging bite of sleet. Somewhere, a drum still sounded, but other than that, the village seemed asleep. Not a single dog barked or person showed himself. Bits of flying debris struck her exposed skin and found their way into her mouth. Shivering, she squinted against the force of the blast.

Counts led her back to the hut where she'd last seen Ready Mary and left her there. "Inside," he commanded.

When she pushed aside the deerskin and entered, Siipu was waiting. Mary lay flat on her back on a blanket near the hearth. Rebecca took one look at her and shuddered.

Mary's face and arms were sprinkled with hundreds of fiery eruptions. Her eyes were shut, and she was moaning, her swollen face flushed with fever.

Siipu knelt beside her and pressed a wet cloth to Mary's forehead. "You know this sickness?" Talon's sister asked.

Rebecca clenched her hands into tight balls at her sides as fear churned her stomach to nausea. Spots could be anything, she rationalized in desperation. Measles . . . chicken pox. But that wasn't what she was looking at, and she knew it. "I do."

"Ah." Siipu motioned Rebecca to her side. "She suffers." Even with the mask hiding most of Siipu's face, Rebecca could still see the strain and worry etched there.

"Yes." Rebecca could feel the heat radiating from Mary's body. "Yes." Rebecca had seen this before, when she was a child in Ireland. She'd come upon one of the maids lying on the kitchen floor . . . a village girl named Margaret. The other servants had been terrified, mostly because the master's precious daughter had been exposed to the dread disease.

"This has name," Siipu said. "In English."

Rebecca nodded.

"You say the word."

Rebecca looked down at the laundress in horror. Ready Mary was bad, very bad. Margaret had been like this. She hadn't died, but Rebecca could remember the stench of the disease and Margaret's groans of pain. Someone had tied Margaret hands to the bed so she couldn't scratch at the weeping sores, and when the scabs fell off nearly a month later, she was blind.

"What you call this plague?" Siipu demanded.

"Smallpox." Rebecca couldn't help flinching as she uttered the dreaded word.

Siipu exhaled slowly. "This is white man's gift."

"A gift?" Rebecca's gaze moved from the fever-wracked woman to the red-rimmed almond eyes above the deerskin mask. "A curse, not a gift," she said. "My people die of this as well."

"No," Siipu said sharply. "This one not know how or why, but know true. White men give. Wind tells this woman's heart. This time sickness be sent. White men want all Indian die. Man, woman, child. All die. White men plant corn where Shawnee clear field. Graze cattle where our ancestors are buried."

A terrible ache swelled in Rebecca's chest, making it hard for her to breathe. "Have you had the pox, Siipu? Those who have it once never do again."

"No have. My brother get. This one—no."

"When I was a little girl, my mother deliberately exposed me to cowpox. I was sick for a few days, but nothing serious. I don't know how or why, but cowpox prevents you from catching smallpox. Have many of your tribe—"

Siipu shook her head. "No cows. I do not know this cowpox you talk of. Indian catch this—" she gestured toward Mary's pain-wracked body—"Indian die quick."

"But you said Talon had the smallpox, and he didn't die."

"Have when small child—at Williamsburg. When stay with white shaman. White man sickness. White man know how make well. Indian not know."

"I know how to treat someone with smallpox, but I don't know how to make them well. No one does," Rebecca said. "Of those who catch it in Ireland, one in every five die, and many more are left hideously scarred or blinded."

"Not so for Shawnee . . . Delaware," Talon's sister answered softly. "Two sick, one die. Bad, much bad. Indian medicine not strong for white man sickness."

"There is something we can do, if you're willing to take the risk. My father had a half-brother who studied medicine in Edinburgh, in Scotland. He was visiting us when one of our maids died of smallpox. Uncle Beatty took scabs from the sick girl and put them under the skin of our other servants. They got sick, but no one died. We could do the same thing, Siipu. We could use Mary's illness to protect the rest of the tribe against the disease."

"White men do this thing?"

"No. Most do not. Most people are ignorant. But I saw my uncle do it, and I know our servants didn't die. Others in the village died, but not those Uncle Beatty treated."

"You have scab in your skin?"

"No," she admitted. "No, I didn't, because I'd had the cowpox, but my little brother Colin did. He was only a few weeks old. Colin was the first person that Uncle Beatty treated."

"And this brother not die?"

"No. He wasn't even very sick. He didn't catch the smallpox then, and he didn't catch it when we came over on the ship or since . . ." Or had he? She realized that it had been many weeks since she'd last seen Colin . . . or was it months? The image of his laughing face rose in her mind. Oh, Colin, she wondered. Where are you?

Mary moaned, and Rebecca was jerked from her

reverie back to this dim wigwam and the reality of their situation.

Siipu murmured a few soothing words in Algonquian as she removed the cloth and dipped it in water, then wrung it out and replaced it on the patient's forehead. "What can we do for her?"

Rebecca shrugged. "What you're already doing. Keep her warm, give her water, pray."

"You say her sickness can keep people from die?"

"I think so." She covered Siipu's hand with her own. "What have we got to lose?"

"You have much. You do and Indian people die, you die. They call you witch. Blame you for all death."

"If we don't do anything, there will be an epidemic," Rebecca argued.

Siipu got to her feet and rubbed her hands on her deerskin dress. "You put scab of smallpox under your skin? How?"

"My uncle made a small cut—with a piece of glass. And yes, I would do it to myself. But it's not necessary. I can't get the pox. I told you. I—"

"This one hear you say. People not trust wife of Simon Brandt. You do, this one do, maybe they do."

"All right. We'll take the chance," Rebecca said. Her father had trusted his brother with Colin's life, and he hadn't let them down. None of them had realized that it was the last time they'd ever see Uncle Beatty. A few weeks later, on his return voyage to Scotland, his ship was caught in a sudden storm and sank with all hands. She still remembered the tears her father shed when he got the letter telling him of Beatty's death.

How different things would have been for Colin

and me, she mused, if Uncle Beatty had been her father's nearest living relative. We might still be living in our own home in Ireland with my mother . . .

But then I'd never have known Talon . . .

"Why?" Siipu's question intruded on her thoughts. "Why you care about Indian?" she demanded. "Why take chance?"

Rebecca looked at her in astonishment. "Why? What else could I do?"

"Let Indian die."

"No," Rebecca answered firmly. "Not if we can help it."

But convincing Siipu was easier than convincing the rest of the tribe. In the end, after much arguing with the chief and council members, and after she and Talon's sister had both endured the crude inoculation, Counts His Scalps volunteered. Gradually, one by one, most of the villagers submitted to the treatment.

Many people ran fevers, some very high. Siipu's fever sapped her strength, but despite all Rebecca's pleading, the Indian woman would not take to her bed. For days and longer nights, Rebecca and Siipu went from wigwam to wigwam tending the sick. Mary died, and then the old woman who had taken care of her threw herself in the river and drowned. Men, women, and children broke out with pustules, but no one showed symptoms as severe as Mary's.

As weeks passed, Rebecca began to doubt her decision. More and more of the Shawnee became ill. One young woman miscarried of a child. Angry grumbling arose against Rebecca, and she heard the whispered word "witch" as she moved from house to house.

She lost all track of time, often missing meals

and falling asleep in a strange wigwam surrounded by coughing, moaning patients. It seemed to her as if the sheer drudgery of nursing, the exhaustion, the stink of illness, and the bitter, gray weather had gone on forever.

So many of the Shawnee were flat on their backs that Simon Brandt could have taken the camp single handed. Supplies of fresh meat were depleted when hunters were no longer fit to seek game. Often Rebecca had to direct family members to tie their loved ones to keep them from running outside to quench their fevers in the snow. It was a time of weeping and of little hope.

"It's useless, Siipu," Rebecca said as she broke down in tears. "We wanted to help and we've only made things worse."

"No quit," Siipu said. "The old chief, Seeks Visions, has not ordered you burned at stake. Council not believe you witch yet. No quit."

"But they should be getting better, not sicker," she protested. "Why are they getting sicker?"

"Indian not white man. White man disease. No quit. Believe in self, Becca. Believe."

"I'm trying," she said. "I am, but sometimes, it all seems hopeless."

Then the next morning, Rebecca awoke to the sound of a child laughing. And when Siipu brought her a bowl of corn mush, she told her that there were no new cases of illness in the night. When Rebecca finished eating, she would have gone to see to those who had suffered the highest fevers, but Siipu bade her sleep some more. And she did; she closed her eyes and didn't open them again until dusk had fallen.

Fresh snow fell that evening. The following day, Counts led two youths to shoot down a woods bison, and there were plenty of meat and bones to make rich soup for the village. After that, two deer were taken, and the hungry period passed.

"You were right," Counts said grudgingly to Siipu, as she and Rebecca sat across from him at his fire pit and dined on grilled venison. "White men have the medicine for white men's sickness."

Siipu nodded. "Becca save tribe from smallpox."

"With the help of a Delaware witch," he said.

"And of Counts His Scalps," Rebecca put in. "You were the first to let us cut your arm."

"Hmmp." He cleared his throat importantly. "After you."

"After Siipu and me, you were the first," Rebecca repeated. "It took great courage."

"No one call Counts His Scalps coward," he boasted, displaying the fresh scar on his arm.

"No one ever will," Rebecca assured him. "Talon will be very proud of you."

There had been no word of him for weeks, not since the day he'd left to bring home his father's body, and Rebecca was worried. What if Simon or one of the soldiers had killed him? What if he'd been captured or had taken sick himself?

Fighting the smallpox had taken all of her energy, but now, she had begun to be concerned about her own future again. It seemed as if the Indian people had accepted her presence without malice. What if she did do as Talon wanted? What if she remained here with him?

Counts was laughing at something Siipu had said. "For a witch—" he began. Then he looked toward the entrance.

A young warrior entered the wigwam. He stood up and looked from Counts to Siipu. Rebecca recognized him as a man named Rabbit Running, a man whose pregnant wife had been one of the sickest.

"Is there something wrong with Sees Sunshine?" Rebecca asked, getting to her feet. "Is the baby coming?"

Rabbit Running spoke in Algonquian. Counts shook his head and replied in a loud voice in the same tongue. Siipu added something, but Rabbit Running wouldn't be swayed. He pointed at Rebecca and repeated the same phrase he had uttered when he came in.

"The high council calls for you," Counts said brusquely. "The war chief has returned. You must come and answer for the death of the shaman."

"Talon's back?" she cried. "He's safe?" Nothing else seemed to matter. If Talon was here then—

Siipu seized her arm and gripped it tightly. "My brother say come," she said. "My brother say soul of medicine man must be honored by life of white hostage."

Chapter 20

Anticipation and excitement crackled in the air, and despite a rising fear for her own safety, Rebecca was struck by the pageantry of the gathering. Even though she'd tended them in the sickness, she hadn't realized that the village contained so many people. Hawk-faced men and handsome women stood side by side, garbed in their finest clothing and adorned with feathers, fur, and jewelry. Faces painted with streaks of black and yellow and red, the proud Shawnee and Delaware crowded close together inside the three finished walls of the Big House. More people waited outside, pressing one upon the other for a view of the center hearth and the dignified council members who sat there in stony silence.

The throng parted for her and Siipu. Counts His Scalps and Rabbit Running followed on their heels, but Rabbit Running got no farther than the edge of the building where he was stopped by his father's forbidding glance. Rebecca caught sight of Fox and Counts' friend, Osage Killer, in the first row behind the council. None sat in the forefront but seasoned warriors and a few older matrons wrapped in bright blankets.

Five drummers formed a smaller circle on the west side of the central post, a skinned log of massive proportions boasting an oval carved face painted half white and half black. One drum was a hollow log, two were as large as washtubs, one as small as a man's palm, and the last painted leather stretched tightly over an open circle of wood, much like a gypsy's tambourine. The throbbing of the small drum rose and fell above the deep boom of the log-drum. The others kept up a steady *bom bom bom-bom*, so that the earth under Rebecca's feet seemed to echo their ancient rhythm.

Wild cherry logs burned in the fire pit; there was no mistaking the pleasing smell. The room was also thick with the scents of damp fur and leather, interlaced with leaf tobacco and the heavy musk of bear grease, but she wasn't repelled by the strong odors. She could detect no hint of human sweat in the throng; church services among the unwashed white settlers smelled far worse. Even as a child in Ireland, she had dreaded winter services, when chapel windows were tightly barred and worshipers reeked of fetid wool garments and rancid hair and breath.

She looked around her at the red-brown faces, and refused to believe that these people would really put her to death. These were the villagers she had tended during the illness; that man's head she had held when he was too weak to drink water, and that infant she had bathed and rocked to sleep when his mother couldn't rise from her bed. She felt a kinship with the tribe then, a human link that ran deeper than the color of their skin or the pale shade of hers.

Where was Talon? Rebecca realized that among all these individuals, she had not recognized the one man she longed to see most. Her gaze moved frantically from one stern warrior to another. Rabbit Running had said that the war chief was here. But where was he?

Siipu led her to stand before Seeks Visions. The old chief was splendid in a tall beaver hat with a British peace medal dangling across the front. A cloak of goose feathers covered his frail shoulders, shoulders that Rebecca had rubbed with ointment to ease the itching of the pox only a few short days ago.

Seeks Visions' eyes were clouded with cataracts, his brown, weather-worn features nearly hidden by wrinkles. His hair was as white as the plumage of a snow goose; it hung in two looped braids on either side of his face. The elderly Shawnee retained a full set of nearly perfect teeth beneath a bony nose so large and jutting that Rebecca wanted to reach out and touch it to make certain it was real.

"Here be the white woman who save our people from smallpox," Siipu said loudly, so that her voice might carry to those standing outside the Big House.

Seeks Visions grunted and raised a hand in salute. Siipu translated his words for Rebecca. "He says he see you," she whispered. "He says this be wife of Simon Brandt."

A ripple spread through the onlookers. Rebecca heard Simon's name murmured repeatedly.

"I am Rebecca Gordon Brandt," she said. Her heart was hammering in her chest so hard that she wondered it didn't sound above the drums, and it was difficult to keep her voice from cracking. "Tell him that, Siipu," she insisted.

Talon's sister did so, and the chief nodded.

Rebecca glanced around for Talon. Where was he? If he was here, why didn't he show himself?

He couldn't blame her for his father's death, could he?

The chief began to speak. He went on for several minutes, and then Siipu cleared her throat.

"Seeks Visions tells of the treaty meeting with English," Siipu explained. "He tells of treachery and death of Shawnee and Delaware. He tells of my brother's vow to trade you for our shaman who be prisoner."

"Where is Talon?" Rebecca whispered.

"Shhh," Siipu answered. "Must show respect for Seeks Visions. He tell of shaman's death by hang ... hanging. He say why war chief no keep promise—kill wife of Simon Brandt as shaman be killed."

Rebecca's mouth went dry. She tried to moisten her lips, but they were as numb as if she'd been drinking strong spirits. She wasn't a fainting woman, but any second, she was afraid she'd disgrace herself by falling flat on her face. "I am not responsible for what Simon Brandt does," she said. "You can't blame me. I don't deserve to pay for what evil ..."

The words died in her throat as heads turned and necks craned to see the tall man in the wolf's head cape who materialized out of the darkness.

"He comes," Siipu said.

Voices cried his name. There was a flurry of excitement, and men and women hastily moved back to let the war chief enter the Big House.

"Talon," Rebecca murmured.

His face was painted with slashes of red and yellow over his cheekbones; his thick black hair flowed loose in shimmering waves down his back. A necklace of bear claws encircled his throat. His chest was bare except for a sheen of oil and a gorget of beaten silver engraved with the fleur-de-lis of France. A simple red loincloth and moccasins completed his attire; he carried no weapons except for the sheathed knife at his waist.

"Talon," she repeated, swallowing the thickness in her throat. His eyes were shadowed with grief. He looked like a man who'd walked through hell.

Without a word or a glance, he strode past her with the arrogance of a prince, stopped in the center of the council circle, and stood before Seeks Visions as rigidly as an obelisk of carved granite.

The chief spoke first.

"He asked my brother if his father's body rests in sacred ground," Siipu whispered to Rebecca.

"*Ahikta,*" Talon answered. Yes.

"Does our shaman go empty handed across the river of spirits?" Siipu continued. She paused a moment, then went on. "No, the shaman does not. He rides a fine black horse and carries a new British rifle with him. And at his belt are the scalps of three enemies, so that those who wait on the far side of the river will know that he is a man of worth."

Rebecca shivered. Scalps. Talon had killed men—perhaps even Simon. Suddenly, she wasn't so sure that these people wouldn't harm her. The chasm between Talon's world and her own loomed wide. Was it possible that only a few short weeks ago they had lain in each others' arms?

Talon pushed back the wolf's head cloak and folded his arms over his chest, then switched easily from Algonquian to English. "I, Fire Talon, war chief of the Mecate Shawnee, have come this night to fulfill the promise I made to the long knives and to my people." He turned toward her and raised an open hand. "I vowed that I would return the wife of Simon Brandt when my father was set free. And I gave my word that if harm came to him, the white woman must die."

"*Yuho*," replied a council member.

"*Yuh*," uttered a second.

"*E-e*," a third declared.

Siipu moved to Talon's side and took hold of his arm. "*Ku!*" she cried. "No. You cannot do this thing."

"She must die," Counts His Scalps called. "A war chief cannot break his word."

"*Chitkwesi!*" Fox said.

Rebecca was surprised that she understood. *Be quiet!* Was Fox taking her side? She hadn't thought he approved of her. Fox and Siipu had spoken for her. But what would that matter when so many joined the shouts calling for her death?

Talon shrugged off his sister's clasp and took hold of Rebecca's shoulders. He leaned close to her, so close that she could feel his warm breath on her face. His black eyes were expressionless. "Know that you die for the sins of Simon Brandt," he said.

The earth dissolved beneath Rebecca's feet. She closed her eyes and tried to hold back the scream of terror that rose in her breast. Talon's lean fingers dug into her arms and her eyes snapped open as rising anger flooded her fear. "Take your hands off me!"

She looked full into his devil eyes, and for the barest instant, something akin to admiration flared. He yanked her against his chest and whispered into her ear.

"Trust me."

Bewildered, wondering if she'd imagined what she'd heard, she let Talon drag her from the Big

House to a cleared area in the center of the village. Too late, she saw the black painted post. Before she could do more than put up a token struggle, three women surged forward and began to tie her to the stake.

"Damn you, Talon!" she screamed. "Damn you to a bottomless hell!"

Other matrons carried armfuls of brush and wood. To Rebecca's terror, they began to pile it around her legs. Holy Mary, Mother of God, she prayed silently. They meant to burn her at the stake.

Frantically she looked around for someone to come to her aid. She caught sight of Siipu and Fox standing at the far side of the clearing. But they made no move to help her, and her Irish pride rose hot and bright. She would not beg for her life—not for her immortal soul.

Shawnee and Delaware braves streamed into the clearing. Drummers moved to take their places near the post. The beat of the drums changed. No longer steady and mournful, the cadence lit the fires of fury in the hearts of men and women. A warrior shouted a shrill whoop. Another followed. The hair stood up on the back of Rebecca's neck as Shawnee war cries echoed through the village.

Talon joined in the terrible dance. Feathered trade ax in his hand, he whirled and dipped, flashing steel and calling upon the spirit of his dead father to witness the death of the white hostage.

English. He was singing in English. Rebecca's eyes narrowed in contempt as she watched him come ever nearer. "I hate you," she mouthed. But no one heard.

Women with the lower half of their faces blackened with ashes filed into the clearing. Brandishing lit torches of pitch pine, they uttered dreadful shrieks of mourning so spine-chilling that Rebecca clenched her teeth to keep them from chattering. The women formed an inner circle that gradually widened to surround the fierce, stomping, twisting warriors. The high keening of the women rose above the fierce war whoops of their savage partners until Rebecca thought they would deafen her with their hellish chorus.

Suddenly, Talon stood over her, tomahawk in hand. "Trust me," he murmured again. "I will let you come to no harm, Becca." The acrid scent of ashes filled her head as he smeared her face with the mark of death.

"Go to hell," she whispered, and closed her eyes to wait for the fatal blow.

Instead, she felt fingers tugging at the ropes that bound her hands. Someone threw a blanket over her head, and she struggled to breathe. Hands shoved her along, half-carrying her over the rough ground. She stumbled and a feminine voice giggled nervously. Strong arms bore her up.

Then she was pushed to her knees, the blanket whisked off her head, and she was thrust through a narrow hole into a hot enclosed area. Before she could regain her senses, a dozen hands stripped off her clothes, leaving her as bare as an egg.

"What are you doing to me?" she shouted in protest.

Siipu's rasping voice came from the darkness. "Do not fear. You safe."

"Siipu? Is that you?"

Rebecca reached out and touched the wall. Wood and animal skin. She was in a wigwam of sorts, but what kind. Why was it so hot? Already, sweat had broken out on her face and arms. "What place is this?" she demanded.

Twitters of laughter came from every side. Soft hands touched her, and she felt the smear of something wet. The steamy air smelled of pine boughs and mint. She tried to twist away, but the women were all around her.

"No have fear," a woman said. "Sweat house. Good. No hurt."

Siipu took her hand and squeezed it. "Trust," she said. She tugged expectantly, and Rebecca tried to stand up. "*Ku*, no stand," she ordered. "Come."

On hands and knees, Rebecca followed her. The floor ran downhill to a glowing fire pit of red-hot rocks. Mats of reeds and thin saplings surrounded the hearth. Rebecca sat upright where Siipu indicated, and the other women took their places around the fireplace and began to sing in Algonquian.

Rebecca couldn't understand the words, but the chanting was no longer sad; it was joyous. The women began to clap, and Siipu guided her hands until she joined them in the rhythm. The one woman threw water on the rocks, and clouds of steam filled the small hut. Rebecca felt as though she was being cooked alive.

Wonderful, she thought. They aren't going to burn me at the stake. They're going to boil me for dinner.

"Good," Siipu said.

Sweat ran off Rebecca's face, and she felt light-headed. She wasn't sure what was happening, and she was almost too weak and emotionally drained to care.

Then as the steam began to thin, another

woman dumped a second bucket of water onto the hearth. Again the room grew heavy with moisture and the temperature rose even higher.

By the third time, Rebecca felt as though her strength was gone. She didn't even try to struggle when someone threw a wrap around her shoulders and pushed her back toward the entrance.

When the deerskin flap was pulled away, a crowd of cheering women waited outside with torches. Siipu grabbed Rebecca's hand and pulled her to her feet. The cold air struck her and she gasped. But Siipu was running, and women were shoving her along. Her bare feet were sinking in the snow, but she was past feeling heat or cold.

Or so she thought.

She changed her mind when Siipu leaped off the riverbank into the ice-encrusted, swiftly flowing water. Rebecca screamed and went under, blanket and all. Gasping for breath, she bobbed up, and someone ducked her again. She came up cursing and swinging her fists, ready to kill anyone who tried to keep her from reaching shore.

But no one tried. The onlookers greeted her with gales of friendly laughter, and a stout woman with shell earrings wrapped her in a dry blanket. Still cheering, the women ushered her to a nearby wigwam where they dressed her from head to toe in new garments of white doeskin. When the stout woman—who Siipu identified as her aunt—laced high, fur-lined moccasins to Rebecca's knees and draped her shoulders with a beaver skin cloak, she embraced her.

"You daughter of Squash Blossom now," the tall woman said, and pressed her cheek to Rebecca's with obvious affection. "Squash Blossom's first-born daughter die by hand of white soldier. Born

now, this night, you be *Weeshob-izzi Kimmiwun,*
Sweet Water."

Rebecca looked for Siipu, and then realized with
a start that Talon's sister was standing beside her.
The mask that had hidden her face for so long was
gone. "Siipu?" she asked.

Squash Blossom laughed. "No Siipu. Siipu die
in sweat lodge with wife of Simon Brandt. This
woman your sister, *Kedata.* Squash Blossom have
no daughter. Now two."

Tears glistened in Talon's sister's dark eyes.
"Siipu go to join mother across the river," she said.
"Kedata—Otter Girl—have mother here. Have sister." Hesitantly, she held out her arms, and Rebecca hugged her tightly.

"Daughters come," Squash Blossom said.
"Council wait. Warriors wait. See new daughters
of tribe."

The women formed a procession with Rebecca
and the newly named Kedata in the center. Clapping and chanting, they moved joyously to the
clearing where Rebecca had faced death only two
hours ago. The men fell silent as they entered the
firelight. Large, heavy snowflakes drifted down,
covering the black post and the dance ground
with a thick white carpet.

Squash Blossom took Kedata's hand and led her
forward. One by one, the council members nodded as the stout woman declared Talon's sister to
be her oldest daughter. A great shout went up
from the watching warriors, and they raised their
weapons in salute.

When the older woman returned to reach for
Rebecca's hand, Talon stepped forward. His face
had been washed clean, and he wore leggings and
a vest decorated with porcupine quills. The wolf's

head cloak was gone. An embroidered band of white leather encircled his head, and two eagle feathers dangled from the left side.

"This is my beloved daughter, Weeshob-izzi Kimmiwun," Squash Blossom said, lifting Rebecca's cold hand high. Again, the council members nodded and the men shouted. Squash Blossom motioned for Rebecca to stay where she was, and then she returned to the line of women.

Talon moved to stand beside Rebecca. He would have taken her hand in his, but she snatched it back.

"Don't touch me," she hissed at him.

He looked full into her face. "I know you don't understand," he said. "But this was the only way to save your life." Then he addressed the tribe in a ringing voice. "On this night, my vow has been kept," he said in Algonquian, and then repeated his words in English for her. "On this night, the wife of Simon Brandt has died. My father's soul will not walk the earth and cry out for vengeance."

Then he lifted the string of bear claws from his chest and placed them over her head. "This woman, Sweet Water, is and forever shall be a daughter of the Shawnee. She who faced the *bear who walks like a man* brings honor to our village no matter where her trail leads."

"What are you doing?" she whispered to him.

"By this act you are free of Simon Brandt," he said. "You are a Shawnee woman—a woman who chooses her own path from this day forth."

"But who will free me from you?" she demanded.

Ignoring her plea, he spoke again to the assembly. Rebecca struggled to understand the Algonquian, but she could grasp only a few words.

"This woman!" Talon proclaimed in his own tongue. "Sweet Water will be offered up to the Red Coats of King George in memory of my father's lifelong struggle for peace between our two nations. I, Fire Talon, war chief of the Mecate Shawnee, do so vow."

Chapter 21

"How could you do that to me?" Rebecca demanded. She was so angry that she could hardly look into Talon's broad face—could barely stand to be in the same wigwam with him. "It was despicable! The act of a monster."

Outside, the tribesmen and women seemed to pay no heed to the falling snow or the cold. The drums still beat, and dancing and chanting continued in the center of the village. Immediately after Squash Blossom and Talon had named her a Shawnee, many of the women had come forward shyly to offer her baskets of food, jewelry, and blankets. Squash Blossom had given her a bone-handled knife and sheath, and a beautiful fringed belt to hang it from. Siipu was showered with presents as well, so many that it required six matrons to help carry both her gifts and Rebecca's to Squash Blossom's wigwam.

Siipu had returned to the dance ground, but Rebecca had lingered behind. Squash Blossom's hut was crowded and unfamiliar, so when Rebecca thought that no one was watching her, she fled to the comparative safety of Counts His Scalp's wigwam.

She had no sooner removed her robe and knelt by the fire before Talon had pushed open the deerskin and entered. Seeing him brought back the fury and helplessness she'd felt since Rabbit Running had come to tell her that Talon was demanding her life in exchange for his father's.

"How dare you come here?" she continued to berate him. "I never want to see you again. Do you know—do you have any idea what you put me through tonight? I thought I was going to die."

He crouched on the other side of the fire pit and added another log to the coals. The flames caught the dry bark and flared up, lighting his face with a red glow. "I did not wish to frighten you," he said mildly.

"Didn't wish to frighten me?" she snapped. She was trembling so badly that she could hardly speak. "Didn't wish to frighten me? Are you crazy?" Her fingers closed around another piece of kindling. "You scared me half to death, damn your red soul!"

"I am truly sorry for that, Sweet Water."

"Don't *Sweet Water* me! My name is Rebecca. Say it! Rebecca."

He shook his head. "No. The woman I knew as Becca is dead. You are Sweet Water of the Shawnee."

"That's so much sheep dung! You don't believe it any more than I do."

His ebony eyes widened in disbelief. "You must accept. It is the truth. I break the custom of my people by even speaking the dead woman's name."

"You . . . you . . ." So great was her frustration that when he smiled at her, she lost all composure and hurled the stick at him. It struck his temple hard enough to open a gash.

He winced as blood trickled down his face.

"Oh, Talon," she cried. "I'm so sorry. I didn't

mean . . ." She wasn't sure if she circled the fire pit or dashed through it to reach him, but seconds later, she was weeping openly and trying to stop the bleeding. A purple knot was rising on his forehead. Without thinking, she bent to kiss his injury. He tilted his head and her lips brushed down his nose and landed full on his mouth.

His response was a kiss that rocked her to the soles of her feet. She was crying and kissing him back and trying to stop the blood all at once. His hands were moving over her and his smell filled her head.

Together, they fell back onto a thick pile of heaped fur robes. A gust of wind blew through the smoke hole sending sparks billowing up into the room, but neither heard nor saw. With anguished murmurs of pent-up passion and deep shuddering breaths, they touched and kissed and entwined their limbs.

Somehow, Talon managed to push the skirt of her deerskin dress up around her waist. His warm, strong hand caressed her inner thigh even as he filled her mouth with his hot, thrusting tongue. She arched provocatively against him and stroked his bare chest and hard shoulders with fevered urgency. His mouth burned a scorching trail across her skin, and she moaned as the waves of sweet aching that coursed through her loins churned into a storm surge of liquid fire.

"I love you, my blue-eyed lynx," he whispered huskily. His fingers sought the curls above her woman's cleft and he planted a damp kiss there and then another.

"Oh." She gasped at the intensity of the sensations that radiated from his caress. Never had she felt so alive. She could feel the silken texture of the warm furs under her bare skin, hear the whoosh of wind and snow outside the wigwam and the quick throb of Shawnee drums. Outside these snug walls, a winter storm reigned, but here with Talon beside her, she felt the enchantment of spring sunshine, green leaves, and bird song.

His seeking touch invaded her soft folds and found a tight bud of throbbing ecstasy. She threw back her head and closed her eyes, letting the wonder of his tantalizing seduction sweep over her. He led her to the brink of the abyss, and then, when the honied rapture was almost in her grasp, he drew back and tugged the doeskin gown over her head.

"You are so beautiful," he said, cupping her breast and nuzzling it with his lips and tongue. "So beautiful." He shrugged off his vest and fumbled with the tie of his loincloth. She could feel his engorged manhood, hot and pulsing, pressed against her bare thigh, and she let her fingers explore the satin flesh.

He groaned with pleasure and kissed her throat and tongued her ear, whispering words of love so daring that she blushed and grew more excited just to hear them. He raised his head to look into her eyes and stray tendrils of hair fell across his face. "Kiss me," he urged. "I want you to kiss me."

Emboldened by his lovemaking, she pressed her lips against his smooth chest. Inch by inch, she moved down, letting her fingers stray to tease his sinewy thighs and graze the dark tangle of hair above his tumescent sex.

"Touch me," he said.

He was silken and hard, huge and full, beautiful and frightening. She leaned close, letting her breath and then her cheek touch him. His fingers tangled in her hair, pushing her down. Her lips brushed his straining shaft, and Talon groaned.

"Is this what you want me to do?" she asked.

"*Ahikta.*"

"And this?"

"Yes . . ."

She marveled at the mystery of his taste and texture, reveled in the sense of power she gained from his shuddering sighs of arousal. This is how it should be between a man and a woman, she thought . . . how it could never have been between her and Simon. "I do love you," she whispered. "More than my own soul."

"And I love you, my Sweet Water," he rasped. He took her shoulders and pulled her up to straddle him. "Now, sit on me," he ordered. "I want to feel you against me."

"Like this?" she asked.

"Just like that."

He kissed first one breast and then the other as she moved slowly against him. Then, with a deep groan, he caught her hips and lifted her out onto his shaft. She cried out as he plunged into her. This was a new sensation for her—to be in control—to take her pleasure as she would, to give and tantalize until his skin took on a sheen of perspiration and his breath grew ragged.

"Enough, woman," he said. Rolling her over, he mounted her and drove deep inside. Thrust for thrust she met him with equal passion until at last an explosion of sheer ecstasy shattered her longing into a thousand shards of sweet sensation. Seconds later, Talon found his own fulfillment and slumped against her with a long, slow sigh of satisfaction.

For a long time, they lay skin to skin, holding

each other, while he whispered words of love in her ear. She drifted into a light sleep, then woke to find her head nestled into the hollow of his shoulder. Talon's hand was on her breast, and a fur robe was pulled up to her chin.

"What will we do if Counts comes back?" she whispered languidly. Lying here like this with Talon was all she wanted in the world, all she wished to think about. And if Talon's friend returned and caught them together, it seemed of little importance.

That proves how brazen I've become, she thought with a low chuckle as she drew lazy circles on Talon's chest with her finger. I am his woman, and I don't care who knows it. I don't care what color he is or what language he speaks—I only know that we belong together.

"If Counts enters this wigwam, we'll throw him out into the snow," Talon threatened.

She giggled. "Out of his own house?"

"E-e," he replied. He lifted a lock of her hair and wrapped it slowly around his finger. "How is it that so many women in your country have hair the color of English foxes?"

"And how is it that you use so many different words for what I think is the same meaning. *Ahikta* is *yes* in Shawnee, isn't it?"

"Lenape, or Delaware, my mother's tongue. I have heard the English call our language *Algonquian*. Delaware and Shawnee are much the same; some sounds are slightly different. To your untrained ear, you would not know the difference. Any Shawnee can speak and understand the words of a Delaware, a Menominee, a Nanticoke, and the other tribes of these hills and woodlands. Most Shawnee do not speak the tongue of our enemies, the Iroquois, and they do not understand us."

"If *ahikta* is yes, then what is *yuho* and *e-e?*" she persisted.

He chuckled. "Do not forget *yuh* or *bischi*, *bischihk* or *kehella la*, or the dozen other ways to express what you English—"

"I am not English," she reminded him tartly.

". . . what your English language," he corrected, "means when you say yes. There are many ways for a man to agree, some lazy, some angry, and some . . ." He pushed down the fur to expose her bare shoulder and kissed it softly. "We are not people of ink and paper; we are people of deeds." He lowered the robe and kissed the top curve of her breast. "We have many words for pleasure between a man and a woman. Would you like me to teach—"

A log in the fire crashed down and the light surged up. Rebecca cut off his offer with a cry of distress. Talon's face was smeared with blood. Streaks marked his throat and chest and, she saw to her horror, her own hands. "Sweet breath of Saint Patrick! You're bleeding to death. I've killed you."

He rose to his knees and held his hands out to the firelight. "It is true," he said in mock seriousness. "Your blow to my head is doubtless fatal." He took a firm grip on her hand and stood up, pulling her out of her warm nest.

She gasped as she looked down at her naked body. Dull red patches marred her breasts and belly; one swathe ran down her thigh. In the heat of their lovemaking and the sleepy lull after, she had completely forgotten hitting him with the piece of firewood. "Mother of God," she whispered. She could see now that his head was no longer bleeding, but she was so shamed by her act of violence that she felt herself blush from head to toe. "I'm sorry, Talon," she began. "My temper has always—"

"You are as fierce as any Mohawk," he said. "But even a Mohawk must pay for his daring."

She blinked in confusion. "I said I was sorry. What more can—"

"You split my head and made free with my injured body," he said. "Now, you must make amends. You shall wash me clean."

"Of course," she stammered, realizing that she was standing there naked. She stooped to grab a robe. Where was her dress? "I'll heat water," she said, covering her bare breasts. "Lie back, and I'll—"

"Not here," he said. "The river."

She shook her head.

He nodded.

"Not the river."

He smiled.

"Talon, you wouldn't. Not again! It's freezing. There's ice and . . . No! No, Talon!" Shrieking and kicking, she struggled against him as he dragged her toward the entranceway. "No!"

Icy wind struck her bottom. Her nipples hardened. "Fiend!" she screamed. "Heartless fiend!" Snowflakes swirled around them as he swept her up in his arms and began to run toward the river. She shut her eyes and burrowed against his chest. Branches tangled in her hair. "No!" she shouted again.

She was in the air. For an instant, it seemed as though she hung there, suspended in the darkness between dark sky and darker water. Then she hit the water with a splash, and Talon plunged in after her.

"You're supposed to bathe me," he shouted as she sputtered and shook water in his face.

"I'll kill you!" She swung her fist at him and he dove under. He grabbed her around the knees and pitched her under again. She gasped for air, but before she could gather her senses, he was carrying her out of the river.

Her teeth were chattering, and she was shaking so hard she couldn't speak as he walked back toward the wigwam. When they reached it, Rebecca crawled on hands and knees to the fire. Talon came close behind her. He wrapped her in a robe of white fox, fur side in, and pulled her into his lap.

"I—I'll never . . . never forgive . . . never forgive you for that!" Somehow, she was sitting on his loins, bare skin to skin, and the robe had fallen to one side. "You . . . you torturer," she accused.

He warmed his hands over the fire and rubbed her feet between his hands. "It is a custom," he said. "Lovers—"

"No. I don't believe anything you say. You're crazy. You're trying to kill—" He silenced her with two fingers over her lips. She caught his fingertips between her teeth and bit down, not hard enough to really hurt. He chuckled and twisted under her, so that she fell onto the fur bed. "Cover me," she said breathlessly.

He moved so quickly that she couldn't have escaped if she wanted to . . . and she no longer wanted to. He kissed her full on the mouth and tugged a bearskin to cover them.

"You're rotten," she whispered. It was dark under the robe, but she was beginning to warm up, and his hard, muscular body pressed against her was not altogether unpleasant. "Remind me never to hit you with firewood again."

"This man does not believe he will have to." He nuzzled her neck.

"Bathing in winter is dangerous to the health," she teased.

"Not to mine."

"Will you spend the rest of our life together throwing me in some stream?"

"Sweet Water—"

"Say it in Shawnee," she whispered.

"Weeshob-izzi Kimmiwun."

"That's very long."

"Kimmi . . ." He kissed the corner of her mouth and traced the curve of her lower lip with the tip of his tongue. And all the while, his hands were warming her in other places.

"Why Sweet Water?" she murmured.

"A man cannot live without it."

The growing pressure against her thigh told her that Talon was regaining his strength as well. She snuggled tighter, reveling in the delights of his flesh and the soft furs under her bare skin. "Have you made love to many women like this?" she asked.

"Only to you, my Sweet Water. Like this, only to you . . . and never again . . . like this . . . to another woman."

"Do you mind that my skin is so pale?"

"I have learned to like pale skin." He lifted her hand and kissed the underside of her wrist.

She felt her pulse quicken as desire washed through her again. "And red hair . . . does it offend you?"

"Red pelts are much rarer than black." He

chuckled, raising her damp hair and kissing the nape of her neck. She squirmed against him and felt her nipples begin to harden. He lowered his head and nuzzled her breast.

Counts' voice startled her. "Oh," she murmured.

"Go away!" Talon ordered.

Counts replied in Algonquian, and Rebecca distinctly heard Osage Killer's gruff laughter outside the doorway.

"I said *go away*," Talon repeated. "I am teaching this new member of the tribe our customs."

Rebecca stifled a giggle.

"Where would you have this man go?" Counts asked in badly accented English.

"Jump in the river," Rebecca suggested.

With a final indignant remark in his own tongue, Counts dropped the deerskin and stalked away.

"Satisfied?" Talon asked her.

"Not yet," she said.

"Then this man will do all he can to make you happy."

"And teach me all the customs?"

"As many as a warrior has vigor for on this night."

She awoke to the smell of corn mush, grilled trout, and maple syrup. The wind still howled around the wigwam, but inside, wrapped in her furs, Rebecca was toasty warm. She yawned and stretched, lazily watching Talon prepare breakfast. This morning, he wore only a leather vest, moccasins, and loincloth, and he'd secured his hair in a single braid down the back.

"You do that as if you're good at it," she teased. "I could learn to enjoy having breakfast in bed."

He smiled at her and handed her a small bowl of hot liquid. The tantalizing aroma that spiraled up with the steam smelled surprisingly like real tea. She lifted it to her lips.

"Careful," he warned her. "It's hot."

She noticed that he still had the lump on his head; it had darkened to a purple-blue bruise, but gave no evidence of further bleeding. "Oh," she murmured. "It is tea. It's delicious." He'd sweetened the fragrant drink with honey, and she drank it slowly, savoring each precious drop. "You spoil me," she said at last.

"Last night, before we came together, while you were being reborn as Sweet Water, I spoke to a hunter named Many Snares. He said he camped two nights with The Stranger and a white boy. The boy had hair as dark as a Shawnee, and his eyes were twin blades of obsidian. Many Snares said that there was laughter between The Stranger and the child. This man believes that the boy was your brother."

"Did he say—did Many Snares know where The Stranger was taking him?"

"The Stranger spoke of trapping furs near the English lakes."

"How long ago?"

"When *pees ka wa nee kee shoxh wh'*, the moon, was full. Two of your weeks."

Hope bubbled up in her chest. "If he's taking Colin north, he may mean to trade him to the French," she said excitedly. "Simon said that the French buy up as many white captives as they can and sell them back to the English in New York."

"*Taktani.*"

"English, Talon. I'm just getting *yes* and *no*

down. If you're going to teach me to speak Delaware, you'll have to go slower."

"*Taktani*," he replied patiently, as he dropped grilled fish onto a wooden slab that served as a plate. "It means *I don't know*." He brought the trout to her. "We have Osage Killer to thank for the fresh fish. He went ice fishing yesterday."

"*Taktani*," she repeated carefully. "I don't know." She looked up at him. "But you must have an opinion. What do you think? Do you think The Stranger will—"

"This man believes that The Stranger has an honorable heart. He is not a boy-lover or one who carries hate in his heart for all those with white skins. If Colin is with him, he is safe—or as safe as any of us is. But what The Stranger will decide to do with your brother . . ." He shrugged. "It would be an untruth to say different to you."

"You promised me—"

"That this man would try and find him. You have my word. If it is possible, and if The Stranger will give him up, he will be returned to you in the white settlements."

The plate slipped from her nerveless fingers. "To me? In the white settlements?" She stared at him in confusion. "What are you talking about? I thought that you and I—"

Talon's features hardened. "Do not pretend that you don't know, Sweet Water. With your own ears, you heard this man tell his people."

"No . . ." she stammered. "I don't know." Her hands clenched into tight fists. The robe fell away, exposing her naked breasts, and she didn't even notice. "Tell me again, Talon. What is it I'm supposed to *know*?"

"Before the tribe. You heard me. This man translated everything—"

"No, you didn't. Not that. You didn't tell me—"

"This man must have." He rose to his feet and
looked down at her with eyes as sad as an open
grave. "When this man went for his father's body,
he prayed for a vision—a spirit guide—to show
him what to do. A vow had been made . . . a vow
that this man could not keep."

"Go on," she urged.

"He was a great shaman, a good man." Talon
exhaled softly. "They threw his body on a dung-
hill, where animals tore at it. This man carried
away what was left of his father, bathed him, and
wrapped him in warm blankets. And when the rit-
uals had been completed, this man sat three days
by his father's grave, waiting for a sign."

"What sign?"

"A voice, not heard here," he touched his ear,
"but here." He laid a bronzed hand over his heart.
"The voice explained how Becca Brandt could die
and be reborn as a free Shawnee woman. A war
chief's promise could be kept without the loss of a
worthy soul. But there was a price . . . Always,
from the spirits, there is a price."

"What price?" she demanded. "What in the
name of God are you talking about?"

"This man cannot keep you by his side. This
man must return you to the English."

"You're crazy. You didn't tell me that." She was
too stunned for anger—too hurt for tears. "What
we did here . . . I did for love. I thought we would
be together as man and wife. I thought you
wanted me—"

"At the council fire the words were said," he insisted. "In Shawnee and again in English—for all to hear and understand."

"Not me. I didn't understand. That last part ... about sending me back ... you conveniently left that part untranslated."

"Then this man has wronged you again, Sweet Water. But know in your heart that giving you up was the price of your life."

"You and your damned Indian logic!" She was screaming at him now—like some dockside fishwife. "If I'm not Rebecca Brandt—if she's dead— then why are you giving me, *a free Shawnee woman called Sweet Water,* back to the English?"

"The white men do not know that you are Sweet Water. They see only the face of a living dead woman. It is not what *is true* that matters. It is what appears to be true. In my father's name, to honor his wish for peace between red men and white, you too must pay the price. You must return to the white world and pretend to be *She Who No Longer Draws Breath.* You must forget this man, and forget what we found together in the shadow of the great bear. You must forget that you ever listened to a turkey bone flute or laughed with a Shawnee warrior under fur robes in the night."

"You think I can forget?"

His voice grew harsh with emotion. "You must try, my fox-haired *ki-te-hi,* you must try."

Chapter 22

"If I am a free woman, then why can't I stay with you?" Rebecca asked for the third time that afternoon. "I won't go back to Simon. No one can make me live with him again."

Talon's only reply was to clench his teeth and stare eastward toward the wooded hills and valleys that marched in misty folds to the horizon. They had paused to rest on a natural lookout, a spill of giant boulders along the lip of a mountain pass. From here the four of them could see farther than they could walk in three days.

Counts His Scalps and Osage Killer had insisted on coming with him, even though Counts hadn't fully recovered from his bullet wound. Fox had remained behind in the village, acting in Talon's stead to direct the braves in safety precautions that were necessary, even in winter. When Iroquois were the only enemy of the people, the time of snow had been relatively secure from warfare, but the battle between French and English had changed all that. Now, attack on a town or a family could come at any time, and danger was a constant companion at every campfire.

"Sweet Water is right," Counts grumbled to Talon in Algonquian. "This is foolishness. You'll get us killed to return a woman who doesn't want to go back, one you don't want to give up."

Talon glared at him. Wishemenetoo knew that they'd gone over and over this. "This is done for my father," he said tersely. "In his honor, and because it is what my spirit guide ordered." Had he made the mistake of not translating for her the night she was adopted by the tribe? She insisted he had. And yet . . . he'd been so certain that he'd told her.

Counts arched an eyebrow cynically. "And you never doubt your interpretations of the spirits' wishes, do you?"

Talon didn't answer. He doubted. What man did not doubt? But a man who agonized too much over what was his will and what came from his guide soon became weak and ineffectual—of no use to himself or to his people.

Giving up Sweet Water would be the hardest thing he'd ever done—harder than laying his father's torn body to earth or hearing the news of his mother's death. This red-haired woman had touched a part of his soul that he'd long believed empty. He had felt the scar tissue in his heart ripping when he'd looked at her, and he'd welcomed the pain. After hating for so many years, it was good to feel love and compassion—to know that he would never again judge a man or woman by the color of their skin.

That much you have given me, Sky Eyes, he thought . . . that will not be taken from this one. No matter how much distance separates us, that much will lie nestled in my heart. Your laughter . . . yes, and even the way you bite your lower lip when you concentrate on a difficult task . . . that a man will remember.

Among the whites, Sweet Water would be safe. They would not realize who she really was, and they would treat her kindly. He had told her not to remain on the frontier, but to go to the settlements beside the sea and live there. He would make certain that Simon Brandt never bothered her again. For no one would sleep safely in their beds until he was dead.

They had traveled four days from the village when they met a man and a woman who had escaped the Corn Creek Delaware town. Simon Brandt and his men had passed that way on their way back to the English fort. Now only ashes marked the place where twenty and four wigwams had stood. Eleven people had died, five of them children. The Delaware woman had seen with her own eyes as Simon Brandt dashed her sister's newborn babe's head against a tree.

These deaths are on my conscience, Talon thought. If he had killed the white scout when he had the chance, that village might still stand and that tiny boy still cry for his mother's breast. So many years he and Simon Brandt had played the game of fox and hare; first one would be the rabbit, then the other. It was time for the game to end. Simon Brandt must die.

Or it might well be him, *Sh'Kotaa Osh-Kah-Shah*—Fire Talon—who would die.

That was another urgent reason for taking Sweet Water to the English. For days, he had felt a sense of foreboding that he'd never experienced before. He'd always known that a man's life may be extinguished as easily as a spark, and as war chief or even before, when he was just a brave of the Shawnee, he'd never shied from taking chances. Men were killed in war. He did not welcome death, but he didn't fear it either.

Now, he heard the rustle of *Wing ee yox qua*'s

dark feathers around his head and the faint echoes of his own death chant. This man will meet his end as a warrior should, he vowed. But he had taken the precaution of asking Fox to hunt meat for his sister and his aging aunt if he didn't return.

He glanced at Sweet Water and thought how short their time together had been . . . not even the turn of a single season. And he wished with all his heart that he and Sweet Water could have seen the wild strawberries blossom in spring and the does lead their young, wobbly legged fawns to the river to drink. He wished they could have lain in each other's arms and watched the sun go down on a warm summer's night. He wanted to show her the morning mist on the Ohio, and the first flight of a young eaglet.

He wanted to make a child with her . . . a child of their love . . . and see that infant nurse at her warm breast and grow strong and wise.

Sweet Water and I could sit by a fire in the autumn of our lives, while shared memories of love and laughter drifted around us like bright fall leaves, he mused . . . while grandchildren tumbled around our feet.

"You think too much," Osage Killer intruded brusquely. "Life is a mountain to be climbed. Sometimes the way is smooth and easy, but most of the time rocks and briers bar our path. When spirits speak, it is good that a man listens. The woman must go back."

Counts laughed and made a show of looking all around him. "Osage Killer has become a poet," he quipped. "Beware when a man of few words begins to spout wisdom. Something unusual is about to happen."

Osage Killer made a sound of derision. "It is

true that I am not a man who wastes words like water," he admitted. "But I have sense enough to heed the spirits."

"Do they speak to you often?" Counts needled.

"Sometimes. And now they tell me that we are being followed."

Instantly, Talon motioned Sweet Water down. "Behind that rock," he ordered her in English. She obeyed without question, and he turned back to Osage Killer. "You saw something?"

The lean warrior shook his head and tapped the nape of his neck. "Here. I feel it here."

"Why didn't you say something earlier?" Talon demanded.

"Whoever comes means us no harm," Counts' companion said.

"Who comes?" Talon asked.

Osage Killer shrugged.

Counts had already slipped away into the surrounding forest. Only the slight quiver of a young cedar gave evidence that something living had passed.

"What is it?" Rebecca asked Talon. "What's wrong?"

"Osage says we're being followed."

"Are we?"

Talon checked the priming on his rifle. "He's never wrong." He listened. Crows chattered in the treetops, and from a little way off, he heard the clear whistle of a white-throated sparrow, two sharp notes followed closely by three quavering ones. Whatever was out there, it hadn't frightened the birds.

"Talon—" Sweet Water hissed.

"Quiet."

Osage looked toward him, and he nodded. The

brave cautiously retraced their trail up the bluff and entered the woods a few hundred yards below the overlook. Talon moved to crouch beside Sweet Water. "Come," he said to her. "This isn't a good spot to—" The whir of a grouse's wings as it broke from cover silenced him. Only seconds later, he heard the cry of a jay. Counts' signal, he thought, letting out his breath with a sigh. "It's all right," he assured Sweet Water.

She stared at him in bewilderment

"Wait," he said, "and you will see. The jay walked on two feet."

Shortly, Osage Killer came into sight. Walking beside him was Talon's sister, now known as Kedata. Counts followed close behind her.

"Brother," Kedata called. She was dressed for travel, with a pack on her back and her bow and hunting bag slung over her shoulder. "*Num ees*—my sister." She waved at Sweet Water.

Anger washed over Talon. "What are you doing here? I left you in Fox's care at the village."

His sister laughed. "Since when do I need a man to watch over me? Meshepeshe and I have come to join you. We thought Sweet Water would need female company with so many sour-faced men."

"You brought the mountain lion?" Talon said. He glared at her. "This is not a pleasure trip. You will go back to the village at once."

"I will not," she said sweetly.

"There will be danger when we near the white settlements."

She scoffed. "And I have lived a life sheltered from danger—have I not, Brother?"

"First the witch invades my wigwam; now she shadows my trail," Counts said. "Send her back where she belongs."

Osage Killer looked grim.

"Kedata—" Talon began.

"I will stay." Stepping around him, she went to Sweet Water and embraced her. "*Num ees* and I have little time together before she leaves us forever."

Talon turned his scowl on Sweet Water. "Tell her she should go back," he ordered in English.

Sweet Water shook her head. "You said that Shawnee women were free," she reminded him. "Surely, *our sister* has a right to decide for herself if she will come or go."

Kedata laughed merrily. "You have taught her our ways too well, Sh'Kotaa Osh-Kah-Shah," she teased. "You have made a proper Indian woman of her, and now you must deal with the consequences."

Rebecca did enjoy the company of Talon's sister in the following days. With her encouragement, Rebecca tried out her newly acquired words of Algonquian. Between her meager Shawnee and Siipu's broken English, they managed, sharing jokes and knowledge about each other's customs. Siipu seemed to have left her sorrow in the sweat house, for she quickly become a cheerful friend.

So much of Rebecca's adult life had been spent alone at the cabin with Colin that she'd never had a real woman friend in America. It was something she'd missed, and the warmth filled some of the void of her sadness and hurt at leaving Talon.

Siipu was full of stories of Talon's childhood, and she was quick to embarrass him with them. One night, by the campfire, she was telling about her brother's desire to capture a young hawk for a pet. ". . . climb tall tree, high—high," she explained in a mixture of gestures, English, and Algonquian. "Mother hawk angry. Fly at bad boy. Boy frightened. Limb break—crack! He fall, catch belt on branch."

Counts laughed. "This one remembers that day well. His father—the shaman whose name we must not say—have much anger to see only son dangle upside down."

"Forty feet from ground," Siipu continued with barely contained giggles. "All while hawk dive at bottom."

"Bare bottom," Counts supplied.

"Yes, it was very funny," Talon said, banking the tiny fire.

"Take three men with rope to get him down," Siipu said.

Rebecca smiled at him. "I wish I'd been there."

"This man is sure you do," Talon answered grimly.

Later, when the fire had died to coals, Rebecca had lain awake staring at the cold stars overhead. Talon was only a few feet away, but he might have been miles. Already, he'd left her. She wondered if he had ever felt for her what he'd said he did . . . what she felt for him.

After tossing and turning, she rose and ventured quietly off into the trees. Osage Killer was standing guard on the far side of the camp. He saw her and waved. She waved back, realizing that he didn't want her to go too far from the fire.

She had no intention of doing so. Siipu's cat was out here in the darkness somewhere, hunting, Rebecca supposed. The animal had rarely showed herself, a glimpse of tawny hide here and there. Once, she had come close to Siipu when they crossed a stream.

"Meshepeshe not like Counts His Scalps," Siipu had told her.

Not Siipu, *Kedata,* Rebecca reminded herself. This Indian business of changing names was confusing. It made no sense at all to her, but Siipu wouldn't answer to her old name, and Talon acted as though Becca had never existed. It's just as well I'm going back, she thought. They can say I'm an Indian, but I'll never understand their ways.

A stick snapped behind her and she whirled around.

Talon stood an arm's length behind her. "I would speak with you, Sweet Water," he said quietly.

"Becca. I'm Becca."

"Your heart is hardened against this man."

"Shouldn't it be?"

He touched her cheek.

She shivered as a lump formed in the back of her throat. "I loved you," she said.

"As this man loves you."

"You can't. If you did, you couldn't send me back to Simon."

"Not to him, never to him."

"It is the same thing." Her chest tightened, making it difficult to breathe.

"No, it is not."

"I would have stayed with you and become Indian," she whispered. "I would have left everything I've ever known behind. I could even forgive you for Colin's loss, but—"

"You must understand," he answered hoarsely. "The ceremony was done not to bring you pain but so that you might go on living."

"Why couldn't you simply admit that you'd made a mistake? Is your pride so important that

you'd throw away my love, our future life together, rather than say you were wrong?" she
flared. "What kind of man are you that you can't
say you were wrong?"

He pulled her into his arms and kissed her. She
stood as stiff as a wooden doll, unwilling to give
him the satisfaction of letting him know how
much she wanted his embrace . . . his touch.

"Sweet Water," he murmured hoarsely. He
kissed her again.

She didn't fight him, but she gave no response
to his caress at all. "No more of your lies," she
said. "You don't love me as I love you. That's the
truth."

"My heart, my little fox-haired lion. Ask anything of this man but his honor. Ask for my eyes
and I will cut them out and give them to you."

"What good would that do?"

"Try to understand, *ki-te-hi*. Try. A Shawnee
man—a warrior—is judged by his word. A solemn
vow may not be broken. This one must keep his
promise or become an outcast, lower than the bile
that spills from a drunkard's lips. By asking that
you be accepted into the tribe and reborn as a
Shawnee woman, this man witnessed the death of
one he swore to kill."

"I can see that," she whispered. "It's not logical
by my way of thinking, but—"

"My love for you is one thing you must never
doubt," he said, caressing her hair with his cheek.
"It is as sure as the rise of the sun and the turning
of the seasons. And it will remain steadfast until
dawn comes no more and the earth has ceased to
give life to her children."

"Then why must I go back?"

"For peace. To honor my father's memory, and

to keep mothers from weeping over the graves of their lost ones. If we do not send you back, more long rifles will come. The English king's soldiers will hunt us, and we will find no place to raise our corn or build our wigwams."

"I don't want to go."

He kissed her mouth, slowly, tenderly. She slipped her arms around his neck and pulled him down to her.

"This man does not want you to go, but there is no other way."

Not forever, she thought. I can't stand it if I'll never see him again. "But if peace comes . . ." she said. "If the killing stops, then why couldn't we . . ."

"In my lifetime there has been no peace," he replied.

"But there could be. Promise me that you'll come for me or that I can come to you if things get better between the whites and the Indians. Promise me, Talon. Please, give me something to hope for."

For a long moment, he stood there holding her in utter silence. "If there is peace, this man will come for you."

"You promise?"

"On my mother's grave. This one will not forget you, my Sweet Water. If we can be together again in honor, it will be."

She sighed deeply and snuggled close to him.

"We should go back to the camp," he said finally. "We have far to walk tomorrow."

"Should we?" she asked. Her lips tingled from his kiss, and tears spilled down her cold cheeks.

He groaned and pressed her roughly back

against a tree trunk. Frantically, his hands moved over her body and his mouth sought hers.

Her blood flared as he strained against her, seeking confirmation of their mutual need. There in the darkness within earshot of the camp, they came together in one last desperate act of loving. And when they finally returned to their blankets by the fire, they walked hand in hand.

Five days later, Rebecca lay belly down beside Talon, Counts, and Siipu, staring at a clearing and two cabins in the valley below. Osage Killer waited in the forest, standing guard.

Far below where they lay, smoke drifted from stone chimneys and from an outdoor fire where a woman stirred a large copper caldron. A youth and a barking dog herded several black and white cows across a stubbled cornfield toward a lean-to stable. From behind one of the buildings came the distinct sound of an ax splitting wood.

"There," Talon said. "Go to the German's house and tell him who you used to be. They will take you to the English soldiers. And when they do, you must say that war between Indian and white is a bad thing. Tell them that they must come no farther west with their roads and wagons. Tell them that many will die on both sides if they break the treaties again."

Siipu touched her hand. "Walk with the sun on your face, sister. We have no word for goodbye. To you, this woman says, when you hear wind in trees, sound be whisper of our love for you."

Counts acknowledged Rebecca's departure with a reluctant nod.

"I don't know what to say," Rebecca admitted stiffly. Now that it was time for them to go their separate ways, she didn't know if she could keep from weeping. She looked into Siipu's solemn face. "Siipu . . ."

The Indian woman smiled and shook her head.

"Kedata," Rebecca corrected. "I will never forget you."

"Do not forget Meshepeshe," she reminded.

"Don't worry, I won't." She knotted her hands into tight balls and glanced at Talon. "I don't . . ." she began awkwardly.

Siipu motioned to Counts and they inched backwards away from the ledge and got to their feet.

"It should be safe enough for you to go the rest of the way alone," Talon said. "Call out loudly in English so that they can see you aren't an Indian."

"Talon—" she whispered.

"It is time," he said, backing down the incline away from the edge. She followed and he took her hand, gripping it so tightly that she thought her bones would crack. His hot liquid gaze burned into her soul.

"Remember your promise," she whispered. "If peace comes—"

"This man remembers," he murmured. *"Inu-msi-ila-fe-wanu* keep you from—"

Without warning, a hound began to bay from the forest behind them. A second dog took up the cry. Then a musket shot shattered the quiet morning.

Rebecca screamed. "No! Don't shoot! I'm English!"

Osage Killer's gun fired a reply.

Talon threw up his rifle just as Rebecca saw several white men dash from the trees. The first man fired. Osage Killer groaned and slumped to the ground. Talon's rifle roared. Counts flung himself over his friend's body and raised his weapon as the yellow-haired German staggered to his knees, struck down by Talon's shot.

"Stop!" Rebecca cried. "Please stop!"

Talon braced the butt of his rifle against the ground and began to reload. Counts fired at the charging white men. "Take cover!" Talon yelled to the women.

"No!" Rebecca shouted. "Stop shooting!"

A tall white man in a striped shirt and fringed hunting coat turned and leveled his rifle at her.

"*Ku!*" Siipu cried. Just as the German pulled the trigger, she threw herself in the path of the bullet.

Rebecca screamed. Something struck her. She put her hand to her breast and drew it away covered with blood. Puzzled, she stared at her hand. She felt no pain, but suddenly, the ground beneath her seemed to sway. "Siipu?" she called. "Siipu?"

Talon's sister turned toward her with dilating eyes. The front of her beautiful deerskin was a red blur. "*Num ees,*" she rasped. "My dear sister, take care of him." Dark red blood trickled from her mouth, then became a stream. She pitched forward into Rebecca's arms.

Rebecca tried to hold her, but her strength was fading. "Siipu," she murmured drunkenly. "What's . . . what's happening?"

Rebecca groaned as the ground came up and hit her. Then she heard Talon's war cry as he threw himself at the Germans. Another shot rang out. A loud buzzing filled her head. "Talon," she cried. It came out a whisper. "Talon . . ." Then the buzzing swallowed her up and she sank into merciful blackness.

Chapter 23

Pennsylvania Colony
March 1752

Nearly three months from the day of Siipu's murder, Rebecca clung to the seat of a farm wagon on the Philadelphia road. Clad in a gray wool skirt and bodice, linen mobcap, and man's shapeless felt hat, Rebecca watched the throng of travelers with a weary apathy.

The wide dirt lane was a morass of mud and potholes, crowded by foot traffic, vehicles, and horsemen. Just ahead, the way was blocked by a herd of pigs and an overturned ox cart with a broken wheel. The driver of the oxen swore mightily and shook his fist at a broom seller. The peddler, not in the least intimidated, was shouting back at him in a language Rebecca had never heard before.

Ernst Byler reined in the bays and motioned for Rebecca to stay where she was. Swearing softly in German, he removed his worn cocked hat and wiped the sweat from his forehead. Climbing down from the wagon, Ernst strode around the head of his team and tested the ground to the right of the road with his boot heel.

A speckled pig broke from the squealing herd and dove between the legs of the horses. Snorting

294

loudly, the bays tossed their big heads and sidled sideways in the harness, but made no move to bolt. Rebecca sat with her hands folded in her lap and waited, not really caring if they went on or sat here all day.

It was warm for March; the sun had broken through the clouds in midmorning and had shone brightly ever since. Two days of rain had soaked the earth, and the air smelled of new grass and freshly turned earth. Already, farmers were plowing the fields, leaves were budding, and the meadows and hillsides were taking on a vivid green hue.

Rebecca didn't notice the vibrant colors of spring or the trilling notes of bird calls. She was still mentally locked in winter and in her prison of grief.

The first few weeks after the tragedy had been lost in pain and fever. Vaguely, she'd been aware of a smoky cabin, the heavy odor of sickness, and unfamiliar white faces peering into hers.

Her self-appointed saviors had spoken only German. She neither understood nor spoke a word of the language. It would be nearly three long months before Ernst Byler came to the farm and explained that her shooting had been an accident. Meinhard Troyer, her host, had believed that she was an Indian. "Because of the clothes, you see," Ernst had translated. "An honest mistake."

The German settlers had believed her mad, too crazed by her terrible experience to realize that she'd been rescued from the savages. It was a belief that had only been strengthened when Rebecca first set foot out of the cabin after weeks flat on her back in bed. She had taken one look at the mountain lion skin stretched on the stable door and flown at Meinhard with hammering fists and round Irish oaths.

And when she'd noticed Talon's prized rifle hanging over the fireplace, she'd cried for hours and not eaten a mouthful for four days.

Dead. They were all dead; Siipu, Osage Killer, Counts His Scalps, and Talon. They were dead. She wished with all her heart that she had died back there on the crest of the hill as well.

Mornings were the hardest. Each day she would wake, and the overwhelming sorrow would grip her. She almost welcomed the pain in her breast. Meinhard's lead slug had torn her flesh and scarred her for life, but all she could think of was that the bullet had passed through Siipu first. Her Indian sister had given her life so that Rebecca could live.

It was the greatest gift a soul could offer another. And Rebecca didn't want it . . .

Strangely enough, she felt no hate for Meinhard Troyer and his family. They were not evil people; they had fired on Osage Killer out of ignorance. In the eyes of settlers, especially those recently come from the old country, Indians were the enemy—to be destroyed as routinely as the forests were cut down. Even if she spoke fluent German, it would have been impossible to convey to them what kind of people Talon and Siipu had been.

The chasm between the two cultures was too great to be crossed. The Troyers were Christians; the Indians—in the immigrants' minds—godless animals who wanted nothing more than to ravish and burn.

She had nearly gotten her wish. Meinhard's wife, Anna, had nearly killed her with her dubious medical skills. Rebecca had suffered poultices of goose grease, *powwowing*, smoke blown in her ear, a concoction of sulphur, molasses, and cow urine, live leaches, and having her hands and feet tied to the bed post for the duration of each night.

Too ill and despondent to have an appetite, she had been forced to eat three large meals a day. Greasy blood sausages, cabbage and potatoes, sauerkraut, boiled turnips, and thick porridge with cream had been spooned into her resisting mouth by a stubborn Anna, and promptly rejected by Rebecca's stomach.

She supposed she should consider herself lucky. If the Troyers had been able to find a physician to attend to her bullet wound, he would have bled her, draining what small reserve of will to live she possessed.

Rebecca shifted on the hard wagon seat and glanced down at her hands. The nails were bitten to the quick, and her fingers were so thin that they seemed to belong to a stranger.

An image of Talon's face rose in her mind's eye, and the familiar pain swept over her again. She dashed away the tears that spilled down her cheeks and stared over the horses' heads at the ox cart without really focusing on anything.

Would he haunt her waking and sleeping dreams forever, this copper-skinned shadow? She had loved him, truly loved him, with a passion that exceeded anything she'd ever felt before. She loved him more than she loved Colin or her parents. She loved him more than her own life.

Without Talon, nothing mattered.

They had told her they were returning her to her husband. She didn't care. Nothing Simon Brandt could do to her could touch her. She was already a ghost inside.

Oh, Talon, she sobbed. If I could only feel your arms around me one more time. If I could only hear your laughter ... or even your boasting, she thought wryly.

So many memories ... so many regrets.

Ernst was climbing back into the wagon again. Without speaking to her, he picked up the reins, clicked to his team, and guided them off the road and around the stalled cart. The cart driver shouted something rude as they passed, but Rebecca didn't catch the words and didn't care.

Ernst Byler was a cousin by marriage to Meinhard Troyer. He'd heard of the trouble at the farm, and he'd come with fresh supplies as soon as the weather eased enough for him to make the trek west.

He'd brought with him news of a smallpox epidemic. Rumors were that Indians had started the spread of the illness. More than thirty settlers had died and no one knew how many soldiers. Fort Nelson had been abandoned and later had burned; no one knew who was responsible, but it was supposed that hostiles had done that as well.

Pennsylvania militias had joined with Maryland to make a united attack on unfriendly Indian villages. Simon Brandt had been ill with smallpox himself, but he'd risen from his sickbed and led an expedition that destroyed three Indian encampments. Simon Brandt was in Philadelphia where, it was reported, he was about to be rewarded for his courage with a huge grant of land and a prize of fifty pounds sterling, collected by grateful citizens.

Rebecca's coming would be a surprise to Simon. Doubtless, the Troyers and Ernst Byler expected to be repaid for caring for her and for transporting her to the arms of her loving husband. With so much hard coin, Ernst had declared repeatedly, Simon Brandt would be in a generous mood. Rebecca couldn't keep a bitter smile from her lips. It would serve them all right if Simon refused to take her. What she would do then, she didn't know . . . or care.

"Watch yer step, Mister Brandt," Ezra Fry, the turnkey, said as he led the way down narrow, slick steps to the cell where the red Indian was imprisoned. A rat squeaked and scurried away as the yellow lantern light cast a feeble glow across the crumbling brick floor. "Watch yer 'ead, sir, them rafters over top is low as well."

Stagnant water pooled in low spots. Simon stepped around a puddle and ducked to avoid a hanging spider web. The cellar smelled of mouse droppings and rotting hay. He paused and squinted into the darkness. The only window at street level had been bricked in, and the single candle burning in the lantern provided poor light. This place gave him the creeps. "Where's the prisoner?" he demanded. Damned if he could even see anything resembling a jail.

" 'Ere, Mister Brandt." The guard sloshed through the water and raised the wooden bar on a board-and-batten door set into the brick wall. "In 'ere." He lifted the lantern so that Simon could see.

A dirt-walled annex, no more than five feet wide, six high, and eight deep, ran back into the side of the hill. The ceiling was of splintered planks, the earthen floor covered with moldy hay. There was no furniture, no blankets, and no candle. The condemned, manacled hand and foot with heavy iron, sat hunched over with his back against the far side.

"No need t' worry," Ezra said. "They's a stake set in the ground. The Injun's chained to it. 'E can't reach us."

The prisoner didn't move. His face was hidden from the light by a fall of tangled black hair. The smell hit Simon's nose and he gagged.

"Bad as a midden, ain't it?" Ezra grimaced. "Be 'ard fer a man to stay down 'ere and keep 'is mind whole. This one don't care. What's 'e know? A filthy Injun. No better'n pigs, they be. Stink to high jezzes, ever one of them."

Simon pulled the knife from the sheath at his waist and moved into the cell.

"No need to arm yourself. I tole ye, sir. 'E's not goin' nowhere."

"I've fought Injuns all my life. Scalped more than you got fingers 'n toes. One thing I learnt. Ye don't take chances." Simon seized a handful of the Indian's hair and lifted it so that he could get a clear view of the man's face.

Talon stared back at him with blazing eyes.

"Mother of Christ!" Simon gasped and jumped back. "That's him, all right. That's Medicine Smoke's son, Fire Talon."

"Simon Brandt."

Simon felt as though a timber rattler had just crawled into his bedroll. Hair pricked on his arms, and a queer sensation knotted his bowels.

"Simon Brandt."

Simon tried to answer, but the lump in his throat would not let the sound come out. That was his enemy's voice, sure as shootin'. It was . . . but it wasn't. No demon from hell could put so much malice into a man's name.

The guard snickered, and Simon threw him a look that made him take a step back. "Leave that light and get the hell out o' here."

"That ain't regulations," Ezra protested. "I'm responsible for—"

Simon flashed the knife, and Ezra set the lantern on the sill so hard that it toppled over and he had to right it. "Yes, sir," he replied. "Whatever ye say, Mister Brandt. Yer the Injun fighter, ain't ye." He mumbled a few more flatteries and backed away, his boot nails clicking on the bricks.

Simon waited until the footfalls faded, then looked back at Talon. The wolfish black eyes still watched him with grim relentlessness.

Simon felt a cold draft on the back of his neck. He stiffened, tasting the metallic flavor of fear in his mouth. Shame lanced through him and he slammed the hilt of his hunting knife down across Talon's head. "Take that, ye swivin' red bastard," he swore.

Blood sprang from the split in Talon's scalp, but the Indian didn't react at all. He just kept staring.

"I watched yer pa swing," Simon said, torn between wanting to hurt him again and reluctant admiration for his grit. "I wanted to be there to watch ye foller him to the gates of hell. But they tell me yore goin' back to England to hang. His Majesty's pleasure, the sheriff said. Whipped through the streets of Philadelphia and delivered to King George's court for execution. What do ye say to that, ye mangy dog's vomit?"

Talon didn't answer. It came to Simon that Medicine Smoke had been the same at the end. Not sayin' a word, just watchin'. It wasn't natural. It proved they weren't human, not like white men.

He wondered if the Shawnee had stared at Rebecca like that before he'd raped her. "Did ye take pleasure with my woman?" he asked. "Was she good? I know it's not the first white woman you've abused. Two wives I've had, both taken by the savages, both ruined by ye."

Talon might have been stone deaf. He didn't blink, and he didn't move a muscle. Blood ran down his forehead, but he ignored it as though it didn't exist.

"Did ye hear me? I said my first woman was stolen by a devil like you. But I found her, and I made her pure as driven snow. I cut her throat. Let God judge her. I always said the Injuns done it, but it was me. I had to. She was ruined, swelling with a red bastard."

Talon stared through him.

"Is Rebecca dead? Did you cut her throat and leave her body in the woods?" Simon demanded. "I hoped ye hadn't. I wanted to punish her myself. I wanted to cut her throat like I did the other one. It's my right, ye see. My duty, as her husband." This time when the Indian didn't answer, he struck him across the face with the knife hilt, opening his cheek with the force of the blow.

Talon's head rocked back, but he tensed, swallowed, and continued to look at him as if he wanted to skin him alive and roast him over a torture fire.

"She better be dead," Simon taunted. "If she's not ... Well, she better be. I don't take leavings." He stepped back and forced a laugh. "Ye won't be lonely fer no squaw on the ship. Them sailors got a taste for red meat, I hear. By the time ye get to London, ye ain't gonna be so high and mighty."

That threat struck home. Talon's visible hand tightened to a fist and his muscles tensed.

"Ye think on that," Simon said. "Ye think on it good. 'Cause I'll be thinkin' about it." He bent and picked up the lantern. "Ye won't be needin' this light," he said. "Ye might as well get used to it. It's gonna be dark in the hold of that ship." He put a hand on the door and ducked his head. "Lucky thing that soldier recognized ye at the German's farm, wasn't it? Otherwise, they might of just strung ye up then and there. This way, his Majesty gets to see why he's spendin' so much money tryin' to make the frontier safe for god-fearin' Englishmen."

Simon slammed the door behind him and threw the bolt. His chest felt tight, and he had the shakes. "No different than being in a pit with a mad wolf," he muttered. "Tomorrow, Fire Talon!" he yelled through the door. "I'm gonna be there in the front row to see them cut the hide offen your back with a cat-o'-nine-tails."

He wished the judge hadn't ordered the Shawnee back to England to hang. Better for it to be done here and now. If Talon ever got loose, he'd leave a trail of dead men behind him, that was as certain as God's sunrise.

"Damn fool," he mumbled under his breath. The English born judge didn't know a thing about Injuns. "No more about Injuns than a skunk knows about preachin'." He climbed the stairs slowly, wishing he'd finished off Fire Talon when he had the chance . . . wishing he had the nerve to go back into the cell and do the job.

Damn if he wouldn't, court order or no court order, if it wasn't for that land grant the Pennsylvania bigwigs were about to give him. That's what happened to a man when he got property; he lost the freedom to do what his instincts told him to do. He reckoned that silver was as much a corruption of a man's soul as the devil could be.

When he stepped into the room at the top of the stairs, there was another man there with Ezra Fry. The newcomer was a Quaker. Simon could tell by the wide-brimmed hat and the sober gray clothes cut of expensive wool cloth.

"Simon Brandt," the Quaker asked.

He nodded. "I am."

"Friend—"

"You're no friend of mine. We don't even know each other," Simon replied. He had no use for Quakers. They talked soft and expected other men to do their fighting for them. Any man that wouldn't do his own scrappin' was yellow as a cur dog.

"I am Jonathan Flanders. There's no need for thee—"

"Spit it out," Simon said. "Ye want Simon Brandt, ye've found him."

"There is a man on the street inquiring for thee, friend, a German by the name of Ernst Byler. He has brought thy wife, Rebecca."

"He's done what?"

"Thy wife, Rebecca. She has been ill, but she's alive and on the way to recovery. Ernst Byler's cousin nursed her back to health after they rescued her from the Indians. You'd best come quickly, Simon." The broad-faced Quaker smiled. "And I do believe a reward is in order."

"Reward, hell," Simon said. "Rebecca's dead." She had to be, he thought, as heat washed up his neck and burned the raw places where the pox had scarred him. "The Injuns killed her," he protested. "Whoever this is, she's not my wife."

"Thee best had come and see for thyself. The Lord works in mysterious ways."

"He does, does he?" He took his rifle from the corner where he'd left it and slung his possibles bag over his shoulder. If it was Rebecca, the whorin' little red-haired bitch, he'd make her sorry she'd ever been born. "If that's my wife and the Germans had her, then why didn't they turn her over to the soldiers, or at least tell them they had her?"

"They did tell them, or at least they tried. Ernst Byler says his cousin has no English. The soldiers looked at your wife, but apparently they thought she was one of the family."

Simon pushed past him and opened the door. Below, on the street stood a farm wagon. On the single board seat sat his Jezebel wife—skinny as last winter's hen, and looking older than he'd last seen her, but Rebecca sure enough. For an instant he toyed with the idea of denying her, but then she looked up and saw him.

"Simon," she said.

"Rebecca."

The Quaker stepped out onto the landing beside him. "Did I not tell thee? The Lord does work in mysterious ways."

Simon gritted his back teeth so hard that he felt the corner of one molar crumble. "Praise God," he said. "It is my sweet Rebecca, come home from the shores of hell."

Chapter 24

"**S**it over there and don't open your mouth." Simon shoved Rebecca roughly toward the lumpy bed under the eaves of the attic room.

Keeping her eyes averted, she did as she was told. She hadn't spoken a word to him since she'd first seen him in the street and called his name. She'd watched in silence as Simon had given Ernst Byler ten pounds and thanked him for returning his wife. Then, she'd followed her husband meekly through the streets of Philadelphia to the modest inn near the Delaware River.

"Where's the boy?" he demanded.

"I don't know." If she looked at him, her shock at his appearance might show. When she'd last seen Simon, his features were considered by many to be handsome. Now, the pox had ravished his skin and left angry red craters and puckered scars extending up into his thinning hair. Simon had aged ten years in the past five months. "Colin was taken prisoner," she continued. "I haven't seen him since the day the farm was—"

"Since the day yer *red lover* burned my house and barn? The boy's dead. Make yer mind up to that."

She kept her head down and made no reply. Colin was alive. Nothing Simon could say would change that.

"All the while ye were spreadin' your legs for that Injun, he had yer brother's scalp on his belt."

She shifted, uneasy. There was something different about her husband besides his looks. He'd always been a hard man ... but now, here alone with him, she was suddenly afraid.

"How does that make ye feel? Knowin' ye took pleasure from his thick, dirty cock—"

A loud rap at the door cut off Simon's tirade. With a scowl, he flung open the door. "Yes, what is it?" he demanded of the plump maid standing there.

"Man t' see ye. In the public room. Simon Brandt, he said. Said it was very important business, sir. To do with a land grant."

He glanced back at Rebecca. "Ye stay here and cause no trouble. And talk to no one."

He closed the door behind him, and the tension in the chamber dissipated. She stretched out full length on the bed and pulled a coverlet over her. The patched quilt smelled of mold and stale beer, but she didn't care. She lay and stared at the raw beams and cedar shingles overhead, wondering why it made her so nervous to be alone with a man she'd been married to since she was fourteen.

Later, the maid returned with a round of bread, a slice of cheese, a chicken leg, and a pint of ale. "Mistress said ye needin' feedin', since ye've been a prisoner of the Indians so long. Mistress said ye need to put some meat on yore bones." The girl eyed her curiously. "I'm Betty, do ye need somethin'."

"Did my husband order this meal for me?" Rebecca asked. It was past the dinner hour. Even when he was angry with her, Simon had never been miserly about food before.

"No'm. My mistress. T'was her idee. Mistress Joan is a good sort, always feedin' stray cats an' such." Her blue eyes grew large in the ruddy face. "Not that yore a cat or nothin'. Just that—"

"Thank Mistress Joan for me, Betty. She is very kind."

The girl bobbed a curtsy and left.

Rebecca took a few sips of the ale and nibbled absently on the bread. It was fresh, but she still had little appetite. Simon was behaving strangely for a man whose wife had just returned from the dead ... It was almost as though he didn't want her back.

She didn't bother to light a candle, but returned to the bed when darkness seeped across the braided rag rug. Sometime in the night Simon came in smelling of rum and tobacco. She came instantly awake, but she forced herself to lie still, pretending to be asleep. Feathers of icy fear brushed her spine as he climbed into the bed.

Don't touch me, she begged silently. If he laid a single finger on her, she didn't know what she'd do. She only knew she couldn't bear the thought of his hands on her ... his mouth pressed against hers. But to her relief, he turned his back and fell into a deep sleep.

She lay awake until the first stirrings of the morning routine began in the inn below. Then she crept cautiously out of bed, put on her shoes, and started for the door.

"Where the hell ye think yore goin'?"

She stiffened. "To the necessary."

"Be quick about it. I've a surprise for ye this mornin' and I'll not be late."

"Yes, Simon."

"I can see the red nigras taught ye some manners. Too little, too late."

"Yes, Simon." She didn't wait for his dismissal. Heart pounding, she hurried downstairs and out into the back courtyard.

Dew covered the patches of grass that weren't worn thin by the coming and going of inn patrons. A tan and black spit dog pranced out of the stable with a dead rat clenched firmly in his sharp, white teeth, his stumpy tail wagging excitedly. From inside the barn, Rebecca heard the neigh of a horse and the restless pawing of an iron-clad hoof against a stall door.

The small structure she was looking for stood beyond the dovecote. As she was coming back toward the inn, she passed the red-cheeked Betty going out with a basket of scraps for the pigs.

"They's a special room for bathin' off the kitchen," the girl informed her. "Mistress Joan usually charges twopence, but she says yore welcome to wash free. On account of—"

"Being with the Indians," Rebecca finished. She almost smiled, remembering that the Shawnee were far cleaner than the German settlers, or even Simon for that matter. "I would like to bathe very much." Memories flashed across her mind . . . Talon throwing her into the stream and then laughing . . . Talon standing in hip-deep running water and scrubbing his lean body with sand until it glowed.

"Hurry then," Betty advised. "Be ye first, the water ain't scummy. They's yellow soap and towels."

"I'll go right away," Rebecca assured her. "And thank you."

Twenty minutes later, hair damp and skin tingling from the hasty scrub, Rebecca gathered her courage and entered the attic room.

"Where the hell have ye been?" Simon shouted.

She stared at the toes of his moccasins and prayed he wouldn't hear her heart banging against her chest. "Bathing."

"Thanks to yer disobedience we'll neither of us get any breakfast." He reached for her arm.

Trembling, she took a step back. He looked at her as though she was something foul rotting in a drainage ditch. Every instinct bade her get out of this room and away from him.

"Come on," he ordered. "I've something special for ye to witness this mornin'."

Puzzled, she followed him back down the stairs and out into the street. She felt better once they were out in the open air. Nothing will convince me to go back in that chamber with him, she thought.

As they rounded the corner and were sheltered from view of the inn by a clump of bushes, Simon grabbed a handful of her hair and twisted until tears welled up in her eyes.

"See that ye don't shame me further this mornin'," he threatened. "Keep your mouth closed and try to look decent." He shook her once more and released his grip.

I'm a free woman, she thought. I don't have to take this from anyone. She smiled at him sweetly. "I'm leaving you, Simon," she said softly.

"What?"

"I said, I'm leaving you. I'll not be beaten like your horse or kicked like a hound. I'm going my own way. You can divorce me if you like."

He stared at her as if she'd suddenly sprouted horns. "Ye ungrateful jade," he said, raising a clenched fist. "Ye Shawnee swivin' bitch. Who are ye to tell me that yer leavin'?"

A carriage turned the corner and came down the street toward them. Rebecca watched the approaching vehicle with relief. He might strike her, but Simon wouldn't do anything really violent in front of witnesses. As long as she was in public view, she felt almost safe. "I don't love you. I've never loved you," she continued frankly. "It's best for us both if we part."

"Ye'll go nowhere I don't give ye leave," he retorted. "I bought yer indenture. Ye belong to me—bought and paid fer."

She scoffed. "I think not. Best you remember what I know. There are many people who'd love to hear talk that the great Indian fighter, Simon Brandt, is less than . . . shall we say heroic?" she taunted him quietly. "Less than heroic in his wife's bed."

He would have struck her then, but the driver of the carriage chose that instant to rein in his team. The door of the vehicle swung open, and the same Quaker Rebecca had seen the day before with her husband leaned out.

"Friend Simon," he called. "I was sent to bring thee to the square. The sentence of public whipping is about to be carried out. Get in. I'll drive the both of thee."

Simon's mouth tightened to a thin ivory line. He threw her a warning glance, but he lowered his fist and pushed her toward the carriage. "I'd appreciate that, Mister Flanders," Simon said, "but I wonder what your interest is in all this."

"I'm merely a merchant who wishes peace on the frontier. And Jonathan will do. We plain folk do not use titles."

Still shaken, Rebecca climbed up and sat next to the far window.

The Quaker glanced at her. "Good day to thee," he said mildly.

She mumbled a reply and looked around. It had been many years since she'd ridden in a carriage, but her father's had been far more luxurious.

Simon seated himself opposite Flanders. "Ye must be more than that," he said, "if ye take so much interest in my affairs."

"Not so, friend. I am a member of the town council and a man of commerce."

"Flanders," Simon mused. "Thomas Edgewater who came to see me last night mentioned yer name. Ye own half the land between here and the mountains."

The Quaker dismissed his wealth with a motion of his soft hand. "It is in the interest of all God-fearing men that the Indians be driven out of Penn's Woods."

"My feelin's exactly," Simon said.

Rebecca stared out the open window as the carriage rattled over the streets. Quakers preached the equality of mankind. They were supposed to stand firm for peace and understanding between cultures. But Jonathan Flanders—for all his religion—was no different from Simon. He wanted the Indians' land, and he didn't care what happened to them in the process.

The city was rapidly coming alive. Milk sellers and fish vendors were noisily advertising their wares. Sailors jostled with apprentices to avoid the muddy spots in the road. Dogs barked, and cart wheels squeaked. Gray-shawled housewives shouted orders to their servants. Here a maid in a white linen cap was busy scrubbing the front steps of a brick house; there a blackamoor shooed a bleating goat as he led a saddle horse to a mounting block for his master.

Rebecca was struck by the smells of the town. Smoke from hundreds of fireplaces, tar and rotting fish from the dock, the sour stench of refuse piled beside a public eating house. Even the Quaker's wool clothing, which showed the effects of many years of wear without benefit of cleaning, gave off an offensive aroma. She sighed, finding herself wishing for the clean scent of pine and the quiet of the primeval forest.

The driver crossed through an intersection and reined the team to a halt. Up ahead, Rebecca saw a throng gathering around a knot of uniformed soldiers. Climbing down from his seat on top of the carriage, the servant opened the door. Simon and the Quaker got out, and Simon looked back at her.

"Let's go. What are ye waitin' fer, woman?"

She jumped down and followed the two men across the open square toward the center of activity. Stern-faced king's soldiers in red coats, white gaiters, and cocked hats stood rigid at attention, Brown Bess muskets gripped in their hands. Beyond the soldiers, several elaborately bewigged civilian authorities surveyed the assembly with bored expressions from the isolation of their sedan chairs.

"Pork pies," cried a wrinkled old woman carrying a basket of steaming pastries. "Hot pork pies! Ha' penny each."

Simon caught hold of Rebecca's arm and forced her to quicken her step to match his longer stride. "Look there," he said, pointing. "I believe ye are well acquainted with the condemned."

Two burly soldiers dragged forth an Indian.

"There's the savage!" someone shouted. "There's the red devil hisself!"

A skinny boy uttered a poor imitation of a war whoop. He and a companion had bedecked themselves with chicken feathers and streaked their faces with ashes. Now they jumped up and down and howled with laughter at their own jest.

"God in heaven," a woman in a wide-brimmed straw hat shrieked. "He's not wearing any clothes."

A soldier carrying a coiled leather whip marched stiffly in front of the guards restraining the Indian captive. Just behind them came two additional privates with muskets.

Rebecca's breath caught in her throat. There was something achingly familiar about the nearly naked prisoner. His body was battered and bloody, his filthy loincloth so dirty that its original color was lost. Long black matted hair, tangled beyond belief, hung below the leather hood that obscured his features.

For a heartbeat, she dared to imagine that it might be Talon, but cold logic drenched her hope. The man she loved was long dead, his bones scattered by wind and rain. This was only another poor soul, trapped by the king's justice, held to account for something that—

The soldier with the whip snatched the hood off the prisoner. The Indian's head snapped up, and her knees turned to jelly. If Simon hadn't supported her weight, she would have fallen. A single glimpse of those defiant black eyes was all it took; she uttered a strangled sound of rejoicing, and her husband's fingers dug into her flesh.

Talon. Sweet Jesus, it was Talon. He was alive.

"Mind yourself, woman," Simon hissed in her ear.

He might have been a pile of cow dung for all the heed she paid him. Tears streamed down her cheeks. Talon hadn't died with his sister and the others. He was alive.

"Rebecca!" Simon shook her.

Talon's gaze found her and the familiar lightning bolt seared her to the core. *"Ki-te-hi!"* she cried.

The flat of Simon's hand stung her cheek, but she didn't feel the pain. Talon was alive. She was alive. Nothing else mattered. Not Simon, not the soldiers, not the king of England himself.

"Friend Simon," Flanders cautioned. "Chastise thy wife in private if thee wish, but not here. Such public display of—"

"Mind yer own business," Simon retorted.

"N'tschutti, ili klebeleche?" Talon shouted.

What was he saying? Rebecca struggled to understand the Indian words. *N'tschutti . . . dearly beloved.* Her heart leaped in her breast. *Ili klebeleche.* That was the Delaware greeting. *Dearly beloved, do you draw breath yet?*

What was the traditional reply? *"N'leheleche,"* she called to him. *Yes, I do exist.*

"K'dahole!" His eyes held hers as the soldiers bound him to a raw oak post, newly set into the ground, and secured his manacled wrists to a spike set high above his head.

I love you. She smiled through her tears. He'd said he loved her. *"K'dahole!"* she shouted back.

People began to notice her and Simon. They pointed and whispered, some recognizing the famous Indian fighter.

"She's talking to him in that Injun gobble-de-gook," a sailor said loudly.

"Who is she?" demanded his comrade.

"Shameless." A woman with a dirty child in tow pushed between two merchants to get a better view of Rebecca.

She heard them all, but nothing they could say was important. Rebecca's eyes and her thoughts were on Talon as an officer stepped forward and began to read from the parchment held in his hands.

". . . guilty of the heinous crimes of murder, horse theft, kidnapping, anarchy, and high treason. It is the sentence of this court that the Indian, known as Fire Talon, alias John Talon, shall suffer twenty lashes on the streets of Philadelphia. Furthermore, the said Fire Talon shall be transported to London. There, at his majesty's pleasure, he shall suffer another twenty lashes before being conveyed to Tyburn gallows where he shall be hanged by the neck until dead. His body shall be taken down and cut into four equal pieces, his head severed and placed on public display so that all good folk may know the folly of sin. It is further the sentence of this court that each quarter of the condemned shall be . . ."

Rebecca knew that a Shawnee woman would listen to the terrible words without showing emotion. But she was a daughter of Ireland, and her grief would not be contained. "No!" she screamed as the soldiers raised the cat-o'-nine-tails to deliver the first blow. "No!"

Simon tried to hold her, but she twisted free and darted through the crowd. She was beyond reason, beyond thought. All she knew was that Talon was helpless and he needed her.

She had nearly reached him when they caught
her. Her cries of rage did not block out the crack
of the whip and the awful sound of leather striking flesh.

For weeks she hadn't had the strength to take a
single step or even lift her head. Now, two soldiers
couldn't subdue her. Sobbing wildly, she kicked
and punched and nearly wrested a flintlock pistol
from an officer before they pinned her to the
ground.

"Seven!" The whip hissed again. Talon uttered
not a sound, but she had known he wouldn't.

Then she heard Simon's voice.

". . . out of her mind . . . a captive of the Indians."

"She needs a physician's care," Flanders said.

"Be still or I'll knock ye senseless," Simon whispered in her ear.

She continued to struggle as they enveloped her
in a man's wool coat and carried her off the square
to Flanders' carriage. As they tried to push her
through the door, she freed a hand and hit Simon
full on the nose. He struck her alongside the head
and shoved her inside. There, the two men
pressed her to the floor, nearly suffocating her
with the heavy coat. Her lungs burned from lack
of air. She kicked and tried to get the cloth away
from her face, then lost consciousness.

When she became aware of what was happening again, she was content to lie still. Exhausted
and sore, she forced herself to remain limp as Simon picked her up. She didn't open her eyes, but
she knew he'd taken her into a house. She didn't
think it was the inn, because there were none of
the usual sounds of patrons in the public room or
odors of mutton and ale.

He walked up a flight of steps, followed a hall, and then put her down on a featherbed. She could hear him talking to someone, but he'd moved back, too far away for her to understand what he'd said.

"What is this?" asked a cultured feminine voice. "Jonathan? Who is this young woman?"

Rebecca opened her eyes a crack and tried to see who was speaking. She saw only the satin drapes of embroidered bed hangings overhead.

". . . hysterical outburst at the public lashing of the Indian murderer."

That was Jonathan Flanders. Could this be his home? Was the woman a member of his household? Rebecca wondered.

"She's lost her wits," Simon said. "I didn't want to bring her here, but your husband—"

"Stuff and nonsense," the woman replied. "Jonathan was right. All Philadelphia is abuzz with word of your poor wife's ordeal and her rescue from the savages. What woman would not be hysterical at the sight of the savage who caused her . . ."

Mistress Flanders, then. And much younger than her husband, Rebecca reasoned, if she was any judge of tone. They had brought her to Flanders' house. And Simon was trying to convince them to let him take her back to the inn.

". . . ain't right to put this burden on yer wife," Simon said. "I can fetch a doctor—"

"We won't hear of it, will we, Jonathan?"

"Now, Rachel," Flanders put in. "If Friend Simon wishes—"

"Double stuff and nonsense," Rachel replied. "Friend Simon is welcome to stay with us as well.

You are a hero to us all. It would be an honor to have you."

". . . the Hebrew physician, Saul—"

Rachel cut off her husband's suggestion. "The poor thing has had enough. She needs sleep and good care. Can you not see how thin she is? She will remain here in this house until she is better."

"But if she needs doctorin'," Simon began, "then—"

"The Lord is the best physician, Friend," Rachel said. "And my cook, Lil, is well versed in medicinal practices. Out, out, both of you. Oh, you did not tell me her Christian name."

"Rebecca," Simon said.

"Rebecca. We shall get her into more comfortable clothes and give her something to make her sleep. She shall be better tomorrow, Friend Simon. You shall see. I'm right, aren't I, Jonathan? Who would know about a woman's ills better than another woman?"

Rebecca heard the sound of footfalls and then a lighter step approaching the bed. Cautiously, she fluttered her lashes and let out a delicate groan.

"Dear Rebecca," Rachel said. "You are safe here." A pink and white porcelain face with wide-spaced china blue eyes appeared at her side. Her cap was of the finest lace, her silk ribbon wide and sparkling white. Mistress Flanders' dress was a subdued gray-blue, but elegantly cut and sewn in the finest silk. A few golden curls escaped from her cap to frame the cupid features. Rachel's nose was tiny and upturned, her bee-stung lips as red and rosy as spring strawberries.

No wonder she has her way in this household, Rebecca thought. She opened her eyes a little more and gave what she hoped was a look of fright. "Where . . . where am I?" she whispered feebly.

"You are safe, dear friend. This is the home of Jonathan Flanders, and I am his wife in God, Rachel. You have . . . you have had a nervous—"

"Oh." Rebecca covered her face with her hands. "Oh. What have I done?" she cried.

"There, there. It will be all right. You've had a terrible strain."

"But the Indian," Rebecca whispered hoarsely. "The Indian. I saw him. Don't let him get me. Please, don't let him—"

"Never fear. The rascal is tied to the whipping post, where he shall remain until he is taken on board the vessel *Endeavor* tomorrow. You are safe in this house. No one will hurt you here."

"No one?" Rebecca let her voice quaver, just a bit.

"No one. Your husband has left you in my care. He will be back to see you tomorrow. For now, you have only to rest."

"Oh, thank you, thank you, dear Rachel," she murmured. "I am . . . so . . . so very tired." She let her eyes drift shut.

"Then I will let you sleep. There is a bell on the table beside the bed. You have only to ring it and a servant will come." Still chattering platitudes, Rachel swept out of the room, closing the door behind her.

Rebecca gave a sigh of relief. She had all of today and the night to come up with a plan to save Talon. She must. She had lost him once, and she never intended to lose him again . . . no matter the cost.

Chapter 25

Rebecca pushed aside the cup of chocolate and lay back against the bed pillows. "No, thank you," she said weakly. Mistress Flanders had tried to administer laudanum to her earlier in the evening, and Rebecca was suspicious of the hot drink. "I'd rather sleep, if you don't mind, Rachel." She put two fingers over her lips in pretended distress. "I hope I'm not troubled by dreams of that savage. Is he far away?"

"Far enough for you not to worry," Rachel soothed. "We are quite a few blocks from the river."

"He's at the river still ... where they ..."

"Yes. Jonathan told me that he will remain under close guard. They will leave him tied to the stake tonight as an example to other wrongdoers."

Rebecca looked around her as though she expected an Indian attack at any moment. "Which way is that? The river?"

Rachel pointed toward the side windows. "Down there, but you need have no fear. There will be soldiers to watch him tonight, and at dawn they carry him aboard ship to sail for England." She offered the chocolate again. "Just take a little," she begged. "You've not eaten enough to keep a bird alive today. Chocolate always helps me to sleep." The corners of her pouty mouth turned up in a forced smile. Then she sipped daintily from her own cup.

"Perhaps later," Rebecca hedged.

"My slave girl, Faith, will sit with you tonight. Your husband was afraid you would be left alone, but I assured him we will take good care of you."

And give me no chance to escape, Rebecca thought.

Rachel finished her chocolate and a sweet biscuit and rose to leave. "I will expect you to come down for breakfast in the morning, dear."

"I'm sure I will feel up to it," she answered.

Rachel murmured a few more words and left the room. As soon as she did, Rebecca switched the Quaker woman's empty cup for her full one.

Seconds later, the door opened, and a tall, willow thin maid entered the bedchamber. "I'm to sit wi' ye, lady," she said. "I'm Faith." She was no more than sixteen and garbed all in black with a white apron and cap. The toes of her black shoes were scuffed and worn and her stockings patched. She came close to the bed and stood wringing her hands as if she were not sure what to do.

Rebecca noticed that the hem of the maid's skirt and her sleeves were inches too short for propriety. Faith is still a growing girl, she decided, and probably has a healthy appetite. Perhaps the charity of this good Quaker household doesn't extend to feeding their servants well.

"You may sit there," Rebecca said. She waved to the chair Rachel had just vacated, the chair next to the bedside table containing the chocolate and the plate of tea biscuits. "Have some chocolate and a sweet if you like," Rebecca said softly. "They're very good."

* * *

An hour later, Faith was dozing in the bed and Rebecca was hastily dressing. She slipped down the back stairs of the Flanders home, sneaked through the kitchen past the snoring cook on her pallet, and went out the back door. She took nothing with her but her own clothing, a few biscuits, and a man's cloak and hat she found hanging on pegs in the hall.

It was a cloudy night with no moon, and black as the inside of the devil's boot. She wasn't certain she could find the place where Talon was still held captive using Rachel's vague directions, but she knew she had to try. Getting him loose once she found him would be another problem. She hadn't bothered to look for a weapon. In a Quaker household, she didn't suppose she'd find a gun.

Behind the house were several smaller structures, a smoke house, and a stable. She slipped into the barn and used her nose and ears to find the nearest horse. Finding a bridle and saddle in the darkness of a strange tack room was even harder. But saddling the animal was easy once she'd fed it the biscuits.

Rebecca couldn't help smiling as she thought about Rachel's plan to drug her with the laudanum. Wouldn't she be surprised in the morning when she found the maid asleep instead of Rebecca.

She patted the horse's neck and whispered to him as she led him out through a back gate and along an alley. She hoped she wouldn't be seen, or that she wouldn't lose complete sense of the direction. Once she was several houses away from the grand Flanders' mansion, she coaxed the gelding over to a mounting block and scrambled up into the saddle, riding astride, despite the disarray of her skirts and petticoats.

Following the street, she rode past large town houses that gradually gave way to smaller dwellings and then what she thought might be places of business. The road ended near the water, but not in the place she wanted to be. Her choice was to turn left or right. She chose right and followed the river for a short ways, then reversed her path when she saw that buildings were farther and farther apart and she seemed to be riding into a marsh.

She had no idea how long it had taken her to come this far, but she couldn't quit now. She was a horse thief, and if they caught her, she'd be tried and hanged. She had to free Talon and they had to make their escape before dawn. If he couldn't ride because of the whipping, she vowed she'd find a way to tie him on the horse.

The cobwebs that had clouded her mind since Siipu had fallen with the musket ball in her back were gone. Her body was still weak, but it didn't matter. She and Talon were both alive, and God willing, they'd both survive to reach the Ohio country again. She wished Simon no harm, but she never wanted to lay eyes on his face again.

The sound of raucous male laughter and breaking glass alerted her to the drinking establishment ahead. Immediately, she dismounted and led the horse into another alley and tied it to the wheel of a large wagon. Keeping in the shadows, she crept close. As she'd suspected, the noise was coming from a waterfront tavern. What better place to find a weapon, she thought, than in a den of rascals?

She crouched next to an adjoining building clutching a barrel stave for the better part of an hour, while sailors and townfolk wandered in and out of the tavern. Some moved with a firm step, others seemed to have lost their sense of balance. But none seemed drunk enough for her purpose.

Finally, a smartly dressed gentleman staggered from the door. When he lifted his arm to bid farewell to a companion inside, Rebecca caught sight of a brace of pistols at his waist.

Come this way. Come this way, she pleaded silently. Why hadn't she listened more carefully to her father's tales of highwaymen? She didn't know what she was going to do, but she didn't intend to let this prize escape. Judging from the cut of his coat and the shine on his boots, he could afford the loss of a pistol.

Sweet Saint Katherine forgive me, she thought. First a horse thief, now a robber. She waited, heart thudding, as the man turned first one way and then the other. She couldn't resist a tiny moan of relief when he began to amble in her direction.

She felt sick to her stomach. If she didn't get a gun, how would she have any chance of saving Talon? But to get the pistol, she'd have to hit an innocent man over the head. Oh, well, she decided. In for a penny, in for a pound. With trembling hands, she lifted the piece of wood.

At that instant, a second figure moved out of darkness not three yards away. "Your money or your life!" he snarled.

Instead of handing over his money, the drunk put up a struggle. Both men fell cursing to the gutter in a tangle of arms and legs. The attacker punched and the victim beat him around the head with one of his pistols. Someone inside the tavern shouted, and two men burst out of the doorway. The thief got to his feet, ran a few steps, stumbled, and fell flat on his face. More men poured out into the street, and someone fired a shot. The drunk got up, fell down, and got up again, all the while yelling for all he was worth. And somewhere in the confusion, a painted whore in a scandalous red gown screamed and a pistol landed at Rebecca's feet.

"Thank you, God," she murmured. She dropped the board, scooped up the flintlock, and ran like the hounds of hell were on her heels. The angry crowd pursued the footpad in the opposite direction down the street. Rebecca arrived at the spot where she'd tied the horse with only a few bruises from bumping into walls in the darkness. She threw her arms around the gelding's neck in relief and managed to get into the saddle on the third try.

She rode away from the river and circled around, turning back toward the docks several streets over. This time, she found the open square. The green seemed deserted except for the slumped figure still tied to the post and a single sentry sitting beside a campfire.

Leaving the horse tied to a tree, she tucked the pistol under her cape and strolled to the edge of the firelight. As soon as he caught sight of her, the redcoat leaped to his feet and pointed his musket at her.

"Halt!" he cried. "Who goes there?"

" 'Tis only Molly McCarthy," she said, in her broadest Irish accent. "Don't shoot me, sir, I beg o' ye. I only wanted to see the red man fer meself." She flashed him her biggest smile. "Sure'n a brawny captain, such as yerself, can't be afraid of a defenseless colleen."

"I'm hardly a captain," he corrected. "There was

a sergeant here, but he went to wet his whistle and left me with the prisoner." He looked around. "Are you alone, woman?"

She laughed. "Not now, I'm hopin'."

He relaxed and lowered his musket. "What are you doing wandering the streets at night?" He scowled at her. "You look too pretty to be a tavern slut, and that's a fact."

"I should hope I'm not. I'm a good girl, I am. I just works nights is all. Me da is a fish dealer. We have to get up early. Folks want their fish at daybreak."

"Come closer, fish girl, and let me get a look at you."

"After what you called me?"

"Want to see the Indian, do you?"

"Aye." She let her skirts sway, just a little. "I do."

"He's a cannibal, they say."

"Do tell." She gave him a long, meaningful look.

"When they caught him, he'd murdered twenty men single handed. They say he ate their livers and made a jacket of their scalps."

"No . . ." Rebecca shivered.

"Come on, have a glance then. He's harmless enough now."

"Is he dead?"

"Save the king a bucket of coin if he was, but a healthy man don't die of no twenty lashes. Fifty now, that's a different tune. I saw a sergeant . . ."

Rebecca ignored his rambling. All she could think of was Talon. She tried to keep from trembling as she followed the soldier away from the firelight toward the whipping post. The March night was damp; fingers of mist crept in from the waterfront laden with the smells of ships and foreign cargo. From somewhere off across the water came the shrill note of a boatswain's pipe.

Four paces away from the stake, Rebecca could stand the tension no longer. She whipped the heavy flintlock pistol out from under her cape and used both hands to ease the hammer back. The ominous click was impossible to mistake.

"What the hell—" the sentry cried.

She jammed the muzzle against his spine. "Not a sound," she said. "Not unless you want to spend the rest of your life crawling on your belly. Untie the prisoner."

"I can't—"

She jabbed him harder. "I mean it, English. I'm an Irish rebel who's already killed more redcoats than Willy Brennan. I'll shoot as quick as I would a rat. I swear, I will."

"Woman . . . don't do this. That red man's dangerous. If I—"

"One more word out of you and they'll send both halves of you back to England in a pickle barrel," she threatened. "Talon?"

"*Yuho.*"

Yes. She was breathless with fear, but the sound of his voice made her want to shout with joy. He was hurt badly, she could tell. But he was strong enough to do what had to be done. "Can you walk if this soldier unties you?" she whispered.

"If you cut the rope, this one can walk on water."

"I don't think we want to cut it," she said. "We'll find better use for it." She dug the pistol into the soldier's back again. "Untie the prisoner. Don't make a sound and you may live through this."

"I'll be court-martialed."

"Better that than claiming six feet of Pennsylvania graveyard. Do it!"

Talon groaned and nearly fell to his knees when the ropes came loose. She wanted to catch him, but she didn't dare take the pistol away from the redcoat's back.

"Talon?"

"My muscles are just stiff," he replied hoarsely.

She bit her lower lip as she watched him pull himself erect and step away from the post. After so many hours with his arms over his head, she could imagine the effort it cost him to keep from screaming with pain.

"Tie him in my place," Talon said.

"Get over there," she ordered the sentry. He obeyed without another word.

Talon's wrists were still manacled, but working together, they managed to tie the soldier to the stake. She handed the pistol to Talon and tore off a section of the soldier's shirt to gag him.

Taking his musket, powder horn, and cartridge pouch, Rebecca led the way through the darkness to the spot where she'd left the gelding. "I have only one horse for us both," she said. "Two would have been better, but I was—"

He made a sound of amusement. "You have freed me, Sweet Water. Should a man complain because you didn't lead a Shawnee war party here?"

"I brought you this hat," she explained, sticking it on his head. "And a long cloak." He winced as she wrapped the garment around his shoulders and the rough wool fibers grated against his lacerated back.

His breathing was loud and labored in the mist.

"Are you all right?" she asked, then felt her face

go hot at her own foolishness. Of course, he wasn't all right. They were both in terrible danger.

Talon's movements were slow and obviously painful. "I'll be all right if I can wash the stink of this *Englishmanake* town off me," he answered.

"There's truth. You smell like a dead goat." She suddenly realized that she'd never seen him on a horse. "Can you ride? If you can't, I—"

"I can ride, Meshepeshe."

Meshepeshe. Lioness. She swallowed the lump in her throat. She didn't care what he smelled like. She wanted to throw her arms around him, to cover his face with kisses, but this wasn't the time or the place. "Talon . . ." she began huskily, "I thought . . . I thought you were dead."

"Counts His Scalps lives as well. He escaped. I don't know if he was wounded."

"They never told me that you were alive."

"A bullet grazed my skull. I was taken captive and turned over to British soldiers. I've been in a cell here in Philadelphia for weeks."

"I didn't know," she repeated. All the time she'd believed him dead and wanted to die herself . . . all those wasted tears . . . "Siipu saved my life at the cost of her own. I'm so sorry she had to die."

"My sister—the one whose name we do not say," he corrected her gently, "has the spirit of Osage Killer to guide her across the river to our father's lodge."

The effort it took for him to mount and help her up behind him brought tears to her eyes, but she would not break down now. She had too much pride to let him see her cry tonight.

"This man believed you dead as well."

"I'm not."

He chuckled. "You mean a ghost did not save this man from the torture stake?"

"Not a ghost, but not Rebecca Brandt anymore, either."

"This one knew that. But you have the courage of that sky-eyed Irish woman."

"I mean to go with you, Talon," she warned him. "Wherever you go, from this day forth. So long as I live, I will follow you."

"*N'mamentschi.* My heart rejoices."

"And mine," she whispered.

"We will be married."

She shook her head. "I can't, not as long as Simon lives. And if I pledge my life to you, I want an end to the bloodshed."

"You ask more than this man can give. If my people need—"

"Not all bloodshed," she said. "Just Simon's blood. I couldn't sleep at night knowing that I bought my happiness with my husband's death. Will you give me that, Talon?"

"You will not be my wife?"

"Not *will not, cannot.* It is my faith, Talon. I can live with you in glorious sin, but I can't marry."

"Another was his wife, not you, not the Shawnee woman, Sweet Water."

"You may pretend that, Talon. You may even believe it, but I'm not that much Indian."

"So." He gave a sound of finality. "Do you still care for Simon Brandt?"

"No. But I won't dirty my soul with hating him. There's been enough hate. Let someone else kill him—God knows he deserves a painful death and a quick trip to hell."

"You ask me to break the vow I made on my mother's grave?"

"If you love me, then—"

"We will live together, Sweet Water. In my heart, you will be my wife."

"And in my heart, you will be my husband," she promised.

He exhaled softly. "Do you know the way out of this city?"

"Straight west."

He looked up at the sky. "Two hours before dawn."

"Will it be enough?"

"I don't know." He turned the animal's head away from the square and dug his heels into the gelding's sides. The horse started forward, and Talon reined him to a trot. "We must go quietly," he said. "There will be time enough for running later."

I hope, Rebecca thought.

They had gone no more than a block when muskets roared behind them. Seconds later came the urgent tattoo of a military drum. "The soldiers," she cried. "They've found out you escaped."

His only reply was to slap the horse's neck. The animal leaped forward, his hooves clattering over the damp cobblestones as he broke into a hard canter. Rebecca clutched tightly to Talon's waist, closed her eyes, and began to pray.

Chapter 26

By sunup, the gelding was winded. Foam sprayed from his mouth, and his neck and sides were streaked with sweat. So far, by changing direction again and again, by cutting through alleys and across private yards, Talon and Rebecca had escaped capture by the king's soldiers and the civilian authorities.

They were no longer riding through the town, but had entered an area of small farms and tradesmen's homes and places of business. Even at a trot, it was clear to Rebecca that the horse she'd stolen from the Quakers wouldn't be able to carry them much farther. And on foot, with Talon still wearing wrist manacles—how long could they stay ahead of the searchers?

Talon had a musket and she had a pistol, but she'd had enough of killing and violence. She wanted only to lose their pursuers in the deep woods. Unfortunately, she knew that many miles of farmland lay between them and the all-encompassing forests.

The sounds of a blacksmith's hammer ringing on steel brought them to a halt. "Listen," Rebecca said. Through the gray dawn, she could make out a crossroads, several modest houses, and what looked like a forge. "Where there's a blacksmith, there are hammers and chisels to break your irons.

"Hmmp." Talon's back muscles tensed. "This man will go to the smith and say 'Cut these chains for me.' And then we will have to kill him or have him summon the soldiers."

"You have to get free of these manacles," she argued.

"Even if we tie him up as we did the redcoat, he will tell them we passed this way. This one's Indian face will hang you."

She knew he was right. Even in the hat and cloak, he'd not fool a blind man. And any who saw him would raise a hand against them. Disappointed, she made no protest when he urged their mount off the road and into an orchard.

They'd ridden no more than half a mile, keeping to the back lanes and outcropping of trees, when she smelled wood smoke where there was no sign of a farmhouse. Talon reined in the gelding and motioned for her to slide down. He dismounted, and as he did, he turned toward her. In the gathering light of morning, she saw that his face was flushed with fever.

"Stay here," he ordered. "I will see who camps ahead in the gully."

"How do you know it's a camp? It may be a poor man's hut or—"

"Wait."

She held the horse's head while he moved away and vanished in the thicket. She stood shivering in the cool air. She was hungry, her head hurt, and both legs were chafed to the thigh from riding astride behind the saddle. She leaned against the tired animal, giving him enough rein to crop the green sprigs of grass that sprang from winter's dry foliage.

Then she heard a twig snap behind her. Frightened, she spun around, pistol in hand, and looked into the eyes of a man as startled as she was.

He was thin and olive skinned, his hair as dark as Talon's. His linen breeches and patched shirt had seen many years of use. His shoes were thick soled and clumsy, home stitched, reminding her of the footwear the poor wore in Ireland.

In his right hand the stranger carried a pair of rabbits, in his left he held a rope snare. "Do not shoot," he said in heavily accented English. "You can have the hares."

Rebecca smiled and lowered the weapon. "You're Irish," she said. And she followed this with a secret password she had learned from the tinkers who camped every summer on her father's land in Ireland.

The poacher's eyes widened in surprise.

She repeated the word, and he broke into a gap-toothed grin and took a few steps in her direction. The horse twitched his ears and nickered softly as Talon stepped out of the trees.

Instantly, both men tensed. Before Talon could frighten the tinker further, she motioned to Talon. "It's all right. This man is my countryman. The Irish call them the *travelers*. Have you heard of gypsies?"

The tinker frowned.

"The English call them gypsies, but they are not Rom," she said firmly. "He is a *white smith*, a worker in copper and tin." She glanced back at the newcomer. "I am Rebecca, and this is Talon. What is your name?"

"I am Keir the Lefthanded," he said in Gaelic.

Rebecca smiled at Talon's puzzled expression. "This time I'm the one who must do the translating," she said.

"Do you know this man?" Talon demanded.

"I know his tribe. They were kind to me when I was a child." She turned back to the smith. "We are in grave danger," she explained in the old Irish tongue.

Keir's bright gaze flicked over Talon, lingering for a few seconds on the manacles that bound the Shawnee's wrists together. The Irishman nodded and raised one bushy eyebrow expectantly.

"British soldiers are after us," Rebecca continued. "My friend is hurt, and we need someplace to hide. Can you help us?"

"I have a poor wagon," he answered. "You would be welcome there and at my woman's cook pot. But . . ." He shrugged. "One of my horses has come up lame. We have camped here longer than is prudent."

"Which direction does the wind take you?" she asked.

"Which direction do you need to travel?" he replied.

She smiled. "West."

He smiled. "And that is exactly the way we intended to go . . . before my old mare picked up a stone in her shoe and—"

Talon moved to Rebecca's side. "What is he saying?"

"Keir says that we are welcome at their fire." She turned her attention to the *traveler* once more. "Do you have the tools to remove the irons from my friend?"

"I would be a poor coppersmith if I did not."

"We bring danger with us," she warned.

Keir's smile became a grin. The lines around his eyes crinkled and his face beamed. "Danger adds salt to a hare stew."

"What are you saying?" Talon insisted.

She touched his arm lightly. "It's all right," she soothed. "I have just traded the Quaker's gelding for a ride in this man's wagon."

"Is he to be trusted?"

She glanced back at the smith. "My friend wants to know if you can be trusted."

Keir laughed. "Within reason, my lady. Within reason."

For three days, Talon lay flat on his stomach as the traveler's wagon rolled over the Pennsylvania roads. Keir's wife, Moya, made a paste of oak bark, moss, and honey to apply to Talon's wounds. For his fever, she made a tea of thistle and willow catkins.

The interior of the vehicle was small, packed tightly with household goods, Keir's tools and forge, and four black-eyed children. But when British troops stopped the family to inquire of a savage and a white woman, no one looked inside the wagon. And no one connected the bay gelding, with the newly cropped mane and tail and the damp white spot on his forehead, with the stolen Flanders horse.

On the fourth day, Talon had recovered enough to sit up, but Rebecca still would not hear of his leaving the safety of their hiding place. Mile by mile, Philadelphia was left farther behind, and the farms became scattered, the areas of virgin forest larger.

By the end of the week, Keir's wagon had come nearly fifty miles. That night, when he unhitched the team and Moya built a campfire, Talon and Rebecca repeated their gratitude and bid them farewell.

"I wish I had more to give you," Rebecca said to the plump, green-eyed wife.

"Your gift of the horse is more than gracious," Moya replied. "But keep a place at your cook pot for travelers."

"We will," Rebecca promised. She hugged each child in turn and shook Keir's hand for the second time.

"Come," Talon said, clearly impatient to put more distance between them and the white settlements. "Simon Brandt will not give up the hunt so easily. We must go from this place."

There were more good-byes, and Moya gave Rebecca a bundle of food for the journey. Then Rebecca and Talon set out, moving west through the forest, walking so swiftly that in an hour's time she suffered a stitch in her side.

"I'm not used to this," she complained. She was wearing a German woman's shoes, too wide and too long, and stiff instead of soft like moccasins. She would be blistered by dawn, but there was no help for it. She knew Talon was right. Sore feet or not, there would be no safety for either of them until they reached Indian country.

For the next week, they continued to walk by night and sleep during the day. They survived on bird eggs, Moya's bread and cheese, and fish that Talon caught with his hands.

"This man will not risk a shot," he said. "You must go hungry, and your bones already stick through your skin."

"They do not," she protested. She was still thin, it was true, but she was gaining in strength every day. With Talon beside her, she knew she could keep going as far as they needed, even to the shore of the great salt sea that lay on the far side of the continent.

When they rested, she curled in Talon's arms, her head on his chest, their fingers entwined. And she slept peacefully, content to feel his heart beating ... his breath warm on her cheek.

But as the days passed, she began to wonder why the man to whom she had given all made no attempt to consummate their love. "Don't you find me attractive?" she asked one morning when he'd turned his face aside from her kiss. "Is something wrong between us?"

He chuckled and captured her hand, moving it down to clasp the straining heat of his swollen manhood. "There is the proof of this one's desire for you," he whispered, "a desire that will never fade so long as we both draw breath."

"But ... if you still ..." She broke off as her cheeks grew warm. "Why can't we ..."

"When this man takes you in that way," he explained huskily, "his eyes see only your fox-colored hair, and his ears hear only your cries of pleasure. He smells only your scent, and tastes only your *totush*. Such a man cannot protect the thing he loves most, when his *mishkwe* rules his head."

"I don't care," she said. "I want you."

"And this one wants you," he assured her. "But we must wait until it is safe. Would you have me face Simon Brandt's musket with only *cin gwe ah* in my hand?"

She made a sound of derision. "By the time you stop looking over your shoulder for Simon, I'll be too old to appreciate your *cin gwe ah*."

"You will never be that old," he teased. "If you

are, this man may take a second wife to help you
with your duties."

"Just try it," she threatened.

Rebecca's German shoes had been worn to
shreds when they turned south and stopped to
rest for several days in the isolated cabin of a
Christian Lenape family. The mother in the household was a clan sister to Talon's aunt and thus to
Rebecca.

Joseph Crow had taken an English name and
traded his bow for a plow. The small homestead
boasted several goats, a horse, and real furniture.
Both Joseph and his wife, Ruth, made them welcome. Ruth found a complete change of clothing
for Rebecca, since the garments the Germans had
given her were much the worse for wear. Rebecca
slid between clean linen sheets and slept the entire
afternoon and night, not waking until the sun was
high the following morning.

Childless and separated from many of their relatives by the new way of life they'd accepted, the
Crows were starved for company. Ruth stuffed Rebecca with fresh peas and corn pudding and insisted on making her a new pair of moccasins.
They had heard nothing of Simon Brandt or a
search for Talon and Rebecca. They promised to
tell nothing if anyone did come by to ask.

"Don't expect me to milk goats and plant turnips," Talon warned when he and Rebecca left the
Crows' clearing.

She gazed back at the small, neat cabin with
longing. "Those walls and that roof would be
warm in winter," she said.

"You can stay with them," he said. "Ruth would
have you gladly."

She shook her head. "No chance," she replied, quickening her step to match his. "You aren't getting rid of me so easily.

It was May when they crossed the Ohio River, far south of where Rebecca had been earlier. They had no canoe, so Talon swam, pushing her and their few belongings over on a log. In the afternoon, they met two hunters. One was Shawnee, the other a Menominee from the Big Lake Country. The Shawnee was not from Talon's band, but he had heard of Talon, and he eagerly shared news of the people.

"They have moved their camp farther south," he said. "Near the Falls. The council smoked a pipe with the elders of Three Tree's Miami. The hunting was good this winter. A good year for deer. We have been hunting bear."

"Sweet Water and I have had our fill of bear," Talon replied. And then he asked the Menominee for news of her brother. "A white boy, half-grown, with Indian hair and eyes. He travels with one known as The Stranger. Have you heard of them?"

Later, when the men had called their dogs and moved on, Talon shared what he had learned with Rebecca. "The Menominee, Wheeling Hawk, says that he did not see the boy, but he has heard of such a man and boy. They wintered in a village near his and took many beaver. He thought it must be them because the man's tribe lies far west across the great prairie. He told wondrous tales of bison, herds so large that they take five days to pass by. And of mountains so high that they make ours look like the curves of a woman's belly."

"It could be Colin," she cried. "It must be. Can we go there? Can we search for him?"

Talon shook his head. "They have already moved on." He hesitated, and Rebecca read the regret in his eyes.

Pain knifed through her breast. "Something's happened to him. Colin's dead, isn't he?" she murmured, feeling suddenly faint.

"No, my foolish jay. Would you borrow trouble? Wheeling Hawk said only that they had gone north into Canada with a trading party. It could be that Colin will be given over to the French after all."

"They wouldn't hurt him, would they?"

"No. He would be traded to the British settlements. There is no war between the French king and the English now."

"Then why do you look so—"

"This man has failed you again. If your brother returns, you will not be there to meet him. And if we went to hunt for him, it would be like seeking one acorn in an oak forest."

"So we're just going to give up? You promised me—"

"And I will not forget that promise, Sky Eyes. This one will ask and he will go on asking. And if a times comes when your brother can be found, we will go to him. His path will cross ours. You must believe that. When the time is right, you will see him again."

"At least he's alive," she said.

"Wheeling Hawk spoke of him as a son to The Stranger, not as a captive. Colin is tough. He will survive to grow to manhood."

"But he won't be the same, will he? He'll be more Indian than white."

Talon's eyes narrowed. "Does that give you sorrow? Have you not chosen the same path?"

"I chose it. He didn't."

"Do not be so sure, my Sweet Water. All paths are chosen." He touched the crown of her head with his hand.

"What is it? Do I have leaves in my hair?"

He laughed. "Only sunlight." He caught her hand and lifted it to his lips. "There is a place this man would show you," he said, brushing her fingers with his lips. "It is not far."

"It's early to make camp. Did you want to—"

"Come and see. Then you can decide if you are ready to unroll your blanket." He looked down at her, and the gleam in his eye made her heart race.

"Lead on," she teased. "As far as you've made me walk, what's a few more miles?"

The day was warm, and Talon had already shed the plain leather vest Joseph Crow had given him. Rebecca walked in his tracks, keeping a few yards behind him. The scars of his beating stood out pale against older marks from the bear's claws and Talon's darker skin, but they had healed without limiting Talon's range of movement. His broad shoulders swelled with sinewy muscle; his waist still narrowed to taut buttocks and thighs, barely concealed by his fringed buckskin loincloth.

His body is still beautiful, she thought, unable to keep her eyes off him. The months of abstinence had not dampened her desire to make love to him. Even now, she felt a familiar catch of emotion in her throat as she thought of those powerful legs intertwined with hers . . . of his full length pressed against her body.

The way became more difficult and her calves ached as they followed a twisting game trail up a steep hill. Thorns and briers created a formidable barrier, but he stooped low and continued on, lift-

ing branches so that she could squeeze underneath. "This had better be worth the effort," she
said. The May sun was warm on her back and
face, and she perspired under the combined volume of her stays, shift, stockings, petticoats, and
heavy woolen gown.

"It will be," he promised.

Beyond the thicket lay an arid area of boulders
and gravel. The path was lost among the sharp
stones, but Talon continued to trudge upward. At
last, they reached the top of the incline, slid and
climbed down the far side, and entered a small
sheltered valley.

Rebecca could not contain her joy as gray rock
gave over to lush green grass interspersed with a
frosting of wild flowers. Golden cornflower and
Solomon's seal, lady's slipper, painted trillium,
wild strawberries, and velvet blue violets sprang
in tufts and fairy circles. And near the center of
the glade a natural pool bubbled, sending wisps of
steam into the sweet-smelling air. "Why is the water smoking?" she cried, dropping to her knees
and picking a single sparkling white violet and
holding it to her nose. The fragrance of the fragile
flower was so sweet and pure that it brought tears
to her eyes. "Is this place real?" she asked.

He laughed and took her hand. "Real enough.
Come. This man will show you how real it is."

Reluctantly, she left the mound of white violets
and let him lead her to the edge of the milky water. The pool gave off its own strong odor. "It
smells like . . . like sulphur," she said.

"You will get used to it." He grinned and laid
his musket down carefully. "It's a hot spring. Even
in winter, the water is warm." He untied his belt
and let his loincloth slide to the grass. "Come,

woman, you complain so about bathing in cold rivers. This is your chance to enjoy all the warm water you can stand."

"You mean it? We can bathe in the spring?"

"You may as well. It isn't fit to drink. There's another spring over there," he pointed to the far side of the glen, "running down from those rocks. That water is good to drink." He smiled at her again. "This one is only good for other things."

She sat down on the grass and pulled off her shoes.

"The stockings too," he said. "Maybe this man should help."

"I can ... oh." She laughed as he knelt beside her and pushed up her skirt and petticoat to reach her garter. "Yes," she said breathily. "Maybe I do need help with this."

Deliberately, he began to roll the woolen stocking, letting his lean fingers brush her skin as he moved slowly down over her knee and calf.

A shiver of excitement ran down her spine, and she touched his cheek with her forefinger. "Talon ..." she murmured.

He slipped the stocking off and massaged her slim foot between his strong hands.

"Don't," she protested. "My foot is dirty and—"

"Not for long." He reached for the other leg and a warmth grew in her loins as he made a ritual of removing that stocking as well.

She closed her eyes and sighed. The hum of bees and the warm breeze on her face added to the languor that spread through her body. She wanted to go into that bubbling pool, but she wanted even more to tumble back into the soft grass and pull him on top of her.

"Now this," he said, as he untied the lacing on her bodice.

Her mouth went dry as he loosened the cords a little at a time, until he could pull the tight-fitting garment over her head. Next, he removed her shirt and undid the back of her skirt so that she could wiggle out of it. Only her shift remained, thin linen, soiled by travel and torn at the hem. He reached for the ribbon at her throat.

"No," she protested. "Not my shift. It's broad daylight."

He chuckled. "This man had thought of that. No one will see you, my violet, no one but the warrior who should be your husband." One hand eased the cloth up over her thighs while his other continued to fumble with the tiny knot.

Unable to stand the tension, she backed away, pulled the shift over her head and knelt, facing him, using the crumpled linen to cover her nakedness. "Are you certain it's safe? The spring?" she mumbled. "Is it deep?"

In answer, he jumped in, then stood up. The cloudy water rose half-way up his chest. "Coward," he dared.

She dropped the shift and splashed in beside him. The water was warm and deliciously soft. Her feet found firm support on the sandy bottom, and she lost her fear immediately. The smell was not nearly as bad, now that the steam surrounded her. She let herself drift back until the water lapped over her hair. "This is wonderful," she murmured. "Wonderful."

He held out his hands to her and she came to him. The milky liquid covered the bottom half of her breasts, leaving the tips of her nipples exposed. She felt Talon's gaze on her bare flesh, and heat greater than the temperature of the pool washed through her.

He gently cupped a round breast, and her nipples hardened into tight buds of tingling sensation. Her knees went weak. "Don't start something you don't mean to finish," she whispered.

Her sky-blue eyes darkened with gathering passion, and Talon felt his own need intensify a hundredfold. "There has not been a dawning or dusk that I have not wanted to do this," he said hoarsely. He bent and kissed first one nipple and then the other, drawing the rosy flesh between his lips and suckling until he thought his throbbing organ would burst from anticipation.

He wanted to plunge his man-spear into her secret place and drive deep. He wanted her woman's soft folds to hold him, caressing his passion until his seed shot out and filled her with his love. "Whatever you ask of this man," he whispered. "Whatever you desire, he will do."

He pulled her close, crushing her against his chest, covering her mouth with his. Her small cries of yearning flooded his mind, igniting a wildfire in his blood. Their tongues touched and met, velvet, wet, and thrusting. A fever possessed him; his hands claimed her pale, smooth skin, exploring, caressing. She clung to him, running her fingers through his hair, kissing his mouth and face.

"I want you," she cried. "I want you inside me ... filling me ... making me part of you."

He could wait no longer. The throbbing of his swollen rod was an agony. He caught her hips and lifted her onto his *cin gwe ah*. She held him tightly, and he slipped into her sheath with a shout of triumph.

A sense of power and strength filled him. He

withdrew slowly and she drew in a deep, shuddering breath. "Sweet Water," he groaned. "Ah ..."
He plunged again, and again her muscles gripped him.

"*K'dahole*," she cried. I love you.

"And I love you, my beautiful Sky Eyes," he answered. And then the madness took him, and he could speak no more until the thunder and rain of glorious release broke over them.

He held her for a long time after that, staring down into her face, wondering at what mysteries the spirits planned for a man trail. That he should find the wife of his greatest enemy and heal his heart of hatred at the same time required some wondrous scheme.

They lay together in the water for nearly an hour until hunger stirred them. Then he made her sit while he gathered handfuls of wild strawberries and fed them to her, one at a time. They laughed together and made love again in the warm sunshine. And his soul was full.

"Did you mean what you said?" she asked him lazily. He was stretched full length on the grass, and she was showering him with blossoms. "In the pool. When you said you would give me anything I wanted ..."

"*E-e.* Yes. Anything my *o tah ais*, my flower."

"Even Simon's life?"

His eyes snapped open. "You asked me that before, in Philadelphia."

"You never gave me a straight answer."

"*Ahikta.*"

"Yes, you didn't give me an answer, or yes, you will spare Simon," she persisted.

"He will hunt us."

"No, he won't," she said. "He doesn't want me. He will say I'm dead. He will—"

"He killed his first wife."

"How do you know that?"

"He told me so. When I was in the white man's prison, Simon Brandt came to taunt me. He said that he had murdered her for the sin of lying with an Indian. He said he wished that he had been able to kill you as well. He is a man crazed with hate. He will not rest until he has found us."

"I was with him in Philadelphia. He didn't kill me then, and he won't bother to come after me now. I told him that I was leaving him, that I would never be his wife again."

"Simon Brandt will come."

"You're as stubborn as a mule when you set your head on something, Talon," she protested. "He'll never find us here."

"We can't stay here, my Sweet Water. This is a place for coming to, not for staying. We must return to my people. They need me." He sat up and pulled her into his arms. "This man has great love for you, but he is still a Shawnee, and still war chief, unless another has been elected in his place."

"You promised me," she reminded him. "Anything. I want Simon's life."

"If he tries to hurt you, no vow between this earth and the land of spirits will hold me." He raised a lock of her fox-colored hair to brush against his lips.

"Nevertheless, I still want your promise. It's my Catholic conscience. You've made me so happy . . . happier than I ever thought to be, Talon. But I can't buy my future with the blood of my husband."

"It means so much to you?"

She nodded, and her blue eyes glistened with moisture.

"Then I give you my word, *nee wah*. So long as your life is not in danger, this man will not send him to the white man's hell."

"Thank you, Talon. Thank you." She threw her arms around his neck and kissed him full on the mouth. Then, laughing, she pulled him toward the mineral spring again. "I think I'd like to bathe again," she coaxed.

He followed willingly, but even in the intense pleasure of their lovemaking, he could not help but question the wisdom of his reluctant promise.

Chapter 27

For two weeks, Rebecca and Talon remained in the valley of the hot spring, renewing their love and resting from the long journey. Every day, at dawn, they would rise from their shared blankets and go to the wonderful pool to bathe and splash like careless children.

Sometimes, the playfulness turned serious, and they would make slow, sensual love. Other times, Rebecca found contentment simply floating in the strong circle of Talon's arms.

He fashioned a hair brush for her of thorns and cedar, and each morning he insisted on brushing out her wet hair with they came from the pool. "The sun is captured in these red-gold tresses," he teased one day. "This is no normal color for a woman's hair. Proper hair should be as black as a crow's wing and straight. Only an English *equiwa* has curls around her face like the tangled vines of wild roses."

"I'll dye my hair dark with walnut juice," she vowed solemnly, "and braid it into submission."

He laughed. "Not yet," he cautioned. "Not until a man tires of feeling it against his lips or sliding it between his fingers."

"And will you tire soon, oh mighty warrior?"

"Not until the blue of your eyes has darkened to a proper brown."

"Then it may be a long wait."

"This man hopes so with all his heart."

There in the enchanted meadow, Talon showed her a world she had not dreamed existed. Where some eyes would see only wild and untended growth, he pointed out a nest of baby rabbits still too young to open their eyes, tucked into a hidden crevice, and a hollow tree where a woodpecker raised her hungry brood.

Together, they lay on their bellies and watched as a dainty mother gray fox brought three tiny kits to drink at a stream. Daily, the vixen hunted and brought her little ones field mice and frogs to add to their diet of mother's milk. Rebecca marveled at the antics of the baby foxes as they tumbled and yipped and chased each other in the warm sun. And she saw that each little kit had a temperament of its own, one shy, one bold, one too wise to tease the turtle that invaded their special nook in the clearing.

"I never thought of animals in this way before," Rebecca said to Talon. "The baby foxes are almost like children."

"Each animal has a spirit," he assured her, "a soul, your people would say. Each spirit is precious to the Creator. We are only a small part of the great circle of life."

"But you hunt animals for food."

"Because we must, as the vixen does and the hawk. We eat of the flesh of our brothers the animals, but we remember their worth and we offer a prayer for each life we take."

"You are different here," she mused.

"And you, my flower. This one sees a radiance in your eyes and a spring to your step he has not seen before."

"It is the peace of this place, and the peace I feel in you, Talon. I've always thought of you as a man of war. I didn't know you could be so gentle."

His sloe eyes dilated with emotion as he fixed her with an unwavering gaze. She drew in a deep breath and swayed with giddiness when he caught her hand, raising it to press her palm against his cheek. "It is true that this one has seen more blood than he wishes to remember," Talon admitted huskily, "but he would never have you believe he thirsts for killing. What this man has done in the past, he must answer for. He has no shame for his deeds . . ." He trailed off as a twinkle appeared in his eyes. "Perhaps a small regret for burning your cabin and frightening you and your brother—"

"Frightened? Who said we were frightened?" she teased. "You're lucky my aim wasn't better. It would have been your scalp stretched over my fireplace."

He laughed then. "Such a fierce woman this man has taken to his sleeping mat. Maybe the Mecate should elect you war chief in my place."

She closed her eyes and stretched up to kiss him, wanting to shut out memories of that other time when she had believed him an enemy . . . when she had not known that he would change her life forever. "Promise me you won't seek out the war trail," she begged, when they had kissed and kissed again.

"There is a time to fight and time to refrain from war," he answered softly. "If the whites will leave us alone, this man will be content. It may be that he grows old, but his father's words of peace and caution seem more reasonable than they did." He kissed the tip of her nose. "But do not think to make of this man what he cannot be."

"I know better than that," she replied. And then she smiled at him. "Didn't I hear something about trout for dinner? With strawberries and—"

"You are always hungry, woman."

"I notice you eat your share."

"A man who has such a demanding woman must eat to maintain his strength."

She sighed. "I suppose he must. I'll get the berries if you'll—"

"As you command, *ki-te-hi*. Unless you'd rather do the fishing?"

She shook her head. "Not without a fishing pole and line. The water in that stream is much too cold. That's your job."

"Always does the wife stay by the fire in comfort while her man must brave cold and danger."

Rebecca glanced about the sunny meadow and erupted into laughter. And only after he had gone to catch the meal did she let the word *wife* rise in the back of her mind like the throbbing of a sore tooth. She was Talon's wife in her heart, but so long as Simon Brandt lived she could never be Talon's wife in the eyes of her church. Or in her own mind . . . not really . . .

But her marriage to Simon was an ache that could be hidden away. She refused to let it spoil this paradise and the golden days and nights with Talon. What couldn't be changed must be lived with, her nurse had always said. She would live with this old pain, and rejoice in the happiness she had found and the new delights she was experiencing every day.

And when Talon finally decided they must return to the Mecate village, Rebecca gathered her few belongings without protest and made ready to travel.

He promised her that they would come here again, and that this would always be their special place of healing. And in Rebecca's mind, her new life as a Shawnee woman began not in the sweatbath of the village, but here in this magical glen.

When they reached the camp, they were welcomed with feasting and dance. Rebecca's adopted mother, Squash Blossom, put aside her mourning for Siipu and organized the women to build a wigwam for the new couple.

Summer days slipped by like raindrops dripping from the lodgepole. Rebecca joined the women in the fields, hoeing the young corn and squash and training bean vines to grow up the cornstalks. She gathered berries and wild grapes and dried them for winter, sharing her recipes for cooking and preserving as she learned new ones from Squash Blossom and Fox's cousin, Shell Bead Girl.

Before Rebecca realized it, the first leaves of autumn had begun to turn red. The air took on a crisp scent, and the men began to hunt deer. It was a good time of the year. The rains had come, and the cornfields stood heavy with grain. There had been no sickness, and no young men had gone away to make war. And day by day, the Shawnee village had seemed more like home to Rebecca.

Often Fox, Counts His Scalps, and Shell Bead Girl would come to Rebecca and Talon's wigwam to share a late evening meal. There would be laughter and good food, and sometimes tears, as the friends shared old memories and made others. Shell Bead Girl was close to Rebecca's age, and she spoke perfect English. A divorced woman, Shell Bead Girl, had returned from her husband's village in late winter. She had married a handsome Mandan, but when they had no children, he had taken a second wife. Shell Bead Girl—Shell, as Rebecca came to call her—had decided that she missed home and family.

"There are three mighty hunters here at this fire," Rebecca teased on one such night after Fox and Talon returned from hunting empty handed. This afternoon, she and Shell Bead Girl had caught a huge catfish in the river and broiled it over the fire. Fresh corn on the cob was roasting in green husks, and a rabbit stew bubbled in the pot. "You might choose a new husband from one of these bachelors," Rebecca continued in broken Algonquian. Her mastery of the Indian language was improving every day, and she could understand most of what was said so long as Talon or Shell filled in the words she didn't know.

Counts scowled. Rebecca was just getting used to his new appearance. Counts wore two black stripes of mourning across his lower face, and he had plucked all the hair from his head except for a handful in the center.

That scalplock Counts had let grow long. He braided it with strips of black fur and hair from the tail of a horse, extending the length so that it fell to his waist. All along the false switch he had woven in tiny bones and eagle claws. He had also plucked his eyebrows completely away and ringed both eyes with yellow circles. Talon had told Rebecca that Counts had assumed this new persona because he took his shaman studies seriously and wanted to appear forbidding. But for a long time, she'd found it hard to keep from laughing when she looked at him.

"There are two hunters at this fire and one holy

man," Fox said with a straight face. "Perhaps my cousin's smile could turn Counts to the appreciation of women."

Counts grunted. "Shell Bead Girl makes a corn cake like no other," he admitted, "and for a woman, she is comely. But this man is in mourning for *another*, the one whose name we may not say. If this man was one who cared for the company of women—which he is not—Shell Bead Girl would not be a bad choice."

"This person wants no husband," Shell said. "At least not yet. In winter, when the cold wind creeps down the smoke hole, who can tell?"

Talon laughed. "More than one woman who thought she did not want a husband has changed her mind." His gaze met Rebecca's, and he motioned toward Fox who struck a pose. Rebecca nodded vigorously as she and Talon laughed together like old married folk who share a secret jest.

"I would have Talon as first choice," Shell mused, pretending to ignore their teasing game, "but he and I are of the same clan and can never marry. Counts is a brave man and a skilled hunter. I know that he will be a great medicine man, but he would never make a good husband. Any woman who married him would be jealous when he was in the company of warriors."

"With good reason," Talon said.

They all laughed at that, even Counts.

"And Fox is Fox," she continued. "He is a good hunter, and they say he is brave in battle—although this woman has never seen this for herself. But it is hard to think of sharing a sleeping platform with a man who has a face like a new moon, a face that every girl fancies. I love him well, my cousin Fox, but he is not the man I would choose for a husband."

"I think Shell comes here to get away from suitors," Fox retorted. "Many Bellies desires her for his second wife. Didn't he give your mother a necklace of copper and an iron pot?"

Shell Bead Girl patted a corn cake and laid it on a rock to cook. "Many Bellies can give my mother a forest of iron kettles. He has breath like a redcoat, and his hands are cold."

"All the more reason to consider Counts' fine qualities," Talon teased.

Rebecca handed him a plate of fish and stew and their fingers brushed as he took it from her. Her pulse quickened at the charge of excitement that passed between them. She raised her eyes to his, thrilling at the sensual promise of the long night to come that she read there. I do love him, she thought. I love him with all my heart and soul.

She had not been sorry that she'd come to Indian country with this good man. He was all the things to her that Simon hadn't been. She didn't know how she could ever have considered Talon a savage.

He was a kind and thoughtful husband, rarely ill-tempered or impatient with her. He went out of his way to be generous with members of the tribe who needed meat or skins, or just a helping hand. And if he spent days with his companions, he also took time with her alone.

Just the week before, they had returned from a three-day trip downstream to gather salt. They had taken food with them in their canoe and had camped beside the river at night. He had shown her the mist on the Ohio as he had promised, and he had taken her to a spot where a pair of eagles nested and raised their young.

No, she was not sorry she had come with Talon. He had awakened in her a passionate nature that she had no idea she possessed. He was a lover such as women dream of—an ardent man who thought of her pleasures before his own. And if she went to hell for her sins of the flesh and for committing her soul to Talon, then she would gladly pay the price.

Her only regret was that she hadn't met him years before. If Colin had grown up at Talon's side instead of Simon's, her brother would have had a much happier childhood.

Thoughts of Colin saddened her, and she forced herself to listen to the joke Fox was telling. After he'd finished and they'd all laughed, Shell Bead Girl complimented her on the seasoning of the fish, and they were soon engaged in a discussion about the merits of wild mushrooms and the best places to find the nonpoisonous ones.

"We tire of this idle cooking chatter," Counts grumbled. "Shell Bead Girl is a reciter of old stories. Tell us a tale, one to hold a warrior's attention."

"Yes," Fox agreed, "Tell us why *maxkw* the brown bear walks on two legs."

"Not that one," Talon said. "Tell us about the bride who wanted to please her husband."

"Who is the story teller?" Shell Bead Girl chided. "Who shall decide? And who shall be still and listen?" She glanced around the circle at the now silent men. "Once," she began, "long ago when the world was young, the Lenape, our grandfathers, lived in a land to the east."

Talon leaned back against the sleeping platform

and took a puff from his pipe. The bowl was carved from a single piece of green stone in the shape of a wolf's head. He passed the pipe to Counts, and the tobacco smoke drifted across the fire to the place where Rebecca knelt on a thick fur rug. It was a sweet odor, not so strong as the Virginia tobacco, and she found it oddly comforting.

Firelight reflected from Talon's dark eyes and again a shaft of desire thrust deep into her core. It was not the Shawnee way for a husband and wife to show public affection for each other, but his love for her filled this wigwam and everyone who entered knew it.

". . . the people forgot the Supreme Being who created them and disobeyed his laws," Shell continued softly. "They argued among themselves and each man and woman greedily kept what food and adornments they had acquired for themselves. But there were among them those wise ones who remembered the teachings . . ."

Rebecca passed a basket of dried berries to Talon. They had found thickets of blueberries on their trip to gather salt. They had picked and eaten until both had lips stained blue like naughty children. Later, Talon had darkened her nipples with berry juice. She sighed with pleasure, wondering if she might someday repeat the process at Talon's expense.

"Mountains cracked and spewed forth molten fire and rock," Shell Bead Girl said. "Many people died horribly. Those who did not fled to the shore of the great sea. There waves . . ."

Rebecca nibbled at a honey-sweetened corn cake. There was a full moon tonight, a hunter's moon, Talon called it. She sometimes lost track of the days of the week, but the moon was constant.

It told her that two full cycles had passed without her bleeding time. And she decided that tonight would be the time to tell Talon that they were expecting a child.

She had doubted that she was in the family way because she'd not been sick, not once. But her appetite had grown tremendously; she was constantly hungry. And now, her breasts felt fuller and more sensitive.

As much as she enjoyed the company of Fox and Shell Bead Girl, yes, and even of grumpy Counts His Scalps, she wanted to be alone with Talon to tell him her wonderful news. She didn't doubt for an instant that he would be as happy as she was. And she didn't doubt that their child, boy or girl, would grow up a Shawnee, as wild and bold as their father and as ignorant of Irish customs as a gray fox.

Shell Bead Girl's voice paused for a few seconds of dramatic silence, then took up the story again. "When all seemed lost, there suddenly arose from the sea a mighty turtle with a back so broad and—"

"Talon!" Someone threw back the deerskin door flap. "Talon," came an urgent whisper from outside.

He came instantly alert. "This man is here," he answered. "Who calls?"

"Mountain Horse." The young brave appeared in the entrance, his face clearly showing his alarm. "White men come," he said. "Arm yourself. We have need of the war chief."

An icy numbness splashed over Rebecca. "Talon, be careful," she said. He reached for his musket, and she quickly gathered his hunting bag and powderhorn.

"Go to Squash Blossom's wigwam," he ordered. "She will know what to do." For an instant, he gripped her hand, and then he was gone. Fox and Counts followed him without a word.

"My mother will need me," Shell Bead Girl said. "You are welcome to come with us."

"Just because white men have been sighted," Rebecca said, "that doesn't mean—"

"It means that we must take care. This is Shawnee country. Any who come here without invitation must be considered enemies."

"We're too far from the settlements," Rebecca continued, trying to convince herself that everything would be as it was ... that Talon hadn't gone out to shoot men and be shot in turn ... that her worst nightmare hadn't come true.

"We are far," Shell agreed, and then she shrugged. "Who knows if it is far enough from the white tide?"

"What must I do?"

"Pack food and ... do you have a weapon?"

"Yes," Rebecca answered. "A pistol."

"Take a skinning knife, your fire kit, and a blanket," Shell Bead Girl said. "Never, never, be without them. If we have to flee the village, they could save your life."

"Pray God, we don't." They could hardly pick up the cornfields or the dried meat and fish and berries and run with that, Rebecca thought. All summer the Shawnee had put away food for the winter. What would they do if it was destroyed? The houses burned? How would the children live without warm shelters and winter clothing? How would any of them?

Squash Blossom met them just outside the wigwam. "Come quickly," she said to Rebecca. "We must take the little ones into the forest. They say that it is Simon Brandt and his militia. Rabbit Running said that—"

Rebecca heard only Simon's name. It was true. He had come to destroy her world . . . her one chance at happiness.

A musket blast echoed through the night, followed closely by another, and a man's scream of pain. Somewhere in a nearby wigwam, an infant began to cry.

"Quick!" Squash Blossom shouted. "There is little time."

More gunshots sounded.

Shell Bead Girl pointed to the sky. "Look," she said. "The moon. Blood spills across the moon."

Rebecca's skin prickled as she stared up at the red clouds that marred the surface of the golden disk.

"A bad omen," Squash Blossom said.

"For them or for us?" Shell Bead Girl murmured.

Women and children ran from the wigwams. Dogs barked. An old man slipped and fell to his knees, and Squash Blossom and Shell Bead Girl hurried to his side to help him up.

"Run," White Stone called to her. The girl had a sleeping baby in her arms. "Run for the cedar thicket."

Another family group dashed by. Rebecca recognized the mother and one of the children. They were tugging at the hands of an elderly, white-haired woman who seemed confused. "It's cold," she protested. "I'm sleepy. I don't want to go out. Let me sleep."

"Come, Grandmother," the oldest girl pleaded. "You must come with us. There is . . ."

Rebecca couldn't make out the last of what was said. She looked from Squash Blossom and Shell back toward the woods where there was obviously a fight going on. Shouts and rifle fire continued to resound through the village.

Then Rebecca heard what could only be the thudding of hooves on the earth and a riderless horse galloped through the town, sending women and children scattering before it. The terrified animal skidded to a halt and reared as the village dogs circled it, barking furiously. As the horse rose up and pawed the air, Rebecca saw an arrow protruding from its neck. She dropped her bundle and tucked the pistol into her belt.

"Whoa! Whoa!" she soothed, walking toward the bay. His eyes rolled back in his head, showing the whites, and foam trailed from his nostrils. "Get back," she commanded the dogs as she grabbed for the trailing reins. "Down!" The dogs ignored her commands until she realized that she was shouting to them in English.

Shell Bead Girl came to her aid, clapping her hand and driving off the fiercest of the curs. Rebecca seized the reins and took a firm hold on the bridle. The horse threw back his head and snorted, but his next attempt to rear up was only a half-hearted one.

From what she could see by moonlight, the arrow was only partially buried in the horse's thick hide. Her hands closed around the shaft, she gave a quick jerk, and the arrow came out. "It's all right," she soothed the horse. "It's all right." She handed the reins to Shell. "Tie him to a tree," she ordered. "I'm going to . . ."

She left the rest unfinished. She didn't know what she was going to do, only that she couldn't stay here and hide like a rabbit in a hole. If Talon was in danger, she had to go to him.

"*Ku!*" Shell Bead Girl called after her. "No! Don't go . . ."

Her words were lost as Rebecca ran past the last wigwam and into the forest. She had no trouble seeing in the bright moonlight, and there was no doubt which way to go. She had gone only a short way when she saw Counts His Scalps bending over a sprawled figure with a knife in his hand.

"Where's Talon?" she cried.

Counts turned toward her. His painted face was a demon's mask of vengeance, and she went cold with fear. "Go with the women!" he said. "This is no place for you."

"Talon?" she begged. A steel trade hatchet lay beside the still figure.

"Spare no pity for this English dog," Counts spat. "He killed Raven Song. The boy had not seen his twelfth summer."

Raven's childish face rose in Rebecca's mind. His eyes were big and brown, and always laughing. She could not contain a sob. "Is Simon Brandt here? Did you see him?" she demanded.

"Who do you weep for, Sweet Water?" He glared at her in disgust. "Go back to the women." He picked up the ax.

She ignored him. Pulling her pistol free, she darted off through the trees.

"Stop!" Counts shouted, but she paid him no heed.

A white man in buckskins loomed up before her. She opened her mouth to scream as he raised the butt of his musket to strike her in the face. Then a musket roared behind her, and her attacker was gone. She dodged his fallen body and ran on.

Hand to hand battle raged around her. The militia were heavily armed, strong men and deadly fighters, but the Shawnee were defending home and family. Only a few hundred yards lay between the white scourge and their helpless women and children. The gunshots had nearly ended. Ax and knife and warclub were the weapons that would decide the winners and the losers. Shrieks of triumph and howls of agony assaulted Rebecca's ears.

She wanted to run and hide, to close her eyes and cover her head, but she couldn't. Somewhere Simon hunted Talon, and in her foolishness she had given her husband an advantage he would not hesitate to use. "Let someone else find Simon," she prayed aloud. "For the love of God, let it be someone else."

A pistol to her left shot fire and lead. She whirled to see Fox on one knee holding the smoking flintlock. Facing him was a short bearded man in a cocked hat. He raised a rifle to his shoulder and pointed it straight at Fox's heart.

Fox leaped sideways at the exact instant Rebecca fired. Her target yelled and clutched his shoulder. His rifle went off, the barrel pointed harmlessly toward the trees. Fox scrambled up and lunged toward his opponent. She didn't wait to see that happened. Still clutching the empty pistol, she kept going deeper into the woods.

Moments later, she found Simon and Talon as she knew she would—together. Simon was bareheaded; his shirt was ripped to the waist, and one sleeve dripped blood. He crouched with a fourteen-inch scalping knife in hand, his hate-filled eyes fixed on Talon.

Rebecca shrank back until she felt the solid bulk

of a tree trunk behind her. Talon's thigh was sliced from hip to knee, and his chest bore a fresh wound as well. He too held a knife as he shifted from one foot to another just out of Simon's arm length.

"Rebecca," Simon called. "If it isn't my dear wife. Wait a while, sweet. I'll get to you as soon as I finish this red bastard."

"Sweet Water." Talon's gaze scalded her. "Go!"

Simon dove at him, slashing upward in a mighty stroke that would have disemboweled Talon if he'd not twisted aside at the last second. Simon recovered his balance and lashed out with a booted foot. Talon tripped him and they went down, rolling over and over on the ground, first Talon on top and then Simon.

Rebecca crammed her knuckles into her mouth and bit down on her own flesh to keep from screaming as Simon's knife blade struck Talon's and snapped it close to the hilt. Talon let the useless weapon drop from his hand and seized Simon's wrist. Simon wrapped his legs around Talon's and Rebecca saw sweat break out on Talon's face. Simon was putting pressure on Talon's leg wound. Blood gushed from the gash. Both men strained and grunted. Then Talon flipped Simon over and rolled on top. Tendons stood out on Talon's forearm as he forced Simon's knife hand back.

Rebecca looked down at her useless pistol. She'd dropped the hunting bag back in the camp and had no way to reload. If the weapon was loaded, she had no doubt in her mind what she would do. Tears were running down her face, as she prayed for Talon to kill him.

Suddenly, Talon released Simon's left wrist and slammed the base of his palm into his chin. Before

Simon could recover, Talon had wrenched the knife from his hand and was holding the point at Simon's throat.

Simon's eyes bulged with terror. Rebecca turned away, knowing what had to be, yet unable to watch.

"You want this thing?" Talon said. "This man gives him to you."

Rebecca spun back around to see Talon on his feet, standing over Simon.

"Never say that the promise went unfilled," Talon said hoarsely. He shoved the knife into his sheath and reached for his fallen musket.

Simon leaped up and grabbed Rebecca before she knew what was happening. He twisted the pistol from her hand and held it to her head. Talon froze, his right hand open, his left clenched at his side.

"I've got ye now, ye son of a bitch," Simon snarled. "I've got one shot. Which one shall it be. Her or you?"

Talon spread his hands wide. "It is a good day to die," he said softly.

"It's not loaded!" Rebecca screamed.

"Liar!" Simon lowered the muzzle until it touched the hollow between Rebecca's breasts and pulled the trigger.

Simon's weight slumped against her. His mouth opened and closed, but he made no sound. Talon pulled her trembling into his arms and crushed her to his chest.

From the corner of her eye, she saw Simon fall forward, an English trade ax buried in his back.

"Do you still draw breath?"

Rebecca understood who had saved them as she

heard Counts' voice. Boastful. Full of self-pride. And as welcome as a candle in the pitch of night.

"Talon," she whispered. "Oh, Talon. I wanted you to kill him. I was so afraid for you."

She heard the pounding of his heart and felt the strength of his arms around her, shielding her from the blood and the pain.

"The fighting is over?" Talon asked.

Counts scoffed. "The cowards who come to kill children and burn villages will see no more dawns."

"All of them dead?"

"This . . . this Simon Brandt was the last."

"His killing will be a deed we will hear about around many campfires, Counts His Scalps. It was worthy of a great warrior."

"And a great shaman," Counts added. "Only one who speaks to the spirits would know how great was the need of his war chief."

"So." Talon rubbed her back gently.

"What would you have us do with the bodies?" Counts asked.

"Strip them. Carry them to the Cave of the Two Winds, and drop them down into the bowels of the earth."

"And . . ."

"Gather their horses, their muskets, and their long knives," Talon said. "And let them be carried far from this place."

"To the hunting grounds of our enemies?"

"Is that your suggestion, my wise friend?"

"The Mohawk could use such good horses," Counts said slyly.

"You will lead the party?"

"Who else could you trust to do it right?"

"No one else, Counts His Scalps. No one else," Talon agreed.

When Counts departed to see to the disposition of the dead, Talon led Rebecca away from the spot where Simon had died.

"What would you have done with him?" she asked. "Alive, he would always be a danger to us."

"You do not care that he is dead?"

"No." She shook her head. "He was an evil man. What will we do now? The village, I mean. Will we be safe here for the winter?"

He exhaled softly. "This man believes so. When the militia does not return, the king's soldiers will search for them. Eventually, the tale will surface. For now, we will spend the winter here, and in the spring—"

"We'll move again?" she asked.

"We?" He tilted her chin up and looked full into her eyes. "This is not an easy life this man offers you."

"Yes, Talon. We. You and I, and the child I'll bear you in springtime."

"A child?" He pulled her close and held her with strong, loving arms, and she heard the joyous throb of his heart. "When, *ki-te-hi?*"

"When the wild strawberries ripen."

"Then we will break camp when the snows melt and take our canoes south so that our son will be born in *Can-tuc-kee.* It is a place of tall trees and is thick with game. The grass and water are sweet, and there are no white men there."

"Our son?" She smiled. "Are you a shaman as well that you can tell the sex of an unborn babe?"

"Our son or daughter," he conceded. "It matters not. I will love our child for your sake and mine."

She clasped his hand tightly. "I must sew that cut on your leg. You've lost a lot of blood."

"Now you sound like a wife."

"I am a wife ... or rather, I soon will be. Unless ..." She pursed her lips. "Can it be that you no longer wish to be my husband, now that I'm going to get fat?"

"This man will have you to wife," he said, bending and kissing her tenderly.

"Even if you have to give my adopted mother many cooking pots as a wedding gift?"

"Two, at least." He put an arm around her shoulders.

Rebecca took a final glance over her shoulder at all that lay behind her and stepped forward beside the man she loved. Her path would not be smooth. There would be sorrow and disappointment, as well as fulfillment and happiness. But that was all part of living, wasn't it? Didn't the Bible speak of a time to laugh and a time to cry, a time to die and a time to be born?

She only knew that she would be content to walk beside this man all the days of her life. And when the time came to leave this earth, she would take the Shawnee trail across the river of souls following in his moccasin tracks.

Avon Romantic Treasures

*Unforgettable, enthralling love stories,
sparkling with passion and adventure
from Romance's bestselling authors*

FORTUNE'S FLAME *by Judith E. French*
76865-8/ $4.50 US/ $5.50 Can

FASCINATION *by Stella Cameron*
77074-1/ $4.50 US/ $5.50 Can

ANGEL EYES *by Suzannah Davis*
76822-4/ $4.50 US/ $5.50 Can

LORD OF FIRE *by Emma Merritt*
77288-4/$4.50 US/$5.50 Can

CAPTIVES OF THE NIGHT *by Loretta Chase*
76648-5/$4.99 US/$5.99 Can

CHEYENNE'S SHADOW *by Deborah Camp*
76739-2/$4.99 US/$5.99 Can

FORTUNE'S BRIDE *by Judith E. French*
76866-6/$4.99 US/$5.99 Can

GABRIEL'S BRIDE *by Samantha James*
77547-6/$4.99 US/$5.99 Can